Special Edition
Books 1–4

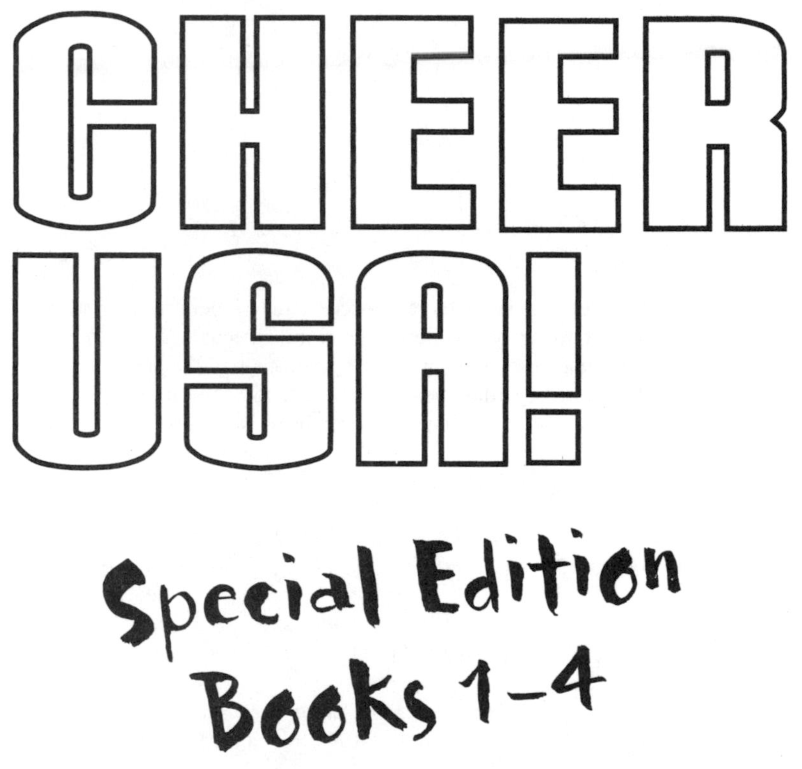

Jeanne Betancourt

SCHOLASTIC INC.
New York Toronto London Auckland Sydney
Mexico City New Delhi Hong Kong Buenos Aires

ISBN 0-439-85200-5

Cheer USA! #1: Go, Girl, Go!

Cheer USA! #2: Fight, Bulldogs, Fight!

Cheer USA! #3: Ready, Shoot, Score!

Cheer USA! #4: We've Got Spirit!

12 11 10 9 8 7 6 5 4 3 2 1 6 7 8 9 10/0

Printed in the U.S.A. 23

First compilation printing, January 2006

Contents

GO, GIRL, GO!

For Carole Halpin

CLAYMORE, FLORIDA.
THE MANOR HOTEL. MONDAY 7:30 A.M.

Emily Granger jumped out of bed, stuck out her arms, and twirled around like a ceiling fan. The first day of middle school was finally here! She was finally starting seventh grade. Denim shorts and a green tank top hung over her desk chair. New sandals stuck out from under the chair. School supplies were neatly piled on the desk next to a purple backpack. Emily ran into the hall. If she hurried, she could beat her sister Lynn to the bathroom.

Returning from the bathroom a few minutes later, Emily met Lynn in the hall.

"Slow down," Lynn said in a groggy voice. "Where's the fire?"

"It's the first day of school!" exclaimed Emily as she rushed past to her room. Lynn isn't one bit excited, thought Emily. Maybe the first day of eleventh grade wasn't as big a deal as the first day of seventh grade in a *whole new school.*

The phone was ringing when Emily came into her room. She picked it up on the second ring. "Hi, Alexis," she said into the receiver.

"Ah, excuse me," said a surprised man's voice on the other end. "I must have the wrong number."

"Sorry," said Emily, "I thought it was my friend. Who is it you were calling?"

"The Manor Hotel," the man answered.

Emily felt herself blush. Just because Alexis said she'd call her before school didn't mean anyone who called would be Alexis. Especially when your family runs a hotel and lives there.

"This is The Manor Hotel," said Emily, "but you have the wrong extension. You want 555-3000. That's the front desk."

As soon as she put the phone down it rang again. "The Manor Hotel," Emily said into the receiver.

"Emily, it's me, Alexis," said the voice on the other end.

"Are you at your dad's yet?" asked Emily.

"I'm still at my mother's," said Alexis. "I'm dressed, and all my stuff is ready. But Mom is taking forever, and she has to bring me and my stuff to Dad's before I can meet you."

"But we'll still meet in front of that juice place at 8:15, right?"

"Squeeze," said Alexis.

"Right," said Emily.

Emily flipped through the blank pages of her new notebook while she talked to Alexis. She always loved the first day of school. It was so much fun to see everybody after the long summer and get off to a fresh start. Seventh grade in a new school would be even better.

Three elementary schools fed into Claymore

Middle School. Emily's parents and her older sister and brother had all gone to CMS. Her mother and sister had been CMS cheerleaders, and her father and brother had been CMS football and basketball players. And best of all, the Grangers always had the Bulldog mascot — a real brown-and-white bulldog. That tradition had started when her father was a boy. The current Bulldog bulldog was Bubba IV, the great-grandson of Bubba I. For Emily, going to CMS was the continuation of a great family tradition.

"I'm so nervous, Emily," Alexis was saying. "I hardly know anyone in the upper grades. And that school is so big."

"We know lots of people," Emily reassured her. "It'll be great, you'll see. We're finally going to be in seventh grade, Alexis! Today! In an *hour*! And we're going out for cheerleading. That's the best."

"Are you still wearing your shorts?" asked Alexis.

"Yes," answered Emily. "And you're wearing that black miniskirt?"

"Uh-huh," Alexis said.

"Then we're all set," Emily told her. "Meet you at Squeeze at 8:15."

As Emily said good-bye to Alexis, her four-year-old sister, Lily, and Bubba burst into the room. Bubba ran circles around Emily until she bent down and gave him a good-morning hug. Lily climbed up on the bed and plopped down next to Emily's cat, Tiger. While Emily got ready for school, Lily played with Tiger and talked nonstop. Bubba sat in the doorway so he could keep an eye on Emily and Lily and, at the same time, check out any action in the hallway. If Lynn or Edward, Emily's ten-year-old brother, came out of their rooms, Bubba would have to choose which Granger he was going to follow. He'd probably charge up and down the hall three or four times before making up his mind. It was dangerous to walk in the hallway when Bubba was making a big decision like that.

Emily checked herself out in the mirror and grinned happily. She was ready for the first day of school.

"Come on," she told Lily. "Let's go get breakfast."

HARBOR ROAD 7:40 A.M.

Alexis Lewis looked around her mother's empty kitchen. At Emily's house, Alexis thought, there would be a whole bunch of people in the kitchen. Alexis wished she had a big family like Emily. *It's always either me and my mother or me and my father,* she thought sadly. Her parents had been divorced for so long she could hardly remember living with both of them at the same time.

"Did you eat your breakfast?" Alexis's mother yelled from her upstairs bedroom.

"Yes," Alexis shouted back. "And I'm ready. My bag is at the door. Please hurry, Mom."

Changeover day. Alexis hated it. But at least her father's apartment was close to Emily's house. And her father let her hang out at the Grangers' more than her mother did. He'd even let her sleep over at the Grangers' on a school night.

Alexis dropped her suitcase and green backpack on the kitchen porch and sat on the top step. She wondered if she should have bought a red backpack instead of a green one. And what about her shoes? Did they look okay with the skirt? Alexis felt tired and sick to her stomach. She'd been awake for hours during the night, nervous and excited about starting middle school. When she did fall asleep, she had nightmares about being lost in the new school. In one nightmare, kids laughed at her and kept giving her the wrong directions to her classes. Alexis wished that her elementary school had a seventh and eighth grade, too. She knew practically everybody in her grade at Claymore Elementary School. She'd been captain of the girls' basketball team and editor of the school paper — and never got lost in the hallways.

Alexis burped. The taste of the cereal she'd eaten for breakfast rose to her mouth. What if she threw up at school? Right in the hallway. With everyone watching.

Alexis's mother finally came outside, and they headed for the car. "Big day for you," she said.

"Yeah," said Alexis.

She didn't bother to tell her mother how nervous she felt. Her mother never seemed to be afraid of anything. Alexis wondered if that was because her mother was an emergency room nurse. Or maybe her mother was an emergency room nurse because nothing scared her. Alexis knew that her mother would never have been nervous about going to a new school, let alone throw up because of it.

Irene Lewis started the car and backed out of the driveway. "When are you and Emily trying out for cheerleading?" she asked.

"I don't know," Alexis said. "Maybe they'll tell us today."

"Cheerleading would be fun," her mother said.

"I'm not very good," Alexis mumbled.

"I'm sure you could be," Irene Lewis assured her daughter. "How many times do I have to tell you, honey? You can do anything you want. You just have to want it bad enough. You really want to be a cheerleader, don't you?"

"Of course, I do," answered Alexis. "Emily is doing it, and we practiced all summer. Her sister Lynn helped us, remember? And she's the best cheerleader."

"Good," said her mother. She stopped for a red light. Alexis looked at her watch. If she was late, she hoped Emily would wait for her.

She'd die if she had to go into that school alone.

DELHAVEN DRIVE 8:00 A.M.

Joan Russo-Chazen looked out her bedroom window. A school bus drove by. Was it going to Claymore Middle School? Joan turned and smiled at her reflection in the mirror. Well, *she* was going to Claymore Middle School! CMS! For three years Joan had attended Spencer Day School in Fort Myers. Spencer was an okay school, but none of her classmates lived in Claymore. Joan had no friends her own age in the town she had lived in for three years! She was glad that Spencer stopped at sixth grade, so she had to go to a public school.

Joan took her brown hair out of the ponytail and shook it loose. Did she look older with her hair down? Maybe. Joan looked at what she was wearing. She thought that wearing jeans instead of a skirt made her look taller. Would she be the shortest girl in her class at Claymore, too?

It would be great not to have to wear a uniform to school. She hoped her parents wouldn't give her a hard time about wearing jeans. Her parents hated jeans. They hated a lot of things that Joan liked — television programs, rock and hip-hop, American movies, and living in the South. Sometimes it seemed to Joan that her mother and father hated everything that she loved.

Joan looked at her watch, grabbed her new red backpack, and headed for the kitchen. Her parents and brother were still at the breakfast table. Her mother was looking over notes for her college lecture and didn't even notice when Joan came into the room. Her thirteen-year-old brother, Adam, glanced up from his cereal and gave Joan the thumbs-up sign. Her father looked up from the book he was reading while he ate breakfast. "Jeans to school?" he said.

"All the girls wear jeans, Father," Adam said. Joan flashed Adam a grateful smile. How lucky that she had a brother who had already been at CMS for a year.

"Mother, we should go," Adam said, "or we'll be late for school."

Michelle Russo looked up from her papers. She seemed surprised to be in the kitchen with her family. Joan wondered if her mother would say something in German or Russian — the two languages she taught at the university.

"Joanie, your hair will fall in your face when you study," her mother finally said — in English. "Shouldn't you put it back?"

"I have a hair clip in my pocket," Joan told her mother.

Ms. Russo put her papers together and dropped them into her briefcase with a sigh. "What a shame there isn't a decent private junior high school around here."

"There are some good teachers at Claymore," Adam said. "Joanie is going to like it there."

"Now that I'm in seventh grade, I want you all to call me *Joan*," Joan told her family. "That's my real name. It's more grown-up."

Paul Chazen smiled at his daughter. "All right, kitten," he said. "Don't forget to sign up for the debate club."

Joan didn't bother to tell her father that she'd outgrown his nickname for her, too.

"The debate club? What is anyone in that school going to have to debate about?" Ms. Russo said. "The merits of basketball versus football? Joanie's and Adam's brains are going to rot in that school."

"Nevertheless," Mr. Chazen told his wife, "the debate club will be good for her."

"Joanie, come on, let's go," her mother said.

"Mother!" Joan exclaimed. "It's *Joan.* That's what you named me, remember?"

"You'll always be *Joanie* to me," her mother insisted. "And as an aside, please do not speak to me in an insolent tone."

Joan knew that there was no way she could win the name battle with her mother.

"Please call me *Joan* at school," Joan told Adam as they walked out of the house together. "That's the way I'm going to introduce myself from now on."

"I'll try," he said and smiled.

Joan looked down at her jeans-clad legs as she climbed into the backseat of the car. All in all, she felt pretty great. She was finally going to CMS. And she was wearing jeans to school.

DOLPHIN COURT APARTMENTS 8:15 A.M.

Melody Max stared at her reflection in the bedroom mirror. She had on a black tank dress. She might be going to school with a bunch of hicks, but she wasn't going to *look* like one. Melody put on her Walkman headphones and hit play. Now, what should she wear on her feet?

Feet. Dancing. Instead of putting on shoes, Melody danced barefoot with her reflection. Suddenly her mother's image appeared in the mirror beside her, scowling and pointing to her watch. Melody pulled off her headphones.

"You are due at your new school in fifteen minutes," Carolyn Sinclair reminded her daughter. "Shouldn't you have some breakfast and get your fancy self moving?"

"It's 8:15!" exclaimed Melody. "Time to see Dad."

Melody grabbed her platform sandals and shoulder bag and rushed out of the room.

Her mother followed. "Do you have to watch him *every* morning on TV?" she asked.

"He's in Miami, and we're over here on the other side of Florida," Melody protested. "It's the only way I can see him now."

"Melody, you know we moved here because I was made editor of the newspaper. That wasn't going to happen in Miami. Please, let's not go over this again." In the sunlit kitchen, Melody saw her mother's beautiful face momentarily crumple into sadness. The divorce had been hard on all of them.

"Sorry," Melody said. "It's just that going to school in Claymore is going to be superboring."

"It's up to you to make it interesting, sugar. Why don't you go out for cheerleading? One of my reporters told me that they have an excellent squad. And it would be a good way to make new friends."

"I miss my old friends, Mom."

"I know," her mother said. She poured a glass of orange juice and put it at Melody's place. "I miss my friends, too. But we'll both be fine. Remember, we come from a family of strong women."

"I know," said Melody.

Melody punched on the kitchen television set and poured some cereal into a bowl.

Like magic, there was her handsome dad telling southeastern Florida the weather. She missed Miami, she missed her father, and she missed her friends. She'd e-mail everybody tonight. She'd tell them all about her first day of school in Hicksville. She'd describe how small the school was and the way the kids dressed. Maybe she'd write a memoir: *Hip Girl in Hick Town.*

"Sunny and cool. High in the seventies, low in the sixties," Sydney Max was telling his viewers. "Now let's take a look at the satellite map."

Carolyn Sinclair leaned over and kissed her daughter on the forehead. "I have to go now. Promise me you'll get yourself to school as soon as your father's off the air. And call me when you come home. Have a great day."

Melody didn't believe for a second that she would have a great day.

How could she, when her father and her best

friends were two hundred miles away and she was starting school with a bunch of strangers?

SQUEEZE 8:20 A.M.

Alexis ran the two blocks from her father's apartment to Squeeze, where Emily was waiting for her. "Sorry I'm late," Alexis said breathlessly.

"It's okay, but let's hurry. We can say hi to everybody and find our lockers before homeroom. It's going to be so much fun to change classes!"

Alexis caught her breath, and the two friends ran up the block. "I wish we were in all the same classes," said Alexis. "The building is so big, and there are so many kids I won't know."

"Don't worry," Emily assured her. "You won't get lost. We got that map of the building that came with our welcome to CMS packet. Remember? They are so organized at this school. I love it already."

The two girls turned the corner and saw the pink stucco school building, two stories high. Emily loved how CMS was U-shaped, with a big courtyard of grass and palm trees in the center. It was a much fancier school than her old elementary school.

"I wish we were in the same homeroom at least," said Alexis.

"Me, too," said Emily. "Can you come to my

house and practice cheerleading after school? Lynn said tryouts will probably be this week."

"Okay," agreed Alexis. "My dad won't mind. I'll leave him a message at his office."

Alexis felt better. She'd go home with Emily after school. She and Emily would practice cheerleading in The Manor Hotel ballroom, just like they had all summer. Maybe Emily's parents would invite her to stay for dinner. Even if she wasn't in a lot of classes with Emily, they'd at least have cheerleading together — if they both made it through the tryouts. Alexis looked at the big building and all the kids coming off school buses. There were so many kids at CMS! What if a lot of girls went out for cheering? And what if they were better at it than she was? What if she didn't make the squad and Emily did? Then she'd hardly *ever* see her best friend. Maybe Emily wouldn't even want her for a best friend if they weren't both cheerleaders.

"Look," Emily told Alexis. "There's Jake."

Alexis saw Jake Feder walking toward them. He waved hello, and Alexis waved back. She'd known Jake most of her life, and she liked him a lot. Jake lived with his grandparents in a house behind The Manor Hotel, and he'd been a good friend of Emily's ever since she was three years old and he was five. Sometimes when Alexis felt sorry for herself because her parents were divorced, she remembered Jake's story. His parents and his baby sister died in a fire when Jake was five years old. That's when Jake moved in with his grandparents, who raised him.

Jake draped one arm over Emily's shoulders and the other around Alexis's. Alexis smiled up at him. She loved how his dark hair framed his tan face. " 'Welcome to CMS, place of great learning and great fun,' " he said, quoting the CMS manual. "You're going to love it here."

Alexis suddenly felt happy and excited. Maybe being at CMS wouldn't be so bad after all.

CMS COURTYARD 8:25 A.M.

Sally Johnson stood in the CMS courtyard watching the stream of kids coming off the school buses. Everyone looked so young. Sally guessed that that's what happens when you're in the ninth grade in a seven-through-nine middle school. As she smiled and said hello to old classmates, Sally reminded herself of her goals for the year. She was sure she would be co-captain of the cheerleading squad. Everyone said she was the best cheerleader in the school — even when she was in the eighth grade. It was going to be a great year in cheerleading. She would see to it that CMS placed in the Cheer USA state competitions. She would run for president of the ninth-grade class and probably win. And she wanted to be queen of the CMS prom, too. That would end the school year nicely.

Last year, in eighth grade, Sally dated Dave Grafton, but they broke up over the summer. Now Dave was in high school. If I'm going to reach all of my goals, thought Sally, I have to have a boyfriend right here, at CMS. She spotted Jake Feder. He was the most popular guy in their grade and a terrific basketball player. He also worked part time at Bulldog Café, which was a cool place to hang out. As editor of the school newspaper, Jake could help her with her presidential campaign. Yes, Jake would make an excellent boyfriend.

Sally was surprised to see Jake talking to what were obviously seventh-grade girls. Oh, well, she thought, he couldn't be interested in *them.* Glancing over her shoulder, Sally noticed Darryl Budd coming in her direction. Darryl was captain of the football team and *very* cute. He should be her boyfriend for sure, at least for the football season. Or maybe she'd let him *think* he was her boyfriend while she worked on Jake.

Sally pretended not to see Darryl and headed straight toward Jake. It would be fun to start off the school year with a little jealousy.

Meanwhile, Joan Russo-Chazen was walking through the courtyard with her brother. Adam said hello to some kids as they passed. "Hey, there's Jake Feder," Adam told Joan. "Come on. I'll introduce you."

Joan recognized one of the three girls with Jake. When she first moved to Claymore, she'd taken a Saturday gymnastics class with that red-haired girl. She even remembered that her name was Emily. Joan had loved gymnastics, but her parents decided it was dangerous and a waste of time, so Joan had to drop out of the class. Joan recalled how she and Emily were about the same size two years ago. Now Emily was way bigger. Joan checked out the kids gathering outside the school building. They all looked taller than she was.

A beautiful girl with a blond ponytail was talking to Jake, too. Joan remembered the girl from the school play that Adam was in the year before. She watched her give Jake a hug.

"Who's that?" Joan whispered.

"Sally Johnson," Adam answered.

Joan noticed that her brother was blushing. Her brother must like this girl. And Joan could see why he would.

"Hey, Adam," Jake called. Before she knew it, Joan was being introduced to Jake and Sally.

"This is my sister, Joanie," Adam said. "I mean Joan."

"Which is it," laughed Sally, "Joanie or Joan?"

"My name is Joanie, but they call me Joan,"

said Joan. As soon as she said it she felt like a jerk. Joan was a real name, and Joanie was the nickname. Everybody knew that.

Sally gave Joan a big smile. She has the most beautiful smile, thought Joan. "I think you look like a Joanie," Sally said. "You're so cute. Do you do gymnastics?"

"I just took a few lessons," said Joan. "But I loved it."

"I hope you go out for cheering," Sally told her. "We need a new flyer. You're just the right size. What you don't know, Coach can teach you."

"We're going out for cheering," Emily said to Joan. "I'm Emily. This is Alexis."

A deep male voice from behind Joan interrupted the introductions. Joan turned and faced a very big, very tall, very handsome boy.

"Hi, Darryl," said Sally sweetly. She put her hand casually on his shoulder, got on her tiptoes, and gave him a kiss on the cheek. Joan noticed that her brother blushed again.

Joan listened to the others talking about what they'd done all summer. I'm so shy, she thought. I don't know what to say. Everybody else looks so much older and is so much cooler than I am. A loud buzzer startled Joan, and she jumped. Nobody seemed to notice her surprise. They compared their class schedules as they headed slowly in the direction of the front door. For the moment even her brother had forgotten her.

Joan felt frightened as she followed Adam and his friends into the building.

NORTH DOOR 8:30 A.M.

Alexis noticed that Joan looked a little lost. She's just as nervous as I am, thought Alexis. Alexis slowed down so she and Emily could walk with Joan. "What homeroom are you in?" Alexis asked.

"Room 210," Joan answered.

"Me, too," said Alexis.

"The only time I was in this school was when my brother was in a play," Joan told her. "I'm a little nervous."

Alexis smiled at Joan. "So let's try to sit next to each other in homeroom," she offered.

"I'm in a different homeroom," said Emily. "But maybe our lockers will be near each other."

As they walked down the corridor of seventh-grade lockers, Emily and Alexis said hi to kids they knew from elementary school. "This is Joan," Emily told a couple of girls standing near a locker. Joan smiled and said hi. It was great to hear someone call her by her real name.

The three girls' lockers were in the same row but not next to one another. When Joan saw

Emily and Alexis put their jackets in their lockers, she did the same. Emily took a CMS pendant out of her backpack and stuck it to the inside of her locker door with some Scotch tape. "That's for good luck," she told Joan. "Because I'm trying out for cheerleading."

Then the three girls compared their class schedules. They weren't in many of the same classes, but they all had the same lunch hour.

Another buzzer rang. "That's the signal to go to our homerooms," Emily explained to Joan. She pointed to the end of the corridor. "You and Alexis go that way and up the stairs. I go to a room on this floor right off the main lobby." She added that she'd meet them in the cafeteria at lunch period. "Whoever is first save places for the other two," she suggested. Alexis and Joan agreed and walked down the hall.

Emily followed a group of kids and went toward the lobby. She didn't know any of them. She didn't know as many people at CMS as she thought she would. Emily suddenly felt a little nervous about being in middle school. Don't be silly, she told herself, you were looking forward to this. You wanted to be in middle school.

When Emily reached the lobby, she noticed a girl holding the welcome-to-CMS envelope that all the new students had received in the mail the week before. The girl didn't seem to know which way to go.

Emily went up to her and asked, "May I help you?"

"Sure," Melody Max said. "Where's room 110?"

"On the other side of the lobby," Emily told her. "I'm going to room 109. I'll show you the way." She smiled at the girl. "I'm Emily Granger. I'm new here. I guess you are, too."

"Yeah," said Melody with a sigh. "I am. I just moved here from Miami."

"You'll *love* CMS," Emily gushed as they walked through the lobby. "Everybody has great school spirit. The football team is the best. And girls' basketball won the state championship in their division. So the cheerleaders are real busy going to games."

Emily didn't feel nervous anymore. This was great. She was talking about CMS as if she already went there. Well, now she did. She was on her way to homeroom.

Melody couldn't believe this girl. She was so bubbly and cheerful. Why did everyone in this school smile all the time? Where was their attitude?

"I'm trying out for cheerleading," Emily continued. "Tryouts are this week."

"Good for you," said Melody. She tried to sound enthusiastic, but she was wondering if Emily Whoever-she-was would make the squad. She didn't look very athletic and seemed so young.

"You can go out for cheering if you want," Emily told her. "The squad is great. They do a lot of tumbling and dancing and compete in the Cheer USA competitions. I'm not a cheerleader — yet. But, like I told you, I'm trying out. I just really hope that I get on the squad."

"Well, good luck," said Melody.

"There's your room," Emily said. "See you around."

Emily went into room 109, and Melody went into room 110.

As Melody walked into the room, the teacher was saying, "Okay, everyone, quiet down and listen up." The room went silent. Melody looked around and took the only empty seat.

The boy in the seat behind her smiled. "Hi," he whispered, "I'm Adam." Melody thought Adam had a handsome, sweet face, especially with that smile. Maybe it's not so bad that everyone around here smiles, she thought as she returned the smile and sat down.

"This is room 110, an eighth-grade homeroom," announced the teacher. "Everyone check your schedule to be sure you're in the right room."

Melody Max quickly reached into her pocket and pulled out the paper with her schedule and read, "8:30 A.M. Homeroom. Room 101."

Room 101! She stood up and grabbed her notebook. Everyone looked at her. They were all smiling. Or were they laughing?

Melody held her head high and walked down the aisle out of room 110. She didn't hurry. And she didn't smile. Maybe she could teach these hicks what cool looked like.

CMS CAFETERIA 12 NOON.

Joan was the first of the three girls to reach the cafeteria for lunch period. She wished Emily and Alexis were already there. It would be embarrassing to go into the cafeteria alone. Joan supposed that Emily and Alexis saw a lot of kids from their elementary school in their morning classes. Maybe they wouldn't want to have lunch with her after all. She felt her body tense up. Would she have to eat lunch all by herself?

Joan finally spotted Emily coming down the corridor with a bunch of kids. They were all laughing and talking excitedly to one another, and Emily was the center of the crowd. Emily saw Joan, left the group, and came over to her.

Joan felt her shoulders relax. Emily hadn't forgotten her after all.

"Have you seen Alexis?" Emily asked, looking around.

"Not since second period English," answered Joan.

"Let's go in," Emily suggested. "Alexis will meet us inside."

In the cafeteria line, Emily introduced Joan to some kids. One of them was a girl who had just moved to Claymore. Joan loved the girl's name — Melody Max. She wondered if anyone ever called her Max, but she decided not to ask. Melody Max wasn't very friendly, and when Emily invited her to sit with them, she said, "No, thanks."

Emily found three empty places at the end of a table. "Alexis has a terrible sense of direction," Emily told Joan. "I hope she didn't get lost in the building."

They'd just sat down with their lunches when Joan spotted Alexis coming into the cafeteria. She looked confused until she saw Joan and Emily waving to her. They were already on their chocolate pudding by the time Alexis got her lunch and joined them.

"Did you get lost finding the cafeteria?" Emily asked her.

"Just a little," Alexis admitted. "But wait until you hear what I saw."

"What?" asked Emily and Joan in unison.

"The cheerleaders," answered Alexis excitedly, "putting up posters about the cheerleading tryouts. There's a meeting tomorrow after school for anyone who's interested in cheering. Tomorrow!"

"Tryouts are tomorrow?" asked Emily in astonishment.

"No," Alexis explained, "tryouts start on Friday. Tomorrow is a meeting to talk about the squad and the first cheerleading clinic. Wait till you see the signs. They are so cool. There's one right outside the cafeteria."

"Hurry up," Emily told her. "Eat. Don't talk. Finish your lunch so we can go see it."

While Alexis ate, Emily told Joan she remembered her from the Saturday afternoon gymnastics class they'd taken together. "You were so good," Emily commented. "Why'd you drop out?"

Joan liked Emily, and she wanted to tell her the truth. But the truth was so embarrassing. How could she say that she had to drop out because her parents thought gymnastics was stupid and dangerous? Instead she said, "It was a scheduling problem. I have a piano class then." Which was sort of true, since she now took piano lessons on Saturday afternoons. "I didn't want to drop out though," Joan added with one hundred percent truthfulness. "I really loved gymnastics. I want to take it again someday."

"Sally Johnson said they need another flyer for the cheerleading squad," Alexis mumbled through a mouthful of sandwich. "She should know. She's the best cheerleader on the squad."

"I'm too big to be a flyer," added Emily. "But you're just the right size, Joan. If you like gymnastics, you'll get to do it a lot in cheering. My sister said that the school hires a special coach to work with the squad on gymnastics."

Joan had seen cheerleaders on television and knew what a flyer did. She imagined herself being tossed in the air by a base of cheerleaders. It would be so much fun. It *would* be like flying. But her parents would never let her do that! Joan could imagine their reaction. "Dangerous!" they'd say. "You don't go to school to be thrown in the air. You go to school to learn."

Emily interrupted her thoughts. "Joan, if you're going out for cheerleading, you should come over to my house after school. We're going to practice. My sister Lynn will help us."

"Lynn's a cheerleader in the high school, and she was co-captain of the squad when she was at CMS," added Alexis.

Joan couldn't believe her good luck. She was being asked to someone's house on the first day of school!

In a few minutes the three girls joined the other seventh-graders leaving the lunchroom. A crowd of girls were gathered in front of the cheerleaders' poster in the hall. Even on tiptoes, Joan couldn't read the poster over the heads of the girls in front of her. Suddenly four hands lifted her into the air.

"You feel like a feather," commented Alexis.

"You *have* to go out for cheering," implored Emily.

The three girls read the poster.

WHAT?	***A meeting and clinic for girls who want to try out for the CMS cheer squad.***
WHEN?	***Tuesday, September 10, at 3:00 P.M.***
WHERE?	***Small gym.***
WEAR?	***Comfortable clothes and athletic shoes.***
WHY?	***Tryouts are Friday, September 13, at 3:45 P.M.***

Are you a girl with spirit?
Then let's hear it,
Go, girl, go!

Emily and Alexis put Joan down on the ground.

"Are you going to the meeting?" asked Emily.

Joan nodded. "And I'll practice with you after school," she added excitedly. "If that's still okay."

"It's better than okay," said Emily. "It's great!"

"We can practice stunts with you," added Alexis. "It's perfect."

It is perfect, thought Joan, as she walked to her first afternoon class on her first day at CMS. I'm going to public school. I have two neat new friends. And I'm going to one of their houses after school. Even one of the ninth-grade cheerleaders told me to go out for cheering.

Then Joan had a thought that made her lunch turn over in her stomach. She wanted to be a CMS cheerleader more than anything she had ever wanted in her life. But what if she didn't make the squad? She'd be so disappointed. Then a second thought. If she did make the squad, how could she keep her cheerleading a secret from her parents? Either way she had a huge problem.

CMS COURTYARD 3:05 P.M.

Joan met her brother outside the school as planned. He was talking to that cute ninth-grader, Jake. When Adam saw her, Joan noticed a worried look cross his face. "What's wrong?" she asked.

"I have a drama club meeting," Adam told

her. "You'll have to go home alone. Do you mind?"

Joan laughed. "I was going to say the same thing to you," she told him. "Emily Granger invited me over to her house."

Adam smiled. "Great, Joanie," he said. "I mean *Joan*."

"Maybe I'll see you there later," said Jake. "The Manor Hotel is my second home."

"Great," said Joan. She couldn't get over how friendly everyone was at CMS. Even kids in the ninth grade, like Jake Feder and Sally Johnson.

"What time do you think I have to be home?" she asked Adam.

"Six o'clock," answered Adam. "That was the rule Mother and Father gave me when I started middle school. It should be the same for you."

"Don't worry. I can take care of myself," Joan told him.

"Good," said Adam with relief. "I have enough trouble keeping track of my own schedule. Just call Father and tell him where you are."

Jake laughed. "You're the only kids I know who call their parents *Mother* and *Father*," he said.

"We're the only kids who have parents like our *mother* and *father*," commented Adam.

Joan saw Emily and Alexis coming in their direction. What if they said something about cheering and the tryouts in front of her brother? She wanted to keep cheering a secret from her whole family — for now. "Gotta go," she said as she quickly took off toward her two new friends.

As the girls walked the ten blocks to the Manor Hotel, Emily and Alexis taught Joan a CMS chant Lynn had taught them. Joan loved walking along Main Street with her new friends, chanting and clapping:

Go, blue X X (clap, clap),
Go, White X X (clap, clap),
Fight, Bulldogs, Fight!

Emily and Alexis stopped in front of a huge white-and-yellow building with a big veranda. It looked like a mansion, but it was The Manor Hotel. "Here we are," Emily announced.

Joan had wondered what Emily's house would be like, but she never imagined it would be a hotel!

"We live on the fourth floor," Emily explained. "The second and third floors are where hotel guests stay. The first floor is the lobby, restaurant, café, and the ballroom."

"That's where we practice," Alexis explained. "In the ballroom."

Joan didn't know where to look first when

she walked into the lobby of the Manor Hotel. There were gilt mirrors and huge plants everywhere. Leather couches and chairs were assembled around a fancy-looking red-and-blue rug. The woman at the front desk called out, "How'd it go, sweetie?"

"Great, Mom," Emily called back.

A cute little girl sat on the rug eating cookies. A bulldog crouched beside her. The child was scolding the dog. When she saw Emily she jumped up and ran over to them, yelling, "Bubba ate my cookie. He did." The dog, barking happily, followed her.

Alexis picked up the girl. "Lexis," the little girl whined. "Bubba's going to be sick all over *everything*. He's a bad dog."

Joan was trying not to smile. But it was difficult because the little girl was so cute.

"Lily, you silly," Emily said. "Bubba eats cookies all the time. They don't make him sick."

Lily laid her head on Alexis's shoulder and sighed, "Okay."

"We're going to practice cheering now," Emily told Lily.

"Me, too," Lily announced as she wiggled to get down from Alexis's arms. "And Bubba."

"Only if you're *very* good," Emily told her. "This is a serious practice."

The girls went down the corridor to the ballroom. Lily walked between Alexis and Joan, swinging hands and chanting a CMS cheer.

THE MANOR HOTEL BALLROOM 4:00 P.M.

Joan thought the ballroom was a perfect place to practice. There were large mirrors along one wall. On the other side, afternoon sunlight poured in through floor-to-ceiling windows. Emily went into a closet and took out three purple exercise mats. "You can use my sister's mat," she told Joan. Alexis pulled open the top drawer of a bureau and removed a file folder. "We keep notes on our workouts," she explained.

Joan looked at the calendar of Alexis's and Emily's summer cheerleading practices. How will I ever catch up? she wondered.

"First, we do warm-up exercises," Emily told her.

For the next fifteen minutes the girls did stretches on the mats. Joan loved the workout and promised herself that she would do those exercises every day, whether she was a cheerleader or not. By the end of the warm-up, Bubba and Lily were bored and went off in search of another adventure in the hotel.

In the ballroom the cheerleading practice continued. Alexis and Emily showed Joan basic hand positions. She learned blades, fists, buckets, and candlesticks.

"You're learning everything so *fast*," Alexis told her.

Then they practiced smiling in the mirror. At first Joan felt weird smiling at herself. But when they added a sideline cheer and pretended they were leading Bulldog fans, it wasn't so hard.

By the time Lynn joined them, Joan had learned some arm movements, a few leg positions, and two jumps — the tuck and the spread eagle.

Lynn's great, thought Joan. Emily is so lucky to have an older sister to show her how to do things, like cheering.

The half hour they spent doing tumbling went by in a flash. Joan had been doing somersaults, cartwheels, and front flips on her own ever since she took gymnastics, so those were easy for her. "You are *very* good," Lynn told her. "You'll make a perfect flyer."

"Lynn is a flyer," Alexis told Joan.

"There are other important positions in cheering besides being a flyer," Lynn pointed out.

Emily and Alexis practiced partner stunts with Joan. I love this, Joan thought.

Before Lynn had to leave to do her homework, she told the girls what they should bring to the cheerleading clinic the next day.

If my parents notice my exercise bag, Joan

thought, I'll tell them it's for gym. It is for gym, since the clinic is in the gym. She felt a twinge of guilt. She had never lied to her parents before.

At the end of their practice, the girls walked around the ballroom to cool down. Joan checked her watch. It was 5:30.

Alexis was glad practice was over. She liked the warm-up stretches and some of the jumping. What she didn't really like was yelling. A cheerleader had to project her voice when she cheered. Alexis also felt a little silly when she put on the cheerleaders' smile. It didn't feel natural to her, no matter how much she practiced it. She wished she could enjoy cheerleading as much as she liked playing basketball. But it was great to hang out at the hotel with Emily and have Lynn helping them. Alexis wasn't so sure about Joan yet. It was hard to share her best friend. She hoped Emily wouldn't like Joan better than her. And what if Joan and Emily made the squad and she didn't?

"I have to go home," Joan said.

Good, thought Alexis. Then it will be just me and Emily.

"Where do you live?" Emily asked.

"Delhaven Drive," answered Joan. "It's going to take me quite a while to walk there."

"My street is right next to Delhaven," said

Alexis. "I live on Harbor Road when I'm with my mother. Which is half the time."

"Then we can go home together now," suggested Joan.

"I'm at my dad's this week," explained Alexis. Besides, she thought, I'm not going home now. I want to stay with Emily and her family for as long as I can.

"Why don't you borrow my bike, Joan?" suggested Emily. "You can ride it to school tomorrow."

"That'd be great," said Joan. "I love to bike ride. In fact I'm planning on riding my bike to school a lot."

"So now you can stay here a little longer," said Emily. "Let's go get a soda at the café and decide what we're going wear for the tryout clinic."

As the three girls walked through the lobby toward the cafeteria, Emily put her arm around Alexis's shoulder and asked her if she could stay for dinner.

Alexis had the happy feeling she always did when she knew she'd be having dinner with the Grangers. She smiled at her very best friend in the whole world. "Sure," she said. "I'll call my dad right now."

Alexis went to the front desk to call her father's office.

"Lewis here," her dad answered.

"It's me, Dad," Alexis said.

"Lexi!" he exclaimed. "How'd it go? First day in middle school. Wow!"

"It was okay, Dad," Alexis told him. "I only got lost once."

"How about the teachers? Do you like your teachers?" he asked.

"They're okay, so far. They didn't give us a lot of homework, like I thought they would."

"Good," he said. "Ease into it. That's the way. You home?"

"I'm at Emily's," Alexis told him. "They invited me to dinner, and Emily and I want to do our homework together."

"Great!" said her father. "I mean great for you. I'll work late and get something to eat around here. So don't worry about your old man. I'll pick you up there about nine, okay?"

"Sure," said Alexis. "See you then."

She hung up the phone. Why did her father always sound so happy when she told him she wasn't going to be seeing him? He's probably going to have dinner with one of his girlfriends, she thought. It's a drag for him to have a kid.

Sometimes Alexis wondered if her father was sorry that he had joint custody of her. She knew he loved her, but she wasn't so sure he liked being with her that much. Maybe he'd like it better if she lived with her mother all the time and only saw him on the occasional weekend. But she didn't want to live only with her mother. Her mother was unhappy a lot of the time. For the next few hours she could pretend she lived with the Grangers.

Which is where she *would* live, if she had a choice.

DOLPHIN COURT APARTMENTS 7 P.M.

Melody's mother reached for a third taco. "Thank you, sugar," she said, "for this wonderful meal."

Melody had prepared chicken tacos, avocado and tomato salad, and rice for dinner. Melody knew her mother would be tired and stressed out from her new job. She was glad she could help by having a good meal ready for her. Both Melody's parents had made sure that she learned to cook. "When you have two working parents, you better know how to cook," her father told her the day he taught her how to make taco fillings.

During dinner, Carolyn Sinclair told Melody some stories from the world news that she'd learned during her day at work. Melody was definitely interested. She thought she might be a journalist some day, too. She loved to write.

When her mom asked her about school, Melody didn't say much. She knew her mother didn't want to hear complaints about her new school and classmates. She'd save her complaints for later, when she e-mailed her friends back in Miami.

After dinner Melody went to her room. The apartment was on the second floor of a two-story apartment complex. They had a terrace overlooking a swimming pool. That was nice. And there were tennis courts in the back. But Melody hadn't found anyone to play with. Her favorite tennis partner was her father, and he was in Miami.

Melody looked around her room. Half her boxes were still unpacked, and the walls were bare. The first week she was in Claymore she thought she still might convince her parents to let her move back to Miami. But crying herself to sleep three nights in a row and driving her mother and father crazy with her complaints didn't work. Both of her parents were adamant that she should spend the next three school years in Claymore with her mother and only spend vacations in Miami. Then if she wanted, she could live with her father and go to high school in Miami.

Melody put on some music, turned on her computer, and went on-line. First she checked for messages. There was one from her dad.

> Maxi's Maxim for the day: Put your best foot forward and you won't fall down.

Melody smiled to herself. Her father was always making up phrases like that. It was his way of giving advice. But that was all he said in his e-mail. Short but sweet, sort of.

There were no other messages. Had her friends forgotten her so fast? Melody reread some old e-mail messages and checked the dates. Two weeks ago, when she first moved to Claymore, her friends e-mailed her almost every day, like they promised. But she hadn't heard from any of them for two days. Well, she'd write to them. She hadn't forgotten *them.*

> Hey, out there. Cheers from the lost girl on the Gulf Coast. I'm marooned here with a bunch of hicks. No soul. No hip-hop. No fun. Where did all the dancing go? Here's the scoop about my first day at Claymore Boremore Middle School. Young. Everyone looks so young. Except a few guys and gals in the ninth grade. Wish I could go home to you all

and the fun we used to have. How's the hip-hop class, and what concerts are you all catching? Write and let me know there's a big old world over there in Miami that will still be there when I finish my three-year prison term. I'll be back for a long weekend at Thanksgiving. Cannot wait to see you all. Love ya. The Max.

Melody sent the letter to five of her best friends in Miami but decided against sending it to her dad. He was sick of her complaints as much as her mother was. Instead, she sent him:

Trying to put that best foot forward. Get rid of the tie you wore on the air this morning. It is way old-fashioned, but not old enough to be cool. Love ya. The Max.

Next Melody tackled her homework. She actually enjoyed the English assignment, reading a short story and answering some questions. She was finished by nine o'clock. What would she do next? She wasn't in the mood for television. She looked around her room. Maybe she'd hang some of her favorite concert posters and put her books on the bookshelves. She opened the blinds. She liked the way the lighted pool bounced aqua light into her room.

Melody revved up the volume on her stereo and went to work unpacking boxes and decorating her room.

CMS SMALL GYM. TUESDAY 3:05 P.M.

After their last class, Emily, Alexis, and Joan went to the locker room and changed into their cheerleading practice clothes. They walked into the gym together and sat on the front row of bleachers.

At 3:30 Emily turned around and made a quick count of the girls. There were about twenty on each of the three rows of bleachers. That meant sixty girls were thinking about trying out for ten positions on the squad! What if they all tried out? With that much competition, what were her chances of making the squad? Or Alexis's? Or Joan's? What were the chances of all three of them making the squad? All the practicing she and Alexis had done during vacation had to pay off. Didn't it?

"There are a lot of people here," Alexis whispered in Emily's ear.

"I know," Emily whispered back.

The door at the side of the gym flung open, and Coach Carmen Cortes came running into the room. She was followed by the six ninth-grade cheerleaders. Emily thought they all looked great in their blue-and-white cheerleading uniforms.

Coach Cortes stopped dead center in front of the stands of girls. The cheerleaders organized themselves in a row behind her.

Coach Cortes looked over the crowd of girls. Her gaze stopped when she saw Emily. "So we have another Granger in the school," she said. "How's Bubba IV?"

"Great!" answered Emily.

"Let's hear it for Bubba," Coach shouted to the cheerleaders.

"Bubba, Bubba," Sally Johnson called out through the megaphone.

The rest of the cheerleaders joined in with:

Bubba, Bubba,
Lead the fight.
Bubba, Bubba,
Help us win.
Fight! Win! Fight!

The girls who knew that Bubba was the CMS mascot cheered. Coach Cortes explained who Bubba was to the rest.

This is great, thought Emily. The school mascot lives in my house. But the great feeling didn't last. She had a terrible thought. What if the other girls thought she thought she'd make the squad because the school mascot was her dog? She knew that wasn't true. The judges for the tryouts came from other towns and wouldn't even know the names of the girls trying out. But did everyone else understand that? Maybe they'd think that Coach Cortes could influence the vote. Could she?

"All right, girls," Coach said. "Here's the drill. First, I'll explain what is required of a CMS cheerleader. By the way, the eighth-graders on the squad have to try out again. That's why they're sitting in the bleachers with you. So, seventh-graders, those of you who make the squad will have to try out again next year." A few people moaned. "The current ninth-graders will demonstrate some of the moves we use in our cheers so you can see what we expect of you. After that we'll conduct the first of three clinics. The clinic sessions run for an hour after school today, tomorrow, and Thursday. Tryouts are on Friday. Results will be posted outside this gym as soon as the votes are tallied."

Coach Cortes took a few steps forward and silently looked over the girls on the bleachers. Did she smile extra special at me? wondered Emily.

"After today," Coach continued, "you may decide against trying out. That's okay. Cheering isn't a sport for everyone. Don't try out unless you want to be a cheerleader with all your heart. Understood?"

Emily looked around. Many girls were nodding their heads.

"So are you ready?" shouted the coach in a strong cheerleader's voice.

"Yes!" shouted the gathering of girls.

"Give us a C," one of the ninth-graders chanted.

"C!" answered the tryout girls.

"Give us an M," chanted all the cheerleaders.

"M!" the crowd shouted back to them.

"S!" called the cheerleaders.

"S!"

"What do you have?"

"CMS!"

"Louder," called the cheerleaders.

"CMS!" chanted the crowd.

OUTSIDE THE GYM DOORS 3:15 P.M.

Melody stood by the gym doors watching. Emily waved for her to come in and sit next to her. She pushed closer to the girl next to her to show Melody that there was enough room.

If I sit down, thought Melody, everyone will think I'm trying out for cheerleading — which

I'm not. She shook her head no. She'd stay right where she was. She wanted to see what else happened at a cheerleading tryout meeting in Boremore. It'd make great material for tonight's e-mail to her friends in Miami.

Melody watched the cheerleaders demonstrate jumps, some tumbles, and lifts. Next they performed some very cool dance moves to an intricate beat of pretty good music. Melody had to admit that the ninth-grade cheerleaders were impressive. The only thing she didn't like was their constant smiling. They could use a little attitude.

As Melody watched the dance, she moved her own body to the beat of the music. When the demonstration was finished, everyone — including Melody — clapped. At the same time she checked out the expressions on the faces of the girls in the bleachers. She'd bet anything a lot of those girls were thinking, I could never do what those cheerleaders did. No way.

But I can, Melody thought. I can do somersaults and cartwheels. And I bet I could learn how to do a flip. I wouldn't be a flyer, but I'd be good at being the base for one. I have strong arms and legs, and I'm very steady. And with practice, I could do that dance routine. Melody wondered if the team had a dance choreographer working with them, because whoever was making up the steps was good.

Two things simultaneously interrupted Melody's thoughts. One was the sudden presence of someone by her side. The other was the voice of the coach saying, "You must all be wondering how our cheerleaders got to be so good."

I am, thought Melody. She ignored the person beside her and listened to the coach.

"How do we do it, squad?" the coach asked her cheerleaders.

"Practice. Practice. Practice," they chanted.

"And more practice," added Coach Cortes. "We also have some outside help. High school cheerleaders assist in our practices. And there is a dance coach and a gymnastics consultant who gives special classes in tumbling."

So there *is* a special dance teacher, thought Melody.

She turned slightly and came face-to-face with a big, handsome guy with the bluest eyes she had ever seen.

"Hey," the boy said in a low voice. "You going out for cheering?"

Melody shook her head no.

"I saw you dancing there a minute ago," he said. "Way cool. You should go out for cheering."

"Who are you?" Melody whispered. "And why are you telling me what I should do?"

Darryl, surprised that she spoke to him so boldly, took a step back.

"Darryl," he whispered back. "I think you're good so you should try out. They lost a lot of great cheerleaders."

"Lost?" Melody asked.

"Not lost-lost," he said. "They graduated. They went to high school." He smiled at her. "Who are you?"

"Melody," she answered. "I'm new here."

"I know," he said.

"How do you know?" she asked.

"I would have noticed you before."

"Darryl," the coach called. "Darryl Budd, the captain of our football team, has a few words to say."

Melody knew that in this school being the captain of the football team was probably a very big deal. "Captain, huh," she commented. "Way cool." She finally gave Darryl a smile — a little one.

When she looked away from him, she saw that everyone in the gym was looking at Darryl . . . and at her.

"Darryl, get over here and tell these tryout girls what it means to the football team to have a cheer squad."

The cheerleaders chanted, **"Dar-ryl. Dar-ryl. Dar-ryl."**

Darryl jogged across the floor to the center of the gym. He stood with spread legs, hands on hips, a big smile on his face. There is no denying that he's cute, thought Melody. And he knows it.

"Try out for the squad," Darryl told the prospective cheerleaders. "We need a strong cheer squad out there helping us win. Then, when the cheer squad goes to Cheer USA competitions, the football and basketball players will be out there cheering for you."

The cheerleaders and the coach broke up laughing. "I better explain," said the coach. "Last year the football team showed up at the state cheerleading competitions in girls' cheerleading uniforms. They even performed a cheer. It was a unique experience. To say the least."

Melody, imagining Darryl in a skirt doing cheerleading motions and jumps, laughed, too. She was glad to see that people at Boremore Middle School had a sense of humor.

"What we did was a joke," Darryl said. "But cheerleading is a serious sport. And the other athletes respect you. So go for it."

Melody was impressed by Darryl. She thought it would take a lot of confidence and a good sense of humor for a football player to put on girls' clothes.

The crowd applauded him as he ran off the floor.

Melody thought Darryl would leave the gym. But he stood next to her while Coach Cortes told the girls to organize themselves in groups of ten around the gym.

"Anyone who knows that they don't want to try out should leave now," Coach announced.

Some girls left the gym. According to Melody's calculations, that left about fifty or so girls to try out for ten positions on the squad.

As the tryout girls were moving into groups, Sally came over to Darryl and draped an arm around his shoulder. "You waiting for me, baby?" she asked Darryl.

She ignored Melody.

"You want me to?" asked Darryl.

Melody was surprised that Sally was ignoring her and that Darryl didn't introduce her. Darryl and Sally seemed to only have eyes for each other.

When Sally did glance in her direction, Melody said, "I'm Melody Max. New here. Seventh grade." Did Sally relax when Melody told her she was in the seventh grade? Melody wondered. Or was that her imagination?

"Sally Johnson," said Sally. "*Ninth* grade."

"Tell Melody she should go out for cheering,"

Darryl told Sally. "I know she'd be good." He gave Melody a huge smile.

Sally smiled at Melody, too. "Are you going to try out?" she asked.

Melody said, "I don't think so."

Sally looked Melody over. She was much too pretty. And Darryl clearly liked her. You may only be in the seventh grade, thought Sally, but I don't trust you. And I sure don't trust Darryl. He loves to have pretty girls falling all over him. Well, I'm the prettiest girl on the squad, and I intend to keep it that way. Sally continued to smile at Melody as she had these thoughts.

Melody was thinking about how friendly Sally was when she noticed Emily and two other girls running toward them.

"Hi," Emily said cheerfully. "Melody, these are my friends. You already met Joan. This is Alexis. We're all going out for cheering."

Melody said hi.

"So aren't the CMS cheerleaders great?" Emily asked.

"They are," Melody admitted.

"Are you going to try out?" Joan asked her.

Before Melody could answer Darryl said, "Sure she is. Aren't you, Melody?" He winked at her.

"She shouldn't do it if she doesn't want to," said Sally.

"At least take the clinic," suggested Emily. "Then you'll know if you like it or not. You'll never know if you don't try."

Coach Cortes walked over to them. "You four," she told Emily, Alexis, Joan, and Melody. "Go over with that group of six." She pointed across the gym to a huddle of girls. "Put a move on. We have a lot of work to do."

The coach thinks I'm doing the clinic, thought Melody. I might as well. I don't have anything else to do this afternoon. Taking the clinic doesn't mean I'll have to try out. What do I have to lose?

CMS SMALL GYM 3:30 P.M.

In a few minutes Coach explained to the cheerleader hopefuls how the clinic would be run. First, there would be a fifteen-minute warm-up for everyone. Then the tryout girls would break up into their groups of ten. The ninth-grade cheerleaders would coach the groups in different parts of the gym. Each group would go from station to station.

Mae Lee, a tall, thin girl with long, straight black hair, would run the jump station. Elvia Gignoux, a short, dark-haired cheerleader, would teach a dance routine. Cynthia Jane Morris, CJ, a small girl, was responsible for teaching tumbling. And Sally would teach the center cheer. Two high school cheerleaders came into the gym. They were there to help CJ with the tumbling.

"All right, everyone," shouted Carmen Cortes to the fifty girls lined up in front of her. "Let's go! Feet hip-width apart. Arms up. Stretch to the right! And breathe out. One. Two. Three. Four."

After the fifteen-minute warm-up, the groups went to the stations. The group that Emily, Alexis, Joan, and Melody were in went to Sally Johnson first to learn a required cheer.

When they went to the jump station, Emily saw that Joan was already jumping higher and better than she and Alexis. And Melody! She practically flew in the air. No one had to tell her to point her toes or the right placement of her head. It was hard to believe she'd never cheered before.

"I studied a lot of ballet," she told Emily as they left Mae's station and headed toward the tumbling station. "And there's a lot of jumping in that." Melody was sweating from the workout and smiling. Emily was glad Melody was finally having some fun at CMS.

Sally watched Melody walking across the gym floor with her friends. She's too pretty and she's too good, she thought. Sally also saw that Darryl was still on the sidelines. She waved to him, but he didn't see her. He was looking elsewhere. Sally followed his gaze and saw that he was watching Melody, too. Darryl was obviously interested in Melody. I can't let that girl make the squad, thought Sally.

I don't know how I'll do it, but I'm keeping Melody Max off my squad.

DOLPHIN COURT APARTMENTS 5:30 P.M.

When Melody got home she was surprised at how terrific her bedroom looked. She'd forgotten that she'd fixed it up the night before. She took off her clothes and put on her bathing suit. Her body felt loose and strong. She'd go for a swim in the pool to cool off. I haven't felt this good since I moved to Claymore, she thought. Cheering is fun. And tonight she and her mom could have a cookout by the pool. It was pretty neat how Dolphin Court Apartments had a gas grill near the pool that all the tenants could use. Maybe one of her new cheerleading friends played tennis. She liked Sally. I'll probably hang out with her and her friends instead of other seventh-graders, Melody thought as she ran down the outside stairs to the pool. And then there was that cute guy, Darryl.

Living in Claymore might not be so bad after all.

THE MANOR HOTEL 6:00 P.M.

Tuesday nights, Emily's mother was maître d' in the restaurant, and her father manned the front desk, so the Granger kids ate in the hotel dining room. Emily's entire body ached, and she'd never felt so hungry in her life. She was tired and cranky from the long day at school, topped by the two-hour cheerleading clinic. Her sister asked her how she did in the tryout clinic.

"It was fun," Emily told her through a mouthful of fried chicken. "Really fun."

Emily didn't tell Lynn that she felt discouraged about her chances for making the CMS cheerleading squad. That it seemed like everyone was so much better than she was. Or that she envied her sister who was already so grown-up and such a great cheerleader. What if I don't make the squad? wondered Emily. What if I'm the first Granger who isn't a Bulldog athlete?

"Is there anything you need extra help with?" Lynn asked. "I can help you after dinner."

"I have a lot of homework," Emily told her. "Maybe tomorrow night."

Emily took the last bite of her mashed potatoes. Eating the smooth, buttery potatoes made her feel better. As she reached for a second helping of potatoes, she eyed the chocolate cake on the dessert table. She could eat more and still have room for dessert.

SEAVIEW TERRACE 6:30 P.M.

Alexis looked in the freezer at her father's house. There were four different frozen dinners for her to choose from. Her father wasn't going to be home until nine. "Microwave yourself something, honey," he said on the message he'd left for her on the answering machine.

Alexis picked out lasagna. As she went to open the microwave she saw her reflection in the glass door. She looked upset. Alexis the worrywart, her father sometimes called her. Well, he should have seen her today at the cheerleading clinic. Her jaw hurt from smiling so much. She placed the frozen meal in the microwave and set the timer for five minutes.

While her meal was being zapped, Alexis stood at the window and stared out at the Gulf of Mexico. Waves tumbled gently against the shore and rolled back out.

"Big blue! Is here! Stand up and cheer!" Alexis chanted loudly.

Yell GO. FIGHT. WIN.
GO, FIGHT, WIN!
Hey Blue! Let's fight!

Yell fight. Bulldogs. Fight!

Go, big Blue and White. Let's win tonight!

By the end of the chant, Alexis's voice had dropped to a whisper and tears filled her eyes. It was no use. She didn't have the spirit. Everyone would know it, and she wouldn't make the squad.

The bell on the microwave rang. Time for dinner. Alone.

DELHAVEN DRIVE 6:45 P.M.

Tuesday was French night in the Russo-Chazen household. Everyone spoke French at dinner. Joan hoped that her parents wouldn't ask her what she did after school. Then she wouldn't have to lie to them.

If I do have to lie, she thought, maybe it will be easier in a foreign language.

Joan kept the French conversation away from her. She asked her father to describe the book that he was translating. She asked her mother about her students. And she asked Adam about his English class and what books they would be reading this semester. She did it all in French, but she didn't pay too much attention to their answers. She was going over chants for cheers in her head as she ate. After each answer she practiced her smile on her family.

"Joanie, why are you grinning like that?" her mother asked in French.

"I smile because I am happy," Joan answered in French. Which was one hundred percent the truth in any language.

When they'd finished dinner, her parents — who had prepared that night's meal — went to the living room to read and listen to classical music. All Joan had to do was clean up the kitchen with Adam. Then she could go to her room to do her homework. She'd be home free, lie free.

Joan knew that sooner or later she'd have to tell Adam that she was trying out for the CMS cheerleading squad. He went to CMS, so he'd find out. Besides, she would need his help to convince her parents to let her be a cheerleader. But tonight she wanted to keep it a secret to herself. Her big, wonderful secret — that Sally Johnson said that of all the girls who were going out for cheering, Joan was the best candidate to be the new CMS squad flyer!

CMS SMALL GYM. WEDNESDAY 5:00 P.M.

At the end of their second day of the clinic, the cheerleading hopefuls lined up in two rows in the center of the gym. Nine girls had dropped out after the first clinic, so now there were thirty-six. The workshop leaders sat on the bleachers with Coach Cortes and watched the girls do the required cheer.

After the last **"Fight, Bulldogs, fight,"** Coach leaned toward Sally and whispered. "Did you see that girl in the center of the back row?"

Sally knew that Coach was talking about Melody Max and nodded.

"I like her style," Coach said. "She has great energy and attitude. Her jumps are high and light with soft, bouncy landings."

Sally thought she had coached Melody so that Coach Cortes *wouldn't* like her. She'd told Melody to show as much attitude as she wanted. She thought that Coach Cortes wouldn't like Melody's jazzy style and that Melody would stick out as not being a good team player. But the plan had backfired! Melody looked good out there. She had a fabulous jump. Keeping Melody off the squad was going to be more difficult than Sally thought. Plan A had not worked. It was time to move on to plan B.

When the tryout girls went to the locker room to change, Sally followed them. She caught up with Melody and Alexis.

"Hey, good work, you guys," she told them. "How do you like cheering so far?"

"Great," said Melody with a big smile.

"Yeah," said Alexis. "And it's fun to be with all your friends after school."

"Well, show that spirit, okay, Alexis?" said Sally. "Give it your all."

"That's what I want," said Alexis. "To give it my all."

"Melody," said Sally. "I think we live in the same direction. You're at Dolphin Court Apartments, right?"

"That's right," said Melody.

"If you're going home now, we could walk together," Sally told her.

"Sure," said Melody. She tried to sound cool, but inside she was thrilled. Sally Johnson, a ninth-grade cheerleader, wanted to walk home with her.

"Meet you in front of the school," Sally said with a big smile.

As Melody quickly changed her clothes, she thought about her first three days at CMS. She liked Emily and her friends much more than she thought she would. Emily and Joan might look young, but they were very sweet and seemed genuinely nice. And Alexis Lewis, who looked more mature, also had divorced parents. She and Melody had already had a talk about that. So I know three seventh-graders who could be my friends, Melody thought.

But to have friends in the ninth grade would be so cool. Darryl Budd seemed interested in her. He had walked her home after the first clinic. She had an interesting talk with Emily's friend Jake Feder about music before school that morning. Now Sally Johnson was walking home with her!

If she made the cheerleading squad, life in Claymore might not be half bad.

CMS COURTYARD 5:10 P.M.

Melody walked out of school a few minutes later. Joan, Emily, and Alexis were standing around talking with two guys. Emily motioned for her to come over. Melody recognized the cute dark-haired guy. He was the eighth-grader who had smiled at her when she was in the wrong homeroom.

"Hi, again," Adam said when Emily introduced them. He smiled broadly. While the other girls were telling Jake Feder about the cheer clinic, Adam whispered to Melody, "You were amazingly cool about homeroom Monday morning."

You're pretty cool yourself, thought Melody.

When Sally came out of the building a few minutes later she saw Jake and Adam talking with Emily, Alexis, Joan, and Melody. They were all laughing and gabbing like best friends. Sally watched them for a few seconds before they saw her. Jake and Adam were paying special attention to Melody, Sally was sure of it. That girl could easily become the most popular girl at school — and she was only a seventh-grader!

As Sally ran up to the group she covered her real feelings with a cheerful laugh, and said, "Hey, everybody."

Minutes later, Melody and Sally were walking along Shore Road. Sally knew that Melody felt like a big deal walking home with a cheerleader. It was time to put part one of plan B into action.

"That was the first time Coach Cortes saw you do the required cheer," Sally told Melody. "She said something about you to me."

"What'd she say?" Melody asked. "I hope it was good."

"I don't want to upset you or anything," Sally said in a concerned tone, "but Coach said that you were showing off. I thought I should tell you she really hates show-offs."

"But you said to show my stuff," Melody protested.

"I said to show your stuff," said Sally. "I didn't say to show off. There's a big difference."

"There is?"

"Oh, yeah," Sally told her. "I thought you understood that, Melody. A cheerleader is supposed to blend in. Keep an eye on how sharp the other girls are doing their motions. How high they're jumping. You stood out too much, Mel. Show you have team spirit."

Melody looked very concerned. "Thanks for telling me," she said.

"Well, I want to help you," Sally told her.

"Did Coach say anything else?" Melody asked warily.

"No," replied Sally. "But I noticed something."

"What?"

"Your jumps," Sally said sadly. "You're jumping higher than the girls next to you. That's the show-off thing. And you're springing too much when you come down. Land with authority. *Stick it* means to *land it*."

"But Mae Lee said to keep the landings light," said Melody, "so you'll be ready for the next move."

"It's difficult to keep it light and land with authority. But that's why everyone who tries out for cheering doesn't make the squad," Sally explained.

"I see," said Melody. But Sally could tell she was confused. Confusion. Lack of confidence. Perfect.

"Do me a favor, Melody," Sally told her. "Don't tell anyone I told you what Coach said or that I gave you advice. I just saw an opportunity to improve your chances for making the squad."

"Thanks for telling me," said Melody.

Sally gave Melody her warmest, most sincere-seeming smile. "I like you," she said. "I'm here to help you, Mel."

NINTH-GRADE LOCKER AREA.
THURSDAY 8:15 A.M.

Sally was talking with her friends, but she kept an eye out for Jake Feder. It was time to put part two of plan B into action. When she finally spotted him, she headed in his direction.

"Hey, Jake," she said when they met. "I'll wait for you. We can go to homeroom together."

Jake's eyes sparkled, and a smile spread across his face. "Okay," he said.

He's thrilled to walk to homeroom with me, Sally thought. I haven't lost my power.

She stood close to Jake as he opened his locker. When he took a Walkman and a tape out of his pocket, Sally noticed the title of the tape. "The Raves," she said. "You like them?"

"Don't know," said Jake. "Melody just lent it to me. They're the hot thing in Miami right now. She went to a concert and got hooked."

"I'll have to check them out," said Sally.

Jake took out a couple of books, put the Walkman and tape in his locker, and slammed the door shut. "Melody's trying out for cheering," he said enthusiastically. "I heard she's good."

"Not," said Sally.

"Not?" he said, surprised.

Sally put on a concerned look. "People should stop telling her she's good. I'm afraid she's in for a big disappointment."

"But Emily and Alexis said . . ." began Jake.

"What do they know, Jake?" Sally said as they started down the hall side by side. "They're seventh-graders. They're just learning about cheering themselves. Melody just isn't good enough, Jake. And even if she was good, I don't think she should be on the squad."

"Why not?" Jake asked with concern.

"I can't say," Sally told him.

Jake stopped on the stairs. "What did she do?" he asked.

"It's not what she did, Jake," said Melody thoughtfully. "It's her attitude. It's what she says."

"Sally, come on, tell me," Jake said.

"Melody Max is a phony," Sally told him. "I hate to say it, but she makes fun of everyone behind their back."

"She does?" Jake said incredulously.

They continued up the stairs. "She does," said Sally sadly. "I was surprised, too. The only reason she's interested in cheering is because it's a way to stay in shape. Basically she thinks we're all a bunch of hicks. She's just killing time until she can move back to Miami."

"But she's so friendly," Jake protested. "Especially to Emily and Alexis."

They'd reached their homeroom, and Sally put a hand on Jake's arm to stop him in the doorway. There was more she wanted to tell him. Besides, Darryl was already in the room, and she wanted him to see her and Jake having an intimate conversation. She took a step closer to Jake. "The thing is, Jake," she whispered, "Melody knows that the Grangers are connected to the CMS sport scene. She also knows that Emily's sister helps them with cheerleading practices. I think she's using Emily to try to get on the squad. But behind Emily's back she makes fun of her. Melody calls her 'that chubette' and thinks Emily's silly with all her school spirit."

"Wow," said Jake.

"At first I was fooled by Melody, too," Sally told Jake. "But trust me, she's not what she seems." She looked at her feet. "I feel just awful for Emily," she muttered.

"And Emily's been so nice to her," Jake commented.

"I don't like to talk about people behind their backs," Sally told him. "Maybe I'm wrong about

Melody. She just moved here and everything. I wouldn't want anyone to be mean to her because of something I said."

"Don't worry, Sally," Jake said. "I won't repeat it. I'm just glad I know."

The second bell rang.

Jake stood back to let Sally go into the room first. He's such a gentleman, Sally thought. It must kill him to think that someone is backstabbing his little friend Emily Granger.

She was right. As Jake went to his seat and listened to homeroom announcements, all he thought about was Emily. She was exactly the age his baby sister would be if she hadn't died in the fire. When he'd moved in with his grandparents, he thought of her as a sister. Now someone was making a fool of Emily and using her to get what they wanted. He had to protect Emily from Melody. But how?

NORTH CORRIDOR 3:05 P.M.

Melody walked slowly through the lobby toward the small gym. The day before, she had been excited and confident about cheering. Now she was disappointed and scared. The tryouts were the next day, and she was doing everything wrong. Last night she tried doing jumps the way Sally described, but they felt awkward and heavy. My first mistake was comparing cheer jumps to ballet leaps, thought Melody. Or maybe my first mistake was going out for cheering. Maybe I'm not cut out to be a cheerleader.

Jake came out of a classroom and cut in front of Melody. She was sure he saw her, but he kept walking. "Hey, Jake," she called out. "Wait up."

He turned and waited for her, but he didn't smile or say hi. Was it her imagination, or was he trying to avoid her?

"Have you seen Emily?" he asked.

"I'm meeting her in the locker room," Melody told him. "We have tryout clinic."

"Oh," he said. He seemed disappointed.

"Is everything okay?" she asked.

"Yeah, sure," he said. He turned and ran ahead of her toward the small gym.

Why doesn't he want to walk there with me? Melody wondered. She quickened her own step. She had to shake herself out of this bad mood. Two days ago she didn't care about the kids at Claymore or about cheerleading. Now her heart was set on being on the cheer squad, and her feelings were hurt because someone didn't say hi to her.

Emily, Alexis, and Joan were already in the locker room when she got there.

Alexis looked up from tying her athletic

shoes. "I'm so nervous," she told Melody. "This is our last chance to learn this stuff before tryouts."

"We're nervous, but we're still having fun," added Joan.

Melody looked around at her new friends. Alexis. Joan. Emily. She would like to become better friends with all of them. But after tryouts tomorrow I probably won't be part of this group, she thought. Everyone will be a CMS cheerleader but me.

Alexis had the same thought.

So did Emily.

Joan was pretty confident she could make the squad. But she didn't know if her parents would let her be a cheerleader.

The four girls went into the gym together and lined up with the other cheerleader hopefuls for the warm-up.

As Emily took her place between Alexis and Melody, she noticed Jake standing near the bleachers. He was motioning for her to come over. Emily was halfway to Jake when Coach Cortes came into the gym blowing her whistle to signal the start of the warm-up. Emily waved to Jake and went back to her place. She wondered what he wanted. She'd call him as soon as she got home.

It was during the jump workshop with Mae Lee that Emily first noticed the change in

Melody's cheering. Her jumps weren't as high as they were the day before. She was also landing with a thud. Maybe it's just jumps that are giving her trouble, thought Emily.

Next they had the center cheer workshop with Sally. Sally told them to take turns performing the cheer in groups of threes. When Melody's group was performing it, Emily noticed that she kept looking at the girls on either side of her instead of at the imaginary crowd. It's like Melody's a whole different cheerleader from the one she was yesterday, thought Emily. There is no way she's going to make the squad if she cheers this way for the tryouts.

Emily also noticed that Melody was quiet when they were leaving the building and saying good-bye to one another outside of school. Emily was nervous about the tryouts, too. And so was Alexis. Even Joan, who was doing so well with the tumbling and had a terrific shot at being picked, seemed to be worried.

As she walked home alone Emily thought over her chances for making the squad and decided they weren't very good. All she could think was, What if I don't make it? From the time she was Lily's age she had wanted to be a CMS cheerleader, just like her mother and older sister. Now it was her turn, and she wasn't going to make it.

Her dream would be gone like a puff of smoke.

BULLDOG CAFÉ 5:45 P.M.

Emily was so distracted by her own mood that she didn't even notice Jake when she walked by Bulldog Café on her way into the hotel.

"Hey, Em," Jake called out. "I've been waiting for you."

Emily turned and saw Jake sitting at the outside corner table. She said hi as she went over and sat in the chair across from him.

"What's wrong?" he asked. "You look sort of sad."

Emily quickly replaced her worried look with a big Emily smile. "Nothing. Nothing's wrong."

Jake leaned forward and looked deep into her eyes. "Emily, it's me," he said. "You don't have to pretend."

"I guess I'm tired and hungry," she said.

"What do you want?" he asked. "I'm having a yogurt smoothie with mango and banana."

"That sounds perfect," she said. "And a donut."

Jake pushed his smoothie toward her and stood up. "Have this one," he said. "I'll get another. Chocolate donut?"

She nodded. "Thanks, Jake," she said. "You're great."

"Sure," he said.

By the time Jake returned with the second smoothie and the donut, Emily was ready to talk about what was on her mind.

"This was our last clinic before tryouts," she began. "I guess I'm real nervous. But all my friends are nervous, too. Especially Melody. Something weird is going on with her."

"I was afraid Melody would upset you," Jake said.

"You were?" she asked. "Why?"

"I have this feeling that Melody might be a little . . . phony," Jake said. "I know you've been really friendly with her. That's why I came to the gym today — to tell you that I thought that."

"Phony?" said Emily with surprise. "Melody? I don't think she's phony. Just the opposite. I think she's honest. And I thought she was going to be a terrific cheerleader. But today she seemed to have lost her confidence, and she was making mistakes all over the place. It's like she's a different person."

"Maybe she *is* a different person from the one you think she is," said Jake. "I mean, we hardly know her. And she did just move here from Miami. I don't think she's so thrilled to be living in Claymore."

"Oh, that," said Emily. "That's the way she felt when she first got here. She told me all about it. But now that she's making friends and trying out for cheering, she's happy. Or she was until today."

"I don't think you should worry so much about Melody," said Jake. "The important thing is that you go out there tomorrow and do *your* best at the tryouts."

"But I'm afraid I'm not good enough, Jake," Emily confessed. "There are so many girls who are terrific. You should see Adam's sister, Joan. She is so great."

"Em," said Jake imploringly. "You practiced all summer. Now all you can do is give it your all. If you don't make it, you don't make it. It won't be the end of the world."

In a flash Emily saw the out-of-town games she wouldn't go to. The Cheer USA competitions she wouldn't be in. The pep rallies. The parades. It would be the end of the Granger family tradition of Bulldog athletes and the life she planned for herself. Tears welled in her eyes.

Jake leaned forward. "Em, we have to get you out of this negative thinking mode," he said. "It's time for some positive thinking. Remember how you helped me when I was so nervous about being in the play last year?"

"How'd I help you?" Emily asked.

"You practiced that play with me for hours," he answered. "You took all those parts."

"Are you going to practice cheerleading with me?" Emily asked with a little giggle.

"No," said Jake. "But I think you should do what my grandmother is always telling me to do. You should write something."

"Write something?" Emily said.

"Write down your thoughts," Jake told her.

"Okay," Emily agreed. She opened her backpack and took out a notebook and pencil. "What do I write?"

"You should probably make some kind of list," he said.

"I know," Emily said. " 'Ten Ways to Cope If I Don't Make the Squad.' "

"You're kidding, right?" said Jake.

"Yes," she admitted. "Sort of." She thought for a second. "I'll make a list of things you should remember when you're going for tryouts. I'll call it 'Tryout Tips.' "

"That's more like it," Jake said.

As Emily made the list she explained why each of her ideas was an important tryout tip.

When she had completed the list, Jake read the whole thing out loud.

CHEERLEADING TRYOUT TIPS

1. Concentrate on your own performance. Don't worry about what the other girls are doing.
2. Have a positive, confident attitude and project it.
3. Look at the judges and smile.
4. Exaggerate your moves. Make it SHARP!
5. Project your voice and emphasize key words in the cheer.
6. Make jumps high, point toes, land light, SMILE.
7. If you make a mistake, go on as if nothing went wrong.
8. Do your personal best, and know that your best is the best you can do.

"I feel better," said Emily. "Thanks, Jake." She took the last sip of her smoothie. "I'm going to call Alexis, Joan, and Melody right away and tell them about my tryout tips. Maybe it will help them keep the tryout jitters under control, too. Especially Melody."

"Don't worry about Melody, Emily," said Jake.

"Jake, that doesn't sound like you!" Emily exclaimed.

"I doubt that she's worrying about you," Jake said. "Call Alexis and Joan. But let Melody Max take care of herself. I am sure she can."

"You really don't like her, do you?" Emily said.

"I just don't want anyone taking advantage of you," Jake said.

"How could she take advantage of me?" Emily asked. "Why would you say that?"

Jake wanted to tell Emily how Melody was making fun of her behind her back, but he didn't want to upset her when she had tryouts the next day. He certainly didn't want to tell Emily the things Melody said about her. That would just hurt Emily's feelings. For now, all he could hope for was that Emily would make the cheering squad and Melody wouldn't. "It's nothing," he said. "Just a feeling."

"When you know Melody better you'll like her, too," said Emily.

She stood up. "See you tomorrow," she said. "Will you hang around for the tryout results?"

"I wouldn't miss it for the world," he said. He gave her a thumbs-up sign. "Go for it, Em," he said.

Emily smiled and waved the paper with the tryout tips. "Thanks," she said. She ran up the steps to call her friends.

DELHAVEN DRIVE 6:30 P.M.

Joan was in the kitchen preparing dinner with her father when the phone rang. He answered it and handed the receiver to her. It was Emily.

"I have a whole bunch of tryout tips for cheerleading," Emily told Joan.

Cheerleading! thought Joan with alarm. What if my father overhears us talking about cheering?

She moved over to the stove, which was as far from her father as the telephone cord would allow. Why couldn't her family have a portable phone like everyone else? With a portable phone she could have had this conversation in another room. Why did her parents have to be so anti anything new? Why did they have to be so different from everyone else's parents?

When Emily was reciting tip number three, Joan's father came over to the stove to check the rice. Joan moved over to the refrigerator.

"Isn't that a good one?" Emily asked.

"Terrific," agreed Joan, but she was hardly listening to Emily. She was too busy avoiding her father.

By tip number seven Joan had moved to the table and back to the refrigerator. Her father was going to become suspicious if she didn't stop dancing around the room. She had to get Emily off the phone.

"That's great, Emily," said Joan. "Thanks for calling."

"There's one more cheerleading tryout tip," Emily said.

"Oh, sorry," said Joan. "What is it?"

" 'Do your personal best,' " Emily told her, " 'and know that your best is the best you can do.' "

"Okay," said Joan. "I'll do that."

"You should feel very confident going out there tomorrow," Emily told her. "You'll make a great cheerleader." She shouted, "The new flyer for CMS! Yes!"

Joan automatically whispered into the receiver, "Sh-sh."

"What did you say?" Emily asked.

"I said 'Sh-hould.' Should I do my homework now or later?"

"I'm going to do mine now," Emily said. "So I can relax before I go to bed. The important thing is to put cheering out of your mind now. Okay?"

"Yeah," Joan agreed. "Thanks. 'Bye."

Joan hung up the receiver and went back to peeling onions for the stir-fry chicken.

"Who was that?" her father asked. "One of your new chums from the debate team?"

"Yes," answered Joan. "She's from the team." As she said it, Joan thought, I mean cheering team, not debate team. But she didn't say that to her father. Does that count as a lie? she wondered.

"So what's the subject of the first debate?" her father asked.

"Ah, we don't know for sure who is going to be on the team yet," Joan answered. "We'll find out tomorrow." She was trying so hard not to lie.

"You must be at least thinking of subjects, with all the meetings you've been having," he said.

"Yes, of course," Joan said nervously. "We're, we're talking a lot about the importance of winning. One side says that to win — at sports — is the most important thing. The other side is arguing that competition isn't the essence of sports. Something like that. It isn't quite defined yet. It's a little hard because we aren't sure who's going to be on the team. But we're practicing a lot."

"Competition and sports sounds like an insubstantial subject to me," he said. "Can't they think of anything besides sports in that school?"

"Guess not," Joan said. She went back to peeling onions. Lying to her parents was awful. But so was not being able to do what she wanted. She loved gymnastics. She wanted to be a cheerleader. Her parents just didn't understand anything that she liked. Jeans. Rock music. Hollywood movies. Public schools. Portable telephones. The list was endless. But now she knew that she definitely agreed with her parents on one thing. They hated lying. And so did she.

Tears streamed down Joan's face as she worked. She always cried when she peeled onions.

This time her weepy eyes were caused by more than the onions.

SEAVIEW TERRACE 6:30 P.M.

Alexis stretched out on her father's easy chair to watch a women's college basketball game on television. A good thing about being at her dad's was that the TV was hooked up to a satellite dish that pulled in great sports channels. She was watching a game between the University of Oregon and Stanford University. Oregon's number twelve was dribbling down the court. Alexis studied the dribble, noticing how far the player bent toward the ball. She'd try dribbling that way the next time she threw baskets with the kids at the playground.

The phone rang as number twelve threw the ball from midcourt. The ball arched through the air and swished down through the net.

"What a shot!" the excited announcer shouted as Alexis hit the mute button but kept her eye on the television screen. She picked up the phone and said hello.

"It's me," Emily told her. "I was so nervous about tryouts tomorrow that I made this list. It's things to help us do our best."

Alexis tried to watch the muted game while Emily read her list of tryout tips. The excitement she'd been feeling while watching the game was replaced by anxiety about the tryouts. What if she wasn't paying enough attention to Emily's suggestions? What if she didn't make the squad because she hadn't learned them?

Alexis turned her back on the TV and took the portable telephone to the dining table where she'd left her notebook. "Start over," Alexis said as she opened the pad to a clean page. "I'm going to write them down. I need all the help I can get."

When Alexis finished writing down Emily's tips, she looked back at the TV. There was only a three-point spread in the score, with Stanford in the lead. Alexis scanned the screen for number twelve. There she was, charging down the court and making another three-point basket! I'd love to be able to play like that, thought Alexis.

"Alexis," Emily said, "are you still there?"

Alexis turned her back on the basketball game again. "Yeah, I am," she said.

"It's going to be so much fun if we both make the squad," Emily said.

"There are a lot of kids trying out," Alexis reminded her. "And a lot of them are good. What if you make it and I don't?"

"It could be the other way around," said Emily. "You might make the squad and I won't."

"I don't want to be a cheerleader if you aren't," Alexis blurted out. She said it almost without thinking. But she knew when she heard herself that it was the truth.

"Alexis Lewis!" Emily exclaimed. "I wouldn't let you not be a cheerleader just because I wasn't."

"Well, it's not going to be a problem, since I'm not going to make the squad," said Alexis.

"No more negative thinking!" Emily scolded. "We've practiced a lot. Now we're both going out there to do our best. That's all we should be thinking about."

"You're right," Alexis agreed. "Do our best."

"But tonight we should put cheering out of our minds and relax," Emily advised. "Don't even practice tonight."

After Alexis hung up the phone, she turned the volume back on the TV, but she was still thinking about cheering.

If I don't make the squad and Emily does, thought Alexis, we'll hardly ever see each other. Emily will always be busy with practices or games. She'll be with her new friends — like

Joan and Melody — all the time. She'll never invite me over. It will be the end of our being best friends. I know it will.

A lump rose to her throat.

Tomorrow her life might change forever.

DOLPHIN COURT APARTMENTS 8:30 P.M.

Melody and her mother climbed the outside stairs to their apartment.

"I thoroughly enjoyed that meal," Carolyn Sinclair said. "But you barely ate yours, sugar."

"I told you," Melody said, "I'm not very hungry."

Carolyn opened the door, switched on the light, and they walked in. "With all the cheerleading you've been doing you should have a huge appetite," she said. She looked deep into her daughter's eyes as if she were trying to read her mind. Melody hated it when her mother did that.

"Melody, you're not on one of those crazy diets, are you?" she asked. "You're not trying to lose weight because you think it will increase your chances for making that squad?"

"No!" Melody answered. "I don't even care about that cheerleading stuff. I hope you didn't tell everyone in your office that I'm trying out."

Her mother broke the eye lock with Melody and looked around the room. Her gaze landed on the blinking answering machine. "There are some messages," she said. "Will you check them?"

Melody knew that her mother had changed the subject because she had blabbed at work about her daughter trying out for the CMS cheer squad. Why did I have to be so enthusiastic about cheering after that first clinic? Melody thought as she walked over to the answering machine. I was such a fool. Why did I tell anyone that I was going out for it in the first place? Why did I e-mail my friends and dad in Miami all about it?

It was all so embarrassing. Maybe she'd just skip school tomorrow. Be sick. Cut. Do anything but go out for cheering and make a fool of herself.

Melody hit the play button on the answering machine and listened.

"Hi, Melody, it's Sally. Just wishing you good luck tomorrow. Remember what I said and you'll be fine. Call me if you have any questions. 'Bye."

The next message was from Emily.

"Melody, it's me, Emily. Hi. Listen, I made up this list of tryout tips to help us get ready for the big day tomorrow. There are a lot of them, and I don't want to fill up your answering machine. So call me, okay? Then I can tell you about them. Also, I wanted to ask you something about . . . I mean . . . please call me. Okay?"

The next message was from her father.

"Check out tomorrow's tie. Oh, yeah, good luck with that cheering business tomorrow. You're the best. They'd be fools not to choose you."

Melody could hear the familiar sounds of the TV studio in the background. Her father had taken time out from his busy day to call her. Too bad she was going to disappoint him. Too bad she wasn't still in Miami. Whatever made her think she should go out for some stupid little cheer squad in Boremore? Forget cheering. Forget new friends. Forget tryout tips. She performed terribly at the clinic today, and she knew it. Even suggestions from Sally didn't help. Nothing was going to help her.

Melody went to her room, closed the door, put on some music, and took out her homework. She wouldn't go out for cheering. She'd be a loner in Boremore, get good grades, and wait it out until she could move back to Miami.

An hour later the phone rang. She didn't answer it. "It's for you, Melody," her mother shouted from her bedroom. "Pick up."

It was Emily. Enthusiastic, friendly Emily.

Melody didn't have the heart to tell Emily that she wasn't going to try out for cheering, so she listened to the tryout tips.

Emily began. " 'Concentrate on your own performance. Don't worry about what the other girls are doing.' "

Emily's first tryout tip totally contradicted Sally's advice about keeping an eye on the other cheerleaders.

Number four didn't make any sense either. " 'Exaggerate your moves. Make it SHARP!' " When I did that, Sally said the coach didn't like it, thought Melody.

And what about Emily's next tip? " 'Make jumps high, point toes, land light, SMILE.' " If I jump as high as I can, thought Melody, I might be higher than the other girls. According to Sally that's not good.

"Here's the last one," Emily continued. " 'Do your personal best, and know that your best is the best you can do.' In other words, don't hold back. Give it your all."

If I do my personal best, thought Melody, I'd be jumping high, landing soft, and making sharp movements. But that's what Sally said not to do.

"That's it." Emily was saying. "Those are my tryout tips. What do you think?"

"Great," Melody said. "Thanks, Emily. That was really sweet of you. Thanks for calling."

"Are you nervous?" Emily asked.

"Not really," Melody said. "I've been thinking I might not go out for cheering tomorrow. I don't like it as much as I thought I would."

"But you were so good. I mean you *are* so good. I mean . . . well, here's what I wanted to talk to you about. You were *great* the first two days. Then today, you didn't seem to be with it."

"I thought I was jumping too high," said Melody. "And I wasn't sticking my landings. My movements were too big. I was trying to improve all that today."

"I think it was much better when you were more relaxed and not thinking about all of those things," Emily told her. "Maybe I shouldn't have said anything, but you were so good before. I just think if you cheer at the tryouts the way you did the first two days, you'll have a great chance of making the squad."

"Thanks for telling me," Melody said.

"I want to help," said Emily.

"I know," said Melody. "Look, I have to go now." She said good-bye and hung up.

Melody sat on the edge of her bed and thought about Emily's phone call. Sally was telling her to cheer one way. Emily was telling her to cheer another way. Whose advice was she going to follow? Another seventh-grader going out for cheering or the best cheerleader on the squad? Wouldn't it make more sense to trust Sally?

She looked around her new room. Her eyes landed on a brown leather notebook on the middle shelf. She took the book off the shelf. Her grandmother had written the family history on the yellowed pages. Melody closed her eyes and flipped through the pages. When she stopped flipping, she put the tip of her index finger on the page and opened her eyes to see where it pointed. She read, "Whenever I don't know what to do next with my life, I remember what *my* mother told me. 'When you need advice, look to yourself. Trust your own heart and mind. Then, sugar, don't hold back. Live life to the fullest.' "

Melody read the passage again and gently closed the book. "Thank you, Grandma," she whispered. "And thank you, Great-Grandma."

Melody looked up and saw her own face in the mirror. Trust yourself, she thought. Don't hold back. Live life to the fullest.

Suddenly, she didn't care about Sally. She didn't care what anyone else thought about how she cheered, even the judges. She was going out for cheering tomorrow and doing it the best *she* knew how. She'd treat it like a dance performance, which meant she would give it her all and show her stuff.

Melody went to the kitchen to get a snack. She was hungry after all.

GIRLS' LOCKER ROOM. FRIDAY 3:10 P.M.

Emily, Alexis, Joan, and Melody picked out lockers next to one another. The locker room was buzzing with nervous energy that went from girl to girl like an electric current.

Emily didn't know how she made it this far through the day without having a nervous breakdown. How was she supposed to keep her pretryout jitters under control when every seventh-grade girl who was trying out was as jittery as she was? It had been going on all day. In the hallways, as they went to and from classes, they exchanged glances that said, "Am I going to make it? Are you going to make it?"

As the tryout girls walked into the gym, Sally handed them each a sticker with a number on it. "Stick it to the upper left-hand side of your T-shirt," she instructed. "And good luck."

Emily was number four.

Alexis was number ten.

Melody was number thirteen.

And Joan was number twenty.

Four judges were seated at small tables set up for them in the four corners of the room. The girls lined up along the side wall. Melody counted twenty-eight girls, which meant that more girls had decided not to try out since yesterday's clinic. Should she have been one of them? Was she about to make a fool of herself?

Coach Cortes, who had been talking to one of the judges, came over to the cheerleading hopefuls and stood facing them. Instead of her usual shorts and T-shirt, she was dressed in a blue skirt, white blouse, and high heels.

"Tryouts are difficult," Coach told the girls. "For all of us. But especially for you. As you know, we only need ten girls to fill out the squad. That means eighteen of you are going to be disappointed today. Before we begin, I want to tell you how very impressed I've been with all of you over the last three days. You are a spirited, hard-working group. I hope that you will bring that spirit and attitude to whatever you do."

Emily tried slow breathing to keep her nerves under control. It wasn't working very well.

"Before I introduce our judges," Coach Cortes continued, "I'll remind you what you are to do for your tryout. When I call your number, you will perform for four separate judges. Look at the signs in the four sections of the room so you know what to do for each of the judges."

Emily looked and saw the four signs: REQUIRED CHEER. JUMPS. TUMBLING. DANCE.

"When you've finished all four tryout requirements, wait in the bleachers. No talking until the last girl has finished her last requirement. Then you will go back to the locker room to change. When you are ready, go to the front lobby, where our ninth-grade cheerleaders will serve snacks. After we've finished tallying the scores, I'll post an alphabetical list of the complete CMS cheer squad on the bulletin board to the right of the gym doors. If your name is on the list . . . well, you know what it means."

Melody's heart was beating like a drum. She wanted her name to be on that list.

Next, Coach Cortes introduced the judges — a high school cheerleading coach from Fort Myers, Florida, the Claymore High School coach, a representative from Cheer USA, and a retired college cheerleading coach.

Finally, Coach said, "Everybody take a deep breath, and let's begin."

The girls sucked in and let out their breaths in a collective swish. A few people, including Coach, laughed at the noise they'd made. Emily checked out the judges. Only one of them was smiling.

"So, are you ready?" Coach asked.

A few girls answered yes. Mostly they nodded silently.

"I said, are you ready?" Coach Cortes shouted.

"Yes!" the girls shouted back.

"Now have fun," Coach Cortes told them. "It's not a funeral."

Maybe not for you, thought Alexis.

Coach picked a small slip of paper from a bowl on the table, read it to herself, and announced, "The first to go is number ten."

Number ten, thought Alexis. That's me! She was frozen in terror.

Emily grabbed her hand and squeezed it. "Go," she whispered. "You can do it!"

Alexis took one last look at Emily before running out to the middle of the floor. How awful, she thought. I'm the first one to go. Her heart pounded. She started the chant. It sounded lonely and hollow. It was so scary to be cheering alone. Alexis thought about Emily's tips and smiled broadly. She tried to remember to have a positive, confident attitude. Smile, she ordered herself.

It was over. Alexis forced herself to flash the dance judge one last smile before leaving the floor. If you pick Emily, please pick me, too, she prayed. Please. She ran off the floor, relieved that it was over.

The sixth girl to try out was Joan.

Forget about your parents and what you'll do if you make the squad, she thought when she heard her number. Just go out there and do it!

As Joan was running to the required cheer corner, she felt light and happy and very excited. **"Give me a C,"** she shouted. Then she went to the jumping judge. Her jumps were high and light. Next, a few somersaults, three cartwheels, and two back handsprings for the tumbling judge. Last, the dance judge. That was fun. And she was done. Emily gave Joan a thumbs-up sign as she ran off the floor.

Five more girls tried out, and it still wasn't Emily's turn. Don't think about how good these other girls are, she told herself. Think about doing *your* best. Do it for CMS.

Finally it was Emily's turn. As she ran over to the required cheer judge, she imagined the bleachers were filled with fans at a basketball game. CMS was three points behind with only sixty seconds left on the clock. It was up to her to fire up the crowd and give the team the confidence they needed to win the game. **"Give me a C!"** she shouted.

Melody watched Emily do her four requirements. Melody was impressed with Emily. She was following her own advice and giving it her best shot. Melody remembered how in dance performances she loved the energy and excitement of going all out.

"Number thirteen," Coach called.

As Melody passed Emily coming off the floor, she heard her say, "Go for it." I will, thought Melody as she took her place in front of the judges and began the chant. She jumped as high as she wanted and landed as lightly as she did when she did ballet leaps. And since she knew how to do a back handspring, she threw that in at the end of her tumbling tryout. She did the dance routine with all her heart and soul and some of her ever-cool attitude.

After the last girl had tried out, they all went back to the locker room. Everyone was talking at once about what they thought they'd done wrong and how well the other girls had done. After they changed they went to the lobby to wait and wait.

And wait.

OUTSIDE GYM DOORS 5:30 P.M.

Finally Coach Cortes came through the gym doors with Sally and Mae. Coach was holding a rolled-up piece of paper. Sally held a small stack of envelopes.

A wave of girls moved toward the bulletin board. Coach Cortes called out, "Hold it. Stay back until I post the notice." They moved a few steps back. "Do not, I repeat, *do not* come up to the bulletin board until I am safely out of here."

Nervous laughter rose from the crowd.

"I have one announcement before I post the list. The CMS cheerleaders are invited to a dinner prepared and served by the football team at seven tomorrow night.

"You will have your first cheerleading meeting after the dinner and you'll be measured for uniforms." Coach looked over at Sally and asked, "What have I forgotten?"

"The parental permission slips," Sally told her. "They have to bring them to the dinner."

"Right," said Coach. "If you make the squad, we will give you a permission slip for your parents to sign. Don't leave here without one, and don't come to the dinner without bringing it back signed. Very important. Essential. Bring it."

A sudden chill ran through Joan's body. Goosebumps rose on her arms and legs. She wasn't just nervous anymore, she was terrified. If she made the squad, her parents had to sign a permission slip by tomorrow!

The lobby became absolutely quiet as Coach Cortes posted the cheer squad list. Emily held her breath.

Coach finally walked back into the gym. The doors closed behind her, and the wave of girls moved forward again. All Joan could see were backs. Suddenly she was in the air above the crowd. Emily, Melody, and Alexis were holding her up.

"Tell us, Joan," Emily yelled. "Who's on the list?"

Joan silently read the list from the top. "Emily! Emily!" she shouted. "You made it!"

Joan almost fell out of the lift as Emily shouted, "I made it. I made it!"

Joan put her hands on Emily's and Alexis's

heads for balance as she continued looking down the list.

"Who else?" asked Emily. "What about Alexis?"

"Oh! Oh!" Joan exclaimed. "I made it. Melody, you made it, too. You're on the squad!"

Melody felt a wave of excitement and happiness charge through her as she helped Joan out of the lift.

"I did it! I did it!" Melody shouted. "I made it!"

Joan and Emily were hugging her. They were all on the list. They were CMS cheerleaders.

Emily broke away from the hug and looked around. "Where's Alexis?" she asked.

The three friends looked at one another in alarm.

"She didn't make the squad!" Emily said with a sudden, terrible realization.

Emily ran over to the list and quickly went down the row of names to double-check. It was true. Alexis Lewis was not on the CMS cheer squad. Emily looked around the lobby. Disappointed, tearful would-be cheerleaders were leaving as quickly as possible. One girl was throwing up in the trash bin. So many people hadn't made the squad. They must all feel awful, thought Emily. And one of them is Alexis.

Emily ran out of the building without waiting for Joan and Melody. She had to find Alexis.

Joan took the permission slip from Sally and walked toward the exit in a daze. Maybe I can sign my parents' names to the slip, she thought. That will give me more time to tell them. But what about the special dinner tomorrow night? And the meeting? She was supposed to be proud and happy because she was chosen to be a CMS cheerleader, but here she was feeling miserable.

Joan walked outside. Where would she go now? What would she do? She saw her brother walking toward her. Jake Feder, on Rollerblades rolled beside him.

"We just heard you made the cheering squad," Jake said as he rolled around her. "Congratulations! That's awesome."

"My kid sister is a CMS cheerleader," Adam said. "I'm so impressed."

"You don't look very happy," Jake observed.

"I'm happy," Joan told him as she flashed the two boys a false smile. "Happy. See."

Adam gave her a surprised look. He knows I'm faking it, she thought.

"Who else made the squad?" Jake asked.

"Emily and Melody," Joan answered.

"Emily must be so psyched," said Jake.

"All the eighth-graders kept their spots on the squad," Joan said. "And the two other seventh-graders are Kelly and Maria. They were really good." Joan let herself enjoy the moment.

She was a CMS cheerleader!

OUTSIDE GYM DOORS 5:45 P.M.

Melody needed to get a permission slip from Sally, but she didn't know what to say to her. After all, she hadn't followed Sally's cheerleading advice. Why did Sally give me such bad advice? she wondered.

Finally, Melody went over to Sally.

"Congratulations," Sally said. "You were great out there today."

"Thanks," Melody replied.

"Don't mention it," said Sally. "I was glad to help. I know I really pushed you, but it worked."

"I sort of did the opposite of what you told me," Melody confessed. "When I tried what you told me I cheered badly."

Sally laughed. "That was the idea, Melody," she said. "I used some reverse psychology on you. It made you really think about cheering and what it's all about. You had to go through that to come out with the great performance you did today. If you had continued cheering the way you were, you never would have made the squad. Believe me."

"I see," Melody said, even though she wasn't

sure she really understood how Sally had helped her. But it didn't make any difference now. The important thing was that she was a CMS Bulldog cheerleader.

Melody and Sally left the school building together. When they came outside, Sally whispered to Melody, "Remember, don't tell anyone that I helped you make the squad. It will look like I was playing favorites."

"Okay," agreed Melody.

They saw Joan, Adam, and Jake and went over to them. Sally put an arm around Joan's shoulder. "Your little sister is amazing!" she told Adam. "You should have seen her out there. She'll be the best flyer CMS ever had."

Adam smiled at his sister and then returned his gaze to Sally. She gave him a big Sally smile.

"And you made it, too," Adam said, turning to Melody. "Congratulations."

"Thanks," Melody said. "I'm so excited. When I first moved here I was homesick for my friends in Miami, but then I met Emily, and she got me to go out for cheering. It's great."

Jake studied Melody. Maybe she had complained about Claymore to Sally because she was homesick. That was normal. And maybe she did call Emily "that chubette," but it was clear that she appreciated Emily. She wasn't faking it. Jake decided that if Emily could be Melody's friend, he could, too. But where was Emily? Jake looked around. "Where's Emily?" he asked.

"I think she went to look for Alexis," Melody told him. "Alexis just disappeared. She must be upset about not making the squad."

"Poor Alexis," said Jake.

"I feel awful that we all made the squad and she didn't," Melody said.

Jake looked into her eyes and knew that she wasn't pretending.

"I'm going home now," Melody told Adam and Joan. "I want to make some phone calls to see if I can find out what happened to Alexis. You going now?"

"Yeah," said Adam.

"I'll walk with you, then," Melody told them.

"Great," said Adam.

"I'll go partway with you," said Jake. "I want to hear all about the tryouts."

Sally noticed that Jake kept looking at Melody. How many guys does that girl need? she wondered.

"You go in the same direction, Sally," Melody said. "You want to walk with us?"

"I still have a few things to do here," Sally told her.

Sally kept her smile going as she said goodbye, but she was cursing to herself. Beautiful Melody Max had made the squad. Melody, who jumped higher than anyone, did a flip like she was made of air, and danced like she was on Broadway. Melody, who had the potential to outshine her.

Not in this lifetime, you won't, thought Sally.

SEAVIEW TERRACE 6:00 P.M.

Emily pressed the buzzer to Alexis's father's apartment. When no one answered the door, she sat on a deck chair and wrote Alexis a note. She'd leave it for her, then she'd go looking for Alexis on the beach. One way or another, she had to find her friend.

When she finished writing, Emily bent down to push the note under the door. A hand fell on her shoulder. She was startled and let out a little shriek of fright.

"Emily, it's just me," a low, sad voice said.

Emily stood up and faced Alexis. Her eyes were puffy and bloodshot from crying. She looked so sad that tears of sympathy sprang to Emily's eyes.

"I was just leaving you a note," Emily told her. She handed Alexis the piece of paper.

Alexis took the note and read it.

Alexis, I'm sorry you didn't make the squad and I did. Maybe you are upset because you think we won't be best friends if one of us is a cheerleader and the other isn't. But that isn't true. Would you stop being my friend if you had made the squad and I hadn't? We didn't stop being friends when you were on the basketball team and I wasn't. Can you come for dinner and a sleep over tonight? I'd be so happy if you would come. I can't be happy about being a cheerleader when you are unhappy. We have to find a way to make you happy, too. That's what friends are for. So please come over tonight. For me. Love always, your very best friend in the whole world, Emily.

"I don't want to ruin your happiness by being sad," Alexis told Emily. "It's just that I wanted to be a cheerleader, too. So we could do everything together in middle school."

"Were you going out for cheering because it was what I wanted to do?" asked Emily. "Sometimes I wondered if you even liked cheering that much."

"I didn't," Alexis admitted.

"That's good to know," Emily said with a sigh. "We still will do almost everything together, you know. Like tonight. Will you come to my house? Please."

"Okay," Alexis agreed. "Come on in. I'll call my dad and get my stuff."

Alexis knew that wanting to be with your

friends wasn't enough of a reason to be a cheerleader. But while she packed her overnight bag, she still couldn't stop thinking about all the times she and Emily wouldn't be together, like all the out-of-town games and whenever Emily had practice. What will I be doing while Emily's busy with cheering? Alexis wondered. Maybe there was something else she could do after school at CMS.

Emily handed Alexis her hairbrush to pack. "What do you want to do after school?" she asked.

Alexis looked at her in amazement. "I was just wondering the same thing," she said. "You read my mind again."

"You're the only person in the whole world I can do that with," Emily told her. She smiled. "That's not going to change."

Alexis smiled back. "I know," she said softly.

"So that's what we have to think about," Emily said in a matter-of-fact tone. "We have to figure out what you do want to do. Okay?"

"Okay," Alexis agreed. "But tonight we're going to celebrate that you made the squad."

"I did, didn't I?" Emily said with delight. She punched the air and shouted, "Yes!"

"Yes!" Alexis cheered. "And the squad is so lucky to have you."

"I just wish you were a cheerleader," Emily

said. Then Emily felt bad about what she said.

Alexis smiled at her best friend. "You know what?" Alexis told her. "I'm really sort of happy that I'm not a cheerleader. I hated all that smiling stuff and the shouting, too. I was dreading it."

"Congratulations on *not* being a cheerleader!" Emily told her.

"Thank you," Alexis said with a giggle.

The two friends broke out laughing.

HARBOR ROAD 6:15 P.M.

When Joan, Melody, Adam, and Jake reached Delhaven Drive, Jake said good-bye to the others. He wanted to swing by The Manor Hotel to see if Emily and Alexis were there.

When he'd gone, Melody asked Adam and Joan if they wanted to go to her place for a swim. "My mom's working late tonight, but I'm sure she won't mind," Melody said. "She's been wanting me to make friends here. She's going to be out of her mind when I tell her I made the squad. We could have a cookout by the pool."

"I don't think so," Joan said. "Dinner is already planned."

"It's my turn to cook with our father," Adam explained.

After they said good-bye to Melody, Adam asked Joan, "Do Mother and Father know that you went out for cheering?"

She shook her head no.

"I didn't think so," he said.

Joan burst into tears. Her brother put his arm around her shoulder. "It'll be okay," he said. "We just need a plan of action. It'll be okay."

"What do you mean, it will be okay?" said Joan as she pulled away from him.

"They won't keep you from being a cheerleader," he said. "We'll explain that it's important to you . . ."

"Just the way we explained that it was important for me to do gymnastics, and they made me drop out?" she asked. "Or how about when I wanted to go to that sleep-away camp for horseback riding, and they made me go to a math camp? How about that? Huh?" More tears came, but now they were angry tears. "They never say no to you, Adam," she shouted. "So of course you don't think it's a problem. Well, don't tell them I made the squad, because I'm not telling them." She shook the permission slip envelope in his face. "I'm forging their names on this permission slip, and I'm going to the dinner and meeting tomorrow, and I'm going to be a cheerleader. I'm going to keep on lying to them. And if you tell . . . if you tell, Adam Russo-Chazen, I am never, ever going to speak to you again."

Before Adam could say anything or stop her,

Joan ran up the street. She'd go in the back door and sneak up the stairs. Her father wouldn't even hear her. He'd be translating and listening to classical music and in another world that didn't include crying daughters and cheer squads and the problems of a kid like her.

BULLDOG CAFÉ 7:30 P.M.

Alexis and Emily were baby-sitting for Lily while Emily's parents worked in the hotel and restaurant. Jake was the café busboy for the dinner shift. When the girls were almost finished eating, Lynn came by on her way home from her high school cheerleading practice.

Lynn leaned over the café railing and congratulated Emily. "I heard you made the squad," she said. "I'm so proud of you. The family tradition continues." She patted Lily on the head. "You're next, pumpkin," she said.

"I'm not a pumpkin," Lily protested. "I'm a human bean."

"Human *being*," Lynn corrected. "Or maybe you are a string bean."

"I'm a human *bean*," Lily insisted.

"Like a Beanie Baby, I guess," Lynn whispered to Emily and Alexis.

"I'm not a baby," Lily grumbled.

"I'm sorry you didn't make it, Alexis," Lynn said.

"It's okay," Alexis told her. "I'm not that upset about it."

After Lynn left, Lily asked, "Lexis, how come you're not a cheerleader?"

"Because I didn't get picked," Alexis told her. "But I'm going to do something else at school."

"What you going to do, Lexis?" Lily asked.

Jake leaned over to put a basket of hot rolls in the middle of the table. Before Alexis could think up something to tell Lily, he said, "Alexis is going to work on the school paper."

"I am?" said Alexis in astonishment.

"I hope you will," Jake told her. "I didn't think of it before because you were so busy with the cheering. What do you say?"

"I say great," Alexis told him.

"Jake, that is perfect," Emily said. "She was editor of our elementary school paper. She practically wrote the whole paper herself."

"I know," Jake said. "I read a couple of the issues. You're a really good writer, Alexis, especially when you're writing about sports. How would you like to cover sports for me? I did it last year, but I can't do that and be editor, too."

"I love sports," Alexis told him. "That would be great!"

"Can you cover the dinner tomorrow night?" he asked.

"Yes!" Emily and Alexis said in unison.

"How come you talk together?" asked Lily.

"Because we're best friends," Alexis and Emily answered — together.

DELHAVEN DRIVE 10:00 P.M.

Joan sat at her desk and tried again to copy her mother's signature from the front of one of her college books. If only she could make it look like her mother had signed the permission slip, that would be one problem solved. But only one — and her problems seemed to be mounting fast. At dinner her parents had noticed that she was upset.

"Have you been crying?" her father asked when she sat down for dinner.

"No," she said. "I'm tired." She told herself that it was only a half lie, because even though she had been crying, she was tired.

"Why aren't you eating your meal, Joanie?" her mother asked. "You love roast chicken."

"I'm not that hungry," Joan answered.

"Why wouldn't you be hungry?" her father asked.

"Don't know," Joan answered.

Adam gave her a look that said, Here's a chance to tell them about cheering. She gave him a look back that said, No way.

In her room now, she practiced writing

Michelle Russo again. Even if she forged her mother's signature for the permission slip, how was she ever going to manage to attend all the practices and games? And what about the out-of-town games?

Someone knocked on her door. Joan quickly stuck the permission slip and the page of forged signatures in her geography book.

"Joanie, it's me," her father said through the door.

"What do you want?" Joan asked.

"Your mother and I would like to speak with you in the living room, please," he said.

Joan's heart started to pound harder than it had before the tryouts. What did they want? Had they guessed her secret? Had Adam told them?

"I'll be right there," she called back.

A minute later Joan was sitting on a chair facing her parents, who sat side by side on the couch. Two against one, thought Joan. It's not fair.

At first her parents just stared at her. Then her mother leaned over and whispered something into her father's ear.

Her father nodded. "Yes," he said. "I agree."

"Agree to what?" Joan asked. "If you're talking about me and I'm here, you shouldn't ignore me. That's rude."

Joan couldn't believe her own ears. She sounded like a bratty kid. That was inexcusable behavior in the Russo-Chazen household. She expected a long-winded scolding from her mother or father, but it didn't come.

Instead, her mother said, "Your father and I are concerned about you, Joanie."

"Why?" Joan asked. There was that bratty-sounding voice again! "I mean," she said in a calmer, softer tone, "I mean, why are you concerned about me?"

"Because you don't seem happy at your new school," her father said. "Adam adjusted so easily when he first went there. We falsely assumed that you would have the same experience."

"But obviously you are not," concluded her mother. "So we wondered what we might do to make a better learning environment for you. We thought that perhaps we could hire a tutor, to enrich your studies."

"We would also consider sending you away to a boarding school in New England this year instead of waiting until you are in high school," her father added.

Joan jumped to her feet. "I don't want to go away to boarding school," she shouted. "I *love* CMS. I *want* to go there."

"You love it!" her mother exclaimed. "Then

why have you been projecting so much unhappiness the past two days? Why did you not eat your dinner?"

"Because I want to be a cheerleader!" Joan told them. "And I'm afraid you won't let me."

Her parents looked at her in shock.

"A cheerleader?" Paul said.

"At sporting events?"

"Yes," Joan told them. "A cheerleader. I love it. I'm not like you. I like to exercise."

"We also enjoy exercise," her father protested. "We go for hikes and walks. But cheering! It's so . . . so . . ."

"So important to me," said Joan completing the sentence. "I want to be a cheerleader, and the squad wants me. Please, please give me permission to be a cheerleader."

"Doesn't that take up a lot of time?" her father asked.

"Not so much," Joan answered.

"What about your studies?" her mother asked. "Won't they suffer?"

"And will you have time for the debate club?" asked her father.

"I'd have plenty of time for studying and the debate club, too," Joan told them. "You have to keep your grades up, or they won't let you stay on the squad. I can manage my time really well, you always say that about me. If I don't get top grades, I'll quit all on my own. I promise."

"Cheering is pretty harmless," her mother told her father. "They just go out there and shout a little. And jump up and down."

"It's probably a peer thing," her father said.

"And cheerleading isn't dangerous like gymnastics," her mother added.

"She'll tire of it," her father concluded.

Joan looked from one parent to the other in amazement. It sounded like they were going to let her be a cheerleader! They thought cheering was just a lot of shouting for the team. Maybe it was like that when they went to middle school, thought Joan. And since they don't watch television or follow sports, they don't understand about the gymnastics and dancing and all the skill that's involved in being a cheerleader. And she wasn't about to tell them.

"Please, may I be a cheerleader at CMS?" Joan asked.

Her father looked at her mother. Her mother nodded. "Yes, of course you may," her father said.

Joan was on her feet again. "Then I need you to sign a permission slip. It's no big deal, just like when there's a class trip. Be right back."

She jumped up and ran out of the room, practically knocking over Adam, who was eavesdropping in the hall.

"Way to go," he whispered. "I was standing by in case you needed me."

"I do now," Joan told him. "Distract them while I have them sign the permission form. I don't want them to read it. They have no idea that it involves gymnastics."

"Sure," said Adam.

Adam went into the living room, and Joan continued up the stairs.

When she came back a minute later she could hear Adam in action. He was reciting Shakespeare's *Hamlet*, taking all the parts. Her parents loved it when Adam did that stuff like that. It was how he convinced them to let him join the drama club.

As Joan came into the living room, she checked to see which parent was more engrossed in the recitation. Her mother was absolutely captivated. Joan put the paper in front of her and slipped the pen in her hand.

"Just sign it," Joan whispered.

Her mother glanced down and quickly scribbled her name and went back to Adam's performance of *Hamlet*.

Her father grabbed Joan's shirtsleeve and pulled her down on the couch next to him. "Watch this, Joanie," he commanded.

Joan slipped the signed permission slip back

in her notebook and sat on the couch between her parents.

She held the notebook to her chest, leaned back, and smiled as she watched her brother complete his recitation of *Hamlet*.

THE MANOR HOTEL 10:30 P.M.

Emily lay across her bed and watched the moon glowing outside her window. A smile spread across her face. "I made it," she thought happily. "I made it."

Lynn rapped on her door and came in. She threw herself across the bed beside Emily and propped herself up on her elbow.

"Hey," said Lynn. "Penny for your thoughts."

"Nothing special," Emily said. "I'm just glad I made the squad."

"I hope it isn't hard on you at CMS," Lynn said.

Emily rolled over on her stomach and faced her sister. "What do you mean?" she asked.

"It's not like you have to do everything that I did," Lynn explained.

"I know," Emily told her. "I'm a cheerleader because I want to be. Not because you were one."

"Good," said Lynn. She sat up and smiled down at Emily. "By the way, I'm really proud of you. I can't wait to tell all my friends that you made the squad."

"Thanks," said Emily. "And thanks for helping me train."

When Lynn left the room, Emily thought about what her sister said. She knew that Lynn was right. One of the reasons she was a cheerleader was because Lynn had been one. She had wanted to do everything Lynn did for as long as she could remember. But it was hard to follow in her older sister's footsteps.

Especially when Lynn was so much better at everything than she was.

CMS. SATURDAY NIGHT 7:00 P.M.

Melody's mother gave Melody and Joan a ride to the school, so they came into the school building together.

They stopped at the cafeteria door and looked around before going in. A long table in the center of the room was covered with a blue tablecloth, gold stars, and napkins. Twists of blue, white, and gold crepe paper hung above the table. And there was Darryl Budd putting out salads. Melody heard the sounds of her favorite group, the Raves, playing. Joan breathed in the delicious smells of spaghetti sauce.

"This is so much fun," she whispered to Melody.

"Wait for us," a voice called out.

Melody and Joan turned to see Emily and Alexis coming toward them. Alexis had a camera slung around her neck, a pencil stuck behind her ear, and a reporter's notebook in her hand.

After they all hugged and said hello, Emily told them that Jake was there, too, helping the football players with the dinner.

"For my article, I'm going to ask all the new cheerleaders the same question," Alexis told them. " 'Why did you want to be a cheerleader?' I need your answer before I leave, which will be after the dinner. Okay?"

"I can tell you right now," Joan said. "I wanted to be a cheerleader because I love gymnastics and I love CMS. I am going to support my new school in any way I can."

After Alexis wrote Joan's answer in her notebook the four friends went into the cafeteria.

Sally saw Melody. Sally knew that she looked great in her blue slip dress. But Melody had on cool cargo pants. Where does she buy her clothes? Sally wondered.

Darryl walked over to Melody. "Cool music," Sally heard him say. "Jake told me you lent him the disc. What other groups do you like?"

Sally skipped eavesdropping on the rest of their conversation and went over to welcome

Joan and Emily. She'd take care of Melody's popularity later.

As Sally greeted the three girls, she wondered what Alexis was doing there.

Alexis saw the question in Sally's expression and explained that she was on the newspaper staff and was writing an article about the new cheerleaders and the dinner.

"Great," said Sally. But she was annoyed that this cute girl was going to be working on the paper with Jake. And Emily. Why did she make the squad? Other girls tried out who were at the same level as Emily. She probably got picked because her family is so involved in CMS sports. Sally wondered if Emily really would be a good cheerleader. If she wasn't, it could interfere with the squad's chances in the Cheer USA competitions.

One of the football players came by with a tray of little franks. Sally noticed that while Emily was eating one frank, she took two more with her free hand. Not a good sign.

"Emily's parents donated the spaghetti sauce," Alexis told Sally. "It's the one they use in the hotel restaurant."

"Smells good," said Sally. She looked over her shoulder. Darryl and Jake were both talking to Melody now. It was time to break up that little trio. She stepped up on a chair and onto an empty table. She clapped her hands, and everyone's eyes turned to her. That's more like it, Sally thought, as she flashed them her best smile. Then she announced that the cheerleaders wanted to thank the football team for preparing and serving them dinner.

"So," she shouted, **"let's hear it for the cooking Blue."**

All the cheerleaders picked up the chant, clapped their hands twice, and repeated **"Blue."** They used arm movements for the next lines:

Let's hear it for the Blue XX Blue.
C, M, S, cook Bulldogs, cook!

Emily loved the way Sally had substituted cook for fight in the chant. Sally is so clever, she thought. She has the best ideas and the best school spirit. Emily hoped she could be half as good a cheerleader as Sally. I'll make her my role model, Emily decided.

"Let's hear it again!" Sally shouted.

"C, M, S, cook Bulldogs, cook!" the cheerleaders hollered.

Sally did a toe-touch jump in her leap from the table to the floor. The football cooks and waiters applauded.

"Let's eat," Coach Cortes shouted.

The cheerleaders ran over to the table and sat down.

Melody sat between Sally and Alexis. Alexis put her narrow reporter's notebook next to her plate. She was here to work.

"I have my answer to your question," Melody told her. "I want to be a CMS cheerleader because cheering is a perfect way for me to be part of my new town and school. I love the school spirit at CMS, and I'm proud to be on the CMS cheer squad."

Alexis wrote it all down, then looked up and smiled at Melody. "Excellent," she said.

Darryl came over with two plates of spaghetti. Sally noticed that he served her before he served Melody. She winked at Darryl and picked up her fork.

After they all had ice cream and chocolate chip cookies, the coach announced that the cheerleaders should go to the gym for the first official meeting of the full squad. As the girls were leaving the table, the boys came over with their own heaping plates of spaghetti. It was their turn to eat.

"I have an idea for a photo for the newspaper," Alexis told Melody. "The new cheerleaders in front of the table where the football players are chowing down."

Melody helped Alexis organize the shot.

Alexis looked through the viewfinder at the six smiling new cheerleaders. In the background she saw guys eating stringy forkfuls of spaghetti. She couldn't wait to see her photo and article in the *Bulldog Edition*.

Joan didn't mind that her picture was going to be in the school paper. Her parents knew that she was a cheerleader, and they had signed the permission slip. She was safe as long as they didn't know what a cheerleader did, especially a flyer.

"Guys, keep eating," Alexis said. "Girls, smile!" She took four shots of the scene.

Melody was eager for the *Bulldog Edition* to come out, too. She wanted to send a copy to her father. Maybe he'd come see her cheer sometime. She hoped their squad would be in the Cheer USA state competitions. Her father and Miami friends would be very impressed by that.

After the photo shoot, the cheerleaders went to the small gym for their meeting. It was time for Alexis to leave. As she was walking toward the front door, Emily came running up to her. "I forgot to say good-bye," she told Alexis.

"That's okay," Alexis told her. "But you know what else you forgot? You didn't answer my question about why you wanted to be a cheerleader. I have everyone's answer but yours."

"I've wanted to be a cheerleader all my life," Emily said.

"Wait a minute," Alexis said. She took out her notebook and pencil. "Okay. Start over."

"I wanted to be a cheerleader all my life," Emily repeated. "And now I am a cheerleader." Her voice was charged with excitement. "I love CMS. I love cheering."

"Got it," said Alexis as she closed her notebook. Sounds of talking and laughter reached them from the small gym. "You better go back. You don't want to miss the meeting."

Alexis watched Emily running happily back to the gym. I spent the whole summer dreaming about being a cheerleader with Emily, she thought. But somehow she felt all right.

She was going to be the best *Bulldog Edition* reporter.

DOLPHIN COURT APARTMENTS 11:00 P.M.

Melody Max turned on her computer and checked her e-mail. There were messages from three of her friends in Miami and one from her father. They all wanted to know how she did in the tryouts. She'd already called her dad with the good news. Now she'd write to her friends.

> Hey, out there, it's me — Melody Max, CMS cheerleader. Yes, I made it! Wow! For a while there I didn't think I could cut it. It's been a super stress scene over here on the west

coast. But with the help of some other seventh-graders, I pulled it out. Cheer tryouts are a who's-going-to-win-you-or-me kind of scene, but you know what? People were still helping one another. Wild, huh? No time to be bored anymore, so I think I'll be okay. Take that back. I KNOW I'm going to be okay. Did I whine a lot the first two weeks I was here? Sorry about that. Now I'm back on track. Still missing you all, but it doesn't feel like prison no more no how. Cheers! And love. The Max.

Melody sent her e-mail, switched off her computer and stared at the blank screen. She was tired and she suddenly felt very sad. Everything she'd said in the e-mail was true. She was excited about being a cheerleader, but she missed being with friends she'd known all her life. Like Tina. She and Tina thought they were so lucky to be best friends and live on the same block. Now Tina was on the other side of the state. Not so lucky. And her dad! She missed her dad so much it made her heart ache.

Melody got into bed and turned off the light.

THE MANOR HOTEL 11:15 P.M.

Emily had been in bed for an hour and was still wide awake. She turned her head on the pillow and faced her bedside table. She took a deep breath and smelled the delicate scent of the bouquet of white tea roses. The flowers, in a blue vase, were there when she came home. A note leaning against the vase read: *"Carry on the tradition! We're so proud of you. Love, Mom and Lynn."*

I'm so happy that I'm a cheerleader, Emily thought. It's my dream come true. She loved how her family was happy for her. And her friends — even Alexis who hadn't made the squad. But what about the people who thought she didn't deserve to be on the squad?

Emily rolled over onto her back and stared up at the ceiling.

She couldn't get the scene out of her mind. She was coming back into the gym after saying good-bye to Alexis when she thought she heard her name being called. She looked to her right and saw Kelly, Maria, and Sally talking together. "Well, the Grangers are a big-deal family in town," she overheard Sally say. "So of course they had to pick her." Emily walked quickly to the other side of the gym before they saw her.

Tears sprang to Emily's eyes and spilled out onto her pillow case. That's what she was afraid people would think if she made the squad.

Is Sally right? Emily wondered. Did I only

make the squad because of my family connections?

SEAVIEW TERRACE 11:25 P.M.

Alexis lay in bed thinking about her sports column. She wondered if Jake had given her the assignment because he felt sorry for her. What if her piece wasn't good enough? It would be so hard for Jake to tell her that. But he'd have to. That was his job as editor. All I can do is my best, she thought. Then she remembered that was what she had said to herself about cheering. She had done her best at cheering, but it wasn't good enough for her to make the squad. Would her best reporting be good enough for the *Bulldog Edition*?

The phone rang. It's Emily, thought Alexis. She's back home from the cheerleading meeting and wants to tell me about it. Alexis smiled to herself. She loved how she almost always knew when it was Emily calling her. Best friends, she thought. It's like we have mental telepathy. Maybe we do.

She reached over and picked up the phone on her desk. "How'd it go?" she asked.

"How did what go?" asked the person on the other end. It was her mother.

"I thought you were Emily," Alexis explained.

She tried not to sound too disappointed. But she was.

"I just called to say good night," her mother said. "I thought you might be alone like me."

"Dad's here," Alexis told her mother. "He's watching television."

"I figured he'd be out," said her mother, "since it's Saturday night."

"Well he's not," Alexis said.

She hated how her mother felt sorry for herself because her ex-husband had lots of dates and she didn't. Why does she have to tell me about it? Alexis wondered.

After she said goodnight to her mother she lay back on her pillow. Emily hadn't called her.

Was she losing her special connection with her best friend?

DELHAVEN DRIVE 11:30 P.M.

Joan had on her pajamas and was lying in bed, but she wasn't ready to fall asleep. There was so much to think about. She played the last two days over and over again in her mind like a favorite movie. She'd made the squad, her parents signed the permission slip, she'd been to a big dinner party at school, and attended her first cheerleader's meeting. She was even measured for her uniform.

The meeting was so great. Coach congratulated the eighth-graders on making it back on the squad and welcomed the seventh-grade cheerleaders. Sally and Mae passed out a schedule of the football games and cheerleading practices. The first game that the cheerleaders would cheer for was the big game between the Bulldogs and the Santa Rosa Cougars.

"We want to look very good at that game, girls," Coach had said. "You're all going to have to work extra hard, especially the new girls."

Joan closed her eyes and imagined herself cheering for CMS at the Bulldog/Cougar football game. She couldn't wait.

Tryouts were just the beginning.

Fight, Bulldogs, Fight!

For Carole Halpin

CLAYMORE, FLORIDA. THE MANOR HOTEL. FRIDAY 7:30 A.M.

Emily Granger took her blue-and-white cheerleading uniform out of its plastic bag. She held up the uniform and smiled to herself. She was a Claymore Middle School cheerleader, and she was going to wear her uniform for the first time. Today was the big pep rally, and the CMS cheerleaders were wearing their uniforms all day. Emily couldn't wait to get to school.

She put on her skirt and pulled up the zipper. It stopped halfway up. Was it broken? She pulled again. It still wouldn't close. She tried to button the waistband. At least two inches separated the button from the buttonhole. But yesterday it fit, Emily thought. I must have gotten bigger overnight!

She tried on the top. It was too small.

Emily mentally listed what she'd eaten since she'd tried on her uniform at school the day before. Last night she'd had a second helping of garlic mashed potatoes with fried chicken. There was apple pie with ice cream for dessert. And a couple of cookies and some milk before bed. Today she'd already had a pancake breakfast. Tears filled her eyes. She ate too much and had gotten so fat overnight that this morning her uniform didn't fit!

The door to Emily's room flung open. Lily, her

four-year-old sister, came running in. Lily had on a miniature version of the CMS cheerleaders' uniform, the same one Emily had worn when she was Lily's age.

Lily twirled around. "I'm a cheerleader!" she shouted. "I'm going to the pep rally. Mom said."

The entire Granger family was involved in CMS sports. Even the Granger dog! Emily's mother and her older sister, Lynn, had both been captains of the CMS cheer squad. Her father and brother played CMS football and basketball. And starting when Emily's father was a kid, the Granger family had owned and raised the CMS bulldog mascot. Over the years there had been three Granger bulldogs. Now they had Bubba IV, great-grandson of Bubba I.

Bubba IV followed Lily into Emily's room.

Emily squatted to give Bubba a hello pat and her sister a kiss. "You look great," Emily told Lily. "It finally fits you."

"I'm a big girl," bragged Lily.

Me, too, thought Emily. Only I'm *too* big.

Lynn poked her head in the door.

"Lily, Mom wants you to go eat breakfast," she said. "Hey, Em, you got your uniform! Let me see."

Emily was embarrassed to show her perfect sister how imperfectly her uniform fit.

"Hurry," Lynn insisted. "Stand up."

As Emily stood she saw the look of surprise on her sister's face.

"It's too small," Emily told her, the tears coming back to her eyes. "It fit yesterday, but now it's too small."

Lynn smiled.

"It's not funny!" Emily told her.

"Emily, that uniform could not possibly have fit you yesterday," Lynn said. "No one grows that much overnight."

"I ate a lot for dinner last night," Emily confessed. "And I had a big breakfast, too."

"It must be someone else's uniform," Lynn told her. "All you have to do is figure out whose it is. I'm sure that girl has yours." She patted Lily on the head. "Come on, Lily."

The little cheerleader took Lynn's hand and they left the room. Bubba didn't follow them. Instead he licked Emily's leg and whimpered. Bubba always knew when Emily was feeling sad.

"Oh, Bubba," Emily said. "What if it *is* my uniform?"

Bubba lay down on the rug, dropped his head on his folded paws, and watched Emily.

Emily looked at the blue-and-white pleated cheerleader's skirt. Yesterday, Coach Cortes handed out uniforms after cheerleading practice, and the whole squad tried them on. Like the other cheerleaders, Emily had put her uniform back in the plastic bag to take home. Then she went with Melody and Joan to Squeeze, the juice bar, for something to drink. That's when we must have mixed up uniforms, thought Emily. Melody and I are about the same size. But Joan is so much smaller than I am. Emily hoped that she was holding Joan's uniform.

She grabbed the phone and speed-dialed Joan.

DELHAVEN DRIVE 7:45 A.M.

Joan Russo-Chazen practiced a tuck jump in front of her bedroom mirror. She loved how the skirt of her cheerleading uniform flew up in the air. She was doing a back standing handspring across the rug when she heard a knock on her door. It was her father telling her she had a phone call.

That was a close call, Joan thought as she ran down the stairs to the only phone in the house. If my father had opened my door he'd have seen me doing a handspring in my uniform. He'd figure out that cheerleaders do gymnastics, and my cheerleading career would end before it began.

Joan's parents were anti most sports, especially sports in which people could be injured. They wouldn't let Joan take gymnastics or her older brother, Adam, play football. Adam didn't care because he didn't want to play football. But I care, thought Joan. I care because I love cheering, especially the tumbling. The only lucky thing about my parents being antisports is that they don't know that cheerleaders do lots of gymnastics.

"Hello?" Joan said into the phone.

It was Emily. She told Joan that they had each other's uniforms.

"But I have my uniform on," Joan told her, "and it fits perfectly. Maybe you have Melody's."

After Joan hung up the phone she ran back upstairs to fix her hair. As she ran up the stairs, her mother was coming down. She held up a hand to stop Joan.

"I can't believe my eyes," she said. "This is *my* daughter in a cheerleading uniform?" She said it with disapproval, as if wearing a cheerleading uniform was some kind of crime. "It totally baffles me that you want to shout and jump around for a bunch of boys fighting over a ball."

"I love football," Joan told her. "And I love cheering."

"Indeed," said her mother. "What time will you be home?"

"The team and cheerleaders are going to Bulldog Café after the pep rally," Joan said. "Adam's invited, too. Then Emily asked me to sleep over."

"Yes to the gathering at the café," her mother

said. “No to sleeping over. Maybe another time. I’ll pick you up on the way back from the university,” she added. “That will be around six.”

Ms. Russo continued down the stairs. “Cheerleading,” she mumbled. Joan couldn’t understand the rest of the sentence, because her mother was muttering to herself in German — one of the languages she taught at the university.

Joan bounded up the rest of the stairs. She was disappointed that her mother wouldn’t let her stay over at Emily’s, but she wasn’t surprised.

She wouldn’t let that ruin her first pep rally.

DOLPHIN COURT APARTMENTS 8:00 A.M.

Melody Max was about to put on her cheerleading uniform when Emily phoned and asked her if she had the right uniform.

“I haven’t put it on yet,” she told Emily. “Hold on, I’ll try it.” Melody lay the phone on her bed and slipped the top over her head. It was too big. She stepped into the skirt and zipped and buttoned it. It was at least a size too large. Melody picked up the phone and told Emily, “It’s too big on me. It must be yours.”

Emily’s heart sank. Her uniform was too big for Melody. I must be so fat, Emily thought.

“I’ll meet you at our lockers so we can exchange before school," she told Melody. "I'll leave in a few minutes."

After Melody hung up the phone she wondered why Emily didn't sound happier that the mystery of the mixed-up uniforms had been solved. Maybe she just wants to be sure it's hers, she decided.

"Hey, sugar," Melody's mother called from the kitchen. "When are you going to show me that uniform of yours? I have to go to work."

Melody went to the kitchen, showed her the uniform, and explained about the mix-up with Emily.

"My, my," chuckled her mother. "She must have had a fright when she put on yours. Sorry I wasn't here when you went to bed last night. It's taking a while to get the newspaper the way I want it. Part of being the new editor, I guess. I'll try to be home early tonight."

"But I won't be here," Melody said. "There's a party at the café after the pep rally. And then I'm sleeping over at Emily's, remember?"

"Right," said her mother. "Is the big game with the Santa Rosa team tomorrow?"

"Next week," Melody told her. "We're having the pep rally today so we can keep building school spirit all next week."

"I'll be sure to be there," her mother said.

"The rivalry with Santa Rosa is certainly a big deal in Claymore."

Melody kissed her mother good-bye and went back to her room to get her books. It was great that her mother would see her cheer at the big Bulldog-Cougar game. She just wished her father could be there, too.

She picked up a framed photo from her desk. Her mother and father had taken her skiing in Colorado last winter and asked a stranger to take their picture when they finished their first run down the mountain. Her parents, each with an arm around Melody, looked so happy in that picture. Two months later they told her they were divorcing, and a week later her father moved out. Three months after that her mother was offered a job as editor of the *Claymore News*.

Melody's father was a meteorologist and television weather announcer in Miami. Her parents agreed that Melody should leave Miami with her mother and move to Claymore on the west coast of Florida for the three years of middle school. After that she could move back to Miami to live with her father while she went to high school. But for now Melody would only be with her father for an occasional weekend and during vacations.

She missed being with both her parents. It

was hard to believe that they would never be a family like that again.

She put the frame back on her desk and grabbed her bag for school.

SEAVIEW TERRACE 8:10 A.M.

Alexis Lewis zipped up her jeans and pulled a CMS Bulldogs T-shirt over her head. Now, where was her reporter's notebook? She found it on her desk and dropped the notebook into her backpack. She was covering the pep rally today and the big game between the CMS Bulldogs and the Santa Rosa Cougars next week. The Bulldog-Cougar game was the most important game of the year. And she was the only seventh-grader covering it for the school paper.

The sports rivalry between the two towns had been going on for as long as anyone could remember. The Bulldogs beat the Cougars two years ago, but the Cougars beat the Bulldogs last year and had the big gold trophy to prove it. The Bulldogs desperately wanted that trophy back in their trophy case.

Alexis took a deep breath to calm herself. If I'm this nervous because I have to write this article, she thought, imagine how I'd feel if I'd made the cheerleading squad. Alexis wondered if any of the other girls who didn't make the squad were as relieved as she was not to be a cheerleader. The only bad thing about not being a cheerleader was that Emily, her best friend in the whole world, had made the squad. Emily was so busy with cheerleading practices that they didn't hang out together after school the way they used to.

Alexis had hardly seen Emily over the past two weeks. But she was invited to a sleepover at Emily's tonight. Alexis was glad that this was a Dad week and not a Mom week in her joint custody schedule. Her mother always wanted her home at night. "I only see you half the time," she'd say. "That's bad enough." But her father would let her stay over at Emily's whenever she wanted.

Tonight would be like the good old days — before Emily became a cheerleader.

CLAYMORE MIDDLE SCHOOL. EAST WING. GIRLS' BATHROOM 8:25 A.M.

Sally Johnson studied her reflection in the bathroom mirror. Her uniform finally looked the way she wanted it — with a co-captain's gold star on the skirt. It was so great being co-captain of the cheer squad. *What makes it even more perfect,* she thought, *is that my boyfriend is Darryl Budd, captain of the football team.* Sally was sure she was the most popular girl in the school now. Mae Lee, the other co-captain, was nowhere near as popular. Mae didn't even seem to care about popularity and was too serious to be fun. And boys love fun-loving girls.

Melody Max emerged from one of the bathroom stalls. Something about that girl irked Sally. For one thing she was too pretty and uppity for a seventh-grader. Be nice to the seventh-graders, Sally reminded herself. You never know who you might need on your side.

Sally exchanged a smile with Melody in the wide mirror over the sinks. "Don't forget to come to the gym during lunch hour," Sally told her. "To help bring the banners out to the field."

"I'll be there," Melody said. She knocked on a stall door. "You okay, Emily? Does it fit?"

"Yup," Emily replied. She opened the door and came out.

"That looks great, Emily," Melody told her.

"I better comb my hair again," Emily said.

The signal for homeroom buzzed over the loudspeaker.

"I have to grab something from my locker before homeroom," Melody told Emily. "Catch you later."

As Sally put on a little lipstick she noticed Emily Granger sneaking glances at her. "This is your first pep rally," Sally said. "You excited?"

"Oh, yes," Emily answered.

"Was there a problem with your uniform?"

Sally asked. "I heard Melody ask you if it fit."

"We mixed up uniforms," Emily said. "We had to switch. But this one's mine." Emily looked in the mirror and tried to shift the waistband so that the pleats were even on both sides. She had to unbutton it to move it around her waist.

"Does that one fit all right?" Sally asked.

"I think so," Emily said. "Does it look all right?"

Sally looked Emily over. Actually her uniform fit fine, but she was the chubbiest girl on the squad. Sally was convinced that the only reason Emily Granger was a CMS cheerleader was because her family was so active in CMS sports. If Emily dropped a little weight, Sally thought, she might cheer better.

"You know," she told Emily, "now that you mention it, it seems a little tight."

"It feels sort of small," Emily admitted.

"Have you been eating a lot?" Sally asked.

Emily blushed. "I guess," she said.

"Maybe you should watch what you eat," Sally suggested. "Go on a diet. That's what I do when I gain a few extra pounds." She flashed Emily a smile. "It's hard, but it's worth it."

"Okay," Emily said. "I will."

Three eighth-graders rushed into the bathroom and came over to the mirror. Sally glanced at her watch. "I have to go to the office. I'm talking about the pep rally over the loudspeaker during homeroom announcements."

Emily followed Sally out to the hall. As Sally bounced down the hallway people smiled and said hi to her. She's so pretty, thought Emily, and she's so thin.

Emily knew that Sally thought she only made the squad because of her family connections. And she knew that other cheerleaders thought the same thing. She would go on a diet, just like Sally said she should. And work harder than ever on her cheerleading moves.

She'd make sure that she deserved her spot on the squad.

CMS GIRLS' LOCKER ROOM 2:00 P.M.

The cheerleaders had left their classes early to warm up and get ready for the pep rally. Soon classes would be dismissed for the day, and everyone in the building would go to the football field. It was the first appearance of the CMS cheerleaders. Sally knew that the new cheerleaders were excited and more than a little nervous. She remembered her first pep rally. I've come a long way, she thought, from nervous seventh-grader to the ninth-grade co-captain of the squad.

Sally's mother was busy helping the girls with a last-minute check on their appearance.

Sally Sue Johnson, the squad mother in charge of uniforms, hair, and makeup, had been a big-deal college cheerleader. She loved cheerleading as much as her daughter Sally did.

"You have the most beautiful skin," Sally heard her mother saying to someone.

Sally went around the last locker in the row and saw her mother applying a light pink gloss to Melody Max's lips. "And Coach tells me you're a smashing cheerleader, Melody," Sally's mother added.

"Careful what you say to her, Sally Sue," Coach Cortes called from the other side of the room. "Don't want her to get a big head."

Melody smiled.

Melody is so smug, thought Sally. Why does everyone think she's so special?

"Well, I'm looking forward to seeing you cheer," Mrs. Johnson told Melody. "Bend your head. I'll put sparkles in your hair."

Sally caught her mother's eye. "Is my lipstick okay, Mom?" she asked.

"Ah, honey," Sally Sue said. "You look perfectly marvelous. And I just love seeing that gold star on your skirt."

"Thanks, Mom," Sally said.

Coach Cortes shouted, "Okay, everybody, line up. We're going out there."

Emily's heart jumped in her chest. It was time

to perform at her first pep rally. The band was already on the field playing the school fight song. Even her snug waistband didn't matter now. She was a *cheerleader*. She had a job to do. She fell in line behind Melody and ran out onto the field.

"And here they are — your classmates and cheerleaders — the CMS Cheer Squad!" the athletic director shouted over the field's sound system.

Joan looked at the crowd in the bleachers, threw a fist in the air to salute them, and did three handsprings in a row. Out of the corner of her eye she saw the rest of the squad running, jumping, and tumbling. On a signal from Sally they all fell into line in front of the crowd. It was time for their first sideline chant. Sally raised the megaphone to her lips and shouted:

We're here. X X (clap, clap)
Let's cheer. X X

Next they led the crowd in a color chant for blue and white. Then they did a competition cheer to see which grade could yell loudest — seventh, eighth, or ninth. By now the crowd was heated up, and it was time to introduce the football team. The cheerleaders picked up their pom-poms and ran toward the entrance of the field. They faced one another in two rows and raised their arms to make an arch of blue-and-white pom-poms.

As each football player's name was announced, the player — in full uniform — ran under the human arch onto the field. The last player to come out had Bubba IV with him. Bubba had on his uniform, too — an extra-small CMS T-shirt and a blue leather collar with silver spikes. The crowd cheered for Bubba as he waddled onto the field and stood in front of the line of players.

Someone in the bleachers stood up and yelled, "Kill the Cougars!"

A few kids laughed, but others picked up the chant, stamping their feet and yelling, "Kill the Cougars!"

It was time for the national anthem and the pledge. Emily looked around to see what they should do. Sally gave the signal to break the arch formation, and the cheerleaders ran to the middle of the field in a line beside the football players.

The crowd quieted down, and everyone stood while the band played "America the Beautiful." Next, everyone said the Pledge of Allegiance.

Then the band played the school fight song, and the cheerleaders led the singing. They were determined to keep the crowd pepped up. At the end of the song the cheerleaders did tumbles and jumps and ran off the field. It was time for the principal and the coach to make speeches.

As Melody ran off the field, Darryl Budd, the CMS quarterback, gave her a thumbs-up sign. Melody loved it. The captain and star of the football team was telling *her* she was great.

Sally, who was already at the sidelines, noticed Darryl's thumbs-up sign and saw Melody's pleased reaction. Sally made sure to catch Darryl's eye and flashed him her best smile. He smiled back, and from the corner of her eye Sally watched Melody's smile fade.

Sally's thoughts of Darryl and Melody were interrupted by a low growl. She looked down. Bubba was standing next to her. What an ugly dog, she thought. Coach Cortes once said, "Bubba is so ugly that he's cute. That pup has the sweetest disposition."

Sweet? thought Sally. Are you kidding me? She hated that dog. She felt like kicking him all the time. She would have, too, if hundreds of people weren't there watching and she wasn't so afraid of the dribbling little monster.

Bubba growled up at her again. Sally looked around. People could see her, but they couldn't hear her over the band music. She leaned over, put on a fake smile, and said between her teeth, "Get away from me, you flat-faced little creep."

Bubba didn't budge. He glared at her and bared *his* teeth.

Sally backed away and listened to what the principal, Mr. Asche, was saying.

"Our rivalry with Santa Rosa is intense," he said. "Things happened at the game last year that are best put behind us. I expect all of you — fans, players, cheerleaders — to represent the best in CMS with good sportsmanship and spirit."

Put last year behind us? thought Sally. No way. The game was at Santa Rosa. CMS lost. The Bulldog players said that the Cougars played dirty. To make matters worse, their cheerleaders had been rude to the Bulldog cheer squad. Whenever the Bulldog cheerleaders led a chant or did a cheer, the Cougar fans shouted over them. And during halftime the Cougar band played so that the Bulldog cheerleaders couldn't do their halftime routine. The Cougar cheerleaders didn't even try to control the crowd.

But what bothered Sally more was that Cougar cheerleaders placed at the CHEER USA competitions in Miami and the Bulldog squad did not. All because one of last year's flyers fell twice. It was all Allison's fault. Well, Allison was in high school now, and the Bulldogs had Joan. We're going to place in Miami this year, thought Sally. And starting at the game next week the Cougar cheerleaders are going to know which squad is on top.

Emily, looking up from the sidelines, noticed her mother and Lily. Lily looked so cute in her cheerleading outfit. Then Emily saw Jake and Alexis sitting together on the top bleacher. Emily waved. She loved that her two best friends in the world were sitting together.

Since Jake was the editor of the school paper, the *Bulldog Edition*, he was Alexis's boss. But Alexis didn't mind. She'd always looked up to Jake, ever since she and Emily had become best friends in first grade and she started hanging out at the Grangers'.

Jake's parents and younger sister had died in a fire when he was five years old. Since that awful accident, he lived with his grandparents in a house right behind the Grangers' home and business, The Manor Hotel. Emily was the same age as Jake's sister would have been. He was especially close to Emily and practically a member of the Granger family.

"There are a lot of adults here," Jake told Alexis. "I've never seen so many people show up for a pep rally or get so worked up over a game."

"I was thinking of interviewing Darryl for the article," Alexis said. "I'd ask him, 'What does the captain of the football team think of the rivalry with the Cougars and what happened at the game last year?' "

"Good idea," Jake said.

The cheerleaders ran out to the center of the field to do their big number. They did a three-minute routine that included tumbling, a dance, and stunts. It ended with Joan and Sally being held at the top of a team stunt pyramid.

Alexis smiled at her friends on the squad. The CMS cheerleaders looked great. The crowd was excited and ready for the Cougars. She just hoped she was ready to be a *Bulldog Edition* reporter.

THE MANOR HOTEL.
BULLDOG CAFÉ 5:00 P.M.

Emily stood in the middle of the outdoor café. It was mobbed with football players and cheerleaders. There was plenty of soda and juice in a big cooler, and Jake and a couple of players were grilling hot dogs and burgers. As people on the street walked by, they stopped to encourage the players. Everyone was having a great time.

Jake came over with a couple of hot dogs and handed one to Emily. "I'm taking a break from the grill," he said. He smiled at her. "Hey, you looked great out there today, Em."

"Thanks," she said, taking a bite of the hot dog. They stood there side by side, talking about the big game and eating. Emily had already had a burger, but she was still famished. She was halfway through the hot dog when she looked up and saw Sally looking at her.

Emily felt embarrassed. Sally said she should go on a diet, and here she was, stuffing her face again. I have to stop eating so much, she thought. But not tonight. Tonight's a party. Tomorrow I'll start my diet.

Sally wasn't thinking about Emily eating. She was looking for Darryl. Her main objective at this party was to keep her boyfriend away from Melody. But where was Darryl? Sally finally saw him, walking across the deck with two sodas. He was headed toward Melody, who stood talking and laughing with Joan and her brother, Adam.

Sally moved quickly and reached the group an instant before Darryl did. "Hey, guys," she said. "How's it going?"

Darryl came up to them, looked from Melody to Sally, and then looked down at the two sodas. He handed one soda to Sally and the other to Melody.

Melody liked that Darryl brought her a soda, but she didn't believe he was interested in her. Why would he be when he had Sally Johnson, beautiful co-captain of the cheer squad and president of the ninth-grade class, for a girlfriend?

Before Sally could figure out a way to get

Darryl away from Melody, Alexis joined them.

"Darryl," she said. "I'm writing an article about the pep rally and game for the *Bulldog Edition*. I'd love to interview you for it."

Darryl grinned. "We're going to destroy the Cougars," he said. "Write that."

"Okay," she said. "But I also have a bunch of questions I want to ask you. Maybe we could go to the lobby, where it's not so noisy. Do you mind?"

"Nah, I don't mind," Darryl said. "Just as long as you start with how we're gonna kill 'em."

"Have you seen Jake?" Sally asked Alexis, even though she knew exactly where he was.

"He's working the barbecue grill," Alexis told her.

"What a guy," said Sally. "Always doing something nice for people. That's what I love about him."

Sally caught the crushed look on Darryl's face before she turned and headed across the deck toward Jake. Good, she thought. It won't hurt to make him think I might like Jake.

In the lobby, Alexis sat on the edge of an easy chair facing Darryl, who sat on the couch. She loved doing the interview with Darryl, but she was surprised at how hostile he was toward the Cougars. "They play dirty," he said, leaning forward. He ground a fist into his palm. "But we're going to teach them a lesson. We're getting that trophy back."

When Alexis finished the interview with Darryl she went back out to the deck. People were starting to leave. Sally was still there, sitting at one of the tables and having a soda with Jake. Alexis wanted to tell Jake about the interview with Darryl. But Jake was busy talking to Sally. Alexis felt funny walking over to them so she looked for her friends. She saw Joan cleaning up.

Joan was throwing empty cans into a recycling bag when she heard a horn honk three times. Joan looked to the street. "My mother," she told Alexis. She turned to Emily, who was clearing away plates from a table. "I have to go. Thanks for the party."

"I wish you could sleep over," Emily said.

"Another time," Joan told her.

" 'Bye, Joan," Melody called.

As Joan waved good-bye to her friends, she wondered when she'd ever be able to go to a sleepover at a friend's house. Would Emily eventually stop asking her?

When Joan reached the car Adam was standing beside it, talking to their mother through the window. "I'll be in by eleven," Adam said as he opened the car door for Joan. At that moment Joan hated her brother. He could stay out until eleven, but she couldn't stay for Emily's sleepover. She glared at him, got in the car, and reached over to close the door herself.

Joan wanted to tell her parents that she felt as old as Adam. She and Adam were both in middle school, even if he was an eighth-grader and she was a seventh-grader. But her parents had a strict set of rules for raising their children. One rule was, "You don't argue with your mother or father." Another one seemed to be, "Adam will always have more freedom than Joanie."

As the car pulled away from The Manor Hotel, Joan turned and looked out the back window.

Emily and Melody were sitting at one of the tables with Emily's little sister. They were laughing about something that Lily was saying.

Darryl and Sally were walking arm in arm down the street. A whole crowd of ninth-graders were bunched behind them. Adam was one of them, the creep.

Jake and Alexis were standing on the sidewalk in front of the café, talking animatedly.

And here I am, Joan thought, going home with my mother.

She couldn't wait until she graduated from high school and could do whatever she wanted.

THE MANOR HOTEL 11:00 P.M.

Alexis lay across Emily's bed. Emily and Melody sat on the floor in front of the TV. They were watching a videotape of last year's CHEER USA competitions in Miami. I'd rather watch a basketball game, thought Alexis. But Melody and Emily loved watching the cheerleading competitions. This was the third time they'd run the tape.

Melody handed Alexis the bowl of chips. "Miami is such a great place," she said. "You guys have got to come when I go visit my dad sometime."

"We'll be in Miami for the CHEER USA competition," said Emily.

"It'll be so much fun," said Melody. "I'll introduce you all to my Miami friends. Really, Miami is so cool. There's this great hip-hop club we can go to."

Emily pointed the remote at the VCR and froze the image on the TV screen. "Look at that flyer!" she shouted. "Check out that basket toss! Joan has to see this tape. I'll lend it to her." Emily pressed the play button, and the flyer landed in the arms of the bases below her. Emily took a handful of chips.

"I don't think Joan has a TV and VCR," Melody said. "Her parents won't allow it. But she and Adam are coming over to swim tomorrow. You should come, too. Bring the tape and Joan can watch it."

"Okay," said Emily.

"You, too, Alexis," Melody added. "It'll be a pool party. Very Miami."

"I can't," Alexis said. "I'm having lunch with my father and my aunt Louise, then I have to work on the article for the school paper." Alexis also wanted to play some basketball Sunday afternoon. She wished she'd spent all the hours she'd practiced for the cheerleading tryouts shooting baskets. It would have been a lot more fun, she thought.

When the tape ended, Emily flipped over on her side and looked at her friends. "What do you want to do now?" she asked. "We could go downstairs and have some ice cream."

"I'm not hungry," Alexis said. "But I'm really tired."

"Me, too," Melody said with a yawn.

"I'll take the sleeping bag, Melody," Alexis offered. "You can sleep in the extra bed."

"I don't mind sleeping on the floor," Melody said.

While Melody and Alexis discussed who was going to sleep where, Emily gathered up the snack dishes and empty glasses and left for the kitchen. It was eleven-thirty. In a half hour her diet would officially begin.

There was time for one last dish of ice cream.

DOLPHIN COURT APARTMENTS. POOLSIDE. SATURDAY 3:00 P.M.

Every time Emily was tempted by the snacks Melody put out, she peered down at her stomach. It was like a big soft mound sitting on her lap. Melody has a totally flat stomach, thought Emily, even when she sits down. Joan — who had just left for her piano lesson — was even skinnier than Melody, and she was *always* eating. It's not fair, Emily thought.

Emily's stomach rumbled with hunger. All she'd eaten so far that day was a small bowl of cereal with skim milk. I'll be as thin as they are, she vowed to herself. I *have* to be, or I won't be a good cheerleader, and we won't place at CHEER USA.

Melody and Adam were splashing around in the water, throwing a ball back and forth.

"Come on in, Emily," Melody shouted.

"Later," Emily shouted back. "I'll come in later."

Emily sat back in a lounge chair and closed her eyes. She could hear Melody and Adam comparing bands and singers they liked as they tossed the ball back and forth. They hummed lines of music, recited lyrics, and laughed a lot.

Emily wondered what Jake was doing. She held her wrist in front of her face and squinted at her watch. Three o'clock. He was just getting off work. He'll probably go home and do his homework, she thought. Maybe he and his grandparents will have dinner with us tonight. Saturday night dinner in the hotel dining room was a Granger family tradition. The Feders often joined them.

Dinner, thought Emily. She imagined the pink tablecloth covered with heaps of delicious food. A basket of hot homemade rolls, fried shrimp with dipping sauce, roast chicken, rice, beans, and salad. Then the dessert wagon would be pushed over to their table. Her mouth watered, she felt so hungry!

She wished she could hate eating as much as she hated dieting.

DOLPHIN COURT APARTMENTS.
SUNDAY 11:45 A.M.

Melody Max went on-line to check her e-mail. There were messages from Miami from Tina and Jackie. They were full of news about her old gang and the dance class Melody had been in with them. The piece of news that surprised Melody most was that Juan Ramirez, the hottest guy in the school, was asking about her. Melody didn't know if Juan, who never used to pay any attention to her, was really interested in her or if it was a figment of boy-crazy Tina's imagination. Tina ended the e-mail with a question.

> So fess up, Max, how dorky are the guys in Boremore? Tell all or you will not hear another word from me. I mean I'll be mean. Love ya, but not if you don't answer the question. The Big T.

Melody was picturing Big T as she'd last seen her, waving good-bye from the sidewalk when Melody and her mother drove away on moving day. Tina was the smallest of Melody's Miami friends. Her nickname was a joke. And the idea of Big T being *mean* was an even bigger joke.

Melody checked her watch. If she was quick about it she could type an answer to Tina's letter before she went out to dinner with her mother and two of her mother's new friends from the paper. If Big T wanted to hear about guys, she'd tell her about guys.

> Big T: How nosy are you? Well, listen up, because I have some guy news for you. Claymore is Boremore no more. The guys are a-okay. Let me tell you about these guys — three of them anyway — who are becoming friends. Two of them are ninth-graders and

the other one is in the eighth grade. You're dying to hear about them, right? First there's Darryl, ninth-grader, football captain, and major hunk. Would like to be better pals with him, but he's got this glory blond cheer captain gal on his arm, which he likes plenty good enough. Darryl's always making eye contact with me of the "Aren't you cute? Aren't I cute?" variety. I suspect he's a bit dim and not in on how complicated Girl Power can be. Next, there's Jake Feder, also in the ninth grade. Now, Jake is what you'd call an all-around smart sweetie pie. Jake's down-to-earth with a golden heart. Good to be around and no snob. Spending time with seventh-graders no prob for him. Last is Adam. Yup. He's the eighth-grader. Adam's sister, Joan, a good friend, is on the cheer squad with me. Adam is the coolest of the guys I've met here — in my terms. He makes me laugh, which is way important on my friendship meter. Adam knows loads about music, even hip-hop, though he's never been to a live concert that wasn't classical music. He has strict-beyond-belief parents. This parent thing is a major prob, but he takes it on and doesn't much complain, which makes him a lot different from Melody-the-Whiner. (Remember when I first moved here and all I did was complain?)

The girls I hang with aren't pairing off with guys. I'm glad. It's so much fun when a big group of guys and girls are hanging together and just being friends. Don't you think? Or are you all gaga over some big dude I would not approve of? Do tell or I'll be mean. Love ya. The Max.:-)

As Melody was signing off on her e-mail she heard the other phone line ring and her mother answer it.

"Melody, it's for you," her mother called.

"Who is it?" Melody called back.

"A boy. Darryl," her mother answered as she opened the door. "Be quick, Mel. We're already late for dinner."

Melody picked up the phone in her room. Why was Darryl calling *her*?

After they both said *Hi* and *How are you?* they talked about the pep rally. He told her she was a good cheerleader and that she would probably be a co-captain when she was in the ninth grade. She thanked him for encouraging her to try out for cheering in the first place. He said again that he could tell she was a good dancer and asked her how old she was.

"Twelve," she answered.

"Oh," he said. "I thought maybe you were older."

"Nope," she said. "I'm twelve for real."

She didn't know what else to say, so she asked him if he liked hip-hop. He said he hadn't heard much hip-hop but would be interested in learning more about it. She promised to lend him a CD.

"Melody," her mother called. "Let's go."

"I have to go," Melody told Darryl.

When she'd hung up she wondered why he had called her. Then she remembered the question, "How old are you?" That must be why he called, she thought. Maybe he hoped that I was older than I am. Maybe if I was older he'd want to go out with me.

She had had crushes on older guys when she was in sixth grade. But none of them showed any interest in her. If I was thirteen would Darryl Budd ask me on a date? she wondered. Maybe he would ask her out anyway. Did she want him to? Melody tried to imagine herself as Darryl's date. What would it be like to be the girlfriend of just about the most popular guy in school?

Well, for now, only Sally Johnson knew the answer to that question.

DELHAVEN DRIVE 7:30 P.M.

Joan was washing the dinner dishes, and her mother was wiping them. Adam and her father had cooked dinner, so it was Joan and her mother's turn to clean up. Joan wanted to ask her mother why they couldn't have a dishwasher like other people. But she knew the answer. Her parents were against anything that had anything to do with high technology. Joan could argue that there wasn't much high-tech about a dishwasher — that it was a rather simple machine that had been around for more than fifty years. If I argued with my parents about everything we disagree about, she thought, all we would do is argue.

Her mother was asking Joan about the readings in her English literature class when the phone rang. At least we have a phone, Joan thought as her mother went to answer it. It's not a portable, and there's only one in the whole house — but it's certainly better than smoke signals for communication.

Joan listened to see if the call was for her. If it was, she knew that her mother would say that she was busy and that Joan would call back later. Or she might say, "Joanie will see you in school tomorrow." But the phone call wasn't for her. It was *about* her. From her piano teacher.

When Joan's mother hung up, she put down the towel and said in a low, serious tone, "I have to speak to your father."

Joan knew they would be speaking about her.

Then there would be a joint assault from her parents about her piano lessons.

She was right. They were waiting for her when she left the kitchen a few minutes later.

"Sit down, Joanie," her father said. "We want to speak to you about your piano lessons."

She sat on the edge of the easy chair, and her parents sat side by side on the couch facing her. Two against one.

"First," her mother began. "You asked to change your Saturday piano lesson to Thursday after school, and Mr. Richter accommodated you."

"Because of cheering for games," Joan said. "You said that was okay."

"It is," said her father. "But what isn't okay is that Mr. Richter says that your playing is not improving at any appreciable rate. He questions whether you've slacked off on your practice sessions. Have you?"

"I practice for half an hour every night," Joan told them.

"What happened to the hour you used to practice?" her father asked.

"That was when I was in elementary school," Joan said. "I have more homework in middle school." Her heart pounded. She was afraid of what they would say next.

"You should come directly home after

school," her mother said. "That way you can practice piano for an hour and still have plenty of time for your homework."

But I have cheerleading practice three days a week after school, Joan thought. When football season started there would be after-school games in addition to weekend games. As a cheerleader she was expected to attend all practices and games. If she was absent more than twice she would be cut from the squad. She didn't say any of this to her parents. Instead, she said, "But there are extracurricular activities after school. Like debate club. You wanted me to join that."

Joan felt her throat tighten the way it did whenever she lied to her parents. She hated lying. She'd only been doing it since she started middle school and decided to try out for cheerleading. When she went to cheer clinics she had told her parents that she was attending debate club meetings. Even after her mother signed the permission slip for her to be a cheerleader, she didn't tell them that she hadn't joined the debate club.

"Maybe this cheerleading business is taking up too much of your time," her father suggested.

"Adam doesn't have to be home till six o'clock," she tried. "And don't say he's older, because that was the rule when he was in seventh grade, too. I remember."

"We didn't have a phone call from his violin teacher," her mother said.

Don't be afraid, Joan told herself. Don't act like a brat. And don't act like a baby. She took a deep breath.

"Please," she said, "give me another chance. I'll be home by five at the latest. I promise I'll practice an hour every day, even on weekends. I love playing piano." That wasn't a lie. She did love playing the piano. "And I love cheerleading. I won't hang out with my friends after my extracurricular activities. I'll come right home. By five."

Her father whispered something in her mother's ear. They looked at each other and nodded.

"Okay," her father said. "We'll have a two-week trial period. If your piano playing improves you may remain in the debate club and on the cheer team."

Joan didn't bother to tell her father that it was called a cheer squad. The less her parents knew about cheerleading, the better.

"Thank you," she said.

The phone rang again. Joan jumped up. "I'll get it," she said. She ran into the kitchen. This time it was for her. Emily wanted to know what they had for math homework. She also asked Joan what she'd had for dinner. "Spaghetti with meatballs and garlic bread," Joan told her. "Oh, yeah, and a salad. Adam makes great salad dressing."

"Did you have dessert?" Emily asked.

Joan said her parents didn't like desserts that much, but that she liked them. She told Emily she was lucky to have her own café and restaurant. That it must be fun to live in a hotel. Joan loved having a chatty phone call with one of her friends, but she knew her parents didn't approve of long phone conversations. So she signed off pretty quickly and went into the living room to practice the piano.

As she opened her sheet music and put it on the piano, Joan was still thinking about cheerleading. But once she began to play, her mind focused on the music. It was a piece by Beethoven that expressed anxiety and joy. This music sounds the way I feel, thought Joan. She played it with all her heart.

CMS COURTYARD. MONDAY 8:20 A.M.

It was a Mom week, so Alexis's mother gave her a ride to school. As Mrs. Lewis pulled the car up in front of CMS she was talking about what they would have for dinner. Alexis only half heard her. She was distracted by a big crowd of kids gathered in the school courtyard. It wasn't unusual for kids to be in the courtyard of the

U-shaped building before school. But usually they were in small groups scattered around the space. This morning they were all bunched together facing the front door.

"Whatever you want for dinner is fine with me," Alexis told her mother as she jumped out of the car. She closed the door and ran to the courtyard. As she approached the crowd she heard kids saying, "That's disgusting." And, "I hate the Cougars." And, "It's *so* horrible!"

Alexis tried to look past the heads of the kids in front of her. Finally she saw what everyone was looking at. A dog was hanging by its neck over the front doors of the building. It looked like Bubba. It *was* Bubba.

She screamed.

"It's a stuffed animal," she heard someone say. She turned to see Jake standing next to her. He put a hand on her elbow. "It's not real."

"The Cougars?" asked Alexis.

Jake nodded.

The life-size stuffed Bubba swung from a rope that was tied around its neck, hangman style. Even though Alexis knew it wasn't real it looked so much like Bubba it gave her chills. On the door behind the Bubba effigy were large spray-painted letters in red and black that read COUGARS WILL WIN!

"Where's Emily?" Alexis asked.

"With the other cheerleaders," Jake said, pointing to the front steps of the school.

The cheerleaders stood facing the crowd. Darryl and some other guys Alexis recognized from the football team were there, too.

Sally came forward with the megaphone and yelled, **"Fight, Bulldogs, FIGHT!"**

The crowd picked up the chant. The football players threw fists in the air and helped lead the crowd. Sally handed the megaphone to Mae, who continued to shout the familiar chant. Meanwhile, a group of cheerleaders held Sally up in an extension so she could reach the stuffed Bubba. She untied the cord around his neck, and he fell into the waiting arms of another cheerleader. Alexis saw that it was Emily.

Emily looked down at the Bubba effigy. It looked so much like her Bubba that she thought she was going to throw up. If I had eaten breakfast, she thought, I'd be losing it right now.

Just then a loud buzzer sounded over the courtyard loudspeaker. It was the CMS signal for immediate silence and attention. Mae gave a signal for the cheerleaders to stop chanting. They did. But some of the football players and the crowd kept chanting **"Fight, Bulldogs, Fight!"** without them. Emily noticed that some teachers were trying to quiet the group down.

The front doors opened, splitting the word COUGARS between the G and the A. The principal, Mr. Asche, came out. He put a hand on Darryl's arm. Darryl saw who it was and stopped chanting. Mr. Asche said something to Darryl. Darryl nodded, raised the megaphone to his mouth, and said in a booming voice, "Listen up! Mr. Asche wants to talk."

There was still an echo of **"Get the Cougars!"** as some in the crowd continued to chant.

"I MEAN IT!" Darryl shouted.

Finally, the crowd quieted down and Mr. Asche spoke. He said that he would be placing a call to the principal of Santa Rosa Middle School. He added that he was depending on the football players, the cheerleaders, the students of CMS, and the citizens of Claymore to behave with more dignity than the people who had defaced the CMS mascot and school building.

A few kids booed, but most of the kids were silent and waited to see what Mr. Asche would do next. CMS was a pretty strict school. A person could be suspended for booing the principal.

When the boos died down, Mr. Asche spoke in a calm, level voice, but you could hear the anger underneath. "Students, go to your homerooms."

The principal stepped aside, and the kids

started moving into the school building. Some of them gently touched the Bubba effigy in Emily's arms as they passed her. One of them said, "Sorry, Emily."

Coach Cortes came over to her. "Why don't I take that to my office?" she said.

"It looks just like Bubba," Emily said as she handed over the stuffed animal.

"I know," said Coach. "I had a fright when I first saw it."

"Me, too," Emily told her as they walked into the building together.

Melody, Alexis, and Joan met her in the front lobby, and the four friends headed for their lockers. The talking in the lobby and corridors was louder than usual.

"Someone has to teach them a lesson they won't forget," one girl said to another as they passed Emily.

"We can't let them get away with this," she overheard a tall, dark-haired boy tell a small group of ninth-graders who had gathered around him.

As Emily looked around, she noticed everyone was talking about the Cougars.

During homeroom, Mr. Asche spoke to the student body over the public address system. He reported that the principal of Santa Rosa Middle School, Ms. Hylton, apologized for the vandalism. She and Mr. Asche suspected that high school kids from Santa Rosa may have been involved. Ms. Hylton intended to find out who was responsible. Mr. Asche said he had assured Ms. Hylton that there would be no retaliation from members of the CMS student body. He instructed his students to spread the word in town that CMS would practice good sportsmanship. He expected the cheerleaders and football squad to set the example for the rest of the school.

Emily took a deep breath. She hoped that everything would be all right.

CMS SMALL GYM 3:30 P.M.

When the cheerleaders came into the gym they were all still talking about the desecration of their mascot and the graffiti on the school doors.

Coach Cortes was waiting for them. "Take your warm-up positions," she announced in a stern voice.

The talking quickly died down as the cheerleaders went to their positions.

As soon as everyone was ready Coach spoke. "I've seen and heard what's been going on in this school today," she began, "and there's too much anger going down. It's our job to turn it around. How many of you can stay for an extra hour after practice to make some posters? I want a positive message in the halls this week. Who can I count on?"

Joan put her hand up and looked around. Everyone's hand was up. All the cheerleaders were going to pitch in and make posters. Everyone but me, Joan suddenly thought. I have to be home by five to practice piano. She put her hand down. She felt like a baby.

Emily felt her stomach rumble. She'd had an upset stomach all day — ever since she first saw the effigy and thought that it was her dog. It was a perfect replica of Bubba, down to the brown tip on his right ear. Whoever made it knew exactly what Bubba looked like.

"Okay," Coach said. "Now let's talk about how we are going to conduct ourselves next week when the Cougars are here. Any ideas?"

"Maybe we shouldn't let them do a center cheer," C.J., one of the ninth-grade cheerleaders, yelled out. "They didn't let us do one when we were on their field last year. Remember?"

"And they chanted over our chants," Kelly added.

Someone called out, "They weren't fair."

Another girl shouted, "Let's treat them the way they treated us."

Coach put up her hand. "Sorry, gang," she

said. "That wasn't the right answer, and I think you know it. Try again."

Sally stepped forward. "It's our responsibility to keep the spirit of sportsmanship alive at every game," she said. "We'll be courteous to the Cougar cheerleaders. We'll give them equal time in the center field. And we won't interrupt their chants."

Coach applauded. The cheerleaders joined in. Sally grinned.

Emily clapped the loudest. Sally's so cool, she thought. I wish I could be just like her. I wish I could look just like her.

"I couldn't say it better, Sally," Coach said. "Did you all hear that?"

"Yes," the cheerleaders shouted.

Maria raised her hand. "But Coach, what they did to Bubba . . ."

"I know," Coach said.

"Only a few people are responsible for that," Mae said. "We shouldn't do anything mean back to them. Two wrongs don't make a right."

Melody raised her hand. "I thought of something we can do with the bulldog they strung up," she said. "We can dress it up in CMS gear and put it in the trophy case."

Everyone applauded again.

As she clapped, Sally thought, they're all falling for this goody-goody business. Santa

Rosa wouldn't get away with this. Not if she could help it.

MAIN STREET 6:15 P.M.

Emily was walking home along Main Street, chanting over and over in her head, *I'm so hungry. I'm so hungry.* That's not going to help me stay on this diet, she told herself. She changed the chant to, *I'm so fat. I'm so fat.* She was going back and forth between *I'm so hungry* and *I'm so fat* as she approached Bulldog Café.

Jake was there with his grandparents. Her father had pulled a chair up to visit with them, and Bubba lay at his feet. He saw Emily and motioned for her to come over. Bubba waddled over to meet her. When they met, Emily squatted and Bubba put his front legs on her thighs. She gave her real-life dog a big hug and carried him over to her father and the Feders.

When Emily sat down, Mrs. Feder said, "Tell us your version of what happened today, dear."

Emily told them how at first she thought it was their actual dog hanging from the rope. Then she reported that the cheerleaders made posters to keep school spirit headed in the right direction and that the stuffed bulldog now sat in the trophy case dressed in a CMS T-shirt and baseball cap. "He's holding a little sign that says 'CMS. We're the best!' " she added.

While Emily spoke she checked out what Jake and his grandparents were eating. Jake had a chicken burrito. She loved the salsa and guacamole that came with that dish. Mrs. Feder was eating a turkey club sandwich — a Bulldog Café specialty and one of Emily's favorite things to eat in the whole world. Mr. Feder was eating an enormous half chicken with french fries.

Emily wondered, How come they're not fat and I am?

Jake's grandmother, who was principal of the Claymore High School, said that the Cougar prank was being talked about all over her school, too. She made an announcement similar to the one Mr. Asche had made in the middle school. "I told them that there was to be no act of retaliation against the Cougars. That the mischief has to stop now before the pranks become meaner and more dangerous. Anyone in my school who becomes involved will be looking at a suspension."

"We have to try to keep a lid on this thing," Jake's grandfather added, "or someone will be hurt."

"A lot of people stopped by the hotel to talk about it today," Emily's father said. "You must have been pretty shocked, honey." He tapped Emily on the arm. "Emily, are you listening to me?"

She reluctantly looked away from the food on the table and at her father. "Yeah," she said. "It was pretty awful."

"Why don't you pull up a chair and eat something?" her father said.

"You look tired, Emily," Mrs. Feder said. "Sit here next to me. You can start by sharing my sandwich while the kitchen makes your meal."

Jake got a chair for Emily from one of the other tables. Before she knew what she was doing she was sitting between Jake and his grandmother and biting into a turkey club sandwich. Her father asked her what she wanted to order. She swallowed the bite in her mouth. "Another turkey club," she answered. She smiled at Mrs. Feder. "We'll split it."

"And let's have some sweet potato fries," Mrs. Feder said. "We both like those."

Emily nodded. "I'll have a mixed fruit smoothie, too," she told her father as he stood up to place the order. Emily smiled as she took another bite.

She couldn't believe how good that sandwich tasted.

CMS LOBBY. TUESDAY 8:25 A.M.

Joan, walking through the lobby, thought that the posters the other cheerleaders made were great. She just wished that she had been able to help. Her favorite had a big football spiraling though a blue sky. Big white lettering read:

> CMS FOOTBALL HAS THE SPIN.
> WE PLAY HARD.
> WE PLAY FAIR.
> WE WIN!

The other posters in the lobby had positive messages, too.

Melody came up behind her. "Did you see Bubba?" she asked.

"Is Bubba here?" Joan asked with surprise. "In school?"

"Not the real one," Melody answered. She pointed to the trophy case. "Look over there."

Joan joined a crowd of kids in front of the glass case. She stood on her tiptoes and saw the cleaned-up, dressed-up Bubba.

"That's great," Joan told Melody.

"Who did it?" someone asked.

"Melody Max," a boy said in a loud voice. Joan looked up and saw Darryl.

Someone in the group of kids said, "Great idea." Someone else said, "Who's Melody Max?" A few kids turned to check out Melody.

Darryl put an arm around Melody's shoulder, whispered something in her ear, and left.

As Joan and Melody walked to their lockers

Joan noticed that Melody looked upset.

"What'd Darryl say to you?" she asked.

"That there are high school kids who will take care of the Cougars," she answered.

"Did he say what they're going to do?" asked Joan.

Melody shook her head. "But it sounds serious. He said, 'They're going to take care of them.' "

"Uh-oh," said Joan. "Should we do something? I mean to stop them."

"I think we should try," Melody answered. "But what can we do?"

"Let's find Emily and Alexis and tell them," Joan said.

"We should have some kind of meeting about this," added Melody.

BULLDOG CAFÉ 4:00 P.M.

Alexis, Melody, and Joan picked out a table where no one could overhear them, while Emily went to the kitchen to get them all lemonade. As she was coming back with the tray of drinks and a plate of chocolate chip cookies, she saw Jake and Adam walking down the street together. The girls at the table saw them, too. Alexis signaled the boys to join them.

Joan came over to help Emily with the drinks. "Alexis thinks that Jake and Adam should be at the meeting," she said.

"Great," said Emily. She held out the tray. "You take this. I'll get them some lemonade."

When Emily joined the meeting Alexis was saying, "Pranks can be fun. The people in my dad's law office are always playing tricks on one another. But it's because they're friends. They'd never do anything really mean."

"Hanging a model of our mascot by the neck is pretty mean," said Jake.

"And not letting our cheerleaders do their center cheer last year," said Joan. "It wasn't a prank. But it was mean."

"I was at that game," Emily told them. "When their cheerleaders kept trying to shout our cheerleaders down, it made our side really angry."

"When I was in Miami," Melody said, "there was this story my mother wrote. It was *bad.* Not the article. What happened. Some fraternity guys at the university threw a can of homemade tear gas through another fraternity house's window. It was awful stuff. The guys who were in that building said their eyes burned for a really long time. But what was worse was that one of the guys died! He had some kind of allergic reaction to whatever they use to make the tear gas."

"Wow!" Jake exclaimed.

"That is out of hand," said Adam.

"What are we going to do to stop whoever it is from doing whatever they're planning to do?" asked Melody.

"First, we have to find out who it is," said Emily.

"And what they're planning to do," added Alexis.

"How?" asked Joan.

"We need to do some major sleuthing," said Alexis.

"My dad might be able to find out something," Emily suggested. "People are always dropping by the hotel and talking to him about CMS sports. I'll ask him to help."

"I'll tell my grandmother what Darryl told Melody," Jake said. "Maybe she can learn more from the kids at her school."

"Don't tell anyone that Darryl is involved," Melody said. "I don't want to get him in trouble."

"Okay," agreed Jake.

"Darryl likes you, Melody," Joan said. "Maybe you could get some more information from him." Joan noticed her brother look at Melody. Does Adam like Melody, too? she wondered. She wished that her brother wasn't at this meeting. These were her friends. Wasn't it bad enough that he had more freedom than she did? Was he going to steal her friends, too? It wasn't fair that she had to be home by five o'clock and he didn't have to be there until six. She looked at her watch. It was already 4:45. She had to get home. Adam could stay, but she'd have to go. She stood up. "I have to go," she told everyone.

"How come?" asked Emily.

Joan didn't want her friends to know that her parents kept her on a short leash. "I have a piano lesson," she said. She gave her brother a quick glance that said, Don't say anything. He didn't.

"You didn't eat your cookie," Emily told her. Emily wondered how Joan could resist the gorgeous cookie on the napkin in front of her. It was taking every bit of willpower that Emily had not to gobble it up.

"You have it," Joan told her. "I'm not hungry. Have to run."

After Joan left, Adam said, "Even if we knew who it was that was going to retaliate, how would we stop them?"

"Good question," said Alexis. "I guess we'll just have to figure that out. Meanwhile, I'll rewrite my sports column. I'll say that the only way CMS is going to get back at the Cougars is by winning that football game."

"And I'll write an editorial," Jake said. "I'll ask everyone to support our decision, as a school, not to try to get back at the Cougars in any other way than by winning the game."

"When is the paper coming out?" Emily asked.

"Friday morning," Jake answered.

"The cheerleaders should give out the papers," Melody said. "We can tell everyone to read the sports column and the editorial."

"That is a great idea," Adam told Melody.

"Thanks," she said softly as she returned his smile.

"But how is that going to stop the pranks?" Emily asked. "The high school kids who are planning them probably won't even see our school paper. They read the *Claymore News*. That's the paper that covers high school sports."

"The *Claymore News* comes out on Friday, too," Melody said. "Maybe my mother will print Alexis's column and Jake's editorial on the sports page. Then a lot of the high school kids will read them, too. I'll ask her tonight."

"Our articles in the town paper?" said Alexis.

"We have to get people to mellow about the Cougars," Adam said. "The papers are one way to do that."

Alexis felt a wave of panic run through her. Was she good enough? "Jake, you have to help me with mine," she said.

"Don't worry," he told her. "The piece you did on the cheer tryouts was really good. This one will be even better."

"Do you think we should ask Sally to talk to Darryl about it?" asked Emily.

"Sally and Darryl are going out," Jake said. "Don't you think she knows already?"

"And Sally would try to put a stop to it," added Melody. "She made a great speech at practice yesterday about school spirit."

"It was amazing," said Emily. "Sally's amazing."

Alexis hoped her friends were right. Maybe Sally could make a difference. And maybe her article would help, too.

MAIN STREET 4:55 P.M.

As Sally Johnson Rollerbladed away from her house, she was listening to her Walkman and thinking about the Cougars. She was headed for the beach where some kids she knew from Claymore High's football team and cheer squad liked to hang out. They'd been Bulldog athletes and played in the Bulldog-Cougar games in middle school. Sally wanted to talk to those guys about what the Cougars had done at CMS. She'd remind them that the Cougars played dirty and how their cheerleaders treated the Bulldog cheerleaders at the game the year before.

Sally was so distracted by her thoughts that she didn't notice Joan coming from the other direction.

But Joan saw Sally. She admired how beautiful Sally looked rolling along the sidewalk, her long blond hair flying out behind her. I'd love to Rollerblade, she thought. But I can't. Not as long as I live with Michelle Russo and Paul Chazen. Rollerblading was just one more thing that they considered frivolous and dangerous.

Joan figured that Sally would roll right by her. But when Sally finally saw Joan, she did a little turn and stopped. As she punched off her cassette player and pulled off her headphones, she said, "Hi, Joanie. What's up?"

"Not much," Joan answered. As soon as the words were out of her mouth, Joan knew they sounded dumb. She thought, If I don't say something interesting, Sally will be sorry she even stopped. Maybe I should tell her about the meeting we just had. She'll want to stop any trouble with Santa Rosa, too.

But before Joan could say anything, Sally picked up the conversation herself. "Joanie, you're doing great at the stunts for the center cheer. I had a captains' meeting with Coach this afternoon. She's thinks you're great, too."

"Thanks," Joan said.

"And," Sally continued, "Sam Paetro is going to run a clinic for the squad."

"Sam Paetro?" Joan said. "The man who works for CHEER USA?"

"Yup," Sally said. "He'll work with us on tumbling and stunts after school on Thursdays."

Joan's heart sank. She had her piano lesson on Thursday afternoons now.

"Isn't that awesome?" Sally said. "We start next week."

"Great," Joan said, forcing a smile.

As Sally bladed off, Joan thought, How can I take those tumbling classes? I can't ask Mr. Richter to change my class again without telling my parents. I have to make up something that I have to do after school that they'll think is really important. I'll have to lie to my parents again. I hate lying, but I love cheerleading. Why do I have to do something I hate in order to do something I love? It isn't fair.

She turned the corner onto Delhaven Drive and walked slowly toward her house.

Sally was already three blocks away from Joan and skating down Main Street. She loved to Rollerblade on the busy street of shops where plenty of people would see her. Things were going great! Darryl was worked up about the Cougars, and she was going to talk to the high school guys.

Now, what can I do to get revenge on those Cougar cheerleaders for what they did to us last year? Sally wondered. Whatever it was, it had to be something no one would guess she had planned. It should be something that would hit the Cougar cheerleaders just before they went out to cheer. Something to shake them up.

She'd teach those cheerleaders that they couldn't push her squad around.

CLAYMORE BEACH 5:30 P.M.

After the meeting at the Bulldog Café, Adam and Melody walked home together.

"You want to walk on the beach partway?" Adam asked.

"Sure," Melody agreed. "Maybe we'll see a dolphin."

"Have you ever tried to keep up with them by running along the beach?" Adam asked.

"I was just thinking about how I used to love to do that," Melody told him.

When they got to the beach they took off their shoes so they could walk in the surf. "I've been meaning to tell you," Adam said. "You were really great cheering at the pep rally."

"Thanks," said Melody. "I'd never been to a pep rally before. It was fun. I just hope the game will be as much fun. I'm so afraid there will be an ugly scene with bad vibes."

"Are you going to try to talk Darryl out of whatever he's got planned?"

"If he mentions it again," she said. "But I figure Sally will take care of that."

They walked along without talking for a while. Finally Adam said, "Has Darryl asked you out or anything?"

"You're kidding, right?" said Melody.

"Just wondered," Adam said. "I mean, if he's been friendly and everything, I thought maybe . . ."

"Come on, Adam," Melody protested. "Darryl is this big deal captain-of-the-football-team, boyfriend-of-a-captain-of-the-cheer-squad ninth-grader. I'm a lowly seventh-grader."

"You seem older than a seventh-grader," Adam said.

Melody remembered that Darryl had said the same thing. But she didn't tell Adam. It seemed like a good time to change the subject. "Joan is an amazing flyer," she said. "Everyone's talking about it."

"Never say anything like that in front of our parents," Adam said.

"How come?" asked Melody.

"They don't know that cheering involves gymnastics," he said, "which they consider dangerous and a waste of time."

"That must be tough on Joan," Melody said. "She's such a great athlete. There must be lots of sports she'd love to do."

"It is tough on her," Adam said. "I think sometimes our parents are stricter with her than they are with me. Most of it is because she's younger. But still, sometimes it seems unfair. She has to be home an hour before I do on school nights. All because her piano teacher said she wasn't improving fast enough."

"Is that why she's having an extra lesson today?" Melody asked.

Adam stopped himself from telling Melody that Joan didn't have a piano lesson at five o'clock. He didn't want Joan's friends to know that she lied to them. But she had. And she'd been lying a lot to their parents lately. He saw trouble ahead for his sister. And he didn't know how to stop it.

Melody spotted Sally hanging out on a blanket with a couple of older guys and a girl. They were talking and laughing. Sally fits right in with those older kids, thought Melody.

"Look!" Adam said, pointing to the water. "A dolphin. Follow my finger. Keep looking."

In a few seconds Melody saw a gray comma-shaped dolphin break through the surface of the water, arch through the air, and knife back into the water.

"Come on!" Melody shouted. "Let's try to keep up with it."

She and Adam laughed as they ran along the beach together. The sea air filled Melody's lungs, and the wind whipped around her body. One of the things she had loved most about living in Miami was living near the ocean. She loved the sea and the life in it — especially dolphins.

She wasn't living in Miami, but she still lived near the water. And she had a new friend who seemed to love it as much as she did.

DELHAVEN DRIVE 9:05 P.M.

Joan had tried to do her homework. She couldn't. Not when all she could think about was her parents and Sam Paetro's tumbling clinic. If I spend all this time worrying, she thought, I won't do my homework. Then I'll get bad grades, and I'll be in really big trouble. There's nothing more important to my parents than school grades.

There was a tap on her door.

"What?" she yelled.

"It's me," Adam answered. "Can I come in?"

"Sure," she said.

He came in, closed the door behind him, and sat on the edge of her bed.

Joan was feeling irritated with her brother. He hasn't done anything particularly wrong, she thought, except maybe slip into my new group of friends.

"What do you want, Adam?" she asked without looking up from her notebook.

"Nothing special," he answered. "Just wondered what you were doing."

"What does it look like I'm doing?" she snapped. "What do we ever do around here at night? Certainly not watch television like normal people."

"Joanie . . ."

She swiveled around and glared at him. How many times did she have to tell him to call her Joan, not Joanie?

"Joan," he said, correcting himself. "I just think . . . I mean, you seem so angry about this cheering stuff and mother and father."

"Sh-sh," she hissed. "They'll hear you."

"No, they won't," he said. "They're in the living room reading and listening to opera."

Joan knew that she was being mean to Adam. She wasn't being fair. After all, Adam was her brother and her friend. Maybe he could help her. She looked up at him and closed her notebook. "I hate the way they don't approve of anything I want to do," she told him.

"Maybe now that you're older they won't mind about the gymnastics," he suggested. "It's not like it's really dangerous. You should try talking to them about it again. I'd help you."

"Talk to them!" Joan exclaimed. "Are you kidding? Or are you completely out of your mind?"

"I just thought . . ." he said.

"Think a little harder," she said. "I'm the one who had to quit gymnastics. I'm the one who has to be home at five. I can't even stay out with my friends. Pretty soon I'll be home all the time, and I won't have any friends."

"Your friends understand," Adam said. "They feel sorry for you."

"What?" Joan shouted as she jumped up from the chair and ran over to him. She glared at Adam.

Adam realized his mistake. His sister had lied to her friends because she didn't want them to know that she had strict parents. And he had told Melody.

"Who did you tell?" she asked angrily. "What did you say?"

"Nothing," answered Adam. "I — "

Joan gripped his arm. "Adam Russo-Chazen," she said. "If you don't tell me what you said I'll tell everyone every little stupid thing I know about you — like that you sucked your thumb until you were *eight years old.*"

"I just talked to Melody," he said. "On the way home. She was saying what a great flyer you are and I said that it was too bad that our parents are so against cheering. I don't think you should be lying to your friends, Joan. I think — "

"I don't care what you think," she said, interrupting him. "You are such a creep. You're as bad as Mother and Father." Tears sprang to her eyes.

She turned away from him. She wasn't going to let Adam see her cry. That would just prove that she was a baby.

"Get out of my room," she shouted. "Get out NOW!"

She heard Adam stand up and walk to the door. "I'm sorry, Joan," he said. "I didn't mean to — "

"You just want Melody to think you're a big shot," she said, "so 'psychological' and kind."

But Adam was gone. He hadn't even heard her. Joan locked the door to her room and threw herself on her bed.

Everybody would know. They'd know that her parents wouldn't let her do *anything* that was fun. They'd think that *she* wasn't any fun. And they'd all be talking about her like she was some pitiful little thing.

I am pitiful, Joan thought as she rolled over and buried her wet face in the pillow.

CMS SMALL GYM. WEDNESDAY 3:30 P.M.

The cheerleaders sat in two rows, their legs stretched out in front of them.

"Reach to the ceiling," Coach instructed. "One. Two. Three. Four. Now drop and reach for those toes. Keep your legs straight."

Emily glanced at her watch as she bent over. Ten more minutes of stretches.

She looked under her right arm. Melody was lying flat out over her legs.

She looked under her left arm. Joan, the human pretzel, had opened her legs in a perfect split and was lying flat on the floor between them. Sally could do that, too. And Mae. But not me, thought Emily. I'll never even come close to doing that. I can't even reach my toes or stretch out my back in this position, because my huge stomach is in the way.

Coach had announced that next week they were starting a clinic with a CHEER USA coach. "Sam Paetro will move your tumbling to a new level," Coach promised.

Everybody's tumbling but mine, thought Emily. I can't even do a handspring. And my jumps aren't as high as the other cheerleaders'. I know they aren't. The only thing I'm good at is yelling the chants and cheers. Big deal.

After warm-ups Sally led them in jumps. Then they tumbled. Finally, Coach called a five-minute break. "There's a cooler by the door," she said. "Hydrate, girls."

Maria, another seventh-grade cheerleader, walked with Emily toward the cooler. "Did you hear what's going on?" Maria whispered in Emily's ear. "About the Bulldogs and the Cougars?"

Emily decided to play dumb. Maybe that way she could learn more. "What?" she asked.

"Some people in town and a couple of guys from the team. They're going to get back at the Cougars — on Friday night," Maria said. "Isn't that great?"

Emily wanted to tell Maria that she didn't think it was great at all. Then, of course, Maria would think she was a wimp or a goody-goody. But if I don't say what I really believe, Emily decided, how can I expect to stop it? By the time she figured all that out, they'd reached the cooler and the rest of the cheerleaders.

"Don't tell anyone," Maria whispered, and she was lost in the crowd of girls reaching for drinks.

Emily picked out an apple juice. She turned it over and read the label. One hundred fifty calories. Even things that were good for you had calories. She put the juice back and took a bottle of water. Zero calories. She noticed that Sally was drinking water, too.

Sally felt someone's eyes on her. She turned and saw Emily. Sally remembered that she wanted to talk to Emily and motioned her to meet in a corner away from the other girls.

I bet she wants to talk to me about the Bulldog-Cougar stuff, Emily thought. I'll tell her about our meeting about what to do to calm things down. And without naming names I'll tell her that some of the cheerleaders don't have the right spirit. That they aren't following what Sally said at the Monday practice.

Emily was about to say all that when she met Sally at the corner of the gym. But Sally spoke first. "I wondered how your diet is going."

Emily was surprised by the question. Sally must think she was really fat.

"Okay, I guess," Emily said. "I'm not eating as much."

"Good for you," Sally said.

Emily wanted to tell Sally how hard it was to diet. How she got so hungry that she stuffed herself and then felt awful after.

"You need to work on your jumps more, Emily," Sally told her. "You need cleaner jumps if we're going to place at CHEER USA."

"Okay," said Emily. She smiled so Sally would know that she was grateful for the help. But she wanted to cry. It was all too difficult.

Sally beamed Emily a big smile. "You can do it, Emily," she said. "I know you can. Get your sister to help you. She's a fabulous cheerleader."

Emily stopped herself from telling Sally that Lynn had worked with her on cheering all summer. Because then Sally would know the truth about her.

She was never going to be a better cheerleader.

CMS COURTYARD 5:00 P.M.

Melody Max sat on a bench in the courtyard and did her math homework. Her mother would be by any minute to pick her up for a big grocery shop.

"Hey," a voice boomed in her ear.

Melody was so startled she jumped and let out a little yelp.

"Sorry," Darryl said. "Didn't mean to scare you."

"It's okay," Melody said. "You just finish practice?"

"Yeah. And we're looking good. We'll whip those Cougars."

Melody felt relieved. Darryl understood that the way to get back at the Cougars was to win the game. "So the pranks are off?" she said.

Darryl laughed. "No way. When the Cougars roll into Claymore they'll already know who is going to win that game."

"What are you going to do?" Melody asked, trying to hide her alarm.

"You'll see," he said. "Everyone will."

"Tell me," she said in a hushed voice.

Darryl shook his head. "It's all a major secret," he said.

"I just wonder what you could do after what they did to us."

Darryl looked around the courtyard. There were still a few kids there, but none of them was within hearing distance. "We're sneaking into Santa Rosa the night before the game," he began.

"Who?" she asked.

"A few of us guys from CMS and some of the high school guys, you know, who used to play CMS football," Darryl answered. "We're going to spray-paint their buses — all of them — with BULLDOGS WILL WIN. Everyone will see it. Kids getting on those buses. People in town. This cool quarterback from Claymore High has this paint that doesn't come off and is, like, impossible to cover up. They'll have to drive those buses here. They bring loads of kids to the game. But that's not all."

"Not all?" Melody said.

"You're going to love this," Darryl began in his slow drawl. "There's this stuff we're going to put under the hoods that will smoke up when they start the buses. It's stinky smoke. Man, you wouldn't want to be on one of those buses when that happens."

Melody noticed her mother driving up to the school. She didn't have time to try to convince Darryl *not* to do all the things he was so excited about.

"Does Sally know about all this?" she asked as she picked up her books.

He nodded.

Melody's mother honked the horn to let Melody know she was there . . . and waiting.

"I have to go," Melody told Darryl.

"Don't tell anybody about the plan," he said. "We want it to be a surprise. I just wanted you to know that we're taking care of things. You don't have to worry."

I'm plenty worried, Melody thought as she went toward the car. She imagined school buses — loaded with kids — filling up with smelly smoke. Smoke that could hurt someone. At least Sally knows, Melody thought as she got in the car.

32 MAIN STREET. 5:15 P.M.

Jake was dribbling a basketball in front of his garage. He stopped, turned, and made a hook shot from under the basket.

As he grabbed the ball, Jake saw Alexis biking across the hotel parking lot and waved.

Alexis waved back. Suddenly she felt a little funny. She'd been to Jake's dozens of times — but never without Emily.

Alexis rode her bike into the Feders' backyard and pulled up to Jake.

"Want to shoot some hoops before we work on the article?" he asked.

"Sure," she said.

They played a little one-on-one.

"You're good," Jake told her after Alexis sunk her third basket.

It was so much fun. Alexis couldn't stop smiling the whole time. She remembered how she hated smiling for cheerleading. But basketball was different.

Basketball was the sport she loved, especially when she was shooting baskets with Jake.

THE MANOR HOTEL. 5:35 P.M.

Emily was at her desk doing her math homework. She looked at the first problem and wrote down some numbers. But all she could think about was food. She was so hungry. And she was mad at herself for going off her diet last night. Well, today she hadn't eaten anything, and she wouldn't later, either. The weird thing was that the only person who knew she was on a diet was Sally. Emily wondered if it would help if she told someone besides Sally that she was trying desperately to lose weight. Someone she could *really* talk to. Someone like Alexis. Alexis was her best friend. Yes, she'd talk to Alexis about it.

Emily picked up her phone and speed-dialed Alexis's father's apartment.

The answering machine picked up after four

rings. "Hi, Alexis," Emily told the machine after the message and beep, "it's me. Call, okay?"

Emily tried to go back to her math homework. It was no use. She couldn't concentrate. Should she tell Jake about the diet? Jake was so sweet he'd just tell her that she wasn't fat and didn't need to lose weight. But being around Jake might make her feel better. She closed her math book. She'd go over to his house and hang out until dinner. She could do her homework later.

When she stood up she felt a little dizzy from not eating. She held onto the desk until her balance came back. Then she went to the window to see if Jake was outside. She saw him dribbling a basketball. Then she saw that Alexis was with him. Alexis! That's where she is, thought Emily as she headed for her door. He must be helping her with her article. She can come over here when they finish, and I'll tell her about the diet.

By the time Emily ran over to Jake's house, Alexis and Jake weren't outside anymore. Emily went to the kitchen door and looked through the screen. They were sitting at the kitchen table having a cold drink and talking about Alexis's article. Their backs were to her so they didn't see her. They were busy working. Emily turned and walked home.

Alexis and Jake had more important things to do than talk to a fat, famished cheerleader.

SQUEEZE. THURSDAY 8:00 A.M.

Melody waited in front of the juice bar. Even though Darryl had asked her not to tell anyone about the plan to strike back at the Cougars, she felt that she had to tell her friends. They couldn't expect Sally to stop the vandalism all on her own. So Melody had called everyone and asked them to meet her at the juice bar before school. She had some more information on the Cougar-Bulldog case.

Melody saw Jake and Emily heading toward her from one direction and Alexis from another. Before they reached her, a car pulled up, and Joan and Adam jumped out.

"Good-bye, Mother," Melody heard Adam say. Joan's mother said something to Adam and Joan in another language. Melody thought it was French.

"I will," Joan told her mother. "I'll be there."

Melody's parents had always given her a lot of freedom. She wondered what it would be like to have parents who were strict.

"Was your mother speaking French to you?" Melody asked Joan and Adam.

"*Oui,*" answered Adam with a grin.

Joan wasn't smiling. She seemed tense and

grumpy. Melody wanted to say something, but she wasn't sure what would make Joan feel better. She just smiled at Joan and walked with her to meet the others.

The six friends went across the street to the park and sat on the grass. Melody told them what Darryl and his friends had planned for the Cougars.

"We have to stop them," Emily said.

"They have everything organized, right down to what kind of paint they're using," Jake pointed out. "Our articles aren't going to change their minds."

"What else can we do?" Alexis asked.

"We should try to talk to Darryl," Adam suggested. "Get him to change his mind."

"He could get in big trouble over this," Melody said. "Like be suspended or even kicked off the team. I wonder if he's thought about that."

"Don't you think Sally will keep Darryl from going ahead with the prank?" Joan asked.

"I'm sure she's tried," Melody said. "But I think she needs help. I mean, Darryl said she knows, but he's still bragging about what he's going to do to get back at the Cougars."

"You should talk to Darryl, Melody," Jake said. "Tell him how serious this is."

"And that it's dangerous for innocent people,

like the kids on those buses," added Emily.

"Tell him the story you told us about the tear gas at that fraternity house," suggested Joan.

"Darryl's a nice guy," Alexis said. "He probably just hasn't thought about all of this."

"Okay," Melody said. "I'll try."

"Maybe you and Sally could talk to him together," said Adam. "You know, join forces."

"Good idea," agreed Emily.

Melody hesitated. Even though Sally was always nice to her, sometimes she didn't think Sally really liked her. It wasn't anything Sally did or that she could put a finger on. Just a feeling. A weird feeling.

"Maybe it's better if Sally and I approach Darryl separately," Melody suggested. "The message could be more powerful that way."

They all agreed. Melody only hoped that she could pull this off.

It was a big responsibility.

CMS COURTYARD 8:25 A.M.

Melody walked with Joan and Emily across the courtyard.

"There he is," Joan whispered to Melody. "Talking to Sally."

Melody saw Sally and Darryl standing under one of the courtyard palm trees. Sally was tilted back against the tree trunk. Darryl put one hand on the tree and leaned forward to whisper something in her ear. Sally laughed, gave Darryl a quick kiss on the cheek, and ran over to a group of her friends.

"Here's your chance, Melody," Joan said. "He's all alone."

Emily gave Melody a little push in Darryl's direction. "Go. Do it," she instructed. "Good luck."

As Melody walked toward Darryl she wondered if she'd be able to stop his plan. She looked at her watch. It was almost time for homeroom. She didn't have much time. She started toward him.

Two of Darryl's friends from the football team ran over to him. Darryl said something to them, and one of the guys hit Darryl on the back as if to congratulate him. Melody was sure they were talking about all the stuff they were going to do in Santa Rosa on Friday night.

She turned back to her friends and shrugged her shoulders. She'd lost her chance. She'd have to find another time when she could talk to Darryl Budd alone.

Emily and Joan came up on either side of her.

"Joan has an idea," Emily said.

"You should write Darryl a note," Joan suggested. "Tell him you have something important to discuss with him. Ask him to meet you someplace — I don't know where — you pick it out."

"But it shouldn't be at school," Emily added. "He's so popular you'll be interrupted."

"He'll think I'm asking him on a date," Melody said. "And I'm not. It's too embarrassing."

"*You* know you're not asking him out," Emily said, "and he'll know it when you meet him."

"*If* he'll meet me," said Melody. "What if he ignores my note but tells everyone I asked him out?"

"This is important, Melody," said Joan. "It's the only way."

The morning bell rang and a bunch of kids swarmed around them as they walked into school. They couldn't talk privately anymore.

"Okay," Melody told her friends. "It's worth a try."

When she reached homeroom she opened her notebook and wrote:

Darryl. I need to talk to you. It's urgent. Could you meet me on the beach in front of Joe's Seafood Shack around 4:00? No need to answer this note unless you can't make it. I hope you can. Melody

Melody folded the paper in half and put it in her pocket. She'd have to slip it to Darryl later. Privately.

Between first and second periods Melody

took a detour through the ninth-grade corridor on her way to math class. She saw Darryl coming down the hall with a bunch of other guys. He noticed her and smiled but kept walking. No way can I give it to him when he's in a crowd like that, she thought. She kept an eye on Darryl until she saw what room he went in. Then she went back to the first floor. Oh, boy, she thought, it is so obvious that I was waiting for him. He really will think I'm chasing after him.

She felt her face flush with embarrassment, and she hadn't even given him the note yet.

Between the next two periods Melody went back to the ninth-grade corridor and headed straight for the room she'd seen Darryl go into at the beginning of the second period. When he came out she was ready. She quickly thrust the note in his hand, whispered, "Private," and disappeared into the crowd of ninth-graders.

CLAYMORE BEACH 4:15 P.M.

Melody sat on the sand facing the ocean. She reviewed in her mind all the things she wanted to tell Darryl. She looked at her watch. Four-sixteen. What if he didn't show up? She'd wait until four-thirty. The next time she looked down the beach she saw Darryl running across the sand toward her.

"Hey," he said. He was breathless from running. The late afternoon sunlight made a halo around his blond hair. He plopped down in the sand beside her. A huge smile spread across his face. "I figured out why you want to see me."

"You did?" Melody said. Please, she prayed, please don't think I want to go out with you. It would be too embarrassing.

He leaned toward her and said, "You want in on it."

"In on it?" she asked with surprise.

"In on the prank we're playing in Santa Rosa," he said. "But we're not bringing girls."

Melody gave a little laugh. "That's not why I wanted to talk to you," she said. "It's something else. Something very important. But I need you to just listen. So don't interrupt me. Okay?"

"Okay," he agreed.

"When I finish what I have to say you can argue with me," she continued. "I like to argue. I think arguing is very cool." Melody watched Darryl's blank expression. She knew that she was babbling.

Darryl ran his hands through his hair. "Melody, what are you getting at?" he said. "I've got stuff to take care of, you know. So hit a point, will you?"

No more stalling, thought Melody. Time to be blunt.

"Darryl, I don't think you should vandalize

the Cougar school buses. You have to stop it from happening."

Darryl put up a hand. "Whoa. This is why you wanted to meet me?"

Melody pushed his hand down with hers. "Darryl, you promised to hear me out. Listen. I want to explain why."

Melody explained her reasons for not vandalizing the buses. Darryl fidgeted and threatened to leave once, but in the end he let her finish what she'd planned to say.

"Okay," she finally said. "Your turn to talk."

At that moment a volleyball hit Darryl on the head.

"Hey, goofball," someone shouted. "Can't you leave the girls alone for five minutes?"

Darryl and Melody looked up. Three guys in bathing suits were running toward them.

Darryl threw the ball back, then turned to Melody and hissed, "Don't say a word about this. Not a word."

"Just think about what I said," Melody told him.

The ball came back. This time it was headed straight for Melody. She reached up, caught it, and tossed it back — not too far since the guys had almost reached them.

Darryl jumped to his feet. "Let's go," he told his friends. "Do we have enough for a game?"

"Yeah. But there's room for your little friend," said a red-haired guy Melody recognized from the football team. He winked at Melody. "If she wants to play."

Before Melody could answer, Darryl said, "She has to go."

As Melody walked off the beach she saw a bunch of guys and girls organizing into two teams on either side of a volleyball net. One of them was Sally.

Sally saw Melody, too. Did Darryl ask Melody to go for a walk on the beach? she wondered. Or was it the other way around? She intended to find out.

Darryl tossed Sally the ball and headed toward her.

"Didn't know you had a hot after-school date," she said in a teasing voice.

Darryl's face flushed. "We were just talking," he said. "She's a seventh-grader."

"I know," said Sally. "I thought maybe you were baby-sitting."

Randy, a halfback on the Bulldog team, overheard Sally and Darryl. "You jealous, Sally?" he asked, teasing.

"Are you kidding?" Sally answered. She smiled, but she was furious. Not at Darryl. But at Randy for thinking she'd be jealous. No way was she going have a reputation for being jealous.

Not over Darryl Budd. Not when she could be dating high school guys. The only reason she was bothering with this ninth-grade crowd was because she wanted to be the most popular, most everything at CMS.

"Randy," she cooed as she threw him her biggest, flirtiest smile, "let's play."

When the game was in motion Sally kept her eye on the ball and did her part to win for her side. But her mind was elsewhere. What had Melody and Darryl talked about? Was the sophisticated seventh-grader from Miami after her boyfriend? Well, she couldn't have him.

Not during football season.

BULLDOG CAFÉ 5:00 P.M.

Adam, Emily, Jake, and Alexis were waiting for Melody. Adam hoped that Melody didn't have a crush on Darryl. He didn't want her to be hurt. After all, Darryl did have a girlfriend. He wished Melody would hurry up. She was very late.

"It's too bad Joan couldn't come," Alexis said.

"How come she couldn't?" asked Jake.

"Piano lesson," Adam said. "Joan's really good."

Adam took a gulp of his lemonade. That was okay to say, he thought. I didn't make Joan look bad, and I didn't lie. Not this time.

Adam looked around the table. Alexis and Jake were talking about the newspapers that were coming out the next day. Emily was half listening to them while she built a little house out of a brownie and broken pieces of chocolate chip cookies. Adam sighed and reached for another cookie. As he took a bite he noticed Melody walking toward the café. "Here she is," he told the others.

"I can't wait to hear what happened," Emily said.

The expression on Melody's face as she came closer already told Adam that her meeting with Darryl hadn't gone well.

"What happened?" Alexis asked as she poured Melody a glass of lemonade. Adam pushed the plate of cookies and brownies in Melody's direction.

"Well," Melody said as she sat down, "I told Darryl what I had to say. But his friends came by as soon as I finished my list of reasons. Darryl was not happy about what I had to say, I can tell you that. He wanted me out of there."

"You told him about maybe getting suspended and thrown off the football team?" Emily asked.

Melody nodded. "I told him everything."

"Maybe he'll think about what you said," added Alexis.

“I hope you’re right,” Melody said. She looked around the table. “So what has been happening here?”

“The *Bulldog Edition* is being printed now,” Jake said. He looked at his watch. “I’m picking it up in an hour. Don’t forget to wear your uniforms to school tomorrow. And be at school fifteen minutes early to hand the papers out.”

“I’ll remind Joan,” Adam said.

“My mother is running Alexis’s article and Jake’s editorial on the sports page of the Claymore and the Santa Rosa editions of the paper tomorrow,” said Melody.

“Great,” said Adam.

“So if the prank does happen,” said Alexis, “both towns will know that most Bulldogs weren’t behind it.”

“What else can we do?” asked Jake.

The five friends looked at one another and thought for a minute.

“I can’t think of anything else,” said Emily.

“Me, either,” said Jake.

Adam looked at his watch. “I have to go,” he said.

“I’ll go with you,” said Melody as she stood up. She smiled at Emily. “Thanks for the great snack. The house you made with the brownie and cookies is cute. You going to eat it now?”

Emily shook her head. "I made it for Lily," she said.

DOLPHIN COURT APARTMENTS 9:00 P.M.

Melody checked her e-mail. No messages from her friends. But there was one from her dad.

> Hey there, Maxi. What'd you think of my new on-air jacket? And check out the tie tomorrow. Let me know if it's too loud. Or too quiet. Or too anything not cool enough for your fancy taste. I miss having you here to help pick out my ties. Miss you period. Good luck with that big game on Saturday. Love. Dad.

The only time Melody could see her father was when he did the weather forecast from Miami at 8:15 each weekday morning. She'd missed him that morning because of the meeting at Squeeze. And she'd have to leave the house early the next day, too. She'd better write to him.

> Missed your spot this A.M. and will tomorrow, too. Have (and had) to be at school early. Lots going on in prep for big game on Saturday. More about that later. But puh-lease

wear that jacket and tie next week. Promise I will check them out. Your Max.

She pointed the cursor at "reply to sender" and clicked the mouse.

Now I'll write to Tina, Melody thought. I'll tell her what's been going down with this Cougar-Bulldog game. She started the letter and stopped to reread what she'd written. All that was going on in Claymore the last few days was just too complicated to put into words. She deleted everything she wrote. Maybe when it's all over I'll be able to write about it, Melody thought. Then the story will have an ending.

But how will it end? she wondered.

CMS COURTYARD. FRIDAY 8:15 A.M.

Joan and Emily held a pile of *Bulldog Edition* copies and stood near the entrance to the courtyard with four other cheerleaders. With each paper Joan handed out she said, "Check out the sports column and the editorial page."

As Alexis walked across the courtyard she saw kids reading the *Bulldog Edition* and knew that a lot of them were reading her column. Would people agree with what she wrote? Would her article make a difference?

Melody walked around the courtyard making

sure everyone had a paper. She spotted Darryl with two of his football friends. She went over to them and asked, “Everybody here get a paper?”

“Yeah, we got it,” said a cute short guy. He patted a folded copy of the *Bulldog Edition* sticking out of his back pocket.

“Well, check out the sports column and the editorial page,” Melody said. “It’s all about the rivalry with the Cougars and the game tomorrow.”

“*We’re* the game tomorrow,” said a big guy the kids called The Truck.

“You sure are,” Melody said.

Darryl didn’t say anything, but he was staring at Melody. She looked him right in the eye and said, “We’re behind you one hundred percent.”

Darryl half smiled as he told her, “We’ll give you a good game. The Cougars are going to know who’s in charge.” He winked at her, turned, and walked away. His friends went with him.

Sally stood across the courtyard watching Melody with Darryl. She needed to know what Melody knew about tonight. Was Darryl talking to her about it right now?

“Melody,” she called. “Over here.”

Melody looked up and saw Sally motioning for her to come over. As she walked toward Sally she hoped that Sally had an idea to stop Darryl.

“Hey,” Sally said as Melody reached her. “Saw

you talking to Darryl. He's pretty worked up over the game, isn't he?"

"That's for sure," Melody said.

"Well, you can see why he would be," Sally said. "It's an important game. Especially after what the Cougars did."

"I just hope kids from Claymore don't play pranks in Santa Rosa tonight," Melody said.

"You don't need to worry about that," Sally told her.

"Did Darryl say they called it off?" asked Melody.

"Called what off?" asked Sally. She'd play dumb with Melody until she found out how much she knew.

"The prank he was planning," Melody answered. "You know, on the Santa Rosa school buses. He told me you knew. I've been trying to convince him to drop it, too."

So Darryl has been blabbing to Melody about the plans to vandalize the Santa Rosa buses, thought Sally. If he told her, he's probably told a lot of other people. And everyone he's told has told others. And that was not cool.

"Don't worry about it, Melody," she said. "I'm sure if you spoke to him he'll do the right thing."

"I hope so," Melody said. "I'm afraid that people could get hurt. And that Darryl would be kicked off the team."

The bell rang for homeroom.

"Don't worry about anything," Sally told her. "Just go out there tomorrow and cheer for CMS."

"I will," Melody promised.

After Melody left, Sally quickly scanned the crowd for Darryl. She finally found him heading toward the school entrance and ran over to him.

"Hey, babe," Darryl said when he saw her.

Sally threw an arm around his neck. "What's up, Darryl? You keeping yourself out of trouble?"

"I'm trying to," Darryl answered. He looked around to be sure no one could overhear them. "Listen, Sally," he said in a low voice, "this whole thing with Santa Rosa. What if I get caught? I could get kicked out of school."

Sally thought, Sure. Now that you've blabbered it all over town. She didn't want a boyfriend who was a loser. Being kicked off the football team, maybe even out of school, was definitely not cool. And not part of her plan.

"Word has gotten out that something is up," she said. "It's possible you could get in trouble. Maybe you should back out."

"Yeah, that's what I've been thinking, too," Darryl told her. "But Dave Grafton and Ray Torres have it all planned."

"You can tell them that a lot of people seem to know about it. Tell them it would be bad for them if they went through with the plan." She gave him her special smile. "I don't want anything bad to happen to you."

"Thanks, babe," he said. "You're the best."

"You, too," she said.

Even though Darryl's backing out, Sally thought, I can still take care of the Cougar cheerleaders tomorrow — and I don't need anyone's help to do it. A genuine smile spread over her face as she walked toward the front door of the school with Darryl.

Joan bent to pick up a pile of extra newspapers from the steps. As she stood she saw Sally and Darryl going into the school arm in arm. That is so sweet, she thought. The captain of the football team and the co-captain of the cheer squad.

The perfect couple giving their all to CMS.

CMS SMALL GYM 4:15 P.M.

It was the last cheerleading practice before the big game. After the warm-up and some jumping and tumbling practice the girls took a short break. Emily felt tired and hungry. I had a good diet day, she told herself. Maybe tomorrow my uniform won't be so tight.

"Time to draw names," Coach announced. She held up a baseball cap. "Mae, explain it to the new girls."

"The football players' names are in the hat," she said. "We each pick a name. If your player gets a touchdown or does something awesome in the game, you'll do the individual cheer for him."

"So gather round," Coach said. "The co-captains will draw names, then we'll go by class, starting with the ninth-graders."

"I want Randy," Maria whispered to Emily as they joined the circle surrounding Coach. "Randy's so cute, and he always makes a touchdown. Who do you want?"

"I don't know," Emily answered.

Melody and Joan moved over to be near Emily.

"I hope Sally gets Darryl," Joan said.

"Me, too," Emily agreed. "It would be so romantic."

Sally opened her slip and rolled her eyes.

"Guess she didn't get him," said Joan.

"The problem is, some guys, like the linemen, never get cheered for," explained Emily. "Nobody wants to draw their names."

"It looks like Sally picked one," Joan said. "I wonder who will pick Darryl."

Next the ninth-graders drew. Then the eighth-graders.

"Who picked Darryl?" C.J. asked as the seventh-graders lined up for their turn.

None of the ninth- or eighth-graders answered.

"It looks like a seventh-grader will be cheering for him," Mae said.

"I hope it's me!" Maria loudly exclaimed.

Everybody laughed, but the noise quieted down while the seventh-graders picked.

Emily drew first. She almost hoped she wouldn't get Darryl. If she did she'd have to do a jump all by herself. Everyone would see how bad she was. She opened the slip and read it out loud. "Willy Stanton," she said.

"He's a linesman," Maria told her.

Melody went next.

Sally watched her carefully.

Melody opened the slip, smiled, and held it up. "Darryl," she said.

Everyone clapped.

I hate that girl, Sally thought as she joined in the applause, I totally hate her.

As soon as the other seventh-graders had drawn names, Coach called out, "Let's go. Line up for the sideline cheer. Let's see toe jumps on the C and M and make them nice and high and point those toes. Then hit the visual formation on the S."

The cheerleaders lined up side by side and shouted, **"HEY, FANS! LET'S CHEER. GO, CMS!"**

Emily jumped on the C and went right back up again for the M. She remembered being in the air and landing. But the next thing she knew, she was lying on the floor and couldn't remember falling. Everything looked blurry. Slowly, Melody's face and Joan's face came into focus.

"Are you all right?" Melody asked.

"What happened?" asked Joan.

As more girls gathered around Emily, Coach pushed past them, told them to back up, and knelt down next to Emily.

Emily propped herself up on her elbows. "When I came down from the second jump everything was kind of spinning," she said as tears sprang to her eyes.

She tried to stand up, but Coach put her hand out to stop her. "Stay there for a minute," she said as she put her fingers around Emily's wrist to take her pulse and asked, "Do you still feel dizzy?"

"Just a little," Emily said softly.

"Are you nauseous?"

Emily shook her head no.

"Did you hit your head when you fell?"

"I don't think so," Emily answered. She felt her head. "It doesn't hurt or anything."

"Pain anywhere else?"

"Uh-uh," Emily answered, shaking her head.

Emily looked around at the faces of the other cheerleaders leaning over to see her. They all looked worried.

"I'm okay," Emily told them. "I'm not dizzy at all anymore."

Coach looked up at the girls, too. "Mae, get me a bottle of water and an orange juice," she ordered. "The rest of you can leave now. Be here an hour before the game tomorrow, that's 12:30. I'm going to take Emily home."

Melody touched Emily on the shoulder and said, "I'll call you later."

"Me, too," added Joan.

"Thanks," Emily told her

Mae brought over the drinks. As Emily drank the water, Coach said, "What have you eaten today, Emily, starting with breakfast?"

"A piece of toast," Emily told her.

"Not enough," Coach said. "And for lunch?"

"An apple."

"Not enough," Coach repeated. She handed Emily the orange juice to drink.

After Emily drank some of the juice she stood up. She felt fine. "I'm okay now," she told Coach. "You don't have to take me home."

"Yes, I do," Coach insisted. "We need to talk."

Emily felt a wave of fear go through her. What was Coach going to say?

COACH CORTES'S CAR 4:45 P.M.

As Coach drove her car out of the school parking lot, she turned to face Emily and asked, "Are you on a diet?"

"Sort of," Emily said.

"You don't need to be," Coach told her. "You're a fine size."

"Everyone else on the squad is smaller than me," Emily said.

"So what?" Coach said. "People come in all sizes. You are not fat, Emily Granger. And not eating enough can affect your cheering. Food gives you energy. You need your energy to be a good cheerleader."

She doesn't think I cheer good enough either, Emily thought.

"Besides," Coach continued, "it's normal for a girl your age to put on a little weight."

She does think I'm overweight, Emily thought. She's just worried about my feelings. She's being extra nice to me because I'm a Granger.

Coach stopped the car in front of the hotel and turned to Emily. "I want you to promise me that you'll eat a good dinner tonight. And breakfast tomorrow and lunch before you come to the game. Okay?"

"Okay," Emily said.

Coach looked her right in the eye. "I'm serious, Emily."

"Okay," Emily said. "I promise."

"You don't want to faint on the field, do you?"

"No," Emily told her. "I'm sorry."

"There's nothing to be sorry about," Coach said. "Just take care of yourself. I'm going to call your mother when I get home. Meantime, you tell her what happened, okay?"

Emily nodded, said thank you again, and got out of the car.

Tears sprang to her eyes. I am fat, she told herself. And now I have to eat so I don't faint. I'll stay fat, and I'll never be a good cheerleader.

BLUE HERON DRIVE 10:00 P.M.

Sally locked her bedroom door and went to her closet. It was time to prepare for the big game tomorrow, and she didn't want her mother, father, or little brother to walk in on her.

She pulled out the duffel bag she'd used for camp. She'd been planning this prank since last summer. Thank you, Liz, she thought as she opened the bag and took out the three little packets that would release a truly disgusting odor into the visiting cheerleaders' bathroom. Liz Cioffi, her bunk mate, had brought stink bombs to camp thinking it would be a fun trick to play on another cabin. In what she considered one of her more brilliant moves, Sally convinced Liz not to use them. "It's a little childish," she'd told her. "I'll hide them so you won't be tempted."

By the end of camp Liz had totally forgotten about the stink bombs, and Sally had the perfect prank to pull on the Cougar cheerleaders. Not big and splashy like vandalizing buses. But it was something. The best part was that no one knew her plan. She was doing this solo.

She stashed the stink bombs in the bottom of her cheerleading bag.

If she was really lucky the school bus prank would still happen, but without Darryl. The high school guys might be spray-painting the buses right now. Yes, it could all work out just fine.

The other cheerleaders might have forgiven the Cougar squad for what happened at the game last year. But they weren't humiliated the way she was.

It was halftime in the game, and the Cougars were ahead. The Cougar cheer squad did an extra-long center cheer, so there were only a few minutes left in halftime when the Bulldogs ran out for their turn. Thirty seconds into the routine Sally's bases threw her up in a Free Heel Stretch. **"Go, Bulldogs!"** she shouted.

At that instant some members of the Cougar

band did an extraloud trumpet and drum fanfare. The bases holding Sally were so startled by the surprising interruption that they loosened their hold on her. She wobbled at the top of the pyramid in front of *hundreds* of people. From her high vantage point she saw Cougar cheerleaders laughing at her as she tried to keep her balance and shout the cheer. The fanfare played again. Then a few of the musicians broke into a swing number. A lot of Cougar fans were shouting, "Win, Cougars, Win!"

Bulldog fans tried to shout the Cougar fans down. But it only added to the noise and confusion.

Lisa, the co-captain of the Bulldogs cheer squad, must have given the signal to stop the cheer and leave the field. By then Sally's bases were off count, so the timing of her Full-Twist Dismount was off. The dismount was awkward and scary. And no one noticed that she lost her balance as soon as she hit the ground. They were already running back to the sidelines.

Sally was alone in the middle of the Cougar field. The Cougar fans were applauding because they had stopped the Bulldogs' halftime cheer, and they were laughing at the cheerleader sitting on the ground.

As she ran — alone — off the field, Sally saw that those Cougar cheerleaders were still laughing at her. By the time she joined her squad at the sidelines, the Cougar coach was talking to Coach Cortes. She apologized for what a few band members did and said that Bulldog cheerleaders should go back out and do the halftime cheer.

Coach Cortes said there wasn't enough time left and the crowd was too riled up. That the best thing would be to go on with the game. They talked some more about what had happened, and later Coach Cortes told her squad that only a few people in the band were responsible. But Sally knew better. She saw the cheerleaders laughing, and she remembered how they had tried to shout over the Bulldog sideline cheers.

It was time for revenge.

CMS GIRLS' LOCKER ROOM.
SATURDAY 12:30 P.M.

It was one hour until kickoff. Mrs. Johnson was putting sparkles in Emily's hair. "Your hair is adorable that way," she told her.

Emily tried to smile. She had followed Coach's instructions, but she couldn't help feeling really fat. She'd eaten a big meal last night and had breakfast and lunch today.

"What's wrong, sweetheart?" Mrs. Johnson asked as she dabbed a few sparkles on Emily's cheek. "You look all worried."

"Mrs. Johnson, do you think my uniform fits okay?" Emily asked.

"Call me *Sally Sue*, dear," she said. "Now turn around and let me see."

Emily turned around slowly in front of Mrs. Johnson. "I'd say it fits perfectly," she said. "But that's how I like to see the uniforms — nice and snug."

Sally's mother thinks my uniform is snug, too, Emily thought. And I ate so much for dinner last night. I have to go back on a diet.

"Could you give Sally a message for me?" Sally Sue asked Emily, interrupting her thoughts.

"Sure," Emily answered.

"Tell her that I have her cheerleading shoes. She forgot them at home, so I brought them with me. I'm afraid she'll think they're still at home."

Emily went back to the hall where some of the cheerleaders were warming up. Sally wasn't there.

Melody, who had been keeping a lookout for the arrival of the Santa Rosa school buses, came out of one of the classrooms and walked over to Emily.

"They're not here yet," Melody whispered to Emily.

"I hope nothing happened to those buses," Emily said.

"I'll check again in a few minutes," Melody told her.

"Have you seen Sally?" Emily asked.

"I think I saw her going down the hall a minute ago," Melody said as she slowly lowered herself into a split.

"If she comes back, tell her that her mother has her shoes," Emily said. "But I'll try to find her."

As Emily walked away, she felt a wet lick on her calf. "Bubba," she giggled as she turned and looked down. Bubba wagged his behind and licked Emily's calf again. He seemed very proud of himself, all decked out in his CMS T-shirt and fancy dog collar.

Some of the cheerleaders called out, "Hi, Bubba." And, "Isn't he cute?"

Emily's mother was right behind him. "Can I leave him with you for a few minutes?" she asked. "Your father will be here soon."

"Sure," Emily said.

"You look great, honey," Mrs. Granger said as she handed Emily Bubba's leash. "Just perfect. The stands are already filling up. Good luck."

"Come on, Bubba," Emily told her dog. "We're going to go find Sally."

Emily and Bubba walked quickly down the length of the hall. Sally wasn't there or in any of the classrooms along the way. I hope she didn't go home to get her shoes, Emily thought. If she gets there and can't find them she'll really panic. Plus she might miss the start of the game.

"Let's check downstairs," she told Bubba.

When they got to the first-floor corridor, Bubba barked. Emily saw Sally at the other end of the corridor in front of the bathroom that was reserved for the Cougar cheer squad.

Sally almost jumped out of her skin when she heard Bubba's bark and saw him and Emily running toward her. She put her cheerleading bag over her shoulder and held it against her side.

"Hi," Emily called out. "I was looking for you."

"What's up?" asked Sally.

"It's about your bag," Emily said.

Does she know I have stink bombs in there? Sally wondered. How could she? "What about my bag?" asked Sally as she clutched it closer.

"Well, if you look in there you'll see that you forgot your shoes," Emily said. "Your mother asked me to tell you that she has them."

"I figured she had them," Sally said. "But thanks anyway."

Bubba pulled on the lead and tried to jump up on Sally.

Emily yanked him back. "Bubba likes you," she told Sally.

Oh, right, thought Sally.

Bubba tried again to jump to Sally's bag.

Sally backed away. How could she get rid of this silly seventh-grader and her ugly dog?

A huge smile spread across Emily's face. "I know why you're down here," she said. "You're welcoming the visiting cheerleaders. That is so great! Can Bubba and I stay and help?"

Sally's heart sank. There was no way she could pull off her prank. Even if Emily and the dog left now, it wouldn't work. Emily had seen her in front of the bathroom for the Cougar cheer squad. Besides, time was running out. The Santa Rosa buses would soon be here. If Emily had come just a minute later, she thought, it would have been a close call.

Suddenly the air filled with an awful smell. Panic raced through Sally's body. Had one of the stink bombs gone off in her bag? How could it without a match?

Emily smelled it, too, and flushed with embarrassment. "Sorry," she said. "Bubba farted. Bulldogs do that a lot."

Just then Melody ran up to them. "Oh, Bubba! Phew!" she exclaimed.

Sally snuck a sniff of her bag. The terrible smell wasn't coming from there. She glanced down at Bubba and thought, He's ugly *and* he farts.

The doors at the end of the corridor opened,

and a stream of girls dressed in black-and-red cheer uniforms spilled into the hall.

"The buses are clean," Melody quickly whispered in Emily's ear. "No pranks."

"Great!" Emily whispered back. Then she shouted hi to the visiting cheerleaders. "Welcome to CMS."

"Hi," a few of the Cougar cheerleaders shouted back.

"Thanks," someone else said.

A pretty girl with shiny black hair ran up to them. "You're Sally, aren't you?" the girl said to Sally.

"Yes," Sally said. She put on her biggest fake smile.

"I'm Cassie Jimenez," the girl said. "Thanks for coming down to meet us." Bubba gave a little bark and wagged his behind.

Cassie squatted down to pet him. "Bubba is so cute," she gushed. "We all feel just awful about what happened with that stuffed animal. Some graduates of SRMS and maybe one or two of the football players did it. But, well, we apologize even though we didn't have anything to do with it."

"Thanks for saying that," Sally said.

"No one thought it was the cheerleaders' fault," Melody added.

"We owe you an apology for last year, too,"

Cassie said, "for not keeping things under control during halftime. We had a nasty co-captain. It was all her idea to shout during your cheers. But it's different this year. We read what you wrote in the paper and totally agree with you. Our coach is talking to your coach right now. She greeted us at the bus. That was really nice."

"I'm so glad," Sally said through a frozen smile.

Emily couldn't believe her good luck. She'd been here to be part of the coming together of the Bulldog and Cougar cheer squads. There would be peace between the cheerleaders at the football game.

Sally looked at the grinning faces of the visiting cheerleaders. "I better get back to my squad," she said. She flashed one last fake smile, turned, and left.

She couldn't bear to smile at those girls for one more second.

CMS FOOTBALL FIELD 1:30 P.M.

Joan was the first to run out onto the field. She looked up at the stands packed with fans. On one side blue-and-white banners waved for the Bulldogs. On the other she saw flashes of red and black. Plenty of Cougar fans had come to the game, too.

The Bulldog fans applauded and shouted as their cheerleaders filed out and formed an arch of blue-and-white pom-poms. A few Cougars booed, but the Bulldog cheers drowned them out.

"And now, Bulldog fans, welcome YO-OUR players!" the announcer shouted over the loudspeaker.

The Bulldog fans rose to their feet and cheered as their football players ran onto the field, between the two rows of cheerleaders.

When Darryl passed Melody he smiled and winked. She smiled back. Everyone was ready for a great game.

The Bulldogs lined up on the track in front of their fans and waited for the Cougars. The Cougar cheerleaders and players ran onto the field, and the Cougar fans were on their feet.

"Please all stand for the national anthem," the announcer instructed.

Everyone in the stands stood at attention with the players and cheerleaders.

After the Pledge of Allegiance the fans sat down, and the referees and football captains tossed a coin to see which side would kick off.

The Bulldogs won the toss, and Randy kicked the ball into play.

Before the first quarter was over the Bulldogs made their first touchdown.

Joan, Mae, C.J., and Sally tumbled as the rest of the squad shook their pom-poms and shouted:

Touchdown. X
Touchdown. X
The Bulldogs scored a
touchdown. X X

Darryl kicked for the extra point, and Melody did an individual cheer for him while a base of cheerleaders threw Joan up in a Free Liberty. Sally walked up and down the sidelines with the other cheerleaders keeping the crowd pumped up, but she kept her eye on Melody Max.

Alexis sat in the stands with Jake, Adam, and some of their friends. She held her slender reporter's notebook in one hand and a pencil in the other.

"Isn't this great?" Jake asked her.

"Yeah," she said. "I like watching the cheerleaders as much as the football game."

"I meant, 'Isn't it great that the buses didn't get vandalized?' " Jake said. "I bet what you wrote helped."

Alexis turned to him and smiled. "You think so?"

"Yeah," Jake said, returning her smile.

"It also helped that your grandmother found

out which high school kids were going to do it," said Alexis.

"Uh-oh!" Adam exclaimed.

Alexis and Jake looked back to the field.

The Cougars had scored a touchdown. Alexis watched nervously as they kicked for the extra point. The score was tied.

When it was four minutes to halftime the Cougars were moving toward another touchdown. The cheerleaders walked up and down in front of the crowd, shouting:

Hold that line! X X
Hold that line! X X

The Cougars didn't advance.

At halftime the score was still tied. It was time for the Bulldog center cheer. As the girls ran out to the field the dance music for their halftime cheer came over the loudspeaker. They started with a stunt. Melody heard some boos from the Cougar side. But other fans and the Cougar cheerleaders were telling them to quiet down.

The Bulldog cheerleaders came out of the stunt and went into the tumbling section of their routine.

After the tumbling, the girls spread out for

the dance portion of their routine. They ended with pyramids and screamed, **"Fight, Bulldogs, Fight!"** The Bulldog fans were on their feet, clapping.

As she ran off the field Emily noticed that even some Cougar fans were applauding. She felt her heart pound and sweat break out on her forehead. The center cheer was a lot of work.

"Over here," Mae told Emily. "Coach said to line up and watch the Cougar cheerleaders. As a good example to the rest of the crowd."

The Cougar cheerleaders were good. Emily decided that Cassie was the best. She was tiny like Joan and a great tumbler and flyer. It must be wonderful to be so small, she thought.

During the third quarter the Cougars scored another touchdown, but they missed the extra point.

At the end of the third quarter the score was Cougars 13, Bulldogs 7.

Joan was hoarse from yelling, but that didn't stop her. **"G-O, let's go, Bulldogs. G-O, let's GO,"** she shouted.

And the Bulldogs did go. In the final thirty seconds of play Darryl scored a touchdown. The score was tied. Melody started to run out to do her individual cheer for Darryl when she felt a hand pull her back. "A captain should do this one," Sally said.

"Of course," Melody told her. "Go ahead."

Sally tumbled out to the sideline and did her cheer with a series of jumps.

The Bulldog fans went wild yelling Darryl's name.

If he made the extra point they'd win the game. Darryl kicked. Emily watched the ball fly between the goalposts.

The band played the school song.

The game was over. Bulldogs 14, Cougars 13.

The Bulldog football players ran up to the Cougar players and shook hands. Emily bent over and picked up Bubba so he could be part of the excitement, too.

"DAR-RYL. DAR-RYL," the Bulldog fans shouted.

The CMS cheerleaders jumped up and down, shouting and hugging. Sally turned to hug the cheerleader behind her. "We did it!" she shouted. The cheerleader she faced was Emily, and she was holding Bubba, who gave Sally a slobbering lick on the cheek.

"Isn't it great!" shrieked Emily.

Sally flashed Emily a forced grin before turning to wipe the slobber off her cheek with the back of her hand. She looked around for Darryl and saw him looking for her. That was her Bulldog!

BULLDOG CAFÉ
5:00 P.M.

Emily, Joan, Melody, Adam, Alexis, and Jake went back to the café after the game. They took a big table near the railing. Jake and Emily went to the kitchen for a pitcher of fruit punch and a big platter of burritos.

"I'm so hungry," Joan said as she took a burrito. "I always get hungry when I cheer."

"Me, too," said Melody as she bit into a burrito.

Emily poured juice for everyone. I won't eat a burrito, she promised herself. I'm starting my diet again right now.

"There's Darryl and Sally," Jake said.

Everyone turned and saw Darryl and Sally walking arm in arm down the street. When they came closer Emily invited them to join the party.

"We're going to a beach party and — " Sally started to say.

"Hey, burritos," Darryl said, interrupting her. "Man, those look good." He climbed over the rail onto the deck before Sally could object. There's no getting out of this now, she thought. Not when Darryl saw free food. She put two hands on the rail and swung herself over.

Jake made room for Darryl to pull up a chair between him and Melody. And Joan made space for Sally between her and Emily. Jake gave each of the newcomers a plate and napkin. Joan poured them juice.

Emily handed the plate of burritos to Sally. "No, thanks," Sally said. Emily was glad she hadn't taken one herself.

"That was one great game, Darryl," Melody said. "You were awesome."

"Thanks," he said. He leaned toward her and whispered, "You gave me some good advice. Thanks."

"I was afraid you were angry at me," she whispered back.

"Nah," he said. "Not really." He smiled and their gaze locked for an instant.

He really is cute, thought Melody. Maybe Big T is right about guys and crushes. Maybe it wouldn't be so bad to have one special guy.

When Melody turned back to face the others she thought Sally was glaring at her. But maybe it was just the way the sun was hitting her sunglasses.

"So where do you hang out when you're not being a cheerleader?" Darryl asked Melody.

"Here at Emily's sometimes," Melody said. "Sometimes people come to my place. Our apartment complex has a pool and tennis courts."

"You play tennis?" he asked.

"I love tennis," Melody told him. As she said

it she had a memory of playing with her father in Miami. They'd played doubles in a celebrity tournament for charity and made it through the semifinals. "Maxi and I have played together since she could hold a racket," her father told the sportscaster covering the event for the evening news. She really missed her weekly tennis games with her father.

"Maybe I'll come by some time and we could play," Darryl told her.

"Okay with me," Melody said.

"Joanie, you did great today," Sally said. "Sam Paetro is going to love working with you."

Sally would never say anything to me about being good, thought Emily, because I'm not good. She looked around at everyone at the table. This was one of those spontaneous after-game parties like her sister used to have. Now she was having one. It was her dream come true. Only in the dream she didn't imagine herself as a fat, not very good cheerleader. But that's what I am, she thought sadly.

Alexis glanced over at Emily and noticed that she was twisting a curl around her index finger — a sure sign that she was upset about something. What is bothering her? Alexis wondered. Usually when something was bothering Emily, she would talk to Alexis about it. She hoped that Emily would ask her and not anyone else to sleep over. That would be a perfect time to talk and be close like they used to be.

Emily looked up and saw Alexis staring at her and smiled. I miss Alexis, she thought. Alexis was right. We're not as close since we don't see each other as much. She thought about inviting Alexis for a sleepover and decided against it. When they had a sleepover they did loads of snacking. And tonight she was back on her diet.

HARBOR DRIVE 10 P.M.

Alexis walked past her mother sitting on the couch. "I'm going to bed now," Alexis said.

"You don't want to stay up and watch a movie with me?" her mother asked. She held up a video. "It's about a guy who has to keep living the same day over and over again." She sighed. "Sometimes I feel that's the way my life is. Too bad my life's not a comedy. Anyway, the movie is supposed to be funny. That's what the video guy said."

"I'm pretty tired," Alexis said as she bent over and kissed her mother good night. She was tired, but mostly she wanted to be alone to think.

Alexis went upstairs to her room. I hope Mom watches a movie and doesn't bother me, she thought as she closed the door behind her. She put on her nightgown, went to the window, and looked out at the sky. I wonder what Jake's doing, she thought. Maybe he stayed late at the Grangers' and was watching a movie with Emily and her whole family. Alexis wished again that Emily had asked her to stay over.

Emily seemed so different now that she was on the cheer squad. Alexis wondered what was wrong with her friend. Things just didn't seem right with Emily or the two of them.

Alexis turned from the window and went over to her desk. The copy of the *Bulldog Edition* lay open to her article. She loved seeing her name in print. Being a reporter was great. But not if she couldn't share it with her best friend.

DOLPHIN COURT APARTMENTS
10:30 P.M.

Melody Max stood on the terrace overlooking the pool, watching the reflections change as the water rippled in the breeze. She remembered how Sally took her turn cheering for Darryl. It's like we're sharing him, she thought. Only Sally's the one at a beach party right now. When they were all at the Bulldog Café had Sally really glared at her? Why? Melody wondered. Doesn't she like me?

If I was in Miami I could talk to Tina about Sally and Darryl, Melody thought. She hadn't talked to Emily, Joan, and Alexis about Darryl.

Now that she thought about it they didn't talk about boys much at all. But Tina did — all the time. She'd already told Tina a little bit about Darryl. But she hadn't told her about the weird vibes she'd been getting from Sally.

She sighed and went back inside.

Maybe it was all her imagination.

DELHAVEN DRIVE 10:45 P.M.

Joan's father pulled the car into the driveway. Her parents were in the front seat, and she and Adam were in the back. They were coming back from a piano concert in Fort Myers.

"That was an amazing performance," Joan's father said as he turned off the engine.

It *was* amazing, Joan thought as she got out of the car. The pianist had given an all-Chopin performance. And Chopin was her favorite composer. The music still rang through her mind.

"I loved it," Joan told her mother as they walked toward the house. "It was awesome."

"I'm sure he practiced more than a half hour a day," her father said as he unlocked the back door.

"And didn't spend all day Saturday at sporting events," her mother added.

"How do you know?" Joan said.

"Maybe he played football *and* practiced the piano," Adam said. "Some people can manage their time very well." Joan threw him a grateful smile.

Her mother turned on the kitchen light. "Someone who is serious about the piano doesn't play football," she said. "Even if he had the time for it, which he wouldn't, he has to protect his hands. A broken wrist can ruin a promising career."

"But — " Joan began.

"That's why we wouldn't let you do gymnastics, Joanie," her father said, interrupting her. "There are so many small bones in the hand and wrist. A young man I knew in college who was so gifted as a violinist — "

"Jared Capek," her mother put in.

"I know about Jared," Joan said. "You already told me about a thousand times."

"So I have," her father said. He smiled at his family. "Anyone want tea?"

"No, thanks," Joan said. She didn't say she was tired, because then they'd say she shouldn't have been at the football game. Instead she said, "Thanks for taking us to the concert. I loved it."

She said good night and went to her room.

I love cheering, and I love the piano, she thought as she closed her door. And I'll do both. I will.

THE MANOR HOTEL.
11:00 P.M.

Emily closed the door to her room. It had been a perfect day. First the game. Next the spontaneous party at the café. Then Jake stayed for dinner.

She looked out the window and saw Jake walking home alone in the moonlight. Tonight they both laughed so hard at a video that tears ran down their faces. Too bad Alexis wasn't here, Emily thought. She'd have loved that movie, too.

Emily put both hands on her stomach. It was puffed out again. She'd wanted to have only salad for dinner. But since the coach had talked to her mother she couldn't get away with it. Her mother insisted she have meat and rice, too. The only meal I can skip now, she thought, is lunch.

There was a tap on her door. "Who is it?" she called.

"Me," answered her mother's voice. "And Bubba."

"Come in," Emily answered.

Her mother came in carrying an old dress box. She put the box on the bed and sat beside it.

Bubba licked Emily's calf. "Hello to you, too," she said as she leaned over and patted his head.

“You looked terrific out there today,” her mother said. “Was it fun?”

“It was great,” Emily answered. “What’s in the box?”

Her mother opened the box and held up a short blue-and-white dress.

“What’s that?” Emily asked.

Her mother stood up and turned the dress around. Across the front of the top Emily read CMS. “It’s my CMS uniform,” her mother said.

“I’ve seen pictures of you in that uniform,” said Emily. “I didn’t know you still had it.”

“How do you think I looked in those photos?” her mother asked. “The truth.”

“You looked great,” Emily said.

“Did I look fat?” her mother asked.

“ ’Course not,” answered Emily.

Her mother handed Emily the uniform. “Try it on,” she said.

“It’ll be too small,” Emily protested.

“Try it,” her mother insisted.

Emily took off her jeans and shirt. Her mother handed her the uniform, and Emily dropped it over her head. It smelled musty from the attic.

“The zipper is in the back,” her mother said. “I’ll do it.”

“It won’t close,” Emily told her.

“Don’t be so sure,” her mother commented.

Emily held her breath as she felt the cool zipper moving upward along her spine.

"For goodness sake, breathe, Emily," her mother said as she closed the hook and eye at the top of the zipper. "It fits fine."

Emily let out her breath. Her mother was right. The uniform fit her perfectly.

Emily looked up and saw her reflection in her bureau mirror. She looked just like her mother in those photos. The same red hair. The same body.

"Now, will you stop this foolish dieting?" her mother asked. "And eat right."

Emily nodded.

After she'd given her mother back the uniform, she put on her nightgown. She was exhausted and ready to go to bed, but there was one more thing she had to do. She picked up her own cheerleading uniform from the chair, clipped the skirt to the hanger, slipped the top over the hanger, and put it in her closet.

She'd only cheered for one game. There would be a lot more pep rallies and games to cheer for before her uniform would be stored in the attic. The new Bulldog cheerleaders had a whole lot of cheerleading to do.

Ready, Shoot, Score!

Thank you to Janine Santamauro Knight, Head Cheerleading Coach for St. Joseph by the Sea.

CLAYMORE, FLORIDA.
THE MANOR HOTEL. THURSDAY 7:45 A.M.

Emily Granger brushed her light brown hair into a ponytail and straightened her bangs with her fingers. The next thing she had to do to get ready for school was pack her cheerleading bag. After school the Claymore Middle School cheerleaders were having a clinic with a coach from the CHEER USA organization, and everyone on the squad was going to wear the squad's official practice uniform.

"Sam Paetro will bring your cheerleading up a notch," Coach Cortes had told the cheerleaders last week at practice. "I see talent on this squad. You have the potential to be winners at the CHEER USA regionals. Work hard and we'll get there."

Worried thoughts ran through Emily's head as she put clean socks, a brush, and extra hairclips in her bag. She didn't think she was as good as the other girls on the squad. What if I can't improve? she wondered. What if I ruin CMS's chances for placing at the regionals in Miami? What if the only reason I made the squad is because my family is involved in CMS sports? Emily shook her head to try to clear it of negative thoughts.

She picked up freshly washed blue shorts and a white T-shirt from her chair. The school's sports logo — a head shot of a bulldog below a blue-and-white CMS — appeared on the front of the T-shirt. Emily smiled to herself as she placed her practice uniform in the bag. The CMS bulldog mascot was *her* dog, Bubba IV.

The Granger family had always been involved in CMS sports. Emily's father had played on CMS football and basketball teams and so had her brother. Her sister Lynn had followed in her mother's footsteps by being captain of the cheer squad. And the bulldog mascot at CMS football and basketball games for the last twenty years was a bulldog owned by the Granger family. As Emily was thinking about Bubba, he waddled into her room, followed by her four-year-old sister, Lily.

"Hi, Bubba," Emily said as she bent over and patted his head. "I was just thinking about you."

"Me, too?" asked Lily.

"Of course," Emily said as she patted Lily's curly hair.

"I'm hungry," Lily told Emily.

"Let's go have some breakfast," Emily said. "I just have to get my books."

Emily went to her desk and put her math and history books in her backpack. When she picked up her notebook, a slip of paper fell to the floor. Bubba sniffed to see if it was something to eat.

Emily picked up the paper before he could decide. She turned it over and read, *"Good luck. You can do it! A."*

It was the note her best friend, Alexis, had put there the day of cheerleading tryouts. I'm glad I saved it, thought Emily. I did have good luck that day. She pinned the note to her bulletin board next to her Bulldog pennant. Emily felt bad that Alexis didn't have good luck herself that day, but Alexis said she didn't mind that she wasn't a cheerleader. Emily remembered that the only reason Alexis tried out was because Emily was doing it. Alexis said it would be hard to stay best friends if Emily was a cheerleader and she wasn't.

"We've been best friends forever," Emily had protested. "That's not going to change." But things *had* changed between them. Emily knew that she wasn't telling Alexis everything the way she used to. And she didn't think Alexis was telling her everything now, either.

Before leaving her room Emily checked out her reflection in the full-length mirror. She thought she looked pretty cute in a V-neck top and cargo pants. I'm going to that clinic today, she told herself, and I'm going to do my very best.

But as she headed down the hall with Lily

and Bubba, a familiar thought popped into her head.

What if her best just wasn't good enough?

DELHAVEN DRIVE 7:50 A.M.

Joan Russo-Chazen pulled the blue-and-white-striped comforter over her pillow. When she'd picked out the duvet her mother hadn't noticed that it was Claymore Middle School's colors. But Joan had thought of it. She'd been looking forward to being a student at CMS ever since her brother, Adam, started there last year. But being a year younger than Adam, she had to finish at the small private elementary school in Fort Myers. This year she was finally at CMS.

I *knew* I'd love going to CMS, Joan thought as she straightened the comforter.

From her first day at CMS, Joan had wanted to be a cheerleader. She loved cheering, especially the tumbling. When she made the squad, cheering became her favorite thing at school and her biggest problem at home. Coach Cortes said she was a natural at gymnastics and a terrific cheerleader. If I'm this good now, thought Joan, imagine how good I'll be with more coaching. And today she was going to be coached by an expert — Sam Paetro from CHEER USA. She couldn't wait. That was the good part of her life.

But the problem at home part was huge, and

it was becoming bigger every day. Her parents didn't approve of gymnastics or any sport that was in the least bit dangerous. The only reason they were letting her be a CMS cheerleader was because she'd made sure they didn't know that it involved gymnastics.

"You can be a cheerleader," her father had told her, "so long as you keep up your grades and stick to your piano practice schedule."

Well, she was keeping up her grades and playing piano. But adjustments had to be made. Like changing her piano lesson from Saturday to Thursday during football season. Her parents hadn't been very happy about that. But now Thursday wasn't a good time for her lesson. It was at the same time that she was supposed to be at Sam Paetro's clinic. If she told her parents about the clinic, they'd say cheering was taking up too much of her time. And they might start asking questions about the clinic. If they found out about the tumbling and flying, they'd say she couldn't be a cheerleader anymore.

"It's dangerous," they would say. "What if you broke your wrist? How would you play piano then?"

Joan was up all night thinking about what to do. Finally, she came up with a plan. She'd call her piano teacher, Mr. Richter, and tell him she was sick and couldn't go to her lesson. Since there was only one phone in the Russo-Chazen household and it was in the kitchen where she could be overheard, she would make the call from school.

Joan's mother taught German and Russian at a university, and her father worked at home translating books from Russian into English. Both her parents spoke fluent French. Joan thought it was neat that her parents knew a lot of languages; she just wished they understood her better. They disapproved of most things that interested her, like movies, fashion, sleepover parties, and gymnastics.

Joan put a quarter for the phone and a piece of paper with Mr. Richter's number in her jeans pocket. She liked how she looked in her jeans and red top. No more school uniforms, like at the private schools she'd attended.

Life would be so perfect — if only her parents weren't so weird and strict.

DOLPHIN COURT APARTMENTS 8:00 A.M.

Melody Max printed out the short story for Mr. Grudin's English class. Before she turned off the computer she went on-line to check for e-mail. She'd gone to bed at ten the night before, but her friend Tina was a real night owl. There might be a message from Tina.

Melody missed Tina and her other Miami friends. But she missed her father the most. She and her mother had moved from Miami on the east coast of Florida to Claymore on the west coast of the state only two weeks before school started. Her mother thought it was convenient that she was offered a job as editor of the *Claymore News* the year that Melody entered middle school. "You'd be going to a new school anyway," she had told Melody.

Melody had argued with her parents a lot about the move. She loved Miami, and she didn't want to live so far away from her father and her friends. But her parents, who were divorced, agreed that it was best for everyone.

"Everyone but me," Melody had told them.

But now that she was in school she was making a whole new set of friends. Like Emily Granger, who had encouraged her to become a cheerleader. And Alexis Lewis, who also had divorced parents. Then there were Joan and Adam Russo-Chazen, who lived nearby and sometimes walked to school with her. It was cool to have two friends in one family. Melody thought that someday she might be as close to Joan as she was to Tina. She also liked Emily's neighbor, Jake Feder, a ninth-grader, who sometimes hung out with them. Melody was surprised that Darryl Budd, also a ninth-grader and captain of both the football and basketball teams, seemed to like her, too. Plus there was his girlfriend, Sally Johnson. She was co-captain of the cheer squad and by far the most beautiful and popular girl in the school. Sally acted as if she liked Melody, but sometimes Melody wasn't sure she meant it. Why should she care about me, anyway? Melody thought. After all, I'm only a seventh-grader, and I'm new in Claymore.

There were a lot of people for Melody to hang out with, but it still wasn't the same as hanging out with people she'd known all her life, like Tina. She moved the cursor across the computer screen and clicked on her Inbox. There were no new messages. Well, I haven't written to anyone in a couple of days, either, thought Melody.

She reviewed her after-school schedule in her mind. Monday and Wednesday were regular cheer practices. Thursday was the clinic with Sam Paetro. And Tuesday and Friday were basketball games. The first game of the season was tomorrow. She couldn't wait.

Melody looked at the little clock on her computer screen before turning it off. 8:14. Her father would be on television in one minute. She'd better hurry. Some people might think it was weird to watch the Miami weather forecast when you don't live there, she thought as she hurried into the kitchen.

But it's not weird when the weather forecaster is your dad, and the only time you see him is when he's on television.

HARBOR ROAD 8:15 A.M.

Alexis Lewis ran into the kitchen. She'd been searching the whole house for her reporter's notebook.

Her mother was putting the breakfast dishes in the dishwasher. "Did you check the recycling bin?" she suggested. "It might be in there with the newspapers."

"Good idea," Alexis told her.

Her mother looked up at the kitchen clock. "We have to leave soon, Alexis," she told her. "I go on duty at the hospital at eight-thirty."

"I know, Mom," said Alexis. "But I have to have that notebook."

"Maybe it's at your father's," her mother said.

Alexis searched through the newspaper pile. "That's what you always say when I can't find something," she said. And usually she's right, Alexis added to herself. One of the big problems about having divorced parents was that her things were in two homes. It was especially hard to keep track of her stuff with her joint custody schedule, a Mom week followed by a Dad week. Week after week. Month after month. Year after year, since she was two years old. No wonder I can't find anything, Alexis thought.

"Can't you just get another notebook?" her mother asked.

Alexis shook her head and continued to search through the newspapers. There wasn't a notebook in the world that could replace the one she'd lost. It was her first notebook as sports columnist for the CMS newspaper, *Bulldog Edition*. Her editor, Jake Feder, gave it to her. She wanted to keep it forever. She put the pile of papers back in the blue recycling bin. Her notebook wasn't there.

"We're leaving in two minutes," her mother reminded her. "So hurry up."

"I have to get my stuff," Alexis said, remembering that she hadn't looked behind her desk. She'd check there next.

As Alexis was running up the stairs her mother's voice trailed after her. "Maybe you left your notebook at Emily's. Did you think of that?"

Alexis had thought of that. But she knew her notebook wouldn't be at Emily's. She hardly hung out there anymore. Not the way she used to. Sometimes a bunch of kids would have a soda or something at Emily's. But that was at Bulldog Café and not upstairs on the fourth floor of the hotel where the family lived. I was right, thought Alexis. We're not as close since Emily made the cheer squad.

The phone rang. As Alexis reached for it she automatically tried to figure out if Emily was calling her. She and Emily had such a special connection that she could usually tell when it was Emily calling her. But now, she realized, she couldn't tell.

"Hello," she said into the receiver.

"Hi, Alexis," said the voice on the other end. "It's Jake."

"Oh, hi," said Alexis. Why is Jake calling me? she wondered.

"Your reporter's notebook was in my backpack," he said. "I must have picked it up by mistake after the meeting yesterday. I thought maybe you were looking for it."

"I was!" exclaimed Alexis.

"I'll bring it to school," Jake said. "See you then."

"Yeah," agreed Alexis. "See you."

She hung up the phone.

"Alexis, let's go!" her mother shouted up the stairs.

"Coming," Alexis called back as she grabbed her backpack and hurried from the room.

She couldn't wait to get to school.

CLAYMORE MIDDLE SCHOOL COURTYARD 8:15 A.M.

Sally Johnson saw Darryl Budd talking to three guys under a palm tree in the courtyard in front of the school. She loved that Darryl, the cutest and most popular guy at CMS, was her boyfriend. Darryl grinned when he saw Sally coming toward him.

"Hi, Sally," a small group of ninth-graders said as they passed her.

She smiled and gave a little wave.

C.J., one of the cheerleaders on her squad, came up beside her. "Sally, how's it going?" she asked.

"Great," answered Sally as they walked side by side. "Ready for Sam Paetro's clinic?"

"You bet," answered C.J. before veering off to the right. "Catch you later."

Mae Lee, Sally's co-captain on the cheer squad, was running up to her.

"I found a bunch of cheerleading sites on-line last night," Mae said. "I got some great ideas for fund-raisers from all over the country."

"Terrific," Sally told her. "Bring them to the meeting." Out of the corner of her eye Sally noticed that a group of seventh-grade girls were watching her admiringly. She flashed them a quick smile. It was great being an upperclassman and the most popular girl in school.

Sally told Mae she was doing a great job for the squad and continued toward Darryl. She kissed him on the cheek before saying hello to the other guys.

Melody was talking with Alexis and Emily when she saw Joan and Adam coming into the courtyard. They waved when they saw her. As Adam walked toward the three of them, Joan went into school.

"How's it going?" Adam asked when he joined the three girls. He was asking everyone, but he was looking at Melody.

Melody smiled and said, "Great," but she was wondering why Joan went into school ahead of them.

Inside the building, Joan was glad that none of her friends had come in with her. She didn't want anyone overhearing her lie to her piano teacher. She went into the administrative office to use the pay phone. A sign over the phone read BUSINESS CALLS ONLY. When the school receptionist saw Joan heading toward the phone she asked, "How come?"

"My piano lesson," Joan told her. "I have to talk to my teacher."

"Go ahead," the receptionist said.

Joan pulled the quarter and the slip of paper with Mr. Richter's number out of her jeans pocket. She hoped he was busy teaching and that she could just leave a message. It was easier to lie if the other person couldn't ask questions.

His machine answered the phone. After the beep, Joan began her message, "Hi, Mr. Richter. It's Joan. Joan Russo-Chazen. I can't make my lesson today because I have a bad cold." She gave a little cough before continuing. "Sorry. I hate to miss a lesson, but I really feel awfully sick. I'll call back later but don't call me. I mean, no one's home. So thanks. Oh, yeah, I meant to tell you I've been practicing a lot lately. That Beethoven piece is hard, but I like it. 'Bye." She coughed one more time before hanging up.

As Joan walked out of the office she had a thought that stopped her in her tracks. She'd told Mr. Richter not to call the house because no one was home. But Mr. Richter knew that her father worked at home. And wouldn't Mr. Richter think it was weird that she wasn't home if she was sick? How could she be so dumb? She'd have to call Mr. Richter back later and say she'd been to the doctor's. Why did lying have to be so complicated?

CMS SMALL GYM 4:15 P.M.

The cheerleaders, dressed in their matching practice outfits, moved to their warm-up positions in the center of the gym. Emily was nervous, but it still made her smile when she looked around at the other cheerleaders and saw fifteen pictures of Bubba on their chests.

"I hope we don't make fools of ourselves," Melody whispered to Emily.

Emily was about to whisper back, "Me, too," when a short, muscular blond man dressed in tan shorts and a white T-shirt entered the gym with Coach Cortes.

"Everyone, welcome Sam Paetro from CHEER USA!" Coach Cortes instructed.

The cheerleaders clapped.

"Call me Sam," he told the girls. "Now, I'd like to know your names. Let's hear them, starting with the girl farthest to my left."

One by one the cheerleaders told Sam their names.

"Now, here's the deal today, girls," he said. "First, the warm-up. Things can happen in your warm-up that lead to problems on the floor. I'll walk around with your coach and make corrections. Then I'll watch your current center cheer and critique it."

There were some moans, and a few girls giggled nervously. The corners of Sam's mouth turned up. Melody couldn't tell if it was a smile or a sneer.

Sally took a few steps forward. "Mr. Paetro — I mean, Sam — as co-captain of the squad, I'd like to say, on behalf of the entire squad, that we think it's great that you're giving us this clinic. We're really looking forward to it, and we're ready to work hard. So welcome, and thanks for working with us."

Sam smiled. Everyone clapped. Coach Cortes beamed at Sally. "And I know you all appreciate that Sam is giving you this clinic for free," she said.

Sam grinned at Coach Cortes. "As a favor to you, Cortes," he said. He turned to Sally and added, "Thank you, Sally." Melody wasn't surprised that Sam remembered Sally's name. She stood out in any crowd.

"Okay, Sally," Coach Cortes called out, "let's warm up."

Sally turned to face her cheerleaders, and they all put their hands on their hips, ready to begin.

Sam and Coach Cortes walked up and down the two rows of girls. Melody listened to Sam's corrections.

"Keep that arm straight, Jessica."

"Straighten that back, C.J."

"No bent knees, Maria."

"Drop your head before you start to roll down, Melody."

That's amazing, thought Melody. He remembers everybody's name.

For the final exercise the girls sat on the floor

and dropped forward over extended legs. Peering under her arms, Emily could see Joan and Melody lying straight on their outstretched legs, like always. Emily, like always, hung over her legs with her chest and hands miles from her knees and toes. A shadow passed across her legs. Sam and Coach Cortes were standing over her. They're watching me do my worst exercise, Emily thought.

Sam squatted behind her. "This exercise would be a lot easier for you, Emily, if you worked from a straight back. Sit tall." He tapped the bottom of her spine. "Straighten your back from way down here." She adjusted her position. "There," he said approvingly. "Now you're in the correct position for this exercise. Reach for your toes, but don't hunch over. Reach!"

Emily felt like crying, not reaching. If she couldn't do the simplest exercise, how could she expect to be a good cheerleader? This clinic was going to prove what Sally and some of the other cheerleaders already believed — that she wasn't good enough to be on the squad. When she reached over, she wasn't any closer to her outstretched legs than before.

But Sam was pleased. "See what I mean?" he asked Emily.

"Right," she said. "Thank you."

"Return to sitting position," Sally directed.

"Keep your back straight coming up, Emily," Sam ordered. Emily did. "And stay up on those sitting bones." As she rolled up she blinked back the tears forming in her eyes.

After the warm-up, Sam asked the squad to do their center cheer. He took a small notebook and pencil out of his back pocket and stood in front of them as they moved into formation. Coach turned on the dance music.

Emily was more nervous than ever as she started the routine, but she smiled and kept going. She hoped that when they did the toe touch jumps, Sam would be watching someone else. But he was staring right at her. And when they finished the series of jumps he wrote something in his notebook. Something like *Emily is no good*, thought Emily.

Following the center cheer, Joan expected Sam to say what was good and what was bad about the routine, and then they'd work on the bad parts. So she was surprised when he had them sit on the bleachers and handed them all little notebooks like the one he was using. Mae handed out pencils.

"I want each of you to write down what you think about your personal performance in that routine," he said. "First write down your strengths. Then your weaknesses. No one's going to look at it but you. Be honest."

Joan had no problem writing down her strong points. But she didn't know what she was weak in. She just wanted to get better and better. So under *My Weaknesses in the Cheer Routine* she wrote: *Single full twist dismount from extension.*

"Okay," Sam announced. "Close your notebooks and leave them on the bleachers. Let's do that center cheer again."

They did it again. Nothing seemed different to Emily. Her toe touch jumps were just as bad, even though she'd written *Toe touch jumps* under *Weaknesses.* How could writing down a problem solve it? she wondered.

But Melody thought writing down her biggest weakness in cheering was a great help. She'd written down, *Pointed toes on toe touch jump.* She was amazed that by thinking about it she'd been able to correct it herself.

When the halftime cheer was finished, Sam told them to go back to the bleachers. "This time write down what you expect to get out of the clinic," he said. "Write it twice. You'll give one copy to me, and you'll keep the other in your notebook. By the way, next week we're videotaping. We'll watch the tape together, make observations and corrections, then film again. Are you all still with me?"

"Yes," a few girls answered.

"I said, *Are you all still with me?*" he repeated.

"Yes!" they all shouted.

"Are you going to become a winning squad?"

"Yes!" they answered.

We won't be a winning squad as long as I'm on it, thought Emily. She opened the notebook and wrote, *I need to become a better cheerleader. This clinic is my only hope.*

"Girls, don't forget we have a special business meeting now," Coach reminded them. "After you've handed in your goals for the clinic, take a five-minute break. Be back here at five o'clock."

Before Joan gave her paper to Sam, she went over to Coach Cortes and told her that she couldn't stay for the meeting. Joan didn't think practicing piano was a good enough excuse for missing a meeting, so she told her she had a piano lesson.

"I'm sorry you won't be here," Coach said.

"Will it count against me?" asked Joan. "I mean, like missing a practice would?"

Coach shook her head no. "It's all right, Joan," she said. "This time."

When Joan handed Sam her paper, he smiled and said in a quiet voice, "Joan, could you wait on the bleachers? I'd like to speak to you before I leave."

Joan went back to the bleachers and sat down. After Emily turned in her paper she came over to her. "Let's go get a drink," Emily said.

"Sam wants to talk to me," Joan told her. "Then I have to go home — I mean, to my piano lesson. Coach said it's okay. But will you tell me what happens at the meeting?"

"Sure," said Emily. "If you tell me what Sam says." She smiled at Joan. "I bet it's about how good you are."

Emily was right. Sam told Joan that she was a talented gymnast. When she told him that she had only taken two gymnastic classes in her life, he was really surprised. His words rang in her ears as she left the gym, "You have great potential, Joan. I know an excellent trainer who runs a camp that would be perfect for you. I'll bring you some literature about it tomorrow. You and your parents might want to contact him."

Right, thought Joan. That's just the sort of thing my parents would want to do.

CMS COURTYARD 4:50 P.M.

Alexis Lewis walked out of the school building alone. While the cheerleaders were at their clinic she helped lay out the ad pages for the *Bulldog Edition*. She looked at her watch. Her mother would be home at five. If Alexis was home, too, her mother would expect Alexis to hang out with her. Her mother called it "keeping her company." Alexis found keeping her mother company a real downer. She's always so depressed, thought Alexis. And she's always criticizing Dad. Alexis didn't want to go home so she sat on a bench to wait for Emily. She hoped Emily would invite her back to the hotel. She loved hanging out with Emily and her family. They were a real family, with two parents and lots of kids.

Alexis took out her history book to do some homework while she waited. Every time she heard the doors to the school open and close she looked up.

She noticed Darryl and Jake and some other guys on the basketball team standing on the grass. Jake noticed her, too, and came over.

Alexis thought Jake Feder was really cute and a great guy. He was tall for his age, had black hair and blue eyes and a cute grin. When she first met Jake she thought he was Emily's brother. Then she learned that he lived in a house behind The Manor Hotel with a man and woman Alexis assumed were his parents. One day Emily told her that they were his grandparents and that Jake's parents and younger sister had died in a fire when he was five. Alexis thought that was the saddest thing she'd ever heard.

Jake came up to her. "Hey," he said. "What's up?"

"Not much," she said. "I'm waiting for cheer practice to end. How was your practice?" She grinned at him. "You guys going to win tomorrow?"

"I hope so," Jake said as he sat on the bench next to her. "Hard to tell. First game of the season, and we lost some key players who were in the ninth grade last year. I don't know if we can fill their shoes."

"I bet you can," Alexis said. "I've seen you make some awesome shots in your backyard."

"I need to work more on my foul shot," he said.

Joan was running across the courtyard toward the street. "Hey, Joan," shouted Alexis, "where's everybody else?"

"A business meeting about how to raise money to go to the CHEER USA competition," Joan called over her shoulder. She waved and continued running.

"Where's she going?" Jake asked.

"She probably has a piano lesson," Alexis answered. "Or has to practice or something. She's really serious about the piano." She stood up.

"But Emily will definitely stay for that meeting. I might as well go home."

"Want to shoot some baskets at my place?" he asked. "You can feed me balls, and I'll practice my foul shot."

"Sure!" Alexis answered. She couldn't think of anything she'd rather do than shoot baskets with Jake Feder.

CMS SMALL GYM 5:00 P.M.

The cheerleaders and Coach Cortes arranged themselves in a circle on the exercise mats.

"All right, girls," Coach began. "You're going to have a fabulous routine. But there's another big job ahead of you. We need to raise money — a lot of money. No matter how well you cheer, if we don't come up with the money for our expenses, we can't go to the CHEER USA regionals in Miami. So let's get some new fund-raising ideas."

"Coach is right," Sally said. "Let's think of some great new ideas. Forget car washes and bake sales for now. Let's do something big. Something everyone in school will want to do badly enough to spend some money. Let's make it fun."

"Yes!" someone shouted.

Sally is so amazing, thought Emily. She is such a great leader.

"Think of what people like to do that could

be turned into a fund-raiser," Sally instructed. "Let's see what we can come up with."

C.J., the secretary of the cheer squad, opened her notebook and was ready to write down their fund-raising ideas.

Melody remembered how the ninth-graders and high school kids were always having parties at night on the beach. A lot of seventh- and eighth-graders would love to go to a beach party, she thought. *She* would. She raised her hand.

Sally nodded at her. "Melody."

"How about a beach party?" Melody suggested. "We could have it at night, with games and food stands."

"Like a carnival," someone called out.

"But it would be on the beach," added C.J., writing in her notebook.

"That's a unique idea for a fund-raiser," put in Coach. "Where would you have it?"

"Maybe we could have it at the town beach," suggested Kelly. "It's close to town, so lots of people can walk there."

"Jake Feder's grandfather is in charge of the beach," Emily told them. "If you want, I can ask him if we can use it. I could talk to him about it tonight."

"Terrific, Emily," Sally said. She flashed Emily a smile while thinking, Emily's connections are good for something.

"Let's make a list of all the games we can think of," suggested C.J. "And see which ones would be good for a beach party."

"How about Spin the Bottle," someone shouted out.

"And Post Office?" giggled Maria.

They all laughed. When the laughter died down, Kelly said, "My friend's school had a photo booth at their fund-raiser. It was really fun and made lots of money."

"Do you think people would pay to have their picture taken at the beach party?" asked Elvia.

"What if they could have their picture taken with Bubba?" asked Melody. "That would be special."

"We could put him on a stool in his CMS outfit," suggested Mae.

"And use an instant camera so they could have the picture right away," added C.J.

"The film costs a dollar a shot," Kelly said. "So we should charge two dollars. Everyone will want to have a picture with the school mascot."

"It's a terrific idea," said Mae. The cheerleaders nodded and smiled in agreement.

Sally looked around at Coach and the cheerleaders. Did they really believe people would pay to have their picture taken with that ugly dog?

"What do you think, Emily?" asked Coach. "Would Bubba go for that?"

"Bubba loves attention," Emily answered. She smiled at Melody. "I think it's a great idea."

In the next half hour the squad put together a list of more ideas for the party, including shooting baskets, horseshoes, and darts.

"We'll need prizes for some of the games," observed Mae.

"We can get donations from local stores," suggested Sally.

"Maybe some local food places, like Squeeze and Bulldog Café, will give us gift certificates to use as prizes," suggested Elvia.

"If some businesses will donate bigger prizes, like dinner for two at Bulldog Café," added Jessica with a smile in Emily's direction, "we could sell raffle tickets."

"Great," said Sally. "You're in charge of raffles, Jess. Anyone who has an idea or a connection for a raffle item, tell Jess."

Melody spoke up next. "I have an idea," she said. "If we could find small stuffed animals that look like Bubba, we could use some of those for prizes and sell the rest. We could call them Bubba Babies."

That dog again! thought Sally.

"That's a great idea, Melody," said Maria. "My mother manages the toy store at the mall. She has a zillion catalogs of stuffed animals. I bet there's one that looks just like Bubba. We can buy them in bulk at wholesale prices and use them as special prizes."

As they continued to brainstorm ideas for the beach party, everyone said how they'd help in the planning stages. Emily said that besides talking to Mr. Feder about using the beach, she'd ask Jake to work a barbecue grill. She also said she'd ask her parents for soda and burger gift certificates to Bulldog Café to use for prizes. She couldn't wait to tell her mother and father about the Bubba Babies and Bubba photo booth.

Sally saved her best idea for the end of the meeting, when it would have the most effect. "How about a volleyball game?" she asked. "Teachers against students. A lot of people would come out to see that. Or to be in it. We'll charge a sign-up fee."

Everyone loved the idea. "We're going to make this the best FUNd-raiser that Claymore has ever seen," Coach Cortes said. She smiled at her squad.

"Yes!" a few girls shouted.

As they stood up to leave the gym, several squad members told Sally that it was a great meeting. No one even remembers that the beach party was Melody's idea, thought Sally. It wasn't much of an idea, anyway. This fund-raiser is turning into something much bigger than a little beach party. Thanks to me. She walked over to Coach to be congratulated on running a terrific meeting.

DELHAVEN DRIVE 6:15 P.M.

Joan was helping her father prepare dinner. She was making the salad while her dad ran out to Joe's to buy fresh fish. As she heard him backing out of the driveway she wiped her hands on a dish towel and picked up the phone to call her piano teacher. This time Mr. Richter answered instead of his machine. He asked Joan how she was feeling.

She made a little cough and answered, "Better, thank you. But I hated to miss my lesson. I was wondering if you've filled my Saturday time? You know, for my lesson?" Her heart beat faster as she waited for the answer.

"No, I haven't," he said.

"Could I come this Saturday then?" she asked. "For a makeup?"

"I could take you at one o'clock," he said. "Will you be well enough in another day?"

"I think I'll be fine by then," said Joan. "And I like Saturday lessons. It's harder to take a lesson when you've been in school all day."

"Too bad you can't come on Saturdays regularly," he said.

Joan felt her heart race again. This time with

excitement. Her plan was working. Mr. Richter had given her the opening she needed. "Actually," Joan said, "if you want me to go back to Saturdays, I could. Football season is over, so I'm free on Saturdays again."

"It would be better for your piano work," Mr. Richter said.

It would be better for my gymnastic work, too, thought Joan. I'll be able to take Sam's clinic on Thursdays without any problem.

"So it's all set," Mr. Richter continued. "Saturdays at one instead of Thursdays at four."

"Okay," she said.

"You know, Joanie," he said, "you have a musical gift. A special talent."

"Thank you," she said. "I'll try to do my best."

As Joan hung up the phone she remembered that Sam had said the same thing about her gymnastics. Excellent gymnast. Excellent pianist. She was excellent at the two things she loved to do most in the world.

She smiled to herself and went back to peeling the carrots.

But she wasn't smiling for long. Once her mother was home and they were all sitting down to dinner, the subject of cheering came up. Joan had only wanted to tell her parents about the change in her piano lesson. But the lesson reminded them of cheering.

"I thought you had those football games to attend on Saturdays," her mother said. "For the cheer club."

"Football's over," Joan explained. "Now it's basketball. And the games are on Tuesdays and Fridays after school."

"What time do these games end?" her father asked. "We expect you to practice piano at five o'clock on school nights."

Joan gave Adam a glance that said, *Help me.* But instead of explaining to his parents that basketball games take more than an hour and that all the kids stayed for them, Adam looked back at his plate and took another bite of fish.

"The games might go longer than five o'clock," Joan explained. "So I might get home a little late. Last year, when Adam was in that play, he didn't always get home from rehearsals by five o'clock." She looked at Adam again. "Most of the time it was later. Right, Adam?"

Adam didn't answer. He didn't even look at her.

"Adam!" Joan shouted. "I'm talking to you."

He finally looked up. "Sorry," he said. "My mind must have wandered."

I hate him, she thought. Why isn't he helping me with Mother and Father?

"Well, pay attention," she told him. "I said that you used to come home later than five o'clock from your play rehearsals last year when you were in *seventh grade.*"

"That's right," he said. "I did." He looked from his mother to his father and added, "Thanks for letting me do that. It was great."

"You were in a Shakespearean play, Adam," said Ms. Russo. "It was a very worthwhile endeavor. It isn't as if you were jumping up and down screaming for some team to win a foolish battle with a ball."

Adam didn't say anything but went back to eating his fish.

"Cheering isn't foolish," Joan told her mother. "It's just different from what you like to do. But I like it."

"Your father and I don't object to your having interests that vary from ours," her mother said. "As long as they are worthwhile."

"Well, cheering is worthwhile to me," Joan practically shrieked. She gave Adam a desperate glance. He didn't react. It's like he isn't here, Joan thought. She wished she was sitting close enough to kick him under the table.

"Joanie, you haven't been acting like yourself since you started at this public school," her father said. "You're acting angry and nervous. I'm concerned that you have too many extracurricular activities."

"I just have cheering," Joan protested.

"And the debate club," her father added.

"Right," Joan said quickly. She'd forgotten that she'd told her parents she was going to debate club meetings when she was trying out for the cheer squad. I'm losing track of my lies, she thought.

"The debate club is more worthwhile than cheering," said her mother, looking at her father. "In debating she works with ideas."

"A point well taken," her father agreed.

"So maybe the debate club is enough," her mother continued, "and she should discontinue the cheering."

They're talking about me as if I'm not even here, thought Joan. She hoped it would stay that way and they wouldn't ask her anything about the debate club. She'd never been to a meeting. She didn't even know when the debate club met.

"What day is it that you have debate club, Joanie?" her father asked.

Joan felt a shiver go through her body. Could her father read her mind? "Uh, it's on . . ." she began.

"Debate club meets Wednesday during lunch period," Adam said matter-of-factly.

"Right," agreed Joan. "Wednesday during lunch."

Joan didn't bother to give Adam a grateful look. As far as she was concerned it was too little, too late.

"And who is the teacher responsible for the debate club?" asked her father.

Joan knew the answer to that one. "Ms. Roth," she said. "She's the school librarian."

"And what topics have you been—" her father began. The ring of the phone interrupted him.

"I'll get it," Joan said as she stood up.

"We don't answer the phone during dinner," her mother reminded her.

"I'm expecting a call," Joan said. "About homework. And I finished eating."

The phone rang again.

Her mother and father exchanged a glance. "Answer it," her mother said with a sigh.

Joan went into the kitchen. She hoped it would be Emily telling her about the meeting. But it was a wrong number. She decided not to go back to the dining room but to stay in the kitchen until the dinner conversation about the debate club was finished.

She could hear her parents and Adam listing topics that would be good to debate. "Should America have dropped the atomic bomb on Japan?" suggested her father. "That was one we did when I was in school."

"How about, Which is more beneficial to society, the sciences or the arts?" offered her mother.

"Should there be capital punishment?" was Adam's contribution.

"I loved debate club when I was a student," her father said. "I could help this Ms. Roth as an adviser. If I become involved in a school activity, perhaps Joanie will adjust better to public school."

Please, Adam, Joan prayed, please help me. Make up something. Tell them that the school doesn't like parents to help out like that.

But Adam didn't say anything.

Joan dropped into a kitchen chair. Her father wanted to help with a club she didn't even belong to. And her brother and only ally in the weirdo Russo-Chazen household wasn't even trying to stop him.

CMS GYM. FRIDAY 4:00 P.M.

Melody and the other cheerleaders were standing along the sidelines when the Bulldog basketball players ran out onto the court for their warm-up. The cheerleaders shouted and clapped:

LET'S HEAR IT FOR THE BLUE
X X (clap, clap)
BLUE!
LET'S HEAR IT FOR THE WHITE

X X
WHITE!
CMS! FIGHT, BULLDOGS, FIGHT!

The crowd joined in. Melody could feel the excitement in the air. Everyone was charged up and ready for a great first game of the season against the Riverton Raiders. She did a toe touch jump and a tuck and another toe touch.

Adam, who was sitting in the stands with some other eighth-graders, gave Melody the thumbs-up sign.

Emily noticed Melody's jump series. And that Joan did a perfect single twist dismount. Everyone is getting better because of the clinic, thought Emily. Everyone but me.

The buzzer rang, and the announcer called out the names of the starting lineup for each team. The referee tossed up the ball, and Jake deflected it to Darryl, who dribbled downcourt. When they were a few feet from the Bulldog basket, Darryl, covered by two Raiders, passed the ball back to Jake. Jake caught it, aimed, and released a soft jump. A Raider guard shoved against him, but Jake kept his cool and scored the first two points of the game. The referee blew his whistle. The Raider guard had fouled him in the act of shooting, so Jake had a chance to make two more points for his team.

Alexis watched Jake go to the foul line. You can do it, Jake, she thought, just stay calm and don't overshoot. Jake squared himself for the shot and pushed the ball into the air. Alexis watched it arc and drop through the net. "Yes!" she shouted as the cheer squad led the crowd in a quick cheer for Jake.

At halftime the score was Raiders 43, Bulldogs 35. Alexis checked her notes. Darryl had made thirteen of those points, and Jake had made twelve. They were the best Bulldog shooters.

The cheerleaders started their halftime cheer with basket tosses. Soon everyone on the Bulldog side was shouting with the cheerleaders, **"LET'S GO, BULLDOGS!"** Alexis had planned to watch Emily throughout the cheer, but she ended up watching Joan, too. She was amazed at how Joan kept getting better and better at tumbling.

Alexis waved to Emily as she ran off the court. But Emily didn't notice her. She was thinking about her toe touch jumps and how they weren't as high as everyone else's on the squad.

In the opening minutes of the third quarter, Jake scored eight more points and so did Darryl. As Alexis watched them she thought about how she would describe the two stars of the Bulldog team in her sports column. She jotted in her notebook, *Darryl is fast, can protect the ball, accurate shooter.* Beside Jake's name she wrote, *good team player, accurate shooter, stays calm.* She thought but didn't write, *very cute, kind, and smart.*

As Alexis watched Jake dribble the ball down the court, a rush of thoughts ran through her head. Having a crush on Jake is ridiculous. Jake is my editor and an old friend. He can't be my crush. He's two years older than I am. He would never, ever think of me as a girlfriend. I can't have a crush on Jake. It's hopeless and embarrassing.

Alexis vowed that she wouldn't tell a soul her thoughts about Jake. Not even Emily.

Darryl made a three-point shot from mid-court. Sally led the cheerleaders and crowd in a chant.

BASKET.
SHOT.
LOOK AT THE ONE
DARRYL JUST GOT!

Alexis wrote, *Darryl — brilliant 3-point basket at end of 3rd quarter.*

In the last minute of the game the score was Raiders 58, Bulldogs 57.

Joan was hoarse from shouting, but she didn't care. She loved basketball and wanted the Bulldogs to win more than anything. They deserved to win. With ten seconds to play, the Raiders called a time-out.

"Let's go," Sally shouted to her squad. The squad lined up facing the stands of Bulldog fans. Joan waved her pom-poms and shouted, "**Go, Bulldogs, Go!**" Then Joan saw something that made the last "**Go**" catch in her throat. Her father had come into the gym. What if he sees me tumble? she thought. What if he sees any of us tumble? It'll be the end of me on the squad!

The ball was back in play, and Jake had it. He dribbled down the court and passed the ball to Darryl. While the Raiders were trying to keep Darryl from making a shot, Jake ran up to the basket.

Darryl passed Jake the ball. It was in the air on its way to becoming the winning basket. Joan's father cheered as the ball swished through the basket. The Bulldogs won. Joan approached her father from behind and tapped him on the shoulder. He turned and faced her so that his back was to the court. As she shouted, "Father, what are you doing here?" the CMS cheerleaders tumbled. The postgame shouting was drowning out Joan's voice, so she gestured to her father that they should go out to the hall.

"I know it's after five o'clock," Joan said when they were in the hall. "But I told you — "

" — I came to introduce myself to the debate club adviser," he said, "but the library was closed. A pity. Students should have access to the library during *and* after school hours. Then I remembered you had this game, so I came in to see it. But all I saw was that last basket."

People were leaving the gym. Joan saw Emily coming toward them. Emily didn't know that Joan's parents disapproved of gymnastics. Joan realized that Emily might say something that would give away her secret. "We're in the way," she told her father, steering him farther down the hall.

Melody spotted Joan and her father with Emily following them. She suddenly knew why Joan hadn't tumbled when they won the game. Adam had told her that his parents didn't approve of gymnastics and weren't aware that there was tumbling in cheering. She had to keep Emily from talking about cheering in front of him. She ran to catch her.

But Emily had already reached Joan and her father. "Are you okay, Joan?" she asked. "How come you didn't — "

"Hi," Melody said, interrupting Emily. She extended a hand to Joan's father. "I'm Melody Max. I'm a friend of Joan's and Adam's. I'm pleased to meet you. You and Adam look so much alike."

"Well, thanks for the compliment," Joan's father said as he shook Melody's hand.

"And I'm Emily Granger," said Emily.

Joan gave Melody a grateful smile. Now if Melody would only take Emily away.

"We better go, Emily," Melody said. "Coach wants to go over a couple of things about the fund-raiser."

"Me, too," Joan told her father. "I'll just grab my stuff and meet you in the car."

"Nice to meet you," Emily shouted over her shoulder as the three girls pushed through the crowd leaving the gym.

"Thanks," Joan whispered to Melody. She'd been angry at Adam because he'd told Melody about the parent problem. But now she was glad.

Melody was a bigger help than her own brother.

CMS COURTYARD 6:00 P.M.

Alexis was waiting outside the locker room door when Emily and Melody came out.

"Wasn't it a great game, Alexis?" Emily said happily. "Wasn't Jake incredible?"

"Definately!" agreed Alexis.

"Darryl, too," added Melody.

"Come on," Emily said. "Let's go back to my

place. I bet lots of players will drop by the café on their way home."

When the three girls were a block away from the hotel, Jake came up behind them. He threw one arm around Alexis's shoulder and the other around Emily's.

"Great game, Jake!" Alexis said.

"You played really well," said Emily.

"That final basket was so amazing," Melody added.

The four friends were still talking about the game when they sat down at a large outside table at Bulldog Café. Soon Sally, Darryl, and Randy showed up. Emily's father brought over a pitcher of lemonade and a plate of cookies. "Tell me about the game," he said.

"Jake made the winning basket," Emily told him. "And the opening points of the game."

"Plus he made all his foul shots," added Darryl.

"Good going, Jake," Mr. Granger said. "Shooting from the foul line is your trouble spot."

Jake smiled at Alexis. "Alexis worked with me last night. I started seeing that I was shooting too hard. She kept saying, 'Softer,' and that was the trick."

Alexis felt the color rising in her face. She blushed easily and knew that right now she was as red as the sun that was setting behind the Gulf Coast horizon.

Emily knew that Alexis sometimes went to Jake's house without her. Of course, she would, Emily told herself. They've known each other since Alexis and I met in kindergarten. Besides, they both love basketball and work on the school paper. Are my two best friends becoming better friends with each other than they are with me? she wondered.

Randy slapped Jake on the back. "Man, what a way to end the game," he said. "*Swoosh.* You really sank that ball. It was a beautiful dunk."

The word *dunk* reminded Melody of an idea she had for the beach party. "A dunking booth," she murmured.

"What did you say?" Emily asked.

"A dunking booth," Melody repeated, louder. "It's an idea I have for the beach party. Someone sits on a special chair above a big tub of water."

"I've seen that," said Darryl. "The fire department always has it at their carnival. There's a target next to the chair, and people pay to try to hit it. If you make the bull's-eye, the chair tilts and the person falls into the water."

"They just keep getting dunked over and over?" asked Sally. "That doesn't sound like much fun for the person in the chair."

"It could be funny," said Randy. "The person in the chair pretends he doesn't want to be dunked. It's a good chance to clown around."

They all looked at Randy and grinned. There was a long pause.

"Me?" he said with fake disbelief. "You want me to be dunked? You're choosing me? I've been chosen? I'm the lucky guy?"

"You'd think we just voted him head of the NBA," joked Darryl.

"Such an honor!" Randy continued. "I can't wait."

They all laughed. Randy was absolutely the best choice.

"We can't leave the girls out," Randy said. "It's a benefit for the squad, so it's only fair that a cheerleader gets dunked, too."

Sally imagined herself being dunked over and over again. Wet hair, running makeup. It was all so messy. But everyone was looking at her. "Melody," she said quickly, "that is such an excellent idea, and you're such a good sport. Would you mind being dunked?"

When Melody had the idea for the dunking chair at the beach party, she never imagined herself being the one dunked. But it was for a good cause.

"We'll have fun, Melody," said Randy encouragingly.

"Okay," she agreed. "I'll do it." She smiled at her new friends.

Sally smiled back at Melody, thinking, I'll be the first in line to dunk Melody Max.

DOLPHIN COURT APARTMENTS. POOLSIDE. SATURDAY 1:00 P.M.

Melody and Adam sat side by side at the edge of the pool, dangling their feet in the water.

"Joan and I hardly ever fight," Adam said. "It's weird that way. I mean, a lot of brothers and sisters fight, but not us."

"Maybe that's because your parents are so strict," Melody suggested. "You and Joan have to stick together."

"Maybe," Adam agreed. "But now she says I'm not on her side. That I'm against her because I won't lie to our parents."

"Lying is going to make things worse," said Melody. "I mean, they're bound to find out sometime."

Adam looked over his shoulder. "Here she comes," he said.

Melody turned around and waved to Joan.

Joan didn't know that Melody had invited Adam over, too. As she walked toward him and Melody, she wished that he wasn't there. When she first went to CMS she was glad she had an older brother at the school. But she hadn't expected him to hang out with her new friends. Maybe he'll go to boarding school in New England next year, she thought.

"How was your lesson?" Adam asked.

"Okay," she mumbled. She didn't want to talk to Adam. She didn't want to even look at him.

"Joan, you have to stop being so mad at me," he told her.

Joan glared at him. She didn't want to fight with him in front of Melody. Didn't he know that? Didn't he understand her at all?

Adam glared back at her.

Melody looked from Joan to Adam and wondered what she could do to help. She remembered how her grandmother always said that people's problems were never solved with silence. "I think you two should talk about what's going on here," she suggested.

"She needs to stop lying," said Adam. "I'm not sure that I believe anything she says anymore. If she — "

"She?" Joan exclaimed, interrupting him. "Don't talk about me like I'm not here. That's just like Mother and Father. You're getting just like them. That's what's so disgusting! Don't you understand? Cheering is the most important thing to me. And if Mother and Father find out about the tumbling, I'm finished. It's easy for you

to be Mr. Perfect, Adam, because you get to do everything you want."

"Maybe if Coach talked to them about safety," suggested Melody. "I mean, if they understood about mats and the spotters?" She looked at Joan. "I think you have to tell your parents the truth."

"You're taking his side!" shrieked Joan.

"I'm not," protested Melody. "I just — "

Joan saw Darryl coming toward them. He had a towel over his shoulder, and he was carrying a tennis racket.

"There's Darryl Budd," Joan hissed, interrupting Melody midsentence. "If you guys talk about this in front of him, I'll never — "

"Don't worry, Joanie," Adam told her. "We won't."

She glared at him again. How many times did she have to tell him to call her *Joan*, not *Joanie*.

"Thought I'd take you up on a tennis challenge, Melody," Darryl said as he walked toward them.

"Right," said Melody, remembering telling Darryl after a football game that she loved tennis and that there were courts in her apartment complex. He'd challenged her to a match and she'd agreed. It was a little weird that he just showed up without calling first, but she smiled up at him. He was cute, and it would be fun to play a few sets with him.

"Have a seat," she said. "We can play later, if you've got time."

"I've got time," he answered, squatting beside her. He smiled at Joan and Adam. "How are you guys doing?"

"Okay," said Adam.

"We could all play water volleyball," suggested Melody.

"Or we could practice dunking you," said Darryl with a grin.

Joan didn't feel like being around Adam. Or Melody. Or even Darryl. "I'll pass," she said. "I'm going home."

Melody watched Joan go around the side of the apartment complex and head toward the street. Now Joan is mad at me, she thought.

Adam stood up. "I better get going, too," he said. "Thanks for the swim, Melody."

Is he angry at me, too? she wondered. "Please stay," she begged as she stood up to face him. "The three of us could play Canadian doubles. You can use my mother's racket."

For a second Melody's eyes and Adam's eyes met, but he switched his gaze to the pool. "I'll pass," he said.

After Adam left, Melody headed to the tennis

court with Darryl. She liked that he'd dropped by to play tennis. She just wished it had been on a different afternoon.

CMS SMALL GYM. THURSDAY 4:00 P.M.

The first thing Emily noticed when she came into the gym was a big TV monitor on a rolling cart and a video camera mounted on a tripod. It's going to record every mistake I make, thought Emily, and everyone is going to see how bad I am. The second thing she noticed was Sally talking to Sam Paetro. She wished she could be as confident as Sally. She wished she could be even half as good a cheerleader.

As Emily took her place on the floor for the warm-up, she mentally reviewed the corrections Sam had made on her forward stretch the week before. I'll pay attention to everything he says, she told herself. She only wished she didn't have to watch herself on videotape.

Forty-five minutes later that's just what Emily was doing — sitting on the floor with the other cheerleaders, watching a tape of the center routine. I was right, she thought as the tape ended, I don't jump as high as anyone else. Especially on the toe touch jumps.

"All right, girls," Sam said when they'd seen the tape for the second time. "Now that you've watched yourselves, I'd like you each to tell me what you see as your weakness. We'll start with the captains."

Sally said she didn't think her motions were sharp enough.

"We can fix that," Sam said. "Just remember to concentrate on each motion individually. Then lock those arms and hit it."

Mae noticed that she wasn't staying in her position in the routine.

"Actually, that's not your problem," Sam told her. "What you really need to focus on, Mae, is having a more natural smile. Your routine is fine. Now let the crowd know that you're enjoying yourself."

By the time it was Emily's turn, her heart was pounding and her palms were sweaty. "I don't jump as high as everyone else," she told Sam in a wavering voice. "Especially on my toe touch jumps."

"We can fix that," he said. "In fact, come up here right now, Emily, and I'll break down the toe touch jump for you. Listen up, girls. This is something everyone should keep in mind."

Emily couldn't believe her bad luck. Sam was going to correct her in public. "Do a toe touch jump," he instructed.

She swallowed the lump in her throat and did the jump.

"You need to roll your hips under and keep

your back straight," he directed. "Lift your legs to your shoulders instead of dropping your shoulders to your legs. This is what you were doing, Emily."

Sam did the toe touch jump with his backside sticking out. He looked so funny that most of the girls laughed. Emily did not. He smiled at Emily. "Don't look so sad," he told her. "Your jump didn't look that bad." He demonstrated rolling his hips under. "Now watch when I jump with my hips under."

Sam did the highest toe touch jump Emily had ever seen. Everyone applauded. "All you need to remember is to roll your hips under for that jump," he explained. "And keep your chest high. Now you try it, Emily."

It took three tries. By the third try, Emily felt like she had more height. Everyone applauded. She was surprised that such a simple thing could make such a big difference.

"Problem solved," Sam told Emily. "Who's next?"

"You were terrific," Melody whispered when Emily sat back down. "I would have been so embarrassed."

"I was," Emily whispered back.

After Sam worked on each girl's problem, he videotaped the center cheer again. Emily watched herself closely when the tape was played back. It was true. She was jumping higher and better. Next time I'll smile when I jump, she promised herself. Cheerleading was beginning to be fun again.

BULLDOG CAFÉ 5:30 P.M.

Emily had almost reached the hotel when she noticed Jake at one of the café tables with her sister Lily. He waved and Emily waved back.

"We're having a date," Lily told Emily when she reached them. Emily and Jake exchanged a smile. Whenever Jake baby-sat for Lily, Lily called it a date. And when Emily or her older sister, Lynn, baby-sat, Lily called it "keeping busy while Mommy and Daddy do the hotel."

"May I join you and your date, Miss Lily?" Emily asked Lily in a mock formal tone.

"O-kay," Lily reluctantly agreed.

Emily couldn't wait to tell Jake about what happened at Sam Paetro's clinic. But the waiter came over as soon as she sat down. "Do you want your usual, Emily?" he asked. "A smoothie and a chocolate-filled donut?"

Emily remembered Coach's advice that she should eat plenty of nutritious foods and skip some of the sweet, fattening ones. "Just the smoothie," she told him. "Thanks."

"About the barbecue for the beach party," Jake told her. "I'm going to meet with your father later to figure out how much food to order. But what will we do about a grill? We can't borrow the café's. They'll need it here, right?"

"C.J. said the firehouse has a huge grill for barbecues," Emily told him. "Her father is a volunteer fireman. She's going to ask her dad if he'll drive it over and set it up for you."

"Great," Jake said.

While Lily ate a grilled cheese sandwich, Emily and Jake decided they'd sell hot dogs, hamburgers, and veggie burgers at the beach party. "Besides food, we'll need paper plates and napkins," Emily told him.

"And we should sell sodas, too," added Jake.

Emily smiled at him. She loved being in middle school with Jake and working on a project with him. *It's more fun than I could ever have imagined,* she thought. She decided that as soon as they finished the list of supplies they'd need for the barbecue, she'd tell him about the cheer clinic.

"Lexi! Lexi!" Lily shouted. Emily saw Jake grin and wave before she turned around and waved to Alexis herself.

"Hey, Lily," Alexis called. She said hi to Emily and Jake when she got closer. Her eyes met

Jake's and she felt herself blush. She quickly turned her gaze to Lily. "How you doing, Lily?" she asked.

"Have a seat," Jake told Alexis as he pulled out the only empty chair at the table.

"I sort of finished my column," she told him as she sat down. "But there are a couple of things I wanted to ask you about."

"Let's see it," Jake said.

While Alexis and Jake went over her column, Emily drank her smoothie and tried to keep Lily from interrupting them.

When they finished working on the article, Alexis said, "Sorry. Were you guys talking about something? Did I interrupt?"

"Not really," said Emily. "Just some stuff about the beach party. We pretty much finished."

"A beach party is such a great fund-raising idea," said Alexis. "I think everyone in school will show up, including the teachers."

"Who will probably bring their kids," added Jake. "Hey, Alexis, you want to help me with the barbecue?"

"Sure," she said.

"I can help you, too, Jake," Emily said. "I mean, if you want."

"Don't you have to do the Bubba photo booth?" asked Alexis.

"Right," agreed Emily. "I forgot."

Alexis looked at her watch. "I better hurry," she said. "I have to meet my mother at Joe's Fish Shack. If I'm even a little late she'll think I was hit by a car or something."

Emily watched Alexis running down the street. There was so much she hadn't shared with Alexis since she became a cheerleader that she wondered if they would ever catch up.

Lily interrupted Emily's thoughts by asking Jake, "Is Lexi your girlfriend?"

"*You're* my girlfriend, Lily," he told her.

"I'm four years old," Lily said sadly.

"I like younger women," Jake said with a laugh.

Does he mean younger like seventh grade? wondered Emily.

DOLPHIN COURT APARTMENTS. SUNDAY 10:05 P.M.

Melody leaned back in her desk chair and read over the answers she'd typed into her computer for history homework. It was hard to concentrate. Her mind kept going back to Joan. She thought about the argument the week before and how Joan had stormed off. She'd thought Joan was going to be her best friend in Claymore, and now Joan was barely talking to her.

Not talking was the worst part. Melody thought about her old friends and how much she missed them.

After dinner Melody typed an e-mail to Tina, her best friend in Miami. She smiled just thinking about Tina. Everyone called her Big T, but she was short and petite, like Joan. In the e-mail Melody tried to explain to Tina how hard it was to make new friends. And how hard it was to figure people out. People like Sally Johnson. "She always *acts* nice," Melody typed, "but I don't feel like she *really* likes me." She went on to explain what happened with Joan. But it was difficult to write about the people in Claymore when Tina didn't know any of them.

Now Melody closed her history homework file and checked to see if Tina had answered her e-mail.

"Yes!" she said out loud when her Inbox revealed a new message from Big T.

> Hey there, Max. What a bummer :-(. All those phony Claymorites. We gotta get you outta there and back home where you belong and everyone loves you. Period. Ya know? So here's the deal. Get a break. Come to Miami next weekend. How? Easy. You remember my Aunt Flora? Well, she is

working in Fort Myers for two weeks, and she's coming home to Miami for the weekend. Now, Auntie Flora says that she could swing by Claymore, which isn't so far from Fort M., around three-thirty on Friday and bring you to and from Miami! Yes! A weekend with your old pals. And there's more! Saturday there's a big dance at the middle school. Everyone you know will be there. And — here's the best part — Juan Ramirez, your old crush who you always said was too old for you and didn't know you were on the face of the earth — asked about you AGAIN! Like my mom says, "Absence makes the heart grow fonder." Maybe that's why you miss us all so much. No! Take that back. We're the best. You should miss us. So come on back for a blast of a weekend. Love ya always. Big T. Auntie's phone number at the hotel is 609-555-7233.

Melody jumped up. Go to Miami for the weekend? How perfect! She could see her dad. And go to the dance with all her friends. She'd seen Juan dance at a hip-hop club and was impressed. If Juan was really asking about her, maybe he'd dance with her. It would be so much fun!

"Mom!" Melody shouted as she ran out of her room. She found her mother on the terrace having a cup of tea.

"What is it?" her mother asked. "What happened?"

When she'd told her the whole story about getting a ride to Miami and going to the dance, her mother asked, "Don't you have that beach party for the cheerleaders next weekend?"

Melody realized that her mother was right. The beach party was on the same night as the dance in Miami. "I forgot," Melody told her mother. "But I could miss it."

"Well, it's up to you, Melody," her mother said. "Of course you can go to Miami if you like."

Melody walked slowly back to her bedroom. Dance in Miami or beach party in Claymore? New friends or old friends?

She sat down at the computer and wrote a message to Tina.

> Miami for the weekend sounds like the best. Would love to. Have a little conflict here in Claymore because of cheerleader stuff. Will try to figure it out and get back to you earliest possible. Say hi to Juan for me, if it's really true he is asking about me and you're not imagining it. That's a big IF. Love ya back.
> Max :-)

DELHAVEN DRIVE. MONDAY 7:45 A.M.

When Joan came into the kitchen, her parents and Adam were there. Her mother was looking over some notes for her lecture at the university. Her father was reading the newspaper and absentmindedly eating a piece of toast. Adam was wolfing down some cereal. The only one who looked up when she walked in was her father.

"There you are," he said cheerfully. "I thought I'd drive you and Adam to school today. I'm sure Ms. Roth will be in the library this morning."

Joan had hoped that her father would forget about volunteering to help the debate club. Even though she had finally joined the club, she didn't want her father coming to school. If he was there he might find out what she was doing as a cheerleader.

"Ms. Roth is really busy before first period," Joan said. "And during first period, too. It's a busy library."

"That's why I think she could use a little help with this debate club," her father said.

Adam looked up from his cereal. "You know, Father," he said, "Ms. Roth is the sort of person who likes to do things her own way. She wouldn't want any interference from a parent."

Joan glanced at her brother in amazement. He was trying to help her.

Their mother looked up from her book. "Interference?" she said. "Your father would be lending some expertise to that debating program. I wouldn't call that interference."

"But — " Joan began, even though she didn't know what to say next.

Fortunately, Adam helped her out. He argued that his father shouldn't advise the debate club and his father argued back, point by point. It was more like a debate than an argument. A really close debate. Adam brought it to a conclusion with his last point. "Father, I think you'd be a bigger help to the club if you coached Joan on the side," he said. "Here at home. You could suggest topics for the club through her and help her with the arguments for her side."

Their mother looked up from her book again. "I agree with Adam," she said.

"Me, too," Joan quickly added.

Mr. Chazen looked around at his family and announced, "I'm outnumbered."

Joan tried to smile at her brother to let him know that she appreciated what he'd done for her. But all his attention was back on his bowl of half-eaten cereal.

Ms. Russo gathered up her papers and put them in her briefcase. "I can drop you both off at school," she said.

"I'm riding my bike today," Adam said.

"Me, too," Joan added. She hadn't planned on riding her bike, but she wanted to go to school with Adam. It would be so great if they could be allies again instead of enemies.

HARBOR ROAD 8:01 A.M.

Adam didn't wait for Joan. He pedaled fast out of the driveway. She caught up with him at the first stoplight on Harbor Road.

Breathless from pedaling so hard, she managed to say, "Thank you, Adam. Your argument was brilliant. You should join the debate club."

He scowled at her. "Did you join?" he asked.

"I told you I did," she said.

"How do I know it's true?" he shot back.

The light changed. Adam sped ahead again. She yelled after him, "Because I wouldn't . . ." The word *lie* stuck in her throat.

Adam skidded to a stop so suddenly she almost ran into him. "Wouldn't what?" he asked. "Lie? You've lied over and over to Mother and Father. Why should I trust you? Why should anyone?"

He sped on. Joan followed, with Adam's questions ringing in her ears.

As Melody walked along Harbor Road an unanswered question was running through her head. Should she go to Miami or stay in Claymore for the beach party? She saw Adam riding his bike past her, but he didn't stop. He must have seen me, thought Melody. So why didn't he stop?

A few seconds later Melody turned and saw Joan speeding toward her. Melody waved and decided that she'd try to talk to her. She was sure Joan saw her, but Joan rode right by without even bothering to wave back.

"Hey, Melody," a voice called. Melody turned and saw Alexis on the next corner.

"How's it going?" Alexis asked when Melody caught up to her.

Melody didn't want to tell Alexis about what had happened between her, Joan, and Adam. So she said, "Fine."

"I heard you volunteered to be dunked," Alexis said as they walked along. "You're such a good sport."

"Actually, I might not be here," Melody said. "The dunking thing is the problem."

Alexis gave Melody a surprised look. "You're leaving town so you won't have to be dunked?" she asked.

"No," laughed Melody. "I have a chance to go to Miami for the weekend. I really want to go, but I'm also supposed to be at the beach party. Getting dunked."

"I went to Miami once with my dad," Alexis said. "It was great."

"It is," agreed Melody. "If I go I'll see my dad. And there's this big dance that all my old friends are going to."

They turned the corner and headed toward school. "Do you have a boyfriend in Miami?" asked Alexis.

Melody smiled at her. "No," she said. "We all just hung out together — the guys and the girls."

"Don't the girls have crushes?" asked Alexis.

"Some of them do," said Melody. "My best friend, Tina, always has her eye on some guy or other. But usually he's older than us. So it's not like she goes out with them or anything."

"So what are you going to do about the beach party?" Alexis asked.

Melody shrugged her shoulders. "Don't know," she said. "But I have to decide. They'll need someone else to dunk."

As they walked into the CMS courtyard, Melody told Alexis that she had to go to the library before homeroom. She took the path that led directly to the front door while Alexis took the route along the side.

As Alexis walked along she noticed Jake standing under a palm tree talking to Mae and

Sally. How could I possibly think he'd like me as a girlfriend? she wondered. I'm lucky that he has anything to do with me at all. Farther ahead she saw Emily talking with C.J., Joan, and Jessica. They're probably talking about cheerleading stuff, she thought. Maybe I'll go to the library, too.

Someone tapped her on the shoulder. She turned and faced Jake.

"Hey," he said.

"Hey," she said back. Her heartbeat quickened. She felt herself blush. Can Jake tell that I have a crush on him? she wondered. Does it show?

"I have to go to the library," she said quickly. "With Melody. 'Bye." And she ran after Melody, calling for her to wait up.

CMS FRONT LOBBY 8:25 A.M.

As Melody was crossing the crowded lobby on her way to homeroom, she met Adam going the other way. He did a one-hundred-and-eighty-degree turn to walk beside her. "I've been looking for you," he said.

"You passed me on the way to school," she said.

"I know," he said. "I couldn't stop or Joan would have thought we were talking about her." He sighed. "I tried to help her with our parents, but we ended up having another fight — sort of."

"Sorry," she said. "She's angry at me, too."

"She's totally changed lately," he said. "It's really weird."

As they reached Melody's homeroom, the final bell rang. "So," she said. "See you later."

He nodded. "I heard you're going to be dunked at the beach party. I promise I won't even try to dunk you."

Melody laughed. "That's what everyone says. There isn't much point doing it if no one pays to try to dunk me."

"Then I'll try," he promised her. "But not that hard."

She was so relieved that he wasn't angry at her that she didn't tell him she might not even be at the beach party.

As Melody walked into homeroom, she noticed a small brown bag on her chair. Is it a present? she wondered. Or a joke? By the time she reached her desk she'd decided that someone had put his lunch on her chair by mistake. She picked up the bag. It was too light to be a lunch.

"Maria put it there," said Tommy, the guy who sat behind her. Melody opened the bag and saw a small stuffed animal and a note. "Bubba," she whispered as she took them both out of the bag. The note read: *Mel. Here's our Bubba Baby.*

Isn't he cute? We have 299 more just like him. Meet me and Emily at lunch to plan how we'll get everyone at CMS to buy one. Maria.

Melody sat the Bubba Baby on the corner of her desk. A few kids around her smiled when they saw the stuffed animal. Melody smiled back. Sally's voice came over the loudspeaker. She made a little speech telling everyone in school about the beach party. "Be there to support your cheerleaders," she concluded. "We need you to come to the beach party and have fun!"

Melody thought, CMS is my school now. But my oldest and best friends are in Miami. She patted the Bubba Baby and wished that on Saturday night she could be in two places at once.

CMS CAFETERIA 12:15 P.M.

Emily carried her lunch tray to a table in the corner of the cafeteria where Melody and Maria were saving her a place.

"The Bubba Babies are *so* cute," Emily said as she put down her tray and sat in the chair next to Melody. "It even has a brown spot on the tip of its ear, just like Bubba."

"I have an idea for making them even cuter," said Melody.

"How?" asked Emily.

"We could tie blue-and-white ribbons around their necks," Melody answered.

"Isn't that a cool idea?" said Maria. "My mother can get us ribbon at wholesale. But it'll take us a long time to cut and tie ribbons for three hundred Bubbas."

"If we have a bunch of people helping us it will go fast," said Emily. "Where are the Bubbas now?" She bit into her turkey sandwich.

"In Coach's office," Maria answered.

"How soon do you think you could get the ribbon?" Melody asked.

"I don't know how much my mom already has in the store," said Maria. "If she has to order it, it'll take a couple of days."

"Maybe we could have a ribbon-tying meeting in the gym on Friday," said Emily. "After the game."

The game! thought Melody. She'd totally forgotten about the game. If Tina's aunt picked her up Friday at three-thirty to go to Miami, she'd miss more than the beach party. She'd miss cheering for the game on Friday, the Bubba ribbon-tying meeting after the game, and setting up for the beach party on Saturday. How could she explain to Coach that she had to miss all those things, plus the beach party?

"Melody," said Emily, interrupting her

thoughts. "Is Friday after the game okay for you?"

Melody nodded. "It's fine," she said. "I'll be there." She smiled at Emily and Maria and added, "It'll be fun."

45 ROOSEVELT STREET.
SATURDAY 12:55 P.M.

Joan sat on a chair in the front hall of Mr. Richter's house while his twelve o'clock student finished a piano lesson in the music room. Joan could tell that the student was a beginner. Listening reminded her of her first piano lesson when she was five years old. After that lesson all she wanted to do was play piano, and no one had to remind her to practice.

"You're our little protégée," her father said proudly after her first piano recital.

"You have a special gift," her mother had told her. "It is your responsibility to develop that gift. And that can only be done with hard work."

Well, I've worked hard at the piano for six years, thought Joan. But I want to do other things, too, like help set up for the beach party today. She wondered if she dared ask Mr. Richter to cut her lesson short.

"Well done, Ryan," she heard Mr. Richter say to his student.

"Can I go now?" asked Ryan.

"Yes," Mr. Richter said. "Your lesson is over."

Ryan left the music room so fast he almost knocked Joan down as she walked in.

"Sorry," Ryan mumbled and kept running. The front door banged behind him.

Joan walked over to the grand piano and sat at the bench. The sooner I get started, she thought, the sooner I can leave.

"Ryan doesn't want to be late for his Little League softball game," Mr. Richter told Joan with a laugh. "I remember that feeling."

"You do?" she said with surprise.

"Sure I do," said Mr. Richter. "When I was his age I played softball or tennis every chance I had." He swung an imaginary racket at an imaginary ball. "Still do. I'm in a tennis tournament tomorrow. Wish me luck."

"Good luck," she said.

Joan never thought of Mr. Richter doing anything but playing the piano and teaching kids. With his gray hair and wrinkled face, she thought Mr. Richter was as old as her grandfather.

"It's important for a musician to be in good shape," Mr. Richter told her. "Playing a musical instrument is strenuous. You're strong, Joanie. Small but strong. I bet you're a good cheerleader."

"I like cheering," she said. She wished she could tell him all about the problems she was having with her parents over cheering and the lies she'd been telling them. But she stopped herself. What if she couldn't trust him?

To change the subject she said, "I had trouble with the last passage of that Chopin piece I've been working on." She opened her music book and put it on the piano.

"Let's get to it then," Mr. Richter said. "Play the piece from the beginning and then we'll deal with the last passage." He smiled at her. "It will be a relief to listen to you after the restless softball player."

When Joan reached the end Mr. Richter helped her with the difficult last passage. "Now play it again," he instructed, "from the beginning. But with more feeling. Chopin knew he had a disease that would kill him when he wrote this. Think how he must have felt knowing it might be the last piece of music he could ever write or play."

That's a little bit like it is for me and cheering, Joan thought as she struck the first chord of the piece. I never know which game will be my last. Before she reached the end of the third line of music she'd forgotten about cheering, her parents, Chopin dying, or the beach party. She only thought of the music she was playing with her whole mind, body, and heart. And the last passage was perfect.

Mr. Richter patted her on the shoulder. "Terrific, Joanie," he said. "Let's do the Beethoven piece you've been working on. There's something I want to show you about the middle section."

Joan turned to the music. She couldn't wait to play it.

MAIN STREET 1:30 P.M.

Melody walked toward the beach along Main Street. It was a sunny, breezy day, and in five hours the beach party would begin. There was a lot of work to do before then.

She saw Adam riding toward her on his bike. This time instead of whizzing by her he stopped.

"Hey," he said. "Where you going?"

"To set up for the beach party," she said. "All the cheerleaders have to help."

"Joan's at her piano lesson," Adam said. "I guess she'll go to the beach from there. Is she still not talking to you?"

"Barely," said Melody. "She mostly avoids me. It's too weird."

He brushed the dark hair off his forehead with his fingers. "Yeah," he said. "I know what you mean."

"When's her lesson over?" Melody asked.

"Two o'clock," Adam answered.

"Where is it?" asked Melody. "Maybe I'll meet

her and we can walk to the beach together. I really want to be her friend."

"Her lesson is on Roosevelt Street," he said. "It's not far. Only about four blocks past The Manor Hotel. It's the big blue house on the right, halfway down the street."

Melody glanced at her watch. "I better hurry," she said.

Adam smiled at her and said, "Good luck."

She smiled back. She wanted so much for her and Joan and Adam to be good friends.

45 ROOSEVELT STREET 1:55 P.M.

Melody sat on Mr. Richter's front steps. Beautiful piano music came through an open window on the side of the house. Maybe the piano teacher is playing a disc for Joan, Melody thought. The music stopped suddenly. A few chords were repeated, then more playing. It's not a disc, Melody decided, so the teacher must be playing. She wondered if Joan was even in there. Had she missed her? She walked over to the side of the house and looked in the window.

Joan was sitting at the piano, playing. An elderly man stood beside her. Melody stared with amazement at Joan's fast-moving fingers. Wow! she thought as she went back to the front steps, she's really good.

The music stopped, and a minute later the

front door opened. Melody stood up and faced Joan. "I came to meet you," she said. "To walk to the beach together."

Joan looked at her suspiciously. "How did you know where to come?" she asked.

"Adam told me," Melody answered as they walked together toward the sidewalk. "I bumped into him on Main Street. I just heard you play the piano. I mean, I had no idea. You're *really* good."

"You heard me?" Joan said.

"Through the window," Melody explained. "It was open. I peeked." She grinned. "Your teacher had his eyes closed while he listened."

Joan couldn't help smiling, too. She pictured Mr. Richter listening to her play with his eyes closed. She knew that from him it was a compliment. It meant he was really enjoying her playing instead of watching her fingering the way he did when she was first learning a piece.

"I never heard anyone our age play like that," Melody said.

"Thanks," Joan said. She hoped Melody wouldn't start preaching to her about how awful it was to lie. She hoped that they could just walk to the beach together like everything was normal and talk about other things.

"I took piano lessons when I was in third grade," Melody said. "But I was terrible and I didn't like it at all. I wanted to play drums."

"Do you?" Joan asked.

"Sort of," Melody answered. "I have these African drums. But mostly I say these poems I write to a beat."

"Cool," said Joan.

Melody told Joan all about the poetry slam she'd been to in Miami and how lots of her friends performed their poems.

"Will you do it for me sometime?" asked Joan.

"Sure," said Melody. "Let me try to make one up for you now. That's what's most fun, just starting something and seeing where it goes." Melody thought of a first line, cleared her throat, and began.

"I love to rhyme
Anytime.
It makes no difference where or when,
If I want, I rhyme right then.
Joan, you have to know
You play cool pi-ano.
You've got talent
Is what I meant.
You play with soul,
Which should be your goal."

Melody stopped rhyming and started laughing.

"That was so great!" Joan said. "Does Adam know that you do that?"

Melody shook her head. "I haven't done it since I moved here," she said.

"I don't know how you can just do it like that," Joan told her.

"Actually, I used to be better. It takes practice," said Melody. "Like the piano."

And cheering, thought Joan, which reminded her of all the lies she'd been telling her parents and how Melody didn't approve. She didn't want to talk about all of that with Melody. Maybe someday. But not now. Now she just wanted to be a normal kid, having a normally great time, and going with a friend to set up for a beach party.

TOWN BEACH. SATURDAY 1:30 P.M.

Emily stood next to a table with a sign that read TAKE A PICTURE WITH BUBBA $2. Bubba, dressed in his CMS T-shirt, lay under the table with his head resting on his paws, waiting for the beach party to begin.

Emily looked up and down the beach. Everything was ready. The big barbecue grill had been delivered and was fired up, strings of colored lights were strung around the trunks of palm trees, and music blared over the loudspeaker system. There was a basketball hoop, horseshoes, and darts. A big tank of water with two dunking chairs was set up for Randy and Melody. Farther down the beach a volleyball court had been set up.

Mae and Maria had their Bubba Babies table near the entrance to the beach. "From here we'll catch them coming and going," Maria had explained to Emily.

Jessica carried a big roll of tickets and wore a sign that listed the raffle prizes. "I hope I can sell all of these tickets," she told Emily as she passed her. The sun will be setting in a few minutes, thought Emily. It's the perfect time for a party to begin.

Just then a huge crowd of eighth-graders walked onto the beach. Emily bent over and told Bubba it was time for him to go to work for CMS. As she put him on a stool she said, "You're our mascot, Bubba. Bring us good luck at this fund-raiser."

Jessica turned back and came over to Bubba and Emily. "Take my picture with him," she said. "I want to be the first." Jessica put two dollars in the jar on the table and stood next to Bubba. She smiled and Emily took their picture. "Give me good luck selling all my tickets," Jessica told Bubba. While she waited for her photo to develop, Kelly had her picture taken with Bubba. "Help us make loads of money," she whispered to Bubba as she put an arm around him and faced the camera.

Melody came over to have her picture taken with Bubba. "Help us get to Miami, Bubba," she told him before Emily took their picture.

Soon, more cheerleaders were at the photo booth. "I heard we're supposed to have our picture taken with Bubba so our squad will make a lot of money tonight," Joan said. Then she added two dollars to the money in the jar and stood beside Bubba.

Bubba wagged his short, stubby tail each time someone stood beside him.

After C.J. had her picture taken, she told Emily, "I heard that all the cheerleaders have to have their picture taken with Bubba or we won't have good luck. Have they all done it?"

"Sally hasn't," Emily answered. "She's probably been too busy. And I don't think Elvia has yet, either."

"I'll go find them," C.J. told her.

Five eighth-graders were lined up to have their pictures taken with Bubba. "Step right up!" Emily announced in a loud, clear voice. "Good luck for two bucks!"

A few minutes later Jake came over to the booth. "I heard that anyone who's working here has to have their picture taken with Bubba to bring good luck for the fund-raiser," he said.

Emily laughed. "It started out with Jessica having her picture taken with him for good luck selling all her raffle tickets," she explained. "Then the cheerleaders all thought they had to do it. Now it's anyone who's working at the party."

"Way to go," Jake said as he handed her two dollars. He put his face right next to Bubba's, and Emily snapped the photo. Jake took his developing photo from Emily. "I'm going back to the grill," he told her. He smiled at Emily. "We're selling lots of food."

Sally saw the crowd lined up waiting to have pictures taken with Bubba and thought, Why would anyone want to have their picture taken with that ugly dog?

"Did you have your picture taken with Bubba yet?" Jake asked Sally as he walked past her. "It's become this good luck charm for the beach party."

"I know," she said. "About a thousand people told me. It's just that I've been busy."

Mae came up beside her. "We're making a load of money," she told Sally. "Thanks to Bubba. Did you — ?"

"Not yet," Sally said, interrupting her. "I'm going now." She went over to Bubba's booth, smiled at Emily, put her two dollars in the jar, and stood next to Bubba. "Move closer," Emily told her. "And bend over a little, so your face is next to his."

Sally leaned closer to Bubba and smiled at the camera. Emily snapped the shot just as Bubba turned toward Sally and licked her cheek.

She quickly stepped back.

"He really likes you," Emily beamed. "That picture is going to be so cute."

"I'll pick it up later," Sally mumbled as she forced herself to smile. "I — uh — have to check on the dunking booth." She ran over to the food stand and grabbed a napkin to wipe her cheek. She reached the dunking booth just as Darryl landed a ball on the bull's-eye, dunking Randy.

Randy stood up in the pool of water, his hands over his drenched head. "Enough, enough," he sputtered.

"Good hit," Sally told Darryl.

Darryl laughed. "It's the third time I've dunked him." He handed money to Joan and took three more balls. "I'm going for the fourth."

"Go for it!" Sally exclaimed.

"You should try it," Darryl said. "It's fun."

It would be fun to dunk Melody, thought Sally. She reached into her pocket for money and shouted to Melody, "Hey, Melody, how many times have you been dunked so far?"

"Ten," Melody answered with a laugh. "I'm one ahead of Randy."

"So let's go for eleven," Sally said. She took the balls from Elvia. I didn't think Melody would look so pretty wet, Sally thought as she wound up and threw her first ball.

She missed.

"Let's throw at the same time," Darryl called over to her. "See if we can make it a double dunk."

"You're on!" agreed Sally. This time, she promised herself, she'd concentrate on the bull's-eye instead of on how Melody looked.

Darryl and Sally exchanged a glance and nodded to each other.

"Ready!" shouted Darryl.

"Aim!" shouted someone in the crowd that was forming around them.

"Shoot!" the crowd shouted in unison.

Darryl and Sally threw their balls. They both hit the bull's-eye. Randy and Melody dropped into the pool. The crowd applauded, and Darryl and Sally bowed. Out of the corner of her eye Sally saw Randy and Melody bowing, too.

"Hey, Darryl, how about you getting dunked for a change?" shouted Randy.

"Dar-ryl! Dar-ryl!" the crowd began to chant.

"Okay, okay, I'll do it," Darryl shouted.

Then the crowd changed its chant to "Sal-ly! Sal-ly!"

Sally looked around at the grinning faces of the crowd that had formed around them. It was part of her plan that she and Darryl would be king and queen of the ninth-grade prom. If this was one step along the way, she'd have to take it. Besides, if she didn't sit on the dunking chair, Melody would stay. Darryl and Melody. It just wouldn't do. "Okay," she told Darryl, "let's do it."

Melody and Randy climbed out of the tub of water as Darryl and Sally took their places on the chairs. Randy took a wet bill out of his pocket and handed it to Joan. "I get the first shot at Darryl," he said.

"Do you want the first shot at Sally?" Elvia asked Melody. Melody wasn't sure she wanted to be throwing balls at Sally Johnson. But since Randy was going to try to dunk Darryl, it seemed like she had to.

"Don't worry," Melody told Sally. "I'm not a good shot."

"The way you hit a tennis ball," Darryl shouted to Melody, "Sally better be ready to swim."

Sally wondered why Darryl knew how Melody hit a tennis ball. Nevertheless, she smiled and told Melody, "I'm ready."

Before Melody could throw her first ball, a shrill voice shouted, “Fire!” Melody turned and saw flames moving along the dry grass near the barbecue pit and Jake stomping out the fire.

“Turn on the hose we used for the pool,” Melody shouted to Elvia, who was nearest to it.

“Throw sand on it!” someone else yelled.

Melody saw a flame leap up toward Jake’s apron. She ran onto the burning grass and grabbed Jake by the arm, shouting, “Get out of there!”

“I have to put it out!” he shouted as he pulled away from her.

Emily and Darryl were beside Melody now, and the three of them dragged Jake away from the flames.

A jet of water dousing the grass splashed against Emily’s leg, and she saw kids throwing handfuls of sand on the smoldering grass. She also saw a wild look in Jake’s eyes that frightened her.

“How’d it happen?” Darryl asked no one in particular.

Alexis, who’d come up beside Melody and Darryl, answered. “I guess coals in the barbecue grill flamed up from the cooking. Suddenly, there was this fire.”

“Well, it’s okay now,” Darryl said.

Sally’s voice came on over the loudspeaker

system. "Listen up," she said. "There was a little fire over by the food tent, but it's out. Remember, you're here to party and spend money for your Bulldog cheer squad. Check out the volleyball court. The teachers versus students game begins in five minutes."

Emily went back to the Bubba photo stand and found Bubba sleeping under the table. She was surprised that Jake had tried to stamp out the grass fire when there was plenty of sand and water nearby. She looked across to the food stand to see what Jake was doing now. She could see Alexis and the four other volunteers cooking and selling food. But Jake wasn't there. She peered to her left and right. No Jake. If he's upset, she thought, I have to find him.

"I'm going to walk Bubba," Emily announced to the kids waiting to have their pictures taken with him. When he heard his name Bubba came out from under the table. Emily bent over and picked up his leash.

She looked around and thought about where Jake might have gone. She remembered that when Jake was upset he liked to walk along the beach. She looked up and down the shoreline. There was a stone embankment to the left of the town beach, so he couldn't have gone that way. But on the right the beach continued for a long stretch past the town beach. Emily turned right and led Bubba across the sand toward the water.

Alexis watched Emily and Bubba running to the edge of the beach. She wondered if Emily was going to look for Jake.

The sandy shoreline made a sharp turn after about a hundred yards. It was difficult for Emily to see very far ahead now that she was away from the bright lights of the party. As she walked along, the party noises grew fainter. There were a few houses overlooking the water, but they were set back and far apart. No one was on the beach. Emily squatted down and studied the packed, wet sand by the dim light of the stars and the sliver of a new moon. She found what she was looking for. Tracks in the sand. Tracks made by sneakers.

"I think he came this way," she told Bubba as she stood up and began sprinting along the beach. A small wave washed in and lapped over her sandals. She looked down and saw that it had taken Jake's tracks with it. She stopped and quickly undid Bubba's leash. If I can't find Jake, she thought as she picked up her pace again, maybe Bubba can.

"Jake!" she called.

After a few hundred yards Bubba ran toward a dock. She was about to call him back when she noticed a large dark shape under the dock. It was big enough to be a person.

"Jake," Emily called softly as she walked toward the dock. Her heart beat fast. The dark figure moved. "Jake," she called again. "I'm scared. Tell me if it's you."

"Yeah," Jake said in a low voice. "It's me."

UNDER THE DOCK 9:00 P.M.

Emily got on her hands and knees and crawled under the dock. First she saw Jake's familiar black-and-white high-top sneakers, then his jeans, and finally his face. Bubba was licking it.

"Sorry," Jake said. "Sorry I-I scared you."

"That's okay," Emily said as she squeezed in and sat beside him.

"Is everybody looking for me?" he asked.

"Just me," she said. "They probably think you're taking a break or that you went home to change your clothes because of the smoke and everything. I thought you might be upset. I mean, because it was a fire and — you know — "

Jake didn't say anything, but she heard him take a deep breath.

"No one was hurt," Emily continued. "It wasn't a dangerous fire."

He mumbled something she couldn't understand.

"What did you say?" she asked.

"It was my fault," he said more clearly.

Emily turned toward him. "Jake, the fire's out. It was no big deal."

"Not that fire," he said.

Emily knew he was thinking about the fire that killed his sister and parents. She put her hand on his arm. "Jake, you were sleeping when that fire started," she said. "You didn't start it."

"I didn't tell the firemen that someone was upstairs," Jake said. "I was crying, so they saved me first. I shouldn't have cried. I could have gotten out by myself or gone upstairs and carried my sister out. If they hadn't been worrying about me they could have saved them. I — "

"Jake," Emily said interrupting him, "you were only five years old. It was a terrible fire. I'm sure there were a lot of firemen and they did everything they could."

Bubba nudged Emily's leg and whimpered. It was hot and stuffy under the dock, and Jake smelled smoky from the fire.

"Let's get out of here," Emily said.

"I don't want to go back to the party," he murmured.

"I know," she said. "We can sit on the beach instead of under here."

Emily gave Bubba a little push before she crawled out herself. Jake followed, and the three of them walked to the edge of the sand. Jake and Emily took off their shoes. As they stood silently in the still, hot night Emily noticed Jake's smoky clothes. That smell must bring back memories, too, she thought.

"Let's go for a swim," she suggested to Jake. "In our clothes. Like we used to when we were little."

Emily didn't give him a chance to reject her idea but ran into the water, calling, "Come on, Jake." She waited for him to join her, then they dove in and swam together. Looking to shore Emily saw Bubba waiting patiently on the sand. "Poor Bubba," she said. "He can't swim."

When they came dripping back onto the sand Jake said, "Thanks, Em. That was a good idea. And thanks for coming after me."

They squeezed out the edges of their clothes and walked slowly along the sand toward the town beach.

"Do you ever talk to your grandmother about the fire?" Emily asked.

"No," Jake said. "I don't want to upset her. My father was her only kid. I mean, it must have been so hard for her and Gramps."

"Even though it was awful," Emily said thoughtfully, "I think you should talk to her or your grandfather. I mean, they probably know stuff about the fire that you don't know."

"Maybe," he said. "But if it was my fault they'd never tell me that."

"Your grandmother would tell you the truth," Emily said. "Whatever it is. She's always talking about how important honesty is. Besides, no matter what happened that night, there is no way it was your fault."

Jake didn't say anything for a few minutes. Emily didn't, either. Finally, Jake broke the silence. "Do you think the party is still going on?" he asked.

"I don't know," she said. She pointed to a big house set back from the beach. "You could cut through there if you don't want to see anybody. Bubba and I could go back the regular way. I'll tell them you went home because your clothes were smoky."

"No, it's okay," Jake said. "I'll go back with you."

As they rounded the bend in the shoreline they were greeted by the colored lights of the party. But the crowds were gone, and the cheerleaders and some helpers were cleaning up.

"Don't tell anyone about me being upset or anything," Jake told her.

"Of course not," she assured him. "I won't tell anyone."

"Especially not Alexis," he said.

"Okay," she agreed. She wondered if Jake said that because he wanted to tell Alexis himself.

TOWN BEACH 10:00 P.M.

"There's Emily and Jake," Melody shouted.

Alexis looked up from packing the unused hot dog and hamburger rolls and saw Jake, Emily, and Bubba walking along the beach.

"Looks like Jake has himself a girlfriend," Alexis overheard C.J. say to Elvia as they walked past her.

"But I thought Alexis — " Elvia started to say.

"Shhh," said C.J., interrupting her. C.J. glanced in Alexis's direction.

"Oops," muttered Elvia.

Do they think I have a crush on Jake? wondered Alexis. Does everybody? She felt her face flush with embarrassment as she walked over to join the group surrounding Emily and Jake.

"So where were you two?" Sally was asking them.

Jake patted his wet T-shirt. "Swimming," he said. "I was all smoky from stamping out the fire."

"Your little fire dance," Randy said. He threw an arm over Jake's shoulder. "Our hero."

Emily leaned over and patted Bubba. "I had to walk Bubba," she said. "And then I saw Jake. How did the rest of the party go?"

"We haven't counted all the money yet," Sally told her. "But I think we did great."

"The Bubba Babies sold out," Maria announced.

"I took the jar from your table after you left," C.J. said. "Bubba made a lot of money."

"The students won the volleyball game," Darryl said. "Fifteen to thirteen."

"That's great," Emily said. "Ya know, I'm all salty and my jeans weigh a ton. Plus, I should take Bubba home."

"I'll go with you," Jake said.

They said good-bye to everyone and turned to go. As Jake passed Alexis he said, "Sorry I disappeared on you."

"That's okay," she said. "There were plenty of people to help."

"Thanks," he said, and he and Emily left.

Alexis watched them walk away.

"Jake and Emily," Darryl said to the group when they were gone. "Wow!"

"Don't be ridiculous," Sally told him. "Emily's a seventh-grader."

Darryl hung an arm over Sally's shoulder. "Good point," he said.

Joan turned to Alexis. "You're Emily's best friend," she said. "Do you think she and Jake are, you know, like, boyfriend and girlfriend?"

Alexis shrugged and tried to swallow the lump in her throat before she muttered, "Emily never said." She turned to go back to her packing. She hoped no one would notice the tears that she couldn't hold back.

MAIN STREET 10:30 P.M.

Melody left the town beach and went out to the sidewalk. Adam and Joan were standing on the curb. Adam turned and saw her. "Hi," he said. "You have on dry clothes."

"Finally," she said. "I was so glad when Sally took my place."

"You were such a good sport to do that," said Joan.

"I'm calling my mother for a ride home," Melody said. "You guys need a ride?"

At that instant Joan and Adam's father drove up to the curb in front of them.

"We can give you a lift," Adam told her.

"Okay," Melody said.

Adam leaned through the open car window and asked his father if they could drop Melody off.

"Melody Max?" his father said with a big

smile. "Certainly." When she got into the backseat with Joan he greeted her with, "Nice to see you."

"You, too," Melody said. "Thanks for giving me a ride, Mr. Russo-Chazen."

"Actually," he said, "I'm Mr. Chazen. My wife is Ms. Russo."

"My mom uses her own name, too," Melody said. "Only I just have my dad's last name."

He seems nice, thought Melody. He doesn't seem like a father you'd have to lie to.

"How was the beach party?" he asked.

"Fun," Adam answered.

"We made a lot of money," Melody said.

"I didn't know that the party was a fundraiser," Mr. Chazen commented. "Who'll benefit from the funds?"

"The cheerleaders," Melody answered.

"To buy uniforms and stuff," Joan quickly added. She shot Melody a pleading glance that said, *Don't say anything about Miami and the CHEER USA competitions.*

Poor Joan, thought Melody. She's a nervous wreck. It must be awful to have a secret from your parents.

"Doesn't the school pay for uniforms?" Mr. Chazen asked.

"The cheer squad doesn't get as much support from the athletic funds as other — " Melody almost said "sports," but Joan interrupted her.

" — activities," Joan said, finishing the sentence for her.

"Right," said Melody. "Other activities get more money than cheering."

"Where exactly do you live, Melody?" Mr. Chazen asked.

"Dolphin Court," Melody answered. She decided not to say anything else to Joan's father. It was the only way to be sure she didn't say something that got Joan in trouble.

The car pulled up in front of Melody's building. She said thank you and good night as she got out of the car. Adam waved to her as the car pulled away.

Melody felt sorry for Joan and Adam, especially since they were fighting with each other. She was glad that she and Joan had a nice time walking to the beach together. But they still hadn't talked about Joan's problem with her parents. As Melody climbed the outside stairs to her apartment, she wondered if, in the end, Joan's lying and the fight between Adam and Joan could keep her from being friends with either of them. *My friendships in Miami weren't so complicated,* she thought. *Maybe I should have gone to Miami this weekend, after all.*

SEAVIEW TERRACE. SUNDAY 6:00 P.M.

Alexis was sitting in front of the television set, watching a women's pro basketball game, when the phone rang. As she ran around the apartment looking for the portable phone, she hoped that Emily was calling to invite her over. If I sleep over at Emily's, she thought, maybe I can ask her if she has a crush on Jake. Even if I don't like the answer, at least I'll know the truth. She found the phone under a dish towel on the kitchen counter. But the caller wasn't Emily. It was her father. "I'm still at the office," he told her. "I have to finish a brief for court tomorrow. I'm sorry I've been so busy this weekend, Lexi."

"I know," she said.

"Why don't you meet me at Bulldog Café in an hour?" he suggested. "We can have dinner together."

I wanted to go to Emily's, thought Alexis. But only if she wants to see me, too. What if she's at the café on a date with Jake or something? I'd be so embarrassed. "Can we go to Joe's Fish Shack instead?" Alexis suggested to her father.

"Actually, I need to talk to the Grangers about this case I'm arguing in court tomorrow," he said. "I thought you'd love to go to the café, Lexi. You can see Emily."

"She might not be there," Alexis told him. "But okay. We can go."

"I'll meet you there at seven," her father said. "If I'm not there by seven-fifteen order for yourself, and I'll be right along. 'Bye."

After Alexis hung up she stood in the kitchen staring at the phone. For the first time in her life she *didn't* want to go to The Manor Hotel.

DOLPHIN COURT APARTMENTS.
SUNDAY 6:30 P.M.

Melody went on-line to check her e-mail. There were three messages. The first was from her father. The second was from Tina. And the last one was from JuanR@kl.com. She double-clicked on the last message and read:

> Hey, girl, where were you? Big T said you were going to the dance. What's with this moving away business? The word is that there is nothing happening where you are. You missed a way cool dance. Next chance you get to come east, do it. These guys I know are planning a poetry slam that will be where it is all going to happen. I'll be doing my poetry. Juan

Melody read the message from Juan three times. It didn't surprise her that he was going to perform. She'd heard his poetry at a poetry slam that she and Tina went to in June, and he was good. She could still picture Juan, with his close-cropped black hair, dark eyes, and cool attitude, rapping his rhymes. She remembered that he said he liked her poetry. But she never thought he'd send her e-mail or want to dance with her.

Why couldn't this have happened when I was still in Miami? she asked herself. Maybe I wasn't ready for a boyfriend last year, anyway. Am I now? she wondered.

She closed the e-mail from Juan and opened the one from Tina.

> Hey, Max. You missed an incredible time, sister. I mean, guess who asked where you were and acted like he was way interested in you? Yes. Juan. Not that he didn't dance with anyone else, you understand. He was out there moving with the beat, against the beat, making up his own beat. And once — this is so very cool — he rapped his poetry using the dj's mike. He is not shy! I'd die before I could do that. Remember how embarrassed I was just reading my rhymes at that poetry slam? I danced so much that I can hardly walk today. Of course my new crush, Tony Jackson, was looking elsewhere. How was your beach party? How many times did you

get dunked? Man, what a trade-off — being dunked when you could have been dancing with Juan and seeing your old friends. Have you lost your mind? That Darryl guy must hold strings around your heart. Or is it Adam this week? Or Jake? Love ya. Come soon. Write back. Big T.

PS: I gave your e-mail address to Juan. Hope you don't mind. Like any girl in her right mind wouldn't want to have Juan on-line. Luv.
Big T :-)

Did Juan really ask for my e-mail address? Melody wondered. Or was it Tina's idea to give it to him? That was just the sort of thing Tina would do. She might have told Juan, "Melody said she wanted you to write to her. Here's her e-mail address."

I bet that's just what happened, Melody concluded.

Melody closed Tina's message and opened up her father's. In it he told her how he spent the weekend, asked her if the beach party was a success, and said that he loved and missed her.

I miss you too, Dad, Melody thought as she shut down her e-mail program. But she wouldn't write back to anyone tonight. There was too much to think about.

BULLDOG CAFÉ. SUNDAY 7:00 P.M.

Emily and Lily sat at a big table near the street. Lily was drawing with crayons on the paper table covering. Emily watched Jake clearing a table at the other end of the café terrace. She remembered when he was in third grade and said that someday he would work at the café. Now he did. She wondered if he was still upset about the fire. Had he talked to his grandparents about it?

"Jake," Lily shouted. "I made you a picture. Come see."

People at nearby tables smiled in Lily's direction, and Jake signaled her that he'd be there in a minute.

"May I see?" Emily asked Lily.

Lily covered the drawing with her arms. "Jake has to see it first," she said. "It's his picture."

When Jake came over to their table Lily smiled up at him and moved her arms away.

"Nice," he said. "I love birds. Are you going to color in the sky?"

"Okay," Lily agreed. She picked a blue crayon out of the plastic cup on the table and went back to work. Meanwhile, Jake came over to Emily's side of the table and leaned over. "Can we talk later?" he asked. "I get off at nine."

"Sure," she answered.

"Meet me behind the hotel," he said. "Near the swings. Okay?"

She nodded.

At that moment, Alexis walked into the café and saw Emily and Jake with their heads together, whispering.

Lily spotted her and shouted, "Lexi, Lexi."

Jake straightened up, and Emily looked in her direction. Alexis could tell she had interrupted a private moment between them. Emily motioned her to come over, and Jake waved before going back to his station.

"I'm meeting my father here for supper," Alexis explained when she reached Emily. "He needs to talk to your parents about some case he's working on."

"Lexi, I made a picture for Jake," Lily told her. "Want to see?"

Lily's brightly colored drawing reminded Alexis of the drawings she and Emily used to do on the café's paper table coverings. One summer day between first and second grade, they'd drawn bouquets of flowers in the middle of every table. When Mr. Granger saw their centerpieces he told them they could do it anytime they wanted. But it had taken them so long to do that they never did it again.

"Remember when we drew flowers in the middle of all the tables?" Emily asked Alexis. "It took us hours to finish."

"Yeah," Alexis said. She didn't tell Emily that she'd been thinking the same thing. "Did you make a lot of money at the beach party?" Alexis asked.

"We did great," Emily told her. "Thanks for helping. We can definitely go to Miami."

"Sit next to me," Lily told Alexis. "I'm having a grilled cheese sandwich and chocolate milk."

Alexis saw her father's convertible pulling up to the curb. He hopped out and walked onto the café deck. People at three tables said hi to him before he reached her. Alexis loved that her father was always so full of life and had a zillion friends. She wished she was more like him and less like her shy mother. Her mother was always so lonely. But her father was always having fun.

Mr. Lewis greeted Emily and Lily. "So where's your dad, Emily?" he asked.

"Right behind you," Emily said with a giggle.

Alexis's father turned around and saw Mr. Granger coming toward him.

"I'm on a break from the front desk," Mr. Granger said as the two men greeted each other. "I'll eat with you."

"Perfect," Mr. Lewis said. "There's something I need to ask you."

Alexis sat between Emily and Lily, and the two men sat side by side. After they all placed their food orders, the men talked business. Alexis looked around the table. She couldn't count the number of times she'd eaten at the café with Emily and other members of the Granger family. She always loved it, especially on Sunday nights when she slept over and she and Emily went to school together on Monday morning.

Emily took a purple crayon out of the plastic glass and made a tic-tac-toe grid on the table covering. Alexis took a red crayon and made the first X. They showed Lily how to play and played with her until the food came.

Alexis had her favorite, spaghetti with meat sauce. She was surprised that Emily didn't have the same thing. That was always what they had on Sunday nights. Instead, Emily ordered grilled chicken breast and salad.

"How's the cheering going?" Alexis's father asked Emily.

"Great," Emily said. She told him about the Sam Paetro clinic and how a little correction made all the difference with her jumps. "I was the worst jumper on the squad before that," she concluded.

Alexis was shocked to learn that Emily didn't think she was a good cheerleader. Why didn't she tell me? wondered Alexis.

"So, who wants dessert?" the waiter asked. He looked from Emily to Alexis. "I bet you two are splitting a brownie à la mode."

Alexis smiled at Emily. They'd had that dessert so often that all the waiters knew it.

"Not for me," Emily said.

"We always — " Alexis began to say.

"I'm pretty full," Emily said, interrupting her.

"I'll split it with you, Lexi," her father offered. "One brownie à la mode," he told the waiter. "Two spoons."

"Are you on a diet?" Alexis whispered to Emily.

"Sort of," Emily answered. "Don't tell anybody."

But why didn't she tell me? Alexis wondered. What else is going on with Emily that I don't know?

Later, as Jake was clearing away the dessert dishes, Mr. Granger asked Alexis, "You staying over with us tonight?"

"That's like asking if the desert is dry," Alexis's father said with a laugh. "Has she ever had dinner here on a Sunday night and *not* stayed over?"

"I don't when I'm at Mom's," Alexis told him.

"I meant when you're with me, honey," her father said.

Alexis was waiting for Emily to say that she

wanted her to stay over. But Emily was playing another game of tic-tac-toe with Lily and ignoring the conversation. Alexis could still read Emily's mind well enough to know that she didn't want her to stay. And that the reason had something to do with Jake.

Finally, Emily looked up and asked, "Can you stay?"

"I can't," Alexis answered. "I have some stuff to do at home. At Dad's."

Her father stood up. "Well, then, we'll be off," he said.

"Please stay, Lexi," Lily begged.

"Not tonight," she told Lily.

I would have stayed if Emily had asked me again, Alexis thought as she left the café.

" 'Bye, Alexis," Emily called after her. "See you at school tomorrow."

Alexis pretended she didn't hear.

DELHAVEN DRIVE 8:30 P.M.

Joan couldn't concentrate on her homework. All she could think about was how to get her parents to let her go to Miami for the CHEER USA regionals. She knew if she said there was a regional competition in cheering, her parents would ask lots of questions like, What is so hard about cheering that you would have competitions? Why would people from all over south

Florida go to Miami to compete in cheering?

Joan looked down at her math homework. The numbers swam in front of her. She felt unhappy and nervous. There was only one thing in the world that would make her feel better and calm her down. She ran downstairs and into the living room.

Her mother was reading, and her father was doing some paperwork. He looked up when she came into the room.

"May I play the piano?" she asked.

"Of course," he answered.

She sat on the piano bench, uncovered the keyboard, and struck the first notes of her favorite piece by Beethoven. She played so fast and so hard that she was sweating when she finished. The last note was reverberating around the room when she looked up and saw her parents staring at her.

Adam burst into the room. "Wow!" he exclaimed. "That was incredible."

"Powerful," her father said.

"Intense," added her mother. "What will you play next?"

Joan stood up and closed the cover over the keyboard. "That's all I wanted to play," she said. "I still have homework to do."

She walked past her brother and out of the room. She felt much better.

THE MANOR HOTEL 9:05 P.M.

Emily sat on a sling swing in the hotel playground and waited for Jake. It's just as well Alexis didn't stay over, she thought. I promised Jake I wouldn't tell anyone how the fire at the beach upset him. Even Alexis. There were a lot of things she hadn't been telling Alexis lately. Alexis didn't know that she'd gone on a crash diet. Or that she'd been worried about being able to improve as a cheerleader. I guess I don't talk to her because we're hardly ever alone together, thought Emily.

She looked up and saw Jake coming toward her under the row of lamps behind the hotel. When he reached her, he said hi and sat on the next swing. He pushed himself gently back and forth by pressing his right foot on the sand. She did the same. For a minute neither of them spoke.

Jake finally broke the silence by saying, "I talked to my grandmother. About the fire. She told me everything that happened that night."

He kicked the sand with the toe of his sneaker.

"What did she say?" Emily asked.

Jake let out a deep breath. "I was sleeping downstairs," he started. "That's where my room was. My sister's room was right next to my parents' room. On the second floor. At around one in the morning, neighbors saw flames shooting out of my sister's window. It was open, and the curtains were on fire. A woman called the fire department while her husband ran over to our house. He had to break a window to get in. The house was filled with smoke, and flames were coming down the stairs. He heard me coughing in my room and went to get me out. By the time the fire department arrived, flames were coming out of the roof. It was too late to save my parents and sister. I was in the hospital overnight. The next day my grandparents had to tell me that my mother, father, and sister were dead. My grandmother said it was the hardest thing she ever did."

Jake and Emily didn't move or speak for a while.

"What caused the fire?" Emily quietly asked.

"It was an old house, and my father was trying to fix it up himself," Jake explained. "The wiring must have been pretty bad. And there were lots of chemicals, for taking off old paint and stuff. They said the wiring started the fire, and because of the chemicals it spread really fast."

Jake was speaking so softly that Emily had to lean forward to hear him.

"Do you know when my grandmother started to cry?" he asked.

"When?" asked Emily.

"When I said I used to think I could have saved everybody. That it was my fault they died," he answered.

"She really loves you," Emily said.

"She said I look just like my father did when he was my age," Jake added. "He played basketball. And after college he worked for a newspaper."

"Just like you," said Emily.

Jake stood up and faced Emily. He grabbed the chains of the swing and pushed her a little. "Anyway, Em, I wouldn't have talked to her if you hadn't told me to."

"You're glad you did?" Emily asked.

He nodded. "Yup. So thanks."

Emily stood up and looked up at him. "You're getting so tall," she said.

"You'll catch up," he said.

They walked through the playground. "You always say that about my catching up," she reminded him. "I used to believe you. But the truth is, I'm going to be short like my mother, and you're going to be tall."

"Like my father," he said.

They reached the driveway and stopped. "I guess it's good you're tall, for basketball," Emily remarked. "You've scored the most points at every game."

"The game on Tuesday will be tough," he told her. "The Cougars are out to get us."

"Are they any good?" Emily asked.

"Too good," he said. "They must have kept a bunch of ninth-graders back just so they could beat us."

"They did?" Emily exclaimed. "Who told you that?"

"No one," he admitted. "But the Cougars are awesome. My grandfather went to one of their games to spy for us."

"You guys are good, too, Jake," Emily said. "And you've been playing great. Your shooting from the foul line is practically perfect."

"Thanks to Alexis," Jake said.

"She loves basketball," Emily commented. "I guess she likes working on the paper, too."

"She's a good writer," Jake said. He looked around. "I thought maybe she'd stay over with you tonight."

"You said you wanted to talk to me," Emily told him. "So I didn't really invite her."

"I could have told you another time," he said. "I mean, if you wanted to have Alexis over." He gave her a little punch on the arm. "Thanks again. See you in school tomorrow."

Jake walked toward the backyard that separated his grandparents' house from the hotel parking lot. Emily walked slowly back to the hotel. She turned once to look back at Jake and saw him do a jump shot toward his basketball hoop with an imaginary basketball.

Will he tell Alexis about the fire, too? she wondered.

SEAVIEW APARTMENTS 9:30 P.M.

Alexis's suitcase was packed for a Mom week, and she'd done her homework. She peered around her room, not knowing what to do next. She wished her father would keep her company, that they'd watch a basketball game together on TV or some silly comedy show. But he was in his room working on his court case for the next day. When he finished he'd probably talk on the phone with one of his girlfriends. Alexis thought of watching television, but she didn't feel like doing it alone.

"I'm always alone," she whispered to herself. Tears sprung to her eyes as she thought, I sound just like my mother.

The phone rang, but Alexis didn't bother to answer it. Now that Emily and I aren't best friends, she thought, it's never for me. The only person who calls me is Mom, to complain about being alone when I'm here at Dad's.

Seconds later her father yelled, "Lexi, pick up. It's for you."

Alexis picked up the phone on her desk and said, "Hi, Mom."

"Hi," said a surprised male voice on the other end. It was Jake.

"Hi," she said. "Sorry. I thought it was my mother."

"I called to thank you for helping with the barbecue last night," he said. "I meant to tell you at the café, but it was so busy, I sort of forgot."

"That's okay," she said. "It was fun. And they made a lot of money."

"I'm sorry I disappeared on you after the fire," Jake continued. "I, uh, needed to get away for a few minutes. Guess it ended up being longer than a few minutes."

Alexis pictured Jake and Emily swimming in the moonlight together and walking along the beach hand in hand.

"That's okay," she said. "We had enough people working the grill."

"Thanks, Alexis," Jake said. "You're a good sport. So. I'll see you in school tomorrow."

As soon as Alexis hung up the phone it rang again. This time it was Emily, asking about the English homework.

"I waited until the last minute," she told Alexis. "It's been so busy with the beach party and everything."

"English homework?" Alexis exclaimed. "I totally forgot about it!"

"We have to answer those questions about that poem with the two roads," Emily reminded her.

"By Robert Winter," Alexis added.

"His name is Robert Frost," giggled Emily. "You want to do the questions together?"

"Sure," agreed Alexis. We're going to do our homework together over the phone, she thought. Just like we always did.

They were halfway through the questions when Emily said, "I'm sorry you couldn't sleep over tonight. Can you tomorrow night? Then we can do all our homework together."

"It's my first night at my mom's," Alexis said. "She never lets me on Mondays."

"Right," said Emily. "I forgot about that. How about Tuesday? After the Cougar game."

"Maybe she'll let me then," Alexis said. "Tuesday's perfect."

Alexis smiled at her reflection in the bureau mirror. She was having a sleepover at Emily's.

CMS GYM. TUESDAY 4:30 P.M.

The score at halftime was Cougars 43, Bulldogs 30. Alexis sat on the front bleacher with Adam and some other eighth-graders. "This is one tough game," Adam said as the two teams left the court for the locker rooms.

"The Cougars are awfully good," commented Alexis. "Number fourteen looks like he's more than six feet tall." She wrote in her reporter's notebook, *overpowered by height of #14*.

"It's hard to believe he's only a ninth-grader," she told Adam.

"Maybe he's an old ninth-grader," suggested Adam.

The music for the halftime cheer began, and the CMS cheerleaders ran onto the court. Alexis sat back to enjoy the show. She watched Melody do a round-off back handspring while Joan and Sally were thrown up in basket tosses. "Your sister is amazing," she told Adam.

Adam hadn't been watching his sister. His eyes were on Melody. She was doing another back handspring. It was perfect.

Alexis checked out Emily's jumps to see if she really had improved. "Emily's jumps are getting so high," she said, mostly to herself. Alexis remembered all the hours she and Emily had practiced cheering over the summer. Now Emily was on the squad, and she was good, very good.

When the halftime cheer was over, Alexis told Adam, "They get better every time I see them. I can't wait until they go to Miami. I bet they place."

Miami, thought Adam. How will Joan lie herself into permission for that trip? And even if she managed to go to Miami, if the squad placed in the regionals, everyone in town would be talking about how they won and how good their stunts were. Joan couldn't keep their parents from knowing she was a flyer forever. He felt angry at his sister, but he also felt sorry for her. The longer she lied, the harder it would be for her when the truth came out.

In the first minutes of the third quarter, the Cougars' number fourteen fouled Jake. Alexis held her breath while Jake took his first try from the foul line. Take your time, she thought. Arc it. The ball swished through the net as Alexis let out her breath. He made his second foul shot, too. And later in the quarter he made a brilliant three-point shot while being double-teamed. He's really good, she thought. But is our team good enough to beat the Cougars today?

They weren't.

The final score was Cougars 57, Bulldogs 48.

The Cougar fans went crazy.

"Too bad," Melody said to Emily.

"The Cougars played better than we did today," Emily admitted. "But I hate it when we lose." She watched Jake shake hands with the Cougars' number fourteen. Jake played a great game, she thought. I hope he knows it. She was still watching Jake when Alexis came up beside her.

"Too bad we lost," Alexis said.

"Yeah," agreed Emily. "But they still played great. We'll beat them next time."

"Meet you out front?" Alexis asked.

Emily nodded. "I'll get my bag and be right there."

Alexis closed her reporter's notebook and put it in her pocket. She hoped that Jake would hang out at Emily's tonight. She wanted to talk to him about the game.

DOLPHIN COURT APARTMENTS 8:00 P.M.

Melody decided to swim a couple more lengths of the pool before stopping. It felt great to stretch her body after all the tension and excitement of the game.

She switched from the breaststroke to the crawl and thought about the game. Even though they'd lost, it had been an exciting game and she loved performing the halftime cheer. Sports at Claymore were really terrific.

She turned at the end of the pool and headed back the other way. She thought about the friends she was making at Claymore. She liked

Alexis and Emily a lot and was getting along great with both of them. At first she'd thought she and Sally might be friends, too, but now she realized that Sally wasn't the type who'd be good friends with an underclassman.

She reached the edge of the pool and flipped herself to swim the next lap underwater. She'd thought Joan and Adam would both be her friends and they'd all hang out together. But Joan's lying was changing everything. The more Melody thought about Joan's situation at home, the sorrier she felt for her. What would I do if I were in her place? Melody wondered.

Melody pulled herself out of the pool. Make new friends but keep the old, she reminded herself. She threw her towel over her shoulder and walked toward her apartment. I'll e-mail all my old friends in Miami tonight, she thought. I'll tell them all about the beach party and being dunked and that I'll be in Miami for the CHEER USA regionals. That's not so far away.

Maybe I'll even write to Juan.

DELHAVEN DRIVE 8:15 P.M.

Joan was reviewing her history homework when a solution to her Miami problem popped into her head. Melody was from Miami. She'd tell her parents that Melody invited her to go to Miami for a weekend. My father likes Melody,

Joan thought. If I'm really good and don't slip up with piano and grades. If I act nicer at home. If Adam doesn't rat on me. If all that happens, I might be able to go to Miami before my parents find out the truth and make me quit cheering.

She was glad that Melody hadn't lectured her about lying. And Adam wasn't saying anything about it anymore, either. I don't need anyone to tell me lying is wrong, she thought. I know.

A knock on her door interrupted her thoughts. "Who?" she called out.

"Me," Adam answered.

"Come in," she said.

Adam opened the door and took a few steps into the room. "You guys put on a great party," he said.

"Thanks," she said with a little smile.

"I just want to say I think you're a sensational cheerleader. And I know you're in a terrible spot with Mother and Father," he added. "That's all."

He left the room before she could say anything. So he didn't see her smile crumble and the tears come into her eyes.

THE MANOR HOTEL 8:30 P.M.

Alexis sat at Emily's desk and Emily sat on the floor with her back against the bed. They'd been working on their homework for an hour.

"Did you do number fifteen?" Alexis asked.

"I just finished it," Emily told her. "The answer I came up with is five thousand."

"That's what I got, too," Alexis commented.

They both went back to work.

"Why do teachers give us so much homework on Tuesdays when they know everybody goes to the basketball game?" grumbled Emily. "They have no school spirit."

"Good point," Alexis agreed. She closed her math book and took out her reporter's notebook to work on her write-up of the game. She had a couple of questions she wanted to ask Jake. She'd hoped he'd be at the café after the game, but he wasn't. Alexis looked out the window at the back of Jake's house. She remembered the day a few years ago when the three of them tried using walkie-talkies between Emily's room and Jake's. They'd finally decided that shouting out the windows or using the telephone was a whole lot easier. She noticed there weren't any lights on in his room. Maybe he's in the café right now, she thought. "You hungry?" she asked Emily.

"I'm still full from supper," Emily answered. "But I'd have a lemonade. You hungry?"

"Not really," Alexis said. "But let's take a break and go downstairs."

They took the elevator to the lobby and

walked out to the café. Alexis scanned the crowded deck but didn't see Jake. Is Emily looking for him, too? she wondered.

As they walked toward the bar to get lemonade, Alexis noticed a group of ninth-graders walking on the other side of the street. Darryl and Sally walked hand in hand a few steps ahead of the others. Five more ninth-grade basketball players and cheerleaders followed. One of them was Jake, walking between Mae and C.J. They were laughing and talking. Jake's a ninth-grader, thought Alexis, so of course he's with other ninth-graders. She was glad she hadn't told Emily she had a crush on him.

In a few minutes the two girls were back in Emily's room with their drinks. They sat on the twin beds and faced each other.

Maybe now Emily and I can get back our old friendship and start sharing secrets again, she thought. Just not secrets about Jake.

"Emily, I didn't know you went on a diet," Alexis said.

"I didn't tell anyone," Emily said. "Except Sally knew. It was a little crazy. I wasn't eating right. Actually, it was really stupid. I even fainted."

"You fainted? Alexis said. "Why didn't you tell me?"

"I was sort of embarrassed about it," Emily told her.

"You shouldn't have been embarrassed," Alexis said.

"But I should have told you," Emily continued. "I'm not really on a diet anymore. I just don't eat as much as I used to, especially fattening foods. It's no big deal."

"How come you went on a diet in the first place?" Alexis asked. "You're not fat."

Emily told Alexis the whole story of how she mixed up uniforms with Melody and thought she'd gained weight. They talked about it for a long time.

"How's your mom been lately?" Emily asked.

"The same," Alexis said. "She didn't want me to sleep over tonight because she'd be alone. But she gave in."

"I'm glad," Emily said.

"I finished my homework," Alexis said. "Did you?"

"Yeah," Emily said. "Finally."

"Middle school is different," Alexis said. "I mean, I knew it would be different, but it's different in different ways than I thought it'd be different."

"Like going to the different classrooms is not such big deal," said Emily.

“Right,” agreed Alexis.

“I’m glad you stayed over,” Emily said.

“I was just thinking the same thing,” Alexis said softly.

Neither of them said anything for a few seconds.

“You tired?” Alexis asked.

“Yeah,” said Emily. “Let’s get ready for bed but still talk.”

“I bet you fall asleep first,” Alexis said as she went to Emily’s closet to get the pajamas she always kept there.

“I bet I do, too,” Emily said. “I’ve been working so hard at cheering.”

“You looked great out there today,” Alexis told her.

“Thanks,” Emily said. “It’s hard, but I really love it.”

In a few minutes they were in bed. The only light in the room was the reflected light from the street. Alexis turned on her side and faced Emily. “That beach party was really great,” she said. “Too bad about the fire.”

“At least no one was hurt,” said Emily. She yawned. “I’m so tired. I think I have to go to sleep.”

“Okay,” Alexis said. “ ’Night.”

Alexis turned on her side and stared out the window over Emily’s desk. She couldn’t see

Jake's house from the bed, only a starlit sky. Being in middle school is changing everything, she thought, but some changes were okay.

Emily turned toward the wall. She was glad that Alexis was there. She stared at the familiar striped wallpaper and remembered how great it was to do the halftime cheer. It was so wonderful to finally get better at cheering. But, she thought as she closed her eyes, I have a long way to go before the regionals in Miami.

We've Got Spirit!

For Martha Shankman—
a woman with great spirit!

CLAYMORE, FLORIDA.
THE MANOR HOTEL. FRIDAY 7:50 A.M.

Emily Granger glanced at her watch before leaning over to tie her sneakers. Only one more day of school, one more cheer practice, one more night's sleep in Claymore and she would be on a bus heading for the CHEER USA Regionals in Miami. Tomorrow the Claymore Middle School cheerleaders would be competing with middle school cheer squads from all over South Florida.

"I hope we get enough points to go to the Nationals," Emily told the Grangers' bulldog, Bubba IV. Bubba moved his tail but didn't bother to open his eyes.

The door to Emily's room suddenly flung open and Lily, Emily's four-year-old sister, ran in, shouting, "I can go. I can go."

Bubba got up and waddled over to Lily.

"Go where?" asked Emily.

"To Miami with Mommy," answered Lily. She squatted down and flung her arms around Bubba's neck. "Bubba, too."

"Did Mom say?" asked Emily.

"Yup," answered Lily. She ran out of the room as fast as she'd come in.

Bubba followed Lily to the doorway and plopped down again. Emily smiled to herself. Yesterday her mother hadn't been sure if she could go to Miami. The Grangers owned a hotel with a restaurant and café, so Emily's mother was busy, especially on the weekends. But last night she told Emily she would be able to go to Miami after all.

Emily leaned over and patted Bubba. She loved that her bulldog was the school mascot. There had been a Granger bulldog as the CMS mascot ever since her father had been a student there. Her whole family was involved in CMS sports. Her father and brother had been big-deal football and basketball players, and her mother had been co-captain of the cheer squad. So had Emily's older sister, Lynn. Now Lynn was on the Claymore High School cheer squad and they were going to the Regionals, too. The high school's squad had been to the Regionals before. But this was the first year that the middle school cheerleaders were going to the CHEER USA competitions.

Emily looked around her room and saw that the notebook and books that she'd used for last night's homework were still scattered across her desk. She was stuffing them in her backpack when Lynn came in.

"Emily, did you take my silver earrings?" her older sister asked.

Emily glanced over her shoulder at Lynn.

“ ’Course not,” she said. “You never let me wear them.”

“I wonder where they are, then?” Lynn muttered, more to herself than to Emily.

“Mom and Lily are coming to the Regionals,” Emily told her excitedly.

“I know,” said Lynn. “You nervous?”

“Yeah,” admitted Emily.

“Me, too,” said Lynn. “It’s entirely normal.”

Emily was glad that her sister was also nervous, but she knew Lynn couldn’t be as nervous about the Regionals as she was. If I were as good a cheerleader as Lynn, I wouldn’t be so scared, either, thought Emily. Lynn was so good that Coach Cortes had asked her to be an assistant coach for the last three middle school practices before Regionals.

“I guess I better tell the rest of your squad that it’s normal to be jittery,” Lynn said.

“I guess,” agreed Emily as she zipped closed her backpack.

“Yesterday you were wobbly getting Mae up in the extension,” Lynn said. “We’ll work on that today.”

“Okay,” said Emily.

Emily remembered how they’d almost dropped Mae at practice the day before. What if that happens at the Regionals? she thought.

What if it’s my fault?

DOLPHIN COURT APARTMENTS 8:00 A.M.

Melody Max stood in front of the mirror and tied a red-and-black beaded choker around her neck. Her best friend, Tina, had given it to her the night before Melody moved to Claymore. One of the worst things about leaving Miami was leaving Tina and her other Miami friends.

Melody remembered how upset she'd been when her parents told her that she and her mother would be moving to Claymore. It had been a summer of upsetting surprises. First the divorce, then moving to Claymore. Her mother explained that she'd been offered a job as editor of the *Claymore News*. "I'd never have an opportunity like this on a big-city paper," she'd said.

"But I'm a big-city girl," Melody had protested to her parents. "I don't want to move. I love Miami."

"Living in a small town won't be as bad as you think," her mother told her.

"You'll make new friends," her father said.

"We'll always be best friends," Tina sobbed when she hugged Melody good-bye.

They'd all been right. Living in Claymore wasn't half bad. In fact, since Melody tried out for cheerleading and made new friends, it had been fun. The kids in Claymore weren't as hip as her friends back home, but they were still cool in their own way. Melody especially liked Emily and her best friend, Alexis. Alexis wasn't a cheerleader, but she wrote a sports column for the school paper, the *Bulldog Edition*, so she went to all the games.

Then there was Joan and her brother, Adam. Joan was an amazing cheerleader, an excellent pianist, and a lot of fun. Adam was in the eighth grade, but he still hung out with Joan and her friends.

Jake Feder, a ninth-grader who was editor of the *Bulldog Edition*, liked to do things with them, too. Melody figured that was because Jake lived in a house right behind The Manor Hotel and was a close friend of Emily.

Melody twisted the choker around so that the knot was at the back of her neck. But Tina's still my best friend, she thought. And I'm going to see her tomorrow. She would also see two of her other Miami friends, Tiffany and Sue, who were going to watch the Regionals and come to the pool party at Melody's father's house after the competition.

Melody's mother appeared in the doorway. She was dressed for work and was carrying a glass of orange juice in one hand and her briefcase in the other. "I have an early meeting," she told Melody. "Be sure you eat some breakfast."

"I will," Melody promised.

"You excited about going to Miami?" her mother asked.

Melody nodded. "I invited some of my Miami friends to the party," she said. "I hope it's okay."

Her mother leaned against the doorway and took a sip of juice. "Didn't your father say you could invite as many people as you wanted?" she asked.

"I mean I hope they'll all get along okay," Melody explained. "You know — my old friends and my new friends."

"They all like you," her mother said. "So they'll probably like one another."

"I guess," said Melody. She hoped her mother was right.

After her mother left, Melody went to the kitchen and flipped on the TV. In a few minutes her father would be doing the weather forecast from Miami. Melody always watched him before she went to school. It was the only way to see him every day, now that she lived on the other side of the state.

Today she had another reason for watching him. She wanted to know what the weather was going to be in Miami tomorrow, for her pool party.

SEAVIEW TERRACE 8:05 A.M.

Alexis Lewis brushed her long dark hair and studied her reflection in the mirror. She couldn't decide whether to wear her hair in a ponytail or let it fall loose. Her best friend, Emily, always said her hair looked best down, so Alexis decided to leave it that way. She studied her outfit, a blue-and-black long-sleeved T-shirt and dark jeans. She'd wanted to wear her red shirt with the V-neck, but that was at her mother's. One of the worst things about living one week with her father and the next with her mother was keeping track of her clothes.

Alexis's parents had been divorced for so long that Alexis couldn't even remember what it was like living with both of them. Some kids thought it was interesting to have two bedrooms and two families. But having your stuff in two bedrooms is confusing, thought Alexis, and it doesn't feel like a family when you live with only one parent at a time. More than anything, Alexis wanted to be a member of a big family — like Emily's. Mr. and Mrs. Granger seemed really happy together and Emily had great siblings. Sometimes, when Alexis stayed over with Emily, she'd think how wonderful it would be if she and Emily were sisters and she could be part of the Granger family, too.

But this weekend she wouldn't be having a

sleepover at Emily's or even hanging out with her. Emily, Melody, and Joan were all going to Miami for the Regionals and staying overnight at Melody's father's house. I'd love to go to the Regionals, too, thought Alexis. It would be so much fun, and it would help me with my article for the school paper. Even though she wasn't going, Alexis planned on writing about the event. She'd interview the squad when they got back and there would be a videotape she could watch. But that's not the same as being there, Alexis thought. A good sportswriter is always on the scene.

Alexis wondered what Jake would be doing all weekend. Would she at least get to see *him*? Maybe I'll drop by the Bulldog Café on Saturday, she thought. Maybe he'll be working at his busboy job.

No, she decided, I can't go there if Emily's not around.

DELHAVEN DRIVE 8:10 A.M.

Joan Russo-Chazen had been ready for school for an hour and was packing her suitcase for the big weekend in Miami. She'd already packed jeans, a pair of shorts, some T-shirts, a pair of pajamas, a dress, and her bathing suit. Joan couldn't believe her good luck. She really was going to Miami and the

CHEER USA Regionals. Her strict parents were allowing her to go to Miami with Melody for the weekend. Of course, they had no idea that she was going to be in a cheerleading competition while she was there. They thought she was just going to spend the weekend at Melody's dad's place. *Well, at least that part is true,* she reminded herself.

Her brother, Adam, had advised her to come clean and tell their parents about the competition.

"I can't," she protested. "They'll ask me lots of questions. They might find out that cheering involves gymnastics and that I'm a flyer. They'd never let me go."

"The longer you wait to tell them, the worse it's going to be," Adam said. "They're bound to find out, sooner or later."

"But at least not before the Regionals," Joan countered.

Adam was right. Someday her parents would find out and she'd have to quit cheering.

It's so unfair, Joan thought as she closed her suitcase. *I do everything else my parents want. I get good grades and practice the piano. I love playing the piano. But I love cheering, too — especially the tumbling part.* Why did she have to have parents who didn't approve of something that she loved so much?

"Joanie, come eat your breakfast!" her father called from downstairs.

"I'm coming!" Joan yelled back.

Going down the stairs, she heard the phone ring. What if it was one of the other cheerleaders who didn't know about the problem with her parents? What if they said something to her mother or father about the Regionals? She ran the rest of the way to the kitchen but slowed down when she saw that Adam had answered the phone. Her father was reading the newspaper and eating toast, and her mother was looking over notes for classes she taught in Russian and German at the university in Fort Myers. As Joan poured herself a glass of milk she listened carefully to what Adam was saying on the phone. "Yeah," he told the caller. "We'll talk about it at school, okay? See you then."

Adam hung up the phone and took his place at the table.

"Who was that?" his father asked.

"A kid from school," Adam answered.

"A *kid*," said his father. "Is he a baby goat?"

"A guy, I mean, a *boy* from school," answered Adam.

His mother looked up from her papers and asked, "What did he want?"

Adam shot Joan a nervous glance before answering. "He was calling about some history homework," he said. "I told him I'd see him at school."

"Is he a good student?" asked his mother.

"A very good student," Adam answered. "We talk about history homework a lot. It's interesting."

Joan knew from the look Adam had given her and from the way he had talked on the phone that he was lying. Whoever had called him hadn't asked about homework at all. Adam just lied to Mother and Father, thought Joan. But why?

"The word *kid* is slang for a young person," Mr. Chazen told Adam. "Try to avoid the use of slang. Respect language."

Adam, who was eating a spoonful of cereal, mumbled an okay.

"Don't speak with your mouth full," his mother and father said in unison.

And don't watch TV, thought Joan. *Don't listen to popular music. Don't wear hip clothes. Don't do gymnastics or any sport that might be even a little dangerous. And never, ever lie.* The never-lying thing was a Russo-Chazen household rule that Joan used to respect. She never used to lie. Not until she wanted to be a cheerleader.

But why was Adam lying?

MAIN STREET 8:20 A.M.

Alexis was waiting for Emily in front of the Squeeze juice bar when she saw Jake riding toward her on his bike. He waved and slowed down as he got closer. He is so cute, Alexis thought. She felt her face redden. She hated that she blushed so easily.

"Hi," he said, stopping beside her. "How'd you like to go to the Regionals?"

"I'd love to," answered Alexis. "But I don't have a ride."

"Now you do," Jake told her. "My grandmother's going. She wants to see the high school squad perform — and the CMS cheerleaders, especially Emily."

"Great!" exclaimed Alexis. "That'd be so great."

A three-hour ride to Miami — and then sitting with Jake at the competitions! She knew she was blushing for sure now.

"Being there will help you with your article," Jake said.

"I know," agreed Alexis.

"But let's not tell Emily," Jake suggested, "so we can surprise her."

"Okay," agreed Alexis. Over Jake's shoulder she saw Emily walking quickly toward them. "Here she comes," she warned.

"I've got to find Adam," Jake said, hopping on

his bike. "I invited him, too. But he didn't say if he'd come or not. I guess he had to ask his parents."

Watching Jake ride away, Emily wondered what he'd stopped to talk to Alexis about. She figured since Jake was editor of the *Bulldog Edition* and Alexis wrote a sports column, it probably had something to do with the school paper.

Jake Feder was Emily's oldest friend. She'd met him when he moved in with his grandparents in the house behind The Manor Hotel, when he was five and she was three. Emily was too young then to understand about the tragedy — that Jake's parents and his three-year-old sister, Anna, had just died in a fire. "You sort of took Anna's place for him," Jake's grandmother once told Emily. "It was a lovely thing for all of us that you two became friends."

And we always *will* be, thought Emily.

When she reached Alexis she said, "Your hair looks great today."

"Thanks," said Alexis.

"We'd better hurry or we'll be late," Emily warned.

"You must be excited about the Regionals tomorrow," Alexis said as she fell in step with Emily.

"I'm really nervous," admitted Emily. "I'm so afraid I'll drop Mae or something."

"You'll be fine," Alexis assured her. "You're getting so good at cheering."

"I wish you were going to be there," said Emily.

Alexis tried not to smile. That might give away the secret. She pulled a sad face and used a forlorn tone when she told Emily, "Me, too."

CLAYMORE MIDDLE SCHOOL COURTYARD 8:25 A.M.

Sally Johnson, co-captain of the CMS cheer squad, stood in the center of a group of her cheerleaders. They were looking to her for leadership. The closer they got to the day of the Regionals the more nervous everyone was. When Coach Cortes took over last year, she told the girls she intended to create a squad that could place at the Regionals in Miami and go to the top CHEER USA competition in the country — the Nationals at Madison Square Garden in New York City. Sally knew that the CMS squad this year was better than last year's squad. There were some terrific new cheerleaders, especially Joan Russo-Chazen, who was a super flyer. Sally knew that her squad was good. But were they good *enough*?

Sally looked around at the other anxious

cheerleaders. She suddenly realized that she wasn't that nervous about how *she* would do. She was mostly concerned that everyone else would be so nervous they'd make mistakes. But she couldn't let them know that, either. She had to keep their confidence up. "We're going all the way to the Nationals," she told the girls around her.

Sally's the best, thought Emily. She's just like my sister Lynn was when *she* was in middle school. Co-captain, the best cheerleader on the squad, the most popular, and the prettiest girl at CMS.

Just then Darryl Budd walked by the circle of cheerleaders. Darryl was the star of both the football and basketball teams, the coolest guy in the school, and Sally's boyfriend.

"Hey, Sal," he said to Sally as he passed by.

She flashed him a smile and called, "See you inside." She looked around at her cheerleaders again. Like everyone else on the squad, she desperately wanted to make enough points at the Regionals to go to the Nationals. But she had another reason for wanting to score high. She wanted her squad to do better than the Santa Rosa cheer squad. The Santa Rosa Cougars and the Claymore Bulldogs had been sports rivals for as long as anyone could remember — in football, basketball, and soccer. Now it was the cheerleaders' chance to show that Claymore was best. If the Santa Rosa cheerleaders came in fourth, Sally wanted Claymore to come in at least third; if the Cougar cheer squad came in second, she wanted the Bulldog squad to come in first. Best of all would be if her squad went to the Nationals in New York City and the Santa Rosa squad didn't place at all.

But we can only beat the Santa Rosa squad if my squad is in top form, thought Sally. We can't afford a single mistake. She looked right at Emily and said, "You and your bases have to be really careful when you put Mae up in the extension. Get her right up in one motion."

"I know," Emily said. "Lynn's going to work with us on it today."

"Great," said Sally. "Lynn's great."

Lynn is and I'm not, thought Emily.

Melody ran up to the group. "What's up?" she asked breathlessly.

"Just talking about the routine," Jessica told her.

"If we place at the Regionals," Maria said to Melody, "your party will be, like, this huge celebration."

"We *will* place," Sally assured all of them. She flashed her cheerleaders one last smile. "See you at practice."

As Sally walked away she could hear Melody

telling everyone that a few of her Miami friends would be at the party, too, and that there'd be all this great Tex-Mex food, like burritos and guacamole.

I never thought I'd be going to the party of a seventh-grader, when I'm in the ninth grade, Sally mused. It was like going backward. She hoped that Darryl and his buddy Randy would find a ride to Miami. If they came she'd make sure to get them invited to Melody's. Darryl and Randy were the best guys to have at a party. If they were there, the crowd wouldn't be so young. And the evening might even be interesting.

CMS ROOM 210 8:30 A.M.

Joan Russo-Chazen was mentally reviewing the moves for the dance portion of the cheer routine during homeroom announcements. She didn't care when the chess club and band were meeting. All she could think about was the CHEER USA Regionals. Her thoughts were interrupted by the principal's last words. "And good luck to our cheerleaders in Miami this weekend," he said. "You've been doing a splendid job for our teams at their games. Now you'll be competing in your own sport, and we want you to know we're a hundred percent behind you. By the way, someone just handed me the new issue of the *Claymore News* and the cheer squad is on the front page. What a fabulous photo! They caught your flyer midair. Again, congratulations and good luck."

Several kids turned and smiled at Joan and Kelly, who were the only cheerleaders in homeroom 210. Joan smiled back, but her heart was pounding. Who was the flyer in the newspaper photo? Lots of people took pictures of the cheerleaders when they performed at games. Some girls' parents even made videotapes. But Joan never thought that a reporter might take a picture and that it would be in the *Claymore News*. Her parents read that paper!

As soon as the bell rang signaling the end of homeroom, Joan sprang out of her seat. She had to see that photo. Kelly ran to catch up to Joan as she dashed from the room. "I hope you're the flyer in the picture," Kelly said.

"It's probably Sally," said Joan. Please let it be Sally or Mae, she prayed. Anyone but me.

"Maybe someone in the lobby will have the paper," Kelly said.

Melody came from the other direction. She exchanged a sympathetic glance with Joan. Melody was the only one of Joan's friends who knew that she'd been lying to her parents about cheering.

"Is it me in the picture?" Joan quickly whispered to Melody. "Did your mom say?"

"She didn't tell me anything about it," Melody whispered back. "I guess she wanted to surprise us."

"Do you think she'd pick out one with me flying?" asked Joan. "I mean, because she knows me."

"That's what I'm afraid of," Melody said.

Two ninth-graders passed them. Joan overheard one say to the other, "It should have been Sally's picture. Or Mae's. Not a seventh-grader's."

Joan stopped in her tracks. She was the only seventh-grade flyer. The photo must be of her. Now her brother was walking toward her. She could tell by his expression that it was true.

"Show it to Joan," someone else was saying.

An instant later Joan was staring at herself in a big front-page photo in the *Claymore News*. She was suspended midair in the toe touch basket toss.

People were congratulating her. But Joan had only one thought: How could she keep her parents from seeing the photo?

CMS SMALL GYM 4:45 P.M.

"Okay, everyone," Coach Cortes called out. "Positions for the final run-through."

The music began and Joan moved into position for the basket toss. But at the moment she hit the high point of the toss she remembered that photo. The next thing she knew she was slipping through her bases' hands and hitting the floor on her backside. She saw her bases' surprised expressions as she righted herself and moved into the next part of the routine.

What if this happens tomorrow? she thought in a panic. What if I'm not even *there* tomorrow? The music suddenly stopped.

Everyone froze, as if they were playing Statues.

"Okay, everybody," Coach said. "Normally, I'd let you keep going after a mistake like that. It's what you'd have to do tomorrow. But this is our last practice and we need to end with a clean run-through. And Joan, please keep your cool. You looked too flustered after you fell. We'll do your toss separately before we go through the entire routine again."

"Sorry," Joan said. "It was my fault." She noticed that a couple of her bases were nodding in agreement. "It happens to everybody, Joan," Lynn said. "The important thing is to make the correction."

After they worked on the basket toss, they did the routine again — from the top. This time everyone stayed focused and the run-through was perfect. Coach Cortes and Lynn applauded, and the cheerleaders smiled at one another as they ran off the floor.

"Yes!" said Maria.

"That was perfect, girls," Coach told them. "It's what I want to see at the Regionals tomorrow. Perform like that and the judges won't find reasons for taking off points. Now, all of you, come over here and listen up. Lynn is going to tell you what it's like at the Regionals — from her own experience. Then you can ask us both any last-minute questions you may have."

When all of the girls were seated in the bleachers, Lynn stood in front of them. "The first thing to expect," she began, "is to be nervous. But you should try to act calm. That way, you can help keep one another from getting more nervous. And be friendly with cheerleaders on the other squads. Don't think of it as competing against them. You're competing with yourselves — "

"— for your top score," Coach continued. "The score that will get you to the Nationals."

Lynn and Coach have got it all wrong, thought Sally. We *should* be cheering to beat the other squads, especially the Santa Rosa cheerleaders. Our basketball and football teams are always trying to beat other teams. It should be the same with cheer squads. Especially when it comes to Santa Rosa.

"Any questions?" Lynn asked.

Melody raised her hand. "Actually, it's not a question," she said. "I just want to remind everyone to bring their bathing suits. For the pool party at my dad's."

Sally looked over at Melody and thought, What a show-off. She's sitting there so proud about her house and pool in Miami. Melody better stay focused tomorrow or she'll mess up at the competition.

CMS COURTYARD 5:00 P.M.

Adam was waiting for Melody and Joan when they came out from practice. "How'd it go?" he asked.

"Okay," Melody answered. "But everyone has the jitters."

"Especially me," said Joan. "What if I can't go?"

"If I'd known my mother was running a picture of the squad," Melody explained, "I'd have made sure it wasn't one of you flying, Joan. She probably thought you'd be thrilled."

"It's not your fault," said Joan.

"Maybe you can keep your parents from seeing it," suggested Melody.

"My father always buys the paper," Joan said. "And my picture is on the front page. He's bound to see it. Then he'll make me —"

"It's on the front page of the *second* section," Melody pointed out.

"Father won't be home until dinnertime," Adam added with a little hope. "He had a meeting in Fort Myers this afternoon. Maybe he won't read the paper until tomorrow. You'll already be in Miami by then."

"They'd probably send the police after me," said Joan glumly. She looked at her watch. "I have to be home to practice piano. I'll be there when he comes in. If he has the paper, I'll hide it or something. Adam, you have to help me."

"I hate this," Adam mumbled.

Joan glared at him. She wanted to yell, "I hate it, too. Don't you know that?" But she didn't want to fight with Adam in front of Melody. Melody already knew enough about her family problems. It was all so embarrassing.

"I'll see you later," Joan said, and started running toward Main Street.

"Shouldn't we go after her?" asked Melody.

"Not when she's mad," said Adam.

"It must be awful for you, too," said Melody. "I mean, that your parents are so strict."

"Yeah," admitted Adam. "Sometimes it is. But this cheerleading thing Joan's going through is the worst."

"We need her at the Regionals tomorrow," Melody told him. "I mean, if we're missing a flyer, the whole routine will be wrecked. We might as well not even bother going if Joan can't be in it."

"I didn't think of that," said Adam.

"I bet Joan has," observed Melody.

Adam started walking a little faster. "I'll try to help," he said. "But I hate all this lying."

Melody liked that Adam cared enough about his sister to help her. But she also liked that he didn't want to lie to his parents. There was a lot about Adam Russo-Chazen that she liked. And about Joan, too.

She just wished that she could help them more.

THE MANOR HOTEL.
BULLDOG CAFÉ 5:30 P.M.

Alexis and Emily were on the café deck having smoothies. Alexis raised her glass. "Let's clink for good luck," she suggested.

Emily touched her glass to Alexis's.

"Good luck at the Regionals tomorrow," said Alexis.

"I just wish you were going to be there," said Emily. "If my mom hadn't offered to bring other mothers you could have gone with her."

"I'll see the videotape," said Alexis. "That'll be cool."

Just then Jake came onto the café deck and walked over to their table.

"You want a smoothie?" Emily asked him. "I'll make it."

"Sure," said Jake. "Thanks."

The second that Emily was gone, Jake moved his chair closer to Alexis and whispered, "Are you at your father's or your mother's this week?"

"My father's," she answered. "I called him already. He said I could go to Miami."

"Great," said Jake. "We'll pick you up at seven-thirty tomorrow morning."

"Is Adam coming?" Alexis asked. "He lives pretty close to me. We can pick him up next." She looked past Jake to be sure Emily wasn't coming back yet.

"He said he can't come," said Jake. "It was really weird. It was like he wanted to come, but he couldn't, and he didn't really give me a reason."

"I thought he'd want to see Joan cheer," said Alexis. "She's this big star."

"Exactly," agreed Jake.

"Their parents are really strict," Alexis commented. "Maybe that's why he can't come." She leaned closer to Jake and whispered, "Shhh. Here she comes."

Emily put a big smoothie in front of Jake. "Surprise!" she said. "I put a mango in it."

"I love mangoes," said Jake. "Thanks."

Alexis sat back and smiled at her two friends.

She couldn't wait until tomorrow when she and Jake would surprise Emily.

DELHAVEN DRIVE 6:10 P.M.

Joan's hour of piano practice was over, but she kept playing. She was going through all the fast, loud pieces she knew. It was the only thing she could do to calm herself down. But her nervous thoughts still chased one another. Did her father stop for groceries on the way home? If he did, did he buy the paper? Of course he would buy the paper, he always did on Friday afternoon. Had he looked at it yet? Had he seen her picture? Was he driving home right now thinking about how she hadn't told them the truth about cheering? Was he remembering how they'd taken her out of gymnastics class because they were afraid she'd injure herself and ruin her chances of being a great pianist? Was he deciding how to punish her for lying?

Adam was in the kitchen making spaghetti sauce and watching for their father to drive up.

Joan was finishing a fast but sad piece by Chopin when Adam shouted from the kitchen, "He's here!"

By the time Joan reached the kitchen, Adam was out the door and heading toward the garage. Joan watched her father and Adam come out of the garage together. Adam carried a grocery bag.

Their father carried his briefcase. The newspaper was probably inside. He was talking animatedly to Adam and smiling. He hasn't seen the paper yet, Joan thought. I'm still safe.

She turned on the faucet to wash her hands so she'd be doing something when her father walked in. Through the window over the sink she saw him take the newspaper out of the grocery bag and stick it in the outside pocket of his briefcase.

When he walked into the kitchen with their father, Adam gave Joan a sympathetic look.

Mr. Chazen sniffed the air. "Adam, you made spaghetti sauce!" he exclaimed. "What a splendid surprise."

Joan put out a hand. "I'll take your briefcase, Father," she said. "Taste Adam's sauce and see if it has enough garlic. I know how much you like garlicky sauce."

"Yes, try it," added Adam. "I could use your culinary expertise."

"*Culinary expertise*," Mr. Chazen repeated as he looked from his son to his daughter. "You two are acting a little strange — like you're about to request a privilege."

"I'm just so excited you're letting me go to Miami — with Melody," said Joan. "That's great."

"I see," said her father.

As Joan reached out to take the briefcase

from her father, he held it back long enough to remove the newspaper.

"I'll just keep the paper," he said. "But you can put my briefcase in my study, Joanie. Thank you." Then he sat down and looked over the front page of the first section of the *Claymore News*.

"I thought you were going to taste my sauce," Adam said.

"I trust you, Adam," said his father. He didn't even look up from his newspaper.

Joan thought of asking for the second section of the paper, but then her father would see her picture for sure. She had no choice. She'd said she'd put away his briefcase, so she had to leave the room. The instant she was out of the kitchen she ran up the stairs to her father's study, dropped the briefcase on his desk, and ran down the stairs. She slowed when she came back into the kitchen. Adam was trying his old trick of reciting Shakespeare to distract their father, who was still reading the paper and had already moved on to the middle of the first section.

"Father, how was your meeting in Fort Myers?" Joan asked.

Adam stopped his recitation midsentence to add, "Yes. How did it go?"

"It was a productive meeting," their father answered. But he still didn't look up from the paper.

"I didn't think you liked the *Claymore News* that much," said Adam. "I mean, it's not very intellectual."

"It's important to know what's going on in your community," his father said as he turned a page. "As you can see, I go through it pretty quickly."

"You know, Joan is a great cheerleader," said Adam.

His father looked up. "What makes you say that?" he asked. "Something you just remembered from Shakespeare?"

"Ah — not really. It's just — I didn't know if you knew that," Adam said.

"I'm sure she is," Mr. Chazen said. "But then, it doesn't take much to yell and jump up and down, now, does it?"

Joan realized that Adam was trying to prepare their father for the moment that he'd see her in the paper. Maybe letting him know a little more about cheering was her only hope.

"We do cartwheels and stuff, too," she said.

"*Cartwheels and stuff?*" her father repeated. "*Stuff* is an imprecise term. It's slang. What is *stuff* referring to? What *stuff* do you do?"

At that very instant her father turned over the

last page of the first section of the *Claymore News* and looked down at the first page of the second section. His mouth fell open as he stared at a photograph of his daughter flying through the air.

At exactly that moment Joan's mother walked in the door.

DOLPHIN COURT APARTMENTS 6:30 P.M.

Melody put her black Lycra dress on top of the rest of the things in her overnight case and zipped it closed. That was done. Now she'd check her e-mail to see if she had any messages from Miami. She sat at her desk and turned on the computer.

There were three new messages: one from her father, one from Tina, and the last one from Juan Ramirez — a ninth-grader she had a crush on last year. She opened the message from Juan first.

> Hey, Melody. So you're finally coming to Miami. Tina told me. Said that you were going to this cheer performance thing at the university. I gotta check that out. Same day — night, that is — I am doing my poetry at this new coffee shop. It's called The Place. Hope you can come. Maybe I'll see you at that cheer thing. Later. Juan.

Melody read the message twice. Juan had written to her once before. She was sure Tina had put him up to it that time. Had she done it again?

Tina and Melody had met Juan at a poetry workshop the summer before. Juan was the star of the workshop, so Melody was thrilled when he'd said he liked *her* poetry. But because he was two years older than she was they really hadn't hung out together. This weekend was going to be different. Juan had invited her to see him perform. He might even come to her party. And he was going to the Regionals. Probably. Maybe.

But does he really want to do all those things? wondered Melody. Or did Tina put him up to it? Boy-crazy Tina was always trying to fix people up. Most of the time it was like a joke. But if Tina was telling Juan that Melody liked him, that wasn't funny.

She opened the message from Tina.

> Hey, Max. Can't wait to see you. Sue and Tiffany are coming with me to the cheer thing. I told a bunch of other people about it, too. And guess who's MOST interested. Juan Ramirez! It was his idea to go. Cross my heart. I didn't say you wanted him there — though I'm sure you do. All I said was,

wouldn't it be cool to go and see you cheer, and he said, "Yeah. Sure." Then he said we should come see him perform his poetry at this cool new coffee shop that night. And I knew you'd want to do that so I said yes. You can bring those Claymore girls who are staying over at your dad's. Oh, yeah, and since he's coming to the Regionals, I thought you'd want to invite Juan to the party. So I did it for you. And of course he said yes, as long as we went to hear him perform after. And I invited Rick — this cool eighth-grader. Hope it's okay. I almost fainted when he said yes. Love ya. Big T. :-) times a million.

P.S. My aunt says no problem giving you and your two cheer friends a ride back to Claymore on Sunday. She drives right through there because of her job.

Melody wondered for about the thousandth time what her new friends would think of her old friends. And vice versa. Tina, Sue, and Tiffany loved to have a good time and could be in-your-face and loud. Her new friends liked to have a good time, too, but in a quieter way. Plus, Melody thought, if we don't place in the Regionals, the Claymore crowd will be depressed. Will my old friends understand that, or will they think that my new friends are a bunch of duds?

Melody realized she was almost as nervous about her party as she was about the Regionals. She opened up the e-mail from her father.

> Maxi, everything's set for your party. Tina called and said to expect about ten people from your old group. Fine with me. The more the merrier. If you want to have your sleep-over in the pool house, be sure that Emily and Joan bring sleeping bags. Can't wait to see you. Love and kisses, Dad.

Should we sleep in the pool house? wondered Melody as she closed down her e-mail. Tomorrow night — according to her father's morning forecast — was going to be clear and warm. And the pool house, with the doors wide open to catch the ocean breezes, was her favorite place in the world to sleep. Joan and Emily would love it. She'd call them right away and tell them to bring their sleeping bags.

As Melody was picking up the phone to call Joan she remembered Joan's problem with her parents. What had happened when Joan got home? Melody wondered. Had her parents seen her picture in the newspaper? Were they making

Joan quit cheering? Melody stopped dialing and put down the receiver. She'd go to Joan's house instead of calling.

DELHAVEN DRIVE 6:45 P.M.

Joan and Adam sat on living room chairs facing their parents, who sat side by side on the couch. The second section of the *Claymore News* lay faceup on the coffee table.

"You know that we don't approve of gymnastics," Ms. Russo was saying. "Especially for a pianist. Why do you think we pulled you out of that class two years ago?"

Joan hadn't looked her parents in the eye since the moment her father saw her picture in the paper. Now she stared at her lap and mumbled, "They don't call it gymnastics."

"What did you say?" her father asked.

Joan looked up. She'd expected to see anger in her father's eyes, but all she saw was hurt. She said, "In cheering we don't call it *gymnastics*. It's called *tumbling*."

"Tumbling or gymnastics," he said, "it's the same thing. And it's dangerous."

Her mother pointed to the paper. "Whatever it is called, you knew we wouldn't approve, so you didn't tell us."

"She's really good at cheering," Adam said.

"Joanie is good at a lot of things," her father

said. “Like playing the piano and speaking French.”

“And lying,” her mother added sadly.

“I’m sorry,” Joan said. “I just wanted so much to do it. I love gymnastics. I mean, tumbling.”

“Do you love it more than piano?” asked her father.

“I love them both,” she answered. “I can do both and keep up my grades. I’ve *been* doing it. And cheering really isn’t dangerous. I haven’t gotten injured. No one on the squad has. I don’t ever fall.” She suddenly remembered that she had fallen that very afternoon. “I mean, I don’t fall and hurt myself. We do the tumbling on mats. It’s very safe. And the coach or someone else stands near us just to be sure we’re safe. It’s called spotting.”

Mr. Chazen turned to Adam. “You’ve been part of this deception, Adam,” he said. “Our own children have formed a coalition against us. It’s very distressing.”

“And you didn’t tell us there was a competition for cheering being held in Miami,” her mother added angrily. “We thought you were simply going for a weekend with a friend.”

“It’s all my fault,” Joan said. “Adam wanted me to tell you the truth. Right from the beginning. He said —” her voice dropped almost to a whisper “— that I shouldn’t lie.”

"Joan hated lying, too," Adam added. "She knew she'd have to tell the truth someday. That she couldn't keep getting away with it." He hesitated and then added in a firm voice, "I think you should let her be a cheerleader. Just because it's the sort of thing you don't like doesn't mean she shouldn't do it."

Joan shot him a grateful look. But Adam didn't see it. He was looking straight at his parents as he continued to plead his sister's case. "Joanie *has* to go to the Regionals tomorrow. The squad needs her to do their routine. They don't have any chance of winning without her. She'd be letting everyone down."

"It's true," added Joan.

Their mother stood up. "I've heard quite enough from you two. Go to the kitchen. Your father and I will discuss this matter privately." She looked at her husband. "In his study."

"We'll finish making dinner," said Adam.

Joan followed her brother out of the room. I won't cry, she promised herself. I won't cry.

But two minutes later, when Melody was at the kitchen door, Joan burst into tears.

Melody put an arm around her friend's shoulder. "Did they say you couldn't go?" she asked.

"They're talking about it now," Joan answered. "It's such a big mess."

Melody heard arguing voices coming from upstairs. Joan and Adam exchanged a worried glance.

"They never argue," Adam told Melody. "Ever."

I'm ruining everything, thought Joan. For the cheerleaders and for our family.

"Maybe I should leave," Melody suggested.

"Maybe," agreed Adam.

"I just came to say I'm sorry, Joan," Melody said. "I thought maybe I could talk to your folks or something. I don't know . . . I was so worried about you."

"Thanks," Joan said through her tears. "I'm pretty sure they won't let me go. But let everyone know how sorry I am."

Before Melody opened the door to leave, Joan's father come into the kitchen. His wife was right behind him.

"Melody Max," Mr. Chazen said when he saw Melody.

Since Mr. Chazen was smiling, Melody smiled back.

Joan's mother looked sad and upset, but she didn't look angry. "Hello," she said to Melody. "I don't think we've met."

"Mother," said Adam. "This is our friend Melody Max."

"Also a cheerleader," added Mr. Chazen.

"Melody, this is our mother," Adam said, concluding the introduction.

"The young lady who invited Joan for the weekend in Miami," said Ms. Russo. "Is Joan actually staying at your father's house, or was that a lie, too?"

"It's true," Melody said. "My dad — father — invited us. Actually we're going to sleep in the pool house." She turned to Joan. "You need to bring your sleeping bag. I mean, if you come."

"Is Joan as important to this competition tomorrow as she and Adam claim?" Mr. Chazen asked.

Melody nodded. "Yes," she said. "She's really important. And, Mr. Chazen, it's safe. I mean, we use mats and — "

" — spotters," Mr. Chazen interrupted. "Yes. We've heard."

"Well, Joanie," Mr. Chazen said, turning to his daughter. "Be sure to thank Melody's father for his hospitality . . ." he paused, "when you're in Miami."

"I can go to Miami?!" Joan exclaimed, looking from her father to her mother. "I can cheer in the Regionals?"

They both nodded.

"Thank you. Oh, thank you," Joan said.

"Don't be too hasty in your gratitude," her mother cautioned.

"We're only letting you go tomorrow because you have a responsibility to your group of cheerleaders," added her father.

"We don't think it's fair to punish everyone because of your poor judgment," said her mother. "After this weekend we will reassess the situation."

"Okay," said Joan. Even if I can never cheer again, she thought, at least I can cheer in the Regionals. She wouldn't be letting her squad down tomorrow.

HIGHWAY 95. SCHOOL BUS 7:30 A.M.

Emily put her feet up on the seat in front of her and looked around. Joan sat next to her. Melody and Maria were in the two seats directly across the aisle from them. Everyone had on their regulation warm-up outfit — loose nylon pants and zip-up jackets. Blue and white for the middle school and black and silver for the high school.

Most of the high school squad was sitting toward the back of the bus. A group of them were quietly counting out their routine together.

Lynn came down the aisle and stopped next to Melody. "How're you doing?" she asked.

"Great," said Melody.

Lynn nodded in Joan's direction. "You did an excellent correction yesterday, Joan," she said. "I know you'll be perfect today."

"Thanks," said Joan.

When Lynn moved on, Joan turned to Emily. "You're so lucky to have a sister who's a cheerleader," she said.

"I guess," said Emily. She wanted to tell Joan that it wasn't always easy to have a sister who was a big deal in cheering when you were a cheerleader, too. That it wasn't so great to have an older sister who was so perfect. She didn't think Joan would understand, though. But Alexis would understand, thought Emily. She wished her best friend was going to Miami with her.

HIGHWAY 95. MRS. FEDER'S CAR
7:32 A.M.

Jake's grandmother was driving the car and his grandfather was sitting next to her. Alexis was in the backseat between Jake and Adam.

"The cheerleaders are going to be so surprised when we show up at the Regionals," Alexis said. "I can't wait to see the expression on Emily's face."

"Joan has no idea, either," said Adam.

"I thought maybe your parents wouldn't let you come," Jake told Adam.

"Actually, they're glad I could come," said Adam. "They like it when Joan and I do stuff together. They're into the family thing."

Alexis noticed that Mrs. Feder's car was about to overtake a bus on the road ahead of them. "There they are!" Alexis exclaimed. "It's our bus. With the cheerleaders. Up ahead of us."

"Slow down, Grandma," Jake ordered. "Don't pass them. They'll see us."

Mrs. Feder moved into the slow lane while the bus continued on. She smiled in the mirror at her backseat passengers. "Close call," she said.

Mr. Feder looked at his watch. "We're making good time," he said. "How about stopping at the next exit for some breakfast?"

"Eggs and pancakes for me," said Jake.

That's my favorite breakfast, too, thought Alexis.

"I'm going to have a cheese omelet," said Mr. Feder. "With home fries and sausage."

"French toast and bacon for me," put in Adam. "What about you, Alexis?"

She didn't want to sound like she was copying Jake, so she said, "Pancakes."

"I guess you all want to stop, then," said Mrs. Feder. "Am I right?"

"Yes," they said in unison. Then they looked at one another and laughed.

This is so much fun, thought Alexis. Being

with the Feders is as much fun as being with the Grangers.

MIAMI. UNIVERSITY GYM 10:45 A.M.

The first thing Emily noticed about the gym was how big it was. She'd never cheered in such a huge space. The next thing she noticed was how many cheerleaders were there. Everywhere she looked she saw girls in warm-up outfits, many of them still lugging their athletic bags and their uniforms in garment bags, just like the CMS cheerleaders.

Loud music blared from the speakers. But Emily could still hear the cheerleaders chatting nervously to one another and someone shouting for a girl named Linda. Emily stared up at bleachers that reached all the way to the high ceiling. The competitions wouldn't start for over an hour, but people were already filling up the stands.

"How many people are coming to watch?" Emily asked Mae.

Mae looked around at the bleachers encircling the gym. "A lot," she answered. "Thousands, I guess."

"Wow!" exclaimed Joan, looking around the gym. "I didn't know it was going to be so *big*." Joan had been so worried about whether she could even *be* at the Regionals that she hadn't had time to be nervous about *performing* in them. But now that she was finally in Miami, her stomach was tied up in knots. She remembered Emily's sister's advice: Act calm. She hiccuped. Staying calm wasn't easy.

As Coach Cortes walked past her squad she said, "The high school squad is scouting out bleacher space. Follow them. I'm going to the coaches' meeting and to sign you up for a warm-up time. I'll meet you at the bleachers." Over her shoulder she added, "Sally, check the program for our place in the lineup."

Sally looked around and noticed a table with a pile of programs near the door. She detached herself from the group and went over to it.

"I hope we're first," Emily told her friends as they followed the high school cheerleaders. "I want to get it over with."

"But if we go later we can see how everyone else does," Maria said. "That might be better."

"What if they're all better than we are?" put in Kelly. "That'd be so depressing."

"No way," said Melody. But what if we *are* the worst squad? she wondered. That would be so embarrassing in front of my Miami friends.

"Over here," Lynn called. She was standing next to a section of bleachers marked B.

The middle school cheerleaders went over to

her. "Since the high school squad isn't on until the afternoon," she explained, "we'll save your bleacher space while you're in the locker room and warming up."

Sally caught up with her squad at the bleachers.

"When do you go on?" Lynn asked her.

"We're seventh," Sally answered.

"Seventh out of twelve," Lynn said. "That's good. Right about in the middle."

Sally thought, The Santa Rosa cheerleaders go on tenth. She hoped it would be an unlucky number for them.

A few minutes later Coach Cortes came up to them waving a piece of paper. Her cheerleaders and Lynn swarmed around her.

"She has the score sheet," C.J. told Emily.

"Okay," Coach told her squad. "We've gone over score sheets very similar to this one during practices. There's nothing new here. But let's just look at this one briefly."

Sally and Lynn moved closer to Coach so they could read over her shoulder.

"There are four categories that make up the one hundred possible points," began Coach.

"Which no one ever gets," commented Lynn.

"Category one is Communication," Coach said. "This includes voice, eye contact with the crowd and the judges, and facial expression. That's given five points."

"You've got to show them that you love cheering," Lynn reminded the squad.

"The second category is Fundamental Skills," Coach continued. "We're talking forty points for that one. But, as you well know, it includes a lot."

"Our motions," said Maria.

"And the dance," added Melody.

"Those are ten points each," said Lynn.

"And twenty points for Cheerleading Gymnastics," said Coach. "Jumps, tumbling, stunts."

"Category three is worth fifteen points," said Sally. "That's Group Techniques. Ten of the points are for synchronization. Five are for formation and spacing."

"That leaves forty points," said Kelly.

"And those points are given for Overall Effect," Coach said. "Which means difficulty of the routine, crowd appeal, choreography, that sort of thing."

"I'm more nervous than ever," said C.J.

"Me, too," said Maria with a shudder.

Coach looked around at the squad. "You'll all be fine," she said. "By the way, we're fifth on the warm-up, so we'd better get over to the locker room."

As the CMS cheerleaders walked across the

gym floor Melody scanned the stands to see if Tina and her other friends were there yet. When she didn't see them she was relieved. There was so much to do now that they were at the Regionals. She didn't really have time for a proper reunion with her friends. She had to fix her hair, change her shoes, and stretch before the warm-up in the performance space. After the warm-up she'd have to change into her uniform and add sparkles to her hair. Sally's mother would be there to help all of the cheerleaders and to do a final check of each girl's hair and to apply some makeup.

Melody followed Kelly and Joan into the locker room. "Over here," Coach called. "Hang your uniforms on this rack."

"Uh-oh," warned C.J. "Santa Rosa."

Kelly turned around and asked, "Where?"

"Over there," whispered C.J. "At the end of the second row of lockers."

Kelly waved in the direction of a group of Santa Rosa middle school cheerleaders who were stretching out near the rack of uniforms. A tall, dark-haired girl who was hanging up her uniform waved back. "That's my friend Carole," Kelly told Melody and Emily. "We go to camp together every summer. We're best friends, but we decided not to talk today. Not until the Regionals are over. Since we're sort of in competition."

She lowered her voice. "I hope both squads place."

"Me, too," said Emily. "I'm sick of the rivalry thing. Lots of kids at our school have friends in Santa Rosa."

I don't, thought Sally. And I never will. You couldn't pay me enough money to be friends with anyone in Santa Rosa, particularly a Cougar cheerleader.

Melody was stretching out in a split when she noticed that the music in the gym had stopped. Seconds later another song began, with a different sound. It was the kind of music a squad would use for a cheer routine.

Sally stood up from a knee bend. "They're starting the warm-ups," she said. "Let's go."

Coach led her cheerleaders back into the gym. Lynn ran over to meet them. "When it's your turn," Coach directed, "line up to go on the floor for your run-through. Remember, you're not throwing up stunts or cheering full-out. Just marking your time. Pay special attention to your spacing for the dance section." She held up an audiotape. "I'll bring your music to the sound booth."

"Next up, Johnson Middle School," announced a voice on the loudspeaker. "On deck, Claymore Middle School."

"That's us," said Sally.

As Lynn led the CMS squad to the sideline to await their turn, Melody watched cheerleaders in green-and-white warm-up pants and T-shirts marking time for their cheer. It looked pretty funny to see them just walking through their routine. You couldn't tell from the warm-up if they were good.

"When you're out there don't let the big space throw you," Lynn told them. "Your routine shouldn't take up any more space than it usually does. So don't spread out too much."

The next thing Melody knew, she was doing a toned-down version of the dance portion of their cheer. It seemed like only seconds later that their warm-up was finished and they were running single file off the gym floor back to the locker room. Melody heard someone call her name. She looked around but couldn't see where the voice was coming from. Just before she reached the locker room door, a hand landed on her shoulder and a voice behind her said, "Girl, do you seriously call that cheering?"

Melody turned to face Tina. Sue and Tiffany came up beside her.

Tiffany tugged on the sleeve of Melody's warm-up outfit. "Is this parachute thing you're wearing a uniform?" she asked.

"We were just doing a warm-up —" Melody started to say.

"Just kidding," her three friends interrupted in unison.

Melody laughed and the four girls hugged. Melody felt tears come to her eyes. She had missed her old friends so much.

"Where are you sitting?" Melody asked as she pulled away from the group hug.

Tina looked around. "Where are *you* going to be?"

Melody pointed to the bleachers where the CMS cheer squad would soon be waiting their turn to perform.

"We'll find a place near you," said Sue. She winked at Melody before adding, "We'll save a place for Juan."

"And Rick," added Tina. "Wait until you see him, Melody. He is beyond-belief hunky."

"That's what you say about all of your crushes," Melody teased. "But seriously, I gotta go. I have to change and fix my hair and everything. I'm really nervous."

"Don't sweat it," said Sue. "You'll be great."

"We just saw," teased Tiffany. She mimicked a cheerleader marking time by putting her arms in a V-formation and jumping about an inch off the floor. Melody laughed.

But heading for the locker room, Melody wondered if it had been a mistake to invite her old friends to the Regionals. What if they made fun of cheering, and her new friends didn't think it was funny? She was supposed to be focused on the routine, not on how everyone would get along. Maybe she should have kept her two groups of friends separate.

LOCKER ROOM 11:45 A.M.

Emily mentally reviewed the counts for the basket toss as she unzipped her garment bag and took out her uniform. She was so nervous that she could feel her heart beating. She wondered if any of the other cheerleaders felt the same way.

Emily was combing her hair back into a fresh ponytail when Coach announced, "We're going back to the bleachers. Mrs. Johnson will do the last-minute check on hair and makeup there. Take all of your things with you."

The CMS cheerleaders were walking through the gym when Lily ran toward them. She had on the miniature CMS uniform that Emily had worn to games when she was Lily's age. Emily remembered how the "big-girl" cheerleaders had always made a fuss over her, saying how cute she was. Well, cute isn't enough today, thought Emily. I have to be a good cheerleader. I have to execute our routine perfectly.

Lily took Emily's hand and they walked along

together. “Lexi’s here!” Lily exclaimed. “It’s a surprise!”

Emily looked around. “Where?” she asked Lily.

Lily pointed ahead of them. “There,” she said.

Emily saw that Alexis really was there. And Jake. Her best friends had made it to the Regionals! As Emily waved to them she noticed that Adam was there, too.

Emily turned to tell Joan and Melody that Adam was there, but they were already waving to the new arrivals.

A minute later the CMS cheerleaders were talking excitedly with all the people from Claymore who had arrived while they were changing — including Darryl and Randy and a lot of high school students.

Joan couldn’t believe her brother was there. “I didn’t know you were coming,” she told Adam.

“Jake asked me yesterday,” Adam explained. “He’s the one who called me before school when I said it was about homework. I couldn’t tell you because Jake and Alexis wanted to surprise Emily.”

“I can’t believe you’re here,” Melody told Adam.

“Hey, Melody!” several voices shouted in unison.

Melody and her friends looked around to see who was calling her.

"Mel-o-dy! Mel-o-dy!" the voices chanted.

Melody finally spotted her Miami friends in the stands. Juan Ramirez and a couple of other guys were with them. They all waved and shouted her name one more time. "MEL-O-DY!"

Melody smiled and waved back.

"Your Miami friends?" asked Adam.

"That's them," Melody said. "And *their* friends."

"And here comes your dad," Emily told Melody.

"He looks even better in person than he does on television," said Maria.

"You saw him?" Melody asked.

"After you told me he was on television," Maria explained.

Melody looked over to see her handsome, wonderful father walking toward her.

She rushed to meet him. They were hugging when the announcer's voice boomed, "Welcome to the CHEER USA Regional Competitions for South Florida."

UNIVERSITY GYM 12:20 P.M.

Four squads had already performed. Emily and the other CMS cheerleaders shouted out the chants for the squads as they performed. Coach had said that it showed good sportsmanship and Emily agreed. She hoped other squads would do the same for CMS when they were on the floor.

"Go, Ravens," Emily shouted with the squad from Fort Lauderdale. She thought that the Raven cheerleaders had done a perfect routine that was energetic and fun.

"But their stunts weren't complicated enough," Lynn told Emily. "Your routine is more difficult. You need that to get enough points for a bid to Nationals."

Our routine might be hard enough, thought Emily. But we'll only make it to the Nationals if we don't make any mistakes. If *I* don't make any mistakes.

As the Fort Lauderdale squad cleared the floor, the announcer said, "Next up, East Naples Middle School. On deck, Claymore Middle School."

The East Naples Middle School cheerleaders' music started and they ran onto the floor. The CMS cheerleaders moved forward to the first position in the lineup. Emily couldn't concentrate on the East Naples routine. All she could think about was that her squad was on next.

Lynn put an arm around Emily's shoulders and whispered, "Don't worry. You'll be great."

"Thanks," Emily said. For the first time that day she was glad that her sister was there.

The crowd was still clapping for East Naples when the announcer said, "Next up, Claymore Middle School. On deck, Saint Agnes."

On the first note of the familiar music for the CMS routine, Emily ran out to her position as a base for the basket toss.

Melody ran onto the floor and did a round off back handspring back tuck before moving into position as a base for Joan's free liberty. They rotated Joan 360 degrees before she came out of her liberty with a full twisting dismount. Melody saw that Mae and Sally had nailed their stunts, too.

Next, the squad built a Big M pyramid. At the end of the stunt they raised their arms and hit a high V as they yelled, **"Bulldogs!"**

As the cheerleaders clapped to signal the beginning of the cheer section of their routine, Alexis shouted to Jake, "They're doing great!"

Jake and Alexis shouted the CMS chant with their cheerleaders.

1, 2, 3, 4 — Let's go, Bulldogs.
Here to cheer and make you yell, we're C-M-S.
You yell it. C-M-S.
Yeah!
Come on, crowd.
Don't stop now.

Now watch the signs
And say it loud.
Yell, Go, Bulldogs, go!
You yell it.
Go, Bulldogs, go!
Let's go, Bulldogs!
Yeah!

After the chant, the music came back on for the dance portion of the routine.

"Every one of Emily's jumps was perfect!" Jake shouted to Alexis.

"I know," Alexis yelled back. "She was great!"

When the dance and tumbling were completed, the cheerleaders ended the routine with a Christmas tree pyramid.

Alexis was on her feet, shouting, "Yeah!" and clapping. To her right, Melody's Miami friends were punching the air and yelling, "Yes! Melody!"

UNIVERSITY GYM. BLEACHERS 12:35 P.M.

The high school cheerleaders greeted the CMS squad, who were coming off the floor, with hugs and congratulations.

"But I wobbled a little in the pyramid," Mae was saying.

"And I lost a beat in the dance," added C.J.

"It was *great*," Coach told them. "Whether you place or not, you know you did an excellent job."

Joan looked around at her fellow performers. Tears sprang to her eyes. She had cheered at the Regionals and the squad had done well. But was this the last time she would cheer?

"Sit down now and watch the rest of the performances," Coach instructed.

Joan sat between Sally and Melody.

"Santa Rosa is next," Melody told her.

Kelly leaned forward and whispered, "I hope they do all right, but not as well as us."

"Me, too," said Joan.

I hope they fall on their faces, thought Sally.

Sally watched the Cougar cheerleaders preparing for a team stunt and prayed that they wouldn't pull it off. Just then their co-captain, Cassie Jimenez, missed her heel stretch.

"Uh-oh," said Kelly.

Perfect, thought Sally.

Sally kept her fingers crossed as the final three squads performed. If none of them was as good as her squad, the Bulldog cheerleaders had a terrific chance of placing in the top five.

The tenth squad on the floor performed with energy and skill. But Sally thought that their program was too simple. In the next performance up, girls fell out of two stunts. And the last squad was so nervous that two of their cheerleaders went to the wrong position for the dance portion of their routine. Sally figured they weren't even in the running for the top five.

The performances were over. In a few minutes the results would be announced. Cheerleaders all over the gym clustered nervously around their coaches to wait for the results. Soon, thought Sally, the suspense will be over. She reminded herself that even if her squad failed to place, she still had to show a positive attitude. That was her responsibility. Everyone would be looking to her for leadership. Her stomach flipped. They *had* to place.

"And now . . . the results of the South Florida Middle School CHEER USA competition," the announcer said.

The auditorium fell silent.

Emily looked over to where Alexis sat in the stands. Alexis raised both arms and waved. Her fingers were crossed for good luck.

"In fifth place, with eighty-four points, Saint Agnes Middle School," the announcer said. The co-captains of Saint Agnes walked over to the CHEER USA official to accept their trophy. One of them was crying. "They didn't have enough points to go the Nationals," Emily whispered to Joan.

"They only missed by one point," moaned Joan. "I'm glad that wasn't us."

"In fourth place, with eighty-six points, receiving a bid to Nationals . . ." the announcer began — *Please let us be higher than fourth,* Sally prayed — "East Naples Middle School."

The East Naples cheerleaders jumped up and down, hugging each other. As soon as their co-captains had accepted the trophy and the invitation to the Nationals, the announcer said, "In third place, with eighty-nine points, receiving a bid to Nationals, Johnson Middle School."

We didn't win third place, thought Sally. Does that mean we'll be second or first? Sally noticed a worried look pass over Coach Cortes's face and realized that Coach was afraid that if they hadn't placed fourth or third they might not place at all.

A terrifying thought crossed Sally's mind. Were there slipups in her squad's routine that she hadn't seen? Maybe Emily's jumps weren't high and clean enough. And maybe Melody didn't do a round off back handspring back tuck, but only a single back handspring. C.J. didn't always remember to smile during the dance and sometimes lost count. Had she today? There were so many things that could have gone wrong that Sally didn't see.

"In second place. Receiving ninety points and a bid to Nationals — " Sally was holding her breath " — Santa Rosa Middle School."

The Santa Rosa cheerleaders screeched joyfully and hugged as their co-captains walked over to accept the trophy and their invitation to the Nationals. Sally knew what Cassie Jimenez must be thinking. If it hadn't been for her error her squad might have been in first place.

"First place!" C.J. was saying excitedly. "I bet we're in first place."

Other girls on the CMS squad thought the same thing and were moving around one another with nervous excitement.

Some of the Santa Rosa cheerleaders were crying. Those aren't all tears of happiness, thought Sally. She caught some of the Santa Rosa cheerleaders looking in her direction. They think we're going to get first place and they hate it, she thought as she flashed them a confident smile. They didn't smile back.

Sally glanced in Coach's direction. Coach still had that worried look and was now biting her lower lip. Only one thought filled Sally's head. What if they didn't place at all?

"In first place. Receiving ninety-one points and a bid to Nationals," the announcer was saying, "Claymore Middle School!"

"That's us," Emily shouted.

All around Sally her cheerleaders were jumping up and down shouting and hugging and even crying with joy.

"Go," Coach said, giving Sally a small nudge toward the prize table.

We *did* it, thought Sally as she walked ahead of Mae toward the officials of CHEER USA to accept the trophy. We're the first CMS squad to go to the Regionals and we're number one. I'm taking my squad all the way to the Nationals. Sally shook hands with the main official before accepting the trophy. As she walked back to her squad she held the huge trophy aloft for all the world to see.

People started leaving the stands. Within a few seconds, Bulldog fans and the Claymore High School cheer squad were swarming around the CMS cheerleaders, congratulating them. Sally was breaking away from Darryl's hug when Cassie Jimenez came up to her.

"Congratulations, Sally," Cassie said with a big smile. "You guys did great."

"Thanks," said Sally. "You, too."

"I'm glad both squads get to go to the Nationals," said Cassie.

"I know what you mean," said Sally.

Sally gave Cassie her warmest, most fake smile. But she was thinking, The only reason I'm glad you're going to Nationals is to have the satisfaction of beating you again.

Emily surveyed the gym. She saw that the other winning squads were as excited as she was. She also noticed that many cheerleaders from squads who hadn't placed were sobbing. She felt bad for them.

"Emily, you were so great!" someone behind her exclaimed. Emily turned around to face Alexis. The two best friends hugged.

"We won!" Emily said. "We're going to the Nationals."

"I know," said Alexis, laughing.

Emily thought, This is super. My dream has come true. We came in number one at the Regionals. She couldn't stop smiling. She hugged Alexis again and shouted, "I'm so glad you're here!"

Melody didn't know who to hug next. Elvia and Maria, who stood on either side of her? Her father, who was making his way toward her through the crowd? Or Tina, who'd just come up to her?

Melody threw one arm around Maria's shoulders and the other around Elvia's and leaned toward Tina to shout, "Tina, this is Elvia and Maria. Elvia and Maria, Tina."

"Hey," said Tina. "You guys were all great. I knew you'd be number one. You were jumping pretty high there, Max."

As Melody was hugging Tina she noticed that two women had stopped her father. Looking in Melody's direction, he shrugged his shoulders as if to say, "What can I do?" Melody smiled to herself. She'd forgotten what it was like to have a dad who was a television celebrity. She ran over to him.

"I watch your weather forecast every day, Mr. Max," a tall, thin woman was telling Melody's father.

"Your coverage of Hurricane Henry was so informative," said the shorter woman who was with her.

Melody's father put a hand on Melody's shoulder. She looked up at him and smiled.

"This is my daughter, Melody Max," her father told the women. "Her squad just came in first place."

"And well deserved it was," said the tall woman. "I loved your routine."

"Such a pretty girl," added the other.

When the women finally left, Melody's father gave her a big hug. "You were terrific, honey," he said. "You looked great out there."

"Thanks, Dad," said Melody.

"I have to go back to the studio for a meeting," he said. "But I'll be at the house to set things up before you and your friends come."

"Everybody's all excited about the party," she told him. "Now it'll be a celebration for being in first place."

"I am very proud of you," he said. He turned

to leave, then added over his shoulder, "See you at home."

Melody was making her way back to the Claymore crowd when someone behind her said, "Good dance. Smooth moves." Even in the noisy gym, Melody recognized Juan's deep, musical voice.

She turned to him and said, "Thanks."

Tina was with him. "We're not going to stick around for the high school thing this afternoon," she told Melody.

Melody hadn't expected Juan to stay for the afternoon Regionals. But she had hoped Tina would hang out with her during the high school competition. She'd imagined sitting with Tina, Joan, and Emily, cheering on the Claymore High School squad. But Tina wasn't staying.

"Let's get something to eat," suggested Tina. "I'm starved."

"How come?" Melody asked.

"I didn't have any breakfast," answered Tina.

"I mean, how come you're not staying?" Melody explained.

"Stuff to do," said Tina. "Meeting some people at the mall. Why don't you come with us? You already did your thing here."

"I should stay with my squad," Melody explained.

"But you're only in Miami for a little while,"

protested Tina. "You can be with those other guys all the time."

Melody wondered if she could miss the afternoon competition. After all, the Claymore High School performance would be videotaped, so she could see it later. And they'd have enough support without her.

"There's a chili wagon out there," said Juan. "I say we *chili* out for the lunch thing."

"Very funny," Tina teased.

"Maybe Emily and—" Melody began to say. But she stopped herself. She didn't want to mix her two sets of friends. Not yet.

Melody spotted Maria and Elvia. She waved to get their attention. "I'm going to lunch," she called to them. "I'll catch you later."

Emily noticed Melody walking away with her Miami friends.

So did Adam. "Where's Melody going?" he asked.

"I guess she wants to be alone with her old friends," Joan answered.

"Is that guy her boyfriend or something?" asked Emily.

"Don't know," said Alexis. "Did she say anything about a boyfriend to you, Joan?"

"No," Adam answered.

Joan hated it when her brother answered for her. She glared at him, but Adam didn't notice.

He was still watching Melody and her Miami friends walking arm in arm toward the exit.

UNIVERSITY LAWN 1:35 P.M.

Alexis and Emily followed Joan, Adam, and Jake across the lawn. They all carried lunches from the barbecue stand.

Kelly, Maria, and some of the other cheerleaders were eating at a large picnic table.

"Let's sit over there," Emily suggested. "Okay?"

Joan had already taken a big bite of her cheeseburger, so she could only nod in agreement. The group at the table made room for them. At first the conversation was about the competition. Then about how terrific it was that Jake, Alexis, and Adam were there.

"Now you can come to Melody's party, too," said Emily.

"If we're invited," said Adam. "I mean, did Melody say she wanted us? Maybe so many of her old friends will be there that — "

"Of course you're invited," Emily assured him.

Jake turned to Adam and Alexis. "I already talked to Melody about it," he said. "She wants us to come. My grandparents will pick us up at her dad's place around eight o'clock so we can head back home."

"Then Melody's taking us to this coffeehouse

where one of her friends is reciting poetry," said Joan.

"Which friend?" asked Adam.

"The guy," said Emily. "The cute one with black hair."

"Oh," said Adam.

"You can have some of my french fries," Alexis told Emily. "If you want."

"Thanks," said Emily. They exchanged a smile. Emily was glad she'd told Alexis she was being careful not to eat too many fattening foods. That's why she hadn't ordered french fries with her veggieburger. But half an order would be perfect. After all, they were celebrating.

Emily still couldn't believe that Alexis came. It seemed too good to be true. She wished Alexis was staying for the sleepover, too.

UNIVERSITY CAMPUS.
SCIENCE BUILDING ROOFTOP 1:40 P.M.

Juan led Rick and the girls up the back stairs of the university science building. "My cousin takes classes here," he told them. "He showed me how to get to the roof. It's got a cool view."

When they stepped out onto the roof, Melody took a deep breath of salt air and looked out at the horizon where the hazy blue of the Atlantic Ocean met a cloudless sky. There were three old iron benches on the roof, all facing east. Melody sat on one of them and removed the lid from her cup of chili. She was surprised that of all the places Juan could sit, he chose to sit beside her. Tina grinned at her. Melody had to stop herself from grinning back. What if Juan saw?

"What are you going to perform tonight?" Melody asked him.

"New stuff," Rick answered for Juan.

Juan turned to Melody and asked, "You been writing much lately?"

"Nothing at all," Melody admitted. "I'm busy with the cheer thing."

"Do any of those Claymore people go to poetry slams?" asked Tina.

"No one that I've met," Melody answered. "It's not that popular there."

"Poor Melody," said Sue. "She's moved to Nowhere Land."

Melody was going to defend Claymore but decided not to. When she was in Claymore she liked it well enough. But now that she was back in Miami, Claymore didn't seem so important.

UNIVERSITY LAWN 1:55 P.M.

Emily was lying on the grass feeling incredibly happy. Some of the cheerleaders had already gone back into the gym, but she and Joan had decided to wait until the last minute to go inside.

Alexis and Jake were talking about the article Alexis would write about the competition. Adam was stuffing their used napkins and paper plates into a big plastic bag. Joan was collecting the empty soda cans.

Emily raised her arm and squinted in the sunlight to read her watch. She sat up, saying, "We'd better go back. The high school competition starts in a few minutes."

"I'll find a place to dump this stuff," Adam told her. "Save me a seat."

"I'll go with you, Adam," Joan said as she stood up. But Adam was already walking away. "Save me a seat, too," she called to Emily as she followed her brother. She wanted to talk to him. Alone.

"What'd they say?" Joan asked when she caught up to him.

"Who?" Adam asked.

"Mother and Father," Joan explained. "About my cheering. After I left."

"Not a whole lot," Adam answered. "Mother was looking at the picture in the paper and listing all the horrible things that could happen to you if you fell. Broken arm. Sprained wrist. Mangled fingers. She even had you paralyzed from the neck down and in a wheelchair."

Joan sighed. "What did Father say?"

"He started in on how you're this great pianist and your important career could be ruined because of cheering. That if anything happened it would be their fault because they allowed it. He said they should stop you from being a cheerleader even if you hate them for it."

"I *will* hate them if they make me quit!" Joan cried. "They've made up their minds that cheering is dangerous. But they don't know the first thing about it. It isn't fair."

"Gymnastics isn't exactly the safest sport," Adam muttered to himself.

Joan grabbed his arm and turned him toward her. "You're taking their side again," she said angrily. She thrust the paper bag of cans at him and added, "I'm going to the gym." Turning quickly, she ran away before he could see that she was crying.

IN FRONT OF SCIENCE BUILDING
2:00 P.M.

"So you'll come with us, Max?" Tina said. "I can tell you want to."

"I do," admitted Melody.

"I know the guy at Evolution Records," said Juan. "He's got some new sounds for us to check out."

I haven't been to Evolution Records in so long, thought Melody. And it would be so much fun to go with Juan and my old friends. Especially since Juan knows someone who works there.

"Evolution is my favorite music store," Melody said.

"So come," urged Tina.

Melody thought for a second. All the other CMS cheerleaders would be in the gym to cheer on the high school squad. No one would even miss her. She smiled at Tina and was about to say, "Count me in," when Tiffany asked, "Isn't that one of the girls who cheered with you, Max?"

Melody looked to where Tiffany was pointing. Joan was sitting alone under a tree, her knees to her chest, her head buried in her arms.

Even from halfway across the university lawn, Melody knew that Joan was upset. And she thought she knew why.

"I can't go with you guys," Melody told her friends. "I have to go to the high school competition."

"Why, Max?" Tina asked.

Melody gestured in Joan's direction. Of all her Miami friends, Tina would understand that when a friend needs you, that takes top priority.

Tina looked at Joan and then back at Melody. "You should probably stay here," she said.

"I'll see you at my dad's place at five," Melody told her friends. "Don't be late."

"Right," said Tina. "See you" — she looked at her watch — "in three hours." She gave Melody a quick hug.

"Later," added Sue.

Melody turned and hurried across the lawn toward Joan. When she reached her, she squatted down and called her name softly.

Joan looked up. "I know I'm going to have to quit," she said sadly. "I won't be at Nationals."

"Did your parents already say that?" Melody asked in alarm. "Did you phone them or something?"

Joan shook her head no and told Melody what Adam had told her.

"They really believe you could get hurt," said Melody.

"I know," agreed Joan. "But where is the squad going to find another flyer before Nationals?"

"Your parents let you go this time," Melody said. "Maybe they'll give in again."

"No way," said Joan.

"Listen, Joan," Melody said. "We won. First place! You should be happy today. Worry about the Nationals later."

After a silence, Joan looked up at her. "You think?" she said.

"I think you should be *very* happy today," Melody answered. "You were terrific out there."

"We nailed it," Joan said softly. She looked up at Melody and smiled when she added, "Wasn't it great to have such a big audience? I mean, at first I was scared, but then I loved it."

"Me, too," agreed Melody. She looked at her watch. "Let's hurry so we can watch all of the high school squads perform. We'll see if we agree with the judges."

"Maybe Claymore High will be number one, too?" asked Joan as she stood up.

"That would be so cool," said Melody. "You ready?"

"Let's go," said Joan.

The two friends ran back to the gym.

UNIVERSITY GYM. BLEACHERS 2:10 P.M.

Lily was sitting between Alexis and Emily in the bleachers with the other CMS cheerleaders to watch the high school competition. Joan and Melody sat next to Alexis. As the seventh squad to perform ran off the floor, Emily leaned toward Alexis. "They're the best so far," she said.

"But Claymore High is better," said Alexis. "And we're up next."

Emily noticed that Alexis had her reporter's notebook out and was taking notes on the high school competition.

"Lynn's the best cheerleader in the world," Lily shouted to Alexis and Emily.

"She sure is," said Alexis.

Alexis saw a momentary look of sadness pass over Emily's face. She didn't have time to figure out why because all of her attention was now on Claymore's performance.

Emily agreed with Lily that Lynn was the greatest cheerleader. She looked perfect in an arabesque high above her bases. The whole squad was giving a flawless performance. They had one stunt left. It was their most difficult and it was going perfectly, too, until the dismount. That's when one of the bases — Carmen Torres — fell. She jumped right up and moved on with the routine.

"Uh-oh," said Melody. "That will cost them points."

"But everything else was perfect," said Emily.

As the squad ran off the floor, the middle school cheerleaders and other Claymore fans were on their feet, clapping.

Alexis noticed that Carmen was holding her left wrist with her right hand. Did Carmen injure herself when she fell? Alexis wondered.

"I'm going to find out what happened," she told Emily. She jumped down from the bleachers and ran over to the edge of the small group gathering around Carmen.

"I ruined it," Carmen sobbed to the cheerleaders who surrounded her. "I — I thought we'd nailed it. I was so happy . . ."

"I might have been too heavy on your side for the dismount," said one of the flyers. "Maybe it was my fault."

"No," said Carmen. "I lost count." She looked around at her fellow cheerleaders. "I'm sorry."

Lynn put an arm around Carmen's shoulders. "It could have happened to any of us," she said.

In the background Alexis heard the next squad on the floor chanting, **"R-H-S! Shout it! R-H-S."**

The high school coach made her way through her cheer squad toward Carmen. "You all did great," she said. "You have an excellent chance to place. But we're making too much noise over here. Go watch the rest of the competition and try to calm down."

While the rest of the CHS squad moved back into the bleachers to watch RHS complete their routine, the coach kept Carmen on the floor with her. Lynn stayed, too. Alexis took a few steps toward them so she could hear what was going on.

"Carmen, why are you holding your wrist like that?" Coach asked. "Does it hurt?"

Carmen, her face still streaked with tears, nodded. "I think I broke it or something," she said.

"I'm taking you to the first-aid station," Coach said calmly. "There's a sports doctor there. You just keep holding it like that."

By the time Alexis was back at her place in the stands, word had spread that something was wrong with Carmen's wrist.

Joan leaned over Melody to ask Alexis, "What happened to Carmen? Did she break her hand or something? Can she move it?"

"I don't know," Alexis told her. "I mean, nobody knows. Coach is having the sports doctor look at it now. I think it's her wrist."

Joan tried to imagine what it would be like to have a broken wrist. Could you still move your fingers? she wondered. Would you have to wear a cast?

Maria, who was sitting in front of them, turned around and said, "C.J. said it was Carmen's left wrist and she's right-handed. She'll still be able to write and everything."

But I need two hands to play the piano, thought Joan. And to cheer. She didn't pay much attention to the last four competing high school squads but kept looking to see if Carmen would come back. She didn't.

As the last squad in the lineup finished their routine, Mrs. Granger came over to Emily in the stands. "I'm taking Carmen to the hospital for X rays," she told Emily. "Can you keep Lily with you? I'll meet you later at Melody's."

"Okay," answered Lily.

"Sure, Mom," added Emily. "Tell Carmen I'm sorry she got hurt."

Joan leaned across her friends to get closer to Mrs. Granger, who stood beside the bleachers. “Is Carmen okay?” asked Joan. “Can she move her fingers?”

Mrs. Granger didn’t hear her. “I have to go before everyone starts leaving the gym,” she told Emily.

“Do you know how to get to Melody’s, Mrs. Granger?” Alexis asked.

“I already gave her directions,” Melody told Alexis.

The announcer’s voice boomed over the loudspeaker. “The winners of the South Florida Regional CHEER USA competitions, High School Level,” he began. Joan noticed that Emily, Melody, Alexis, and Lily all had their fingers crossed for good luck. She crossed her fingers, too.

“Fifth place. Receiving eighty-seven points and a bid for Nationals,” the announcer continued, “Key West High.”

As the Key West co-captains strode out to receive their trophy and an invitation to the Nationals, Emily told Alexis, “Maybe CHS will win fourth place.”

But they didn’t. Glancing over at the nervous Claymore High School squad, Alexis wondered if they still hoped to place. She was watching them when the announcer said, “Third place. Receiving eighty-nine points and a bid for Nationals, Claymore High School."

The Claymore High School cheerleaders shrieked and jumped up and down excitedly.

"Yes!" Emily shouted.

"They did it!" Melody screamed.

Lynn and the other high school co-captain, Melissa, broke away from a hug with their coach to walk out for their trophy.

Melissa took the trophy and Lynn accepted the invitation to perform in the Nationals. Joan hoped that Carmen heard that her squad had placed before she left the gym for the hospital.

As Emily watched Lynn jumping up and down and hugging her fellow cheerleaders she thought, I really am happy she's happy. I am. I just wish I could be as good at everything as she is.

The high school cheerleaders were surrounded by people congratulating both squads. When the noise finally died down, Emily was standing with Joan, Melody, and Alexis. Lily was sitting on Alexis's shoulders.

"We're going to two parties," Lily announced. "Mom and me and Bubba."

"We'll have our mascot at the party," said Melody.

"How come you're going to two parties, Lily?" asked Joan.

"We're going to Emily's party *and* Lynn's party," Lily answered.

"But you're going to Melody's party first," said Alexis. "With us. Your mom will come there."

"Then I'm going to Lynn's party," said Lily.

"Where's Bubba now?" asked Melody.

Emily explained to her friends that animals weren't allowed in the gym building, so her mother had dropped Bubba off at a friend's house.

"I hope you brought your bathing suit, Lily," Melody told her. "Because one party is on a beach and mine is at a swimming pool."

Lily nodded. "I know," she said. "I'm going swimming two times. Mom said." She looked serious. "But Bubba doesn't know how to swim."

"He doesn't?" said Melody. "I thought all dogs could swim."

"Not bulldogs," Emily explained. "They sink."

Coach blew a whistle. "Okay, everyone," she announced. "It's party time. Go to the parking lot. The bus leaves in five minutes. Middle school cheerleaders will be dropped off at their party first."

Melody looked around to see that all the CMS cheerleaders were there. "Where's Kelly?" she asked Emily.

Emily pointed to where the Santa Rosa

cheerleaders were organizing to leave. "She's saying good-bye to her friend from Santa Rosa," Emily explained.

"Let's go get her," suggested Melody.

The two friends ran over to the Cougar crowd. They congratulated Cassie and the other cheerleaders on placing in the Regionals.

"But you guys deserve to be number one," Cassie told them. "You didn't make any mistakes."

"The neat thing is that both squads are going to Nationals," said Melody.

Kelly joined them and asked, "What's up?"

"Time to go to Melody's," Emily told her.

As the three CMS cheerleaders turned to go back to their own squad, Emily told Cassie and the other Cougar cheerleaders, "See you at Nationals!"

"You'll see us next Friday," Cassie reminded her. "At the Cougar-Bulldog basketball game."

"I forgot," said Emily with a laugh. "See you then."

"I totally forgot, too," Melody told Emily and Kelly. "I've been so excited about the CHEER USA competitions that I forgot we have a game next week."

"I can't wait for that game," said Kelly.

"Me, too," said Melody.

Emily locked arms with Kelly and Melody,

and the three of them ran to catch up with their squad.

12 PALM COURT. MELODY'S BEDROOM
5:00 P.M.

Emily, Joan, Maria, and Kelly were in Melody's room getting ready for the party. The rest of the cheerleaders were changing in other rooms of the house.

Melody wore shorts and a sleeveless red shirt over her bathing suit. Emily had an oversized T-shirt over her bathing suit. Maria put blue minibarrettes in Emily's hair.

Alexis sat cross-legged in the middle of Melody's bed with Lily, watching the cheerleaders get ready.

"Mommy's got my bathing suit," Lily told her. "She's going to bring it and I'm going swimming. Where's your bathing suit, Lexi?"

"I didn't bring anything to wear for the party," Alexis answered. "I didn't even know I was going."

Melody turned to Alexis. "We're about the same size," she said. "I have an extra bathing suit. And I have the perfect dress to wear over it."

"Thanks," said Alexis.

"I still keep stuff here," Melody explained as she opened the door to a half-filled closet. She didn't tell her Claymore friends that she'd left a lot of her stuff in Miami because she'd hoped to move back there when her parents saw how miserable she was in Claymore. As it turned out she wasn't miserable in Claymore, but she still missed Miami. Especially now that she was home. She missed her old friends. And her father. And the pink stucco house that she'd grown up in.

Melody took a purple sundress out of her closet and handed it to Alexis. "Here, try this on while I look for the bathing suit."

Alexis stood in front of the mirror and held the dress up in front of her. She studied her reflection and said, "It looks sort of old."

"I only wore it a couple of times," said Melody.

"I meant *old* like grown-up," explained Alexis, "not *old* like worn-out."

"Try it on," said Kelly.

"It'll look great on you," added Joan.

"And I have an idea for your hair," said Maria.

Alexis blushed, but she loved that her friends were helping her get ready for the party. She tried on the dress and everyone agreed it was perfect, especially after Maria put her hair back in a French braid.

"You look great," said Emily.

Alexis smiled at her. "Thanks," she said. Alexis wondered if Jake would think she looked great, too. Just then Tina came into the room. Sue and Tiffany followed her.

"Party time," said Sue.

Tiffany held out a little bag. "A present," she said. "From us."

As Melody took the bag she looked around and asked, "Does everybody know everybody else?"

"Nobody knows anybody," said Tina. "Except we met some of the other cheerleaders outside. That captain one and someone named T.J."

"Was it the captain with blond hair?" asked Emily.

Tina nodded.

"That's Sally," said Kelly.

"And T.J. is probably C.J.," added Joan. "It's short for Cynthia Jane."

Emily stepped forward. "Hi," she said. "I'm Emily."

Each of the other girls in the room gave their names, too.

When they'd finished the introductions Tina turned to Melody and said, "Open your present."

Melody opened the bag and held up a disc by one of her favorite groups, the Raves. "Just came out," said Tina. "We got it at Evolution Music."

"Thanks," said Melody. "We'll use it for the party."

"You got a poem for tonight?" asked Sue. "Juan said there might be an open mike."

"No way," said Melody. "I haven't written anything since I moved."

"You made up that poem for me," put in Joan. "When you met me at my piano lesson. That was terrific."

"I was just fooling around," Melody explained. "I couldn't perform that in public. It was nowhere good enough."

"It sounded pretty good to me," said Joan.

"Wait until the poetry slam tonight," said Melody.

"So you're all coming to the coffee shop for the poetry slam?" asked Tina.

"Some of us have to go back on the school bus at eight o'clock," said Maria. "With the high school cheerleaders."

"Joan and I are the only ones staying over," explained Emily.

Melody looked out the window. Cheerleaders were gathering around the pool, and Adam and Jake had arrived. Her father was putting out a big ice chest of sodas and juices, and a delivery truck from Best Tex-Mex was pulling in the driveway with the food. It was party time.

A party for my two groups of friends who have absolutely nothing in common, thought

Melody as she turned from the window to go downstairs.

12 PALM COURT. FRONT HALL 5:05 P.M.

Joan and Emily were coming down the stairs when they heard Lily running through the living room, shouting, "Mommy, Mommy, I want my bathing suit."

"My mother's here," said Emily.

"Let's find out about Carmen," shouted Joan as she ran down the stairs ahead of Emily.

Alexis, Lily, Maria, and Kelly were already in the front hall talking to Mrs. Granger when Joan reached her.

"Carmen's going to be fine," Mrs. Granger was saying. "She tore a tendon in her wrist. It hurts now, but they gave her some medication for the pain."

"How long before she can cheer again?" asked Kelly.

"A month or so," answered Mrs. Granger.

"Poor Carmen," said Maria.

"Does she know that her squad placed third?" asked Emily. "That they're going to the Nationals?"

Mrs. Granger smiled at the girls. "We heard it as we were walking out of the gym. It made her feel a lot better."

"Can she move her fingers?" asked Joan.

"Yes," said Mrs. Granger. "But she has to keep her wrist immobile while it heals."

Joan imagined not being able to move her wrist. She'd played the piano almost every day of her life since she was a little girl. Her teacher and parents said she could be a great pianist. But what if she broke or sprained her wrist? Would an injury like that affect her playing for the rest of her life? Were her parents right? Was she risking her piano career by doing gymnastics?

POOLSIDE 6:30 P.M.

Melody looked over the scene around the pool before going into the house for another platter of burritos. Alexis, Jake, Emily, Mae, and Adam were tossing a Frisbee on the back lawn. Randy, Darryl, Sally, and the ninth-grade cheerleaders were laughing and talking around the diving board. But Melody's three Miami friends were hanging back near the cooler, talking only to one another. As far as Melody could tell the only thing her two groups of friends had said to one another were things like, "You cheered great." And "Miami is nice."

Tina ran up to Melody. "Okay," she said. "We figured out who the ninth-grade hunk is that you have a crush on. Darryl. Right?"

"I don't have a crush on him," Melody

protested. "I just know him, and I played tennis with him once."

"Well, you should have a crush on him," said Tina. "He's to die for."

"He's Sally's boyfriend," Melody told her. "So don't go around saying I have a crush on him."

"I knew you did," said Tina gleefully. "And the eighth-grader you like is that Adam guy, right?"

"He's just a *friend*," Melody said. "I hang out with him and his sister, Joan. They live near me. That's all."

"Well, pretend he's more than just a *friend* when Juan comes," suggested Tina. "That way Juan will be jealous. So will Darryl."

Melody saw Sue and Tiffany look in the direction of the big group near the end of the pool. They were cracking up about something that Randy had said. Sue and Tiffany laughed, too. Are they laughing *with* my Claymore friends, wondered Melody, or *at* them?

"The jealousy thing works great," continued Tina. "You'll end up with a boyfriend in Miami and one in Claymore, with that Darryl guy jealous of both of them."

"Tina, stop it," said Melody sharply. "I don't want a boyfriend."

Tina looked hurt. "What's happened to you?" she asked. "You got some weird attitude going on."

"Sorry," said Melody. "I just don't want to do this thing about guys right now. I have to get more burritos."

"I was just fooling around," said Tina, turning away. Melody heard her mumble, "You used to have a sense of humor."

And I used to live in Miami, thought Melody as she went through the sliding doors into the house.

Her father and Mrs. Granger were in the kitchen warming up burritos and putting more chips and salsa into bowls. Coach Cortes was sitting at the table with Lily on her lap. They were putting bean dip and cheese on tortilla chips. Bubba was lying on the floor in the middle of the room.

Melody put the empty platter on the counter near the stove.

"How's it going out there?" her father asked.

"Okay," she answered. "I came in to get more burritos." She glanced at the work going on at the table and added, "And chips. Lily's chips are a big hit."

Melody loved being back in her own house after living in the small apartment in Claymore. Her bedroom in Miami was twice as big as the one in Claymore. All the rooms were bigger, and they had their own pool and a pool house.

"You got a new table," she said to her father.

"You and your mother took the other one to Claymore," her father reminded her. "I had to replace it."

"Sorry," said Melody. "I forgot."

Her father smiled at her. "Don't be sorry," he said. "I had to replace a lot of stuff and your mother had to buy a lot of stuff. That's what divorce is. Things are split down the middle."

That's how I feel about the divorce sometimes, thought Melody, split down the middle.

As Melody laid hot burritos on the platter she thought about how different her life would be if her mother hadn't taken the job in Claymore. I could have stayed in Miami and lived half the time here and half the time with Mom, she thought. Like Alexis does with her parents. But then I wouldn't have all these new friends in Claymore. Or be a cheerleader on the number one middle school squad in South Florida.

Bubba looked up at Melody as she walked around him with the platter of burritos.

Emily met Melody and took the platter from her. "I'll pass these," she said. "It's such a great party."

Melody looked over the party scene before deciding what to do next and thought, Something's missing. What was it? Juan and Rick weren't there yet. But that wasn't what was bothering her. Suddenly she remembered what she'd forgotten. Music. She'd forgotten to put on the CD player. She ran back inside to the living room, threw open the window, and turned the speakers around so that they faced outside. I'll play the new Raves album, she decided.

When the music came on the kids around the pool looked toward the house to see where it was coming from. Melody waved and Darryl gave her a thumbs-up sign. Sally began to dance.

Over by the cooler, Tina, Sue, and Tiffany began to move to the music, too. Now, if I can just get everyone to dance together, thought Melody as she walked toward the kitchen to get another platter of burritos.

When she came back outside she saw the gate to the yard open and five more of her Miami friends come in. They looked around, then walked straight over to Tina, Sue, and Tiffany.

Melody looked toward her Claymore friends, then back to her Miami friends. There were five new people who hadn't had anything to eat, so she headed in their direction. The two guys among the new arrivals — Will and Lee — lit up when they saw the platter of burritos.

Melody smiled at them and said, "Great to see you guys."

"Hey, Max," said Lee. "Tina said you'd have great food."

"Like the party after graduation," added Will as he picked up a burrito.

Melody had loved her sixth-grade graduation party. There were more than fifty kids there and everyone said it was the best party of the year.

Tina told the new arrivals all about the Regionals while they were reaching for burritos. By the time they'd finished that conversation the platter was empty again. She'd have to fill it up for the Claymore crowd. "Be right back," she said.

Emily saw Melody going toward the house again. "Let's help Melody," she shouted to Jake as she threw him back the Frisbee.

"I'll go with you," said Adam.

Melody was walking into the kitchen when Adam and Emily caught up with her. A few minutes later they came out with two platters of burritos and one of chips. "I guess I'll bring this platter over to the people at the cooler," said Melody. "You can — "

"Why don't we just put all this stuff on the table and let them come and get it," suggested Emily. "That way maybe people will mix a little."

Melody smiled gratefully at Emily.

"Good idea," said Adam.

It *was* a good idea, thought Emily as the two groups of kids came toward the fresh supply of food. But it's not a good-enough idea, she concluded, when the two groups stopped at opposite ends of the table and continued to ignore each other.

"Alexis," Emily whispered. "I think Melody's unhappy that the Claymore kids and Miami kids aren't making an effort to get together."

"You think?" said Alexis.

"Let's go talk to Tina," Emily suggested.

Sally noticed Coach Cortes coming out of the house with Melody's father, Mrs. Granger, Lily, and Bubba.

"Here comes Bubba!" exclaimed C.J. "He's so cute."

Cute? thought Sally. How can C.J. think he's cute? He's totally ugly. That dog gives me the creeps.

Looking away from Bubba, Sally saw Coach Cortes smiling at her cheerleaders. Mae waved to her and Coach waved back. Time for some brownie points, thought Sally. She pointed at Coach Cortes and shouted, "Give us a C!"

A few cheerleaders shouted back "C!"

"Give us an O!" Sally continued.

The rest of the cheerleaders joined in on the O and they all turned toward Coach Cortes.

"We're cheering for our coach," Emily explained to Tina before she joined the others in shouting "R."

When they had spelled out C-O-R-T-E-S, Sally, Mae, C.J., and Elvia ran toward their coach and surrounded her. They lifted her up and dropped her — clothes and all — into the pool.

When Coach broke through the surface of the water she shouted, "Where are my captains?"

Sally looked around for an escape route, but she was already surrounded by cheerleaders. It'll ruin my hair, she thought, but I might as well be a good sport. She hadn't finished the thought before she hit the water. She turned herself around underwater and swam a few strokes along the bottom of the pool. When she surfaced she was in the middle of the pool, and Coach and Mae were already swimming toward the edge.

"And here comes Bubba!" shouted Randy.

Sally watched Bubba flying through the air toward her, his short legs beating at the air. As he fell with a huge splash beside Sally, Emily screamed, "He can't swim."

Sally watched in amazement as Bubba sank like a rock.

"Sally, get him," someone shouted.

"She's a lifeguard," Sally heard someone scream as she upended herself in a surface dive.

She swam straight down toward the lump of dog on the bottom of the pool. When she reached him she grabbed hold of his collar and put her arm around his body to pull him toward the surface. She was aware that other people had jumped in the pool, too.

When she emerged from underwater someone was shouting, "Sally's got him."

Sally turned Bubba over on his back and held him around the neck with her arm. He's even uglier wet, she thought as she tried to keep a firm grip on the squirming, frightened dog. What if he needs mouth-to-mouth resuscitation? she thought. Will everyone expect me to do it? The idea was so revolting that she almost lost her grip on him. But she held on. People jumped into the pool to help. "I've got him," Sally said breathlessly.

Emily and Mrs. Granger knelt at the edge of the pool and leaned over to help Sally lift the dog out of the water. "Bubba, oh, Bubba, are you all right?" Emily said as she grabbed hold of her pet.

Lily was beside her, crying, "Is he drowned? Is he drowned?"

Everyone was talking at once. Suddenly, Bubba barked. The partygoers burst into happy shouts and applause. Sally felt hands clamp around her waist from behind. Over her shoulder she saw that it was Darryl. He lifted her up, straight out of the water.

"Give us an S!" Mae shouted.

"S!" everyone repeated.

"Give us an A!"

"A!" the crowd chanted.

Sally decided that it was worth saving Bubba if this was her reward. She kept her toes pointed and smiled at her audience. I not only saved that stupid dog, she thought, but I'm captain of the CMS squad the first year that they placed in the Regionals. That's what they should be cheering me for. As the crowd chanted "Sally! Sally!" she vowed to herself that when she was captain of the high school squad she'd make sure they were number one in the Regionals, too. She wasn't going to settle for third place.

When the cheer was over, Emily hugged Bubba and told him, "Sally saved your life."

"Everybody in the pool for water volleyball," shouted Melody. "I'm choosing teams." And I'm making sure to mix up my two sets of friends, she vowed to herself. She turned to Tina. "You know where the net is," she said. "Can you get it?"

In five minutes there were two teams facing off in the pool. Each side was a good mix of Melody's Claymore friends and her Miami friends. Adam stood next to Melody in front of the net. "Where's that Juan guy?" he asked. "I thought he was coming."

"He didn't say for sure," Melody said before punching the ball into play. And I'm glad he's not here, she thought, as Alexis hit the ball back over the net. If Juan were here Tina would embarrass me for sure. I have enough to worry about without that. Melody turned to see Tiffany whack the ball back to the other side. I've put together two evenly matched teams, she thought. It was going to be a good game.

UPSTAIRS BATHROOM 7:30 P.M.

Alexis had been waiting outside the bathroom for at least five minutes. She wondered if she should try the door again. Maybe it wasn't locked. Maybe she just hadn't pushed it hard enough. Or maybe nobody was in there after all. She was about to call out, "Is anybody in there?" when she stopped herself. What if a guy was in the bathroom? It would be so embarrassing. She was about to go back downstairs when she thought she heard crying on the other side of the door. She leaned closer and listened. Someone *was* crying.

Should I tell Melody? Alexis wondered. Then she thought of how embarrassed she'd be if she was upset and everyone made a big deal out of it. I'll just wait and see who it is, she decided — in case the person needs help.

Alexis went into Melody's room, which was across the hall from the bathroom, and left the door open. By facing the mirror over Melody's bureau, she'd be able to see who was coming out of the bathroom. Then, when she saw who it was, she could decide what to do. She was thinking about this plan when the door to the bathroom opened. Alexis looked in the mirror and saw Joan walk out into the hall. At that instant, Joan saw her.

Alexis turned away from the mirror to face Joan. "Are you all right?" she asked.

Joan tried to smile. "Fine," she said. "I'm fine." But her voice cracked.

"I heard you crying," Alexis whispered. "What's wrong?"

Joan was trying to think of a lie to tell Alexis about why she was crying, but she stopped herself. I might as well start telling the truth, she decided. Everyone will know what happened anyway when I have to quit cheering. Joan stepped into Melody's room and closed the door behind her. Loud music from the pool party came in through the open window.

"Was someone mean to you or something?" asked Alexis.

"Sort of," said Joan. "My parents." She leaned against the closed door and she told Alexis the whole story. She started at the beginning, from the first time she lied to her parents about going to debate club meetings when she was really trying out for cheering.

When Joan finished telling her story, Alexis told her that she had trouble with her parents, too. That sometimes she hated living in two different places, especially when she was at her mother's. That her mother was lonely and sad a lot of the time and wanted Alexis to keep her company. "She's always saying how Dad has this great life because he's this successful lawyer and he's got a lot of friends. And that she has a terrible, lonely life. It gets me down when she talks like that."

"So do you like it better at your father's house?" asked Joan.

"Well, yes," said Alexis. "But not always. It's lonely there because Dad does have a lot of friends — like my mom says — so he's not there very much."

"Oh," said Joan. "But your parents let you do all the stuff you want to do, don't they?"

"That part's cool," said Alexis. "Except when I'm at my mother's, she doesn't let me stay over at Emily's so much. You know, because then she'll be alone."

"If my parents make me quit cheering I'll miss the Nationals and everything. It'd be awful."

"It would," agreed Alexis. "But maybe they won't make you quit. You can't be sure. They could change their minds when they see how good you are."

"That will just convince them I shouldn't do it," Joan said. "They'll freak out when they see me doing a basket toss. They don't understand how special it is to love a sport. Neither of them are into that sort of thing. And if they hear that Carmen hurt her wrist, forget it. I'll never cheer again."

"That'd be so awful," said Alexis.

Joan walked over to the window and looked out to see what was going on at the party. "I felt sorry for you when you didn't make the squad," she told Alexis.

"I was pretty upset at first," Alexis said, moving toward the window. "But then it was okay."

"I would have been really unhappy for a long time," said Joan. She noticed that Tiffany, Sue, and Lee were dancing with Randy, Jake, and C.J. Lots of kids were dancing now.

"I didn't like cheering that much," Alexis answered. "I just wanted to do what Emily did. You know, because she's my best friend." Alexis saw Jake's grandparents come into the Maxes' backyard. She hoped they wouldn't want to leave right away. "But it's different for you, Joan," Alexis continued. "You really want to be a cheerleader because you love it. And you're so great at it."

"Thanks," said Joan.

The door flung open and Melody, Emily, and Tina came running into the room. "Jake's grandparents are here," said Melody.

"And they want to leave right away," added Tina.

"I have to go," said Alexis.

"We've got a better idea," said Emily.

"You should stay over," said Melody.

"There's plenty of room in my aunt's car for you to go back tomorrow," said Tina.

"Then you can go to the poetry slam," added Emily.

"And sleep over in the pool house," said Tina. "It's really cool."

"*Cool cool*," explained Melody. "Not *cool cold*. And Tina, Tiffany, and Sue are staying, too."

Emily handed Alexis the phone on Melody's desk. "Call your father," she instructed.

"Please," said Joan. "You have to stay."

Alexis smiled at the girls around her. "I'll stay," she said as she started dialing her father's number.

12 PALM COURT. FRONT LAWN 8:00 P.M.

Everyone from the party was standing on the lawn and sidewalk in front of Melody's house. The cheerleaders were waiting for the school bus. Jake and Adam were waiting for Jake's grandparents.

Emily watched Melody say good-bye to her Miami friends who weren't going to the poetry slam. She imagined how awful she'd feel if her parents suddenly divorced and her mother told her she had to move someplace totally new and different — like Miami. Even if I made new friends, Emily thought, I'd miss my old friends. Especially Alexis.

Alexis came up beside her and whispered, "It must be hard for Melody to have friends in two places."

"That's just what I was thinking," Emily whispered back.

Jake and Adam went over to Melody. "Thanks for the party," said Jake.

"It was fun," added Adam.

"Have fun at that poetry thing tonight," Jake said.

"It's a poetry slam," Melody explained.

"You going to perform some poetry?" asked Adam.

Melody shook her head. "I only performed at this class we took. Not at a coffee shop or anything. Anyway, I'm not writing poetry anymore."

"Tina said you were good at it," Adam said.

Joan, meanwhile, was motioning to her brother that she wanted to talk to him. She led him to the side of the house, where they could talk privately. When they were alone she asked nervously, "What are you going to tell Mother and Father about the Regionals?"

Adam put his hands in his pockets and thought for a second before answering. "That your squad came in first. That you were really good and they should be proud of you."

"What about Carmen's accident?" she asked. "Will you tell them?"

He shook his head no. "But they might ask me if anyone was hurt," he said.

"You don't have to lie for me anymore," Joan told her brother.

Mr. Feder leaned out the car window and called, "Jake, Adam. Come on, boys."

"Gotta go," Adam said as he gave Joan a friendly punch on the arm. "See you tomorrow."

She watched him run back to say good-bye to Melody and thank her father.

Jake wrapped an arm around Emily and gave her a quick hug. He smiled at Alexis before running to the car. Even though he hadn't hugged her, Alexis still felt herself blushing as she stood with Emily watching the Feders drive away.

"Here comes the bus," someone called out.

"Is everybody out here?" shouted Coach Cortes. "Let's have a count-off."

The cheerleaders called out their assigned numbers of one through seventeen. When they'd finished the countdown Melody reminded Coach that she and Joan and Emily were going back the next day.

The bus with the high school cheerleaders pulled up in front of Melody's house. While the middle school cheerleaders filed onto the bus for the ride back to Claymore, Lynn hung out a window to talk to Emily.

"How was your party?" Emily asked her.

"Great," Lynn answered. "We went to this neat barbecue place in South Beach. Very cool. Being a cheerleader in high school is even more fun than in middle school. You'll see."

Emily heard the bus driver call out, "Everybody in their seats. We're taking off."

The doors to the bus closed.

" 'Bye," said Lynn as her friend pulled her back into her seat.

Emily and Alexis watched the bus roll down the street. "Why is everything she does better than anything I do?" mumbled Emily.

Alexis couldn't hear what Emily said over the roar of the bus engine. But she could tell by the expression on Emily's face that she was unhappy about something. "What'd you say?" she asked.

"Everyone's always saying how lucky I am to have Lynn for a sister," Emily answered. "But sometimes it's a drag."

Melody turned and called to Emily and Alexis. "You guys coming? We have to change for the poetry slam. I have a great skirt for you, Alexis."

"We'll be right there," Alexis called back. She turned to Emily, "What do you mean?"

"Everything Lynn does is always the best," Emily explained. "When I went to nursery school, she was a bigger deal because she was in first grade. When I finally got to first grade, she was in fifth grade. I'm a middle school cheerleader, but she's a high school cheerleader. She's even a flyer and a co-captain, which I'll never be. I might not even make the high school squad."

"You're worried about being a high school cheerleader *now*?" asked Alexis. "You're only in seventh grade. That doesn't make sense."

"It does if you have a big sister who's older than you and is the best in everything," said Emily.

"I never thought of it like that," Alexis said. "But I can see how it could be a drag."

"The worst part is feeling that way when she's so — so nice," Emily said.

"She's not always so nice," Alexis said. "I don't think she was so nice when she said being a high school cheerleader was better than being a middle school cheerleader."

"You don't?" said Emily.

"No. And I don't always like Lynn. She was really bossy when she helped us with cheering this summer."

"You noticed that, too?" asked Emily.

Alexis nodded. "Besides, when Lynn was in middle school her squad didn't even go to the Regionals. Did you think of that?"

Emily smiled at her. "No," she answered. She paused before adding, "But you're always saying you wish you had a big sister like Lynn."

"That's just because I hardly have any family at all," said Alexis. "But you know what I really wish? Most of all?"

"What?" asked Emily.

"I wish you and I were sisters," Alexis answered softly.

"We're better than sisters," Emily told her. "We're best friends."

Alexis smiled at her. "And Lynn is on her way back to Claymore," she said. "But we're in Miami and we're going to a poetry slam. I bet she's never been to a poetry slam."

Emily laughed as she grabbed Alexis's hand,

and the two friends ran across the lawn toward Melody's house.

KENNEDY STREET. THE PLACE 8:30 P.M.

Joan stood next to Sue waiting to get into The Place. There were a dozen or so kids in front of them — including Melody, Tina, and Tiffany. And more people were lining up behind them. Through the big front window, Joan saw that the coffee shop was already crowded with teenagers. She hoped they'd be able to get in. Even from the street the coffee shop looked like a great place. She loved how the whole room was bathed in warm orange light. A percussion band was performing on the small stage. The music, with its intricate rhythms, reached them on the street.

"All of these people are going to be listening to Juan," Joan heard Tina tell Melody. "I'd be so nervous."

"The way you go on about Juan," Melody teased Tina, "I think you're the one with the crush on him."

"Tina has a million crushes," Sue whispered to Joan.

Joan smiled at Sue. She loved that she was in Miami and that she was going to a poetry slam with a bunch of girlfriends. She felt the most grown-up she'd ever felt in her life. Her parents probably had never even heard of a poetry slam.

The line moved forward.

"Next," the man at the door told Joan.

Joan handed him the entrance fee and Melody led the way into the crowded, dark room. It was even more crowded than it looked from the street.

"The art on the wall is the work of middle and high school kids," Sue told Joan.

Joan looked around at big, colorful paintings. Some were street scenes and others were portraits. They were all good and very professional. "Cool," she replied as they followed Melody to one of the few tables that wasn't already taken. Joan squeezed into a chair between Melody and Sue.

As soon as they'd ordered sodas from the waiter, a young woman walked up to the microphone at the center of a small stage in the front of the room. "Hi," she said. "I'm Batsheba, your host tonight. Welcome to another Saturday night at The Place. Lots of talent here tonight, so let's get started with Lyric Smith. Lyric, come on up here."

A girl, who Joan guessed was at least as old as Emily's sister Lynn, came out of the audience and stepped onto the stage. Joan loved how pink and yellow stage lights made a beautiful pattern on and around Lyric.

"She was in our poetry workshop, too," Melody whispered to her Claymore friends.

Lyric looked around at her audience.

If I were Lyric I'd be so nervous, thought Joan. Then she remembered that she'd just done a cheer routine in front of hundreds of people and had played the piano in a lot of recitals.

Someone called out, "Tell it, Lyric!"

A couple of people shouted, "Lyric."

Lyric cleared her throat, but she waited until the room was totally silent before beginning her poem.

TALKING MUSIC

Rhythm and blues?
Jazz-zzz?
Rock and Ro-oll?
Or rolling words that are talking rhymes,
Like mine,
That keep the time,
And keep you thinking
As words are s
i
n
k
ing
Into that special space,

That brainy place between your ears.
Let the words in
And find the connect
With respect
To the ideas that came before.

Then find the way
To say
What's on YOUR mind.
In rhyme.
That keeps time.
Line by line
Like mine.
DO IT!

Joan loved how Lyric performed the words of her poem by saying some words louder than others and pausing after some of the lines.

The crowd broke into applause. Someone shouted, "Yes, Lyric."

Lyric smiled, put the mike back on its stand, and left the stage.

While the next poet was taking the stage, Melody spotted Juan with a group of friends at a table toward the front of the room. She wondered if he even knew she was there. Just then he looked back and saw her staring at him.

He waved.

Tina elbowed her.

"I know," Melody told Tina under her breath. "I saw him."

Melody didn't recognize either of the next two performers, but she loved their poetry. She vowed to herself that she would start writing poetry again soon. It would be a lot easier to be a poet if I still lived in Miami, she thought. My friends here are interested in poetry. And I'd come to The Place all the time.

Batsheba was at the mike again. "Next up is a newcomer to The Place's Saturday Night Poetry Slam. Please welcome Juan Ramirez."

"Go, Juan!" shouted Tina.

A few people turned around to check out Juan's big fan. But Melody knew that Tina didn't care. She wasn't shy. Melody thought it wouldn't be long before Tina started performing at poetry slams.

Juan walked onstage carrying a small drum, which he put down on a stool that was in the center of the stage. Melody wondered if he was nervous. He probably is, she thought, but he's so cool he doesn't show it. She remembered how nervous she was at the Regionals. How nervous the whole squad was. They'd acted cool, too.

Juan looked confidently around the audience as he adjusted the mike to his height. Then he began an even beat on the drum. His drum riff became softer as he began his poem.

THE BEAT

Beat
Beat
Beat
I hit the beat,
        The street beat
            That moves my feet
To where I want to be.

Uptown
Downtown
Out of town
Going to hit the road
To see a load
Of new spaces,
        Places I've never been.
When?
Whenever I can
Because I am a moving man
        A fan
            of all the peoples of the world.
Africa,
Latin America,
Australia, Asia, and Iceland, too.
Want to . . . want to . . . want to
Go places,
Hear things,
The ring of the words of many peoples
And feel their beat

The heartbeat that says,
"I am here
And so are you.
How do you do?"
Do.
Do.
Do meet
And keep the beat
The heartbeat
Of the world.

After Juan recited the last line, he kept drumming a heartbeat. It was the only sound in the room. Melody felt her own heartbeat keeping pace with the drum.

When Juan stopped there was a second of silence, then the audience applauded loudly. Melody knew that Juan's first appearance at The Place was a big success.

During a break in the poetry performances, Juan came over to Melody and her friends to say hi and thank them for coming.

"You were great," Melody told him.

"You going to do something next Saturday?" asked Tina.

"Hope so," he said.

"I'll be here," Tina told him.

But I won't, thought Melody sadly.

Emily noticed that lots of kids came over

to the table to say hi to Melody. No wonder she wasn't happy when she first came to Claymore, thought Emily. She left a lot of friends behind.

VAN 10:30 P.M.

Tina's mother was waiting for Melody and her friends outside The Place. Melody, Tina, and Joan took the backseat. Alexis sat with Emily and Sue in the middle seat. And Tiffany sat up front with Tina's mother.

When the van slowly made its way down a wide, busy street, Alexis studied the passing scene through the window. To her left, she saw a boardwalk along a sandy beach that led to the ocean. Even though it was late at night, people were skateboarding and Rollerblading on the boardwalk. On the other side of the street there were colorful and brightly lit hotels and restaurants as far as she could see. The outdoor restaurants and cafés were crowded with people. Miami was a lot different from quiet Claymore, where there was only one hotel.

Alexis asked Sue, "Do you do stuff like this every weekend?"

"There's always something fun to do in Miami," Sue answered. "But I'm mostly busy with the swim team. Melody was on the swim team, too."

"And now I'm a cheerleader," said Melody.

“Give us an M!” shouted Tina.

“M!” everyone in the van hollered.

“E!” shouted Tina.

“E!” the rest of the girls repeated.

But instead of continuing to spell out Melody’s name by shouting L, Tina next shouted, “What does it spell?”

“Me?” the girls asked in unison.

“Louder!” shouted Tina.

“Me!” everyone yelled back to her.

Then they broke out laughing.

Melody noticed that her Claymore friends were laughing just as hard as her Miami friends. They appreciated Tina’s offbeat sense of humor, too. Maybe her two sets of friends weren’t so different after all.

12 PALM COURT. POOLSIDE 11:30 P.M.

Melody sat at the edge of the pool, her feet dangling in the water. Emily and Sue were talking about the poetry slam and treading water at the deep end. Alexis and Tiffany had just climbed out of the pool and were drying off while they talked about their favorite women pro basketball players. Tina and Joan were arranging the sleeping bags in the pool house and talking about Adam. Tina said that Joan must love having an older brother because then she’d meet all these cool older guys.

"Adam likes to hang out with my friends," Melody heard Joan telling Tina.

Melody smiled to herself. She was glad that Adam liked to hang out with them. She slipped into the water for one last swim before going to bed. After swimming a few strokes she rolled over on her back to float and look at the stars. A poem she'd written last summer came into her mind.

Split.
Separated.
Divorced.
Mom, Dad, and me
Are not a family of three
Like we used to be.
Now it's Mom and me
Or Dad and me.
Only two at a time.
So why this rhyme?
Because I can't see
Why it has to be
That we are no longer three.

Melody had never shared that rhyme with anyone. Reciting the poem to herself reminded her of all the confusion and hurt she'd felt when her parents told her they were divorcing. I hate it, she thought.

"Hey, Melody," Tina called. "Do you want to

sleep on the end or in the middle, between me and Joan?"

"In the middle," Melody called back to her. At least I got my two sets of friends together, she thought. They don't have to be separated all the time like my parents.

As Melody watched Emily and Sue climbing out of the pool she had an idea. She swam over toward the edge of the pool herself and called to them, "Go over to the pool house. I want to take a group picture. Tell the others."

By the time Melody got out of the water, her best friends from Miami and her best friends from Claymore were at the pool house talking and having a great time together while they waited for her. She took her camera out of her backpack and went over to them.

"Okay," she directed, "Joan and Tina up front, since — "

" — since we're the shortest," Joan and Tina said in unison.

"And I'll sit in front of them," suggested Sue, "because I'm the — "

" — ugliest," teased Tiffany.

"I was going to say *tallest*," explained Sue, pretending her feelings had been hurt.

"You're the *prettiest*, Sue," Emily said.

"Thank you, Emily," said Sue, still acting offended. "You have good taste."

Emily, Tiffany, and Alexis stood behind Tina, Joan, and Sue. Tina held up a blue-and-white striped towel like a flag. "CMS colors," she said. "For the day your squad was number one in all of South Florida."

"Yea!" Melody's six friends yelled.

At that instant Melody took a photo of her three friends from one coast of Florida — where her father lived — and three from the other coast — where she and her mother lived. Six friends who knew and liked her and now liked one another.

POOL HOUSE 11:55 P.M.

Emily lay thinking in her sleeping bag. It had been such a special day she didn't want it to end. But no one was talking anymore, and she could tell by the slow breathing coming from Tiffany's sleeping bag that she was asleep. The only other sound was the water gently lapping against the sides of the pool. Emily sat up on her elbows for one last look at the starlit sky before going to sleep.

"'Night, Emily," whispered Alexis in a sleepy voice. "Congratulations. You were great."

"Thanks," Emily whispered back as she slipped down into her sleeping bag. "Good night."

As soon as Emily closed her eyes she felt like

she was at the Regionals again. Running out to take her position. Hoisting Mae up in one smooth motion. Smiling at the crowds and shouting out the chant. She'd loved every minute of it.

Alexis turned over to make herself more comfortable. It had been a fabulous day — from the moment that Jake picked her up early that morning. Now that all the cheering and partying were over, she was thinking about her article for the *Bulldog Edition*. She'd made lots of notes and would be writing a firsthand account — both from her notes and her memories. Claymore Middle School had placed first in the Regionals — that made her column especially important. I'll work on it as soon as I get home tomorrow, she told herself. I'll write about the high school competition, too, but not about Carmen getting injured. I don't want to make a big deal about it in case Joan's parents read my article. That was Alexis's last thought before falling asleep.

Joan wasn't sleeping yet. She was also thinking about Carmen's injury. What if it had happened to me? she wondered. Would I still be able to play the piano? Were her parents right? Was she really risking her career as a pianist by being a cheerleader? But she'd be so unhappy if she couldn't cheer. She'd have to do everything she could to convince her parents to let her stay on the squad. Everything but lie. Joan promised herself that she wasn't going to lie again. Not to her parents. Not to Adam. Not to her friends.

Melody lay awake long after her friends had fallen asleep. The events of the day kept going through her head. She tried counting sheep, but the sheep turned into tumbling cheerleaders. Finally, she slid out of her sleeping bag and went into the house. As she walked through the rooms she was flooded with memories of her life here. In the living room she remembered how her parents played board games with her when she was little. They always had a great time — the three of them together. In the kitchen she remembered how her father had taught her to cook. And how happy her mother was when she came home late from work and found dinner ready. They'd always fooled around and joked together — the three of them. As hard as Melody thought about it, she couldn't remember her parents fighting. Not once.

She climbed the stairs to her old room, went to her desk, and turned on the light. Her friends' clothes and overnight bags were scattered all over the place. She took Tina's black skirt off the back of the desk chair and Emily's bag off the desk. But before sitting down she carried her chair over to the closet door, stood on the chair, and reached up along the top of the molding. Her fingers found the key she'd left there. She used it to open the bottom right-hand drawer of her desk. Inside was a pile of diaries she'd started keeping when she was seven years old. She took out the last diary, but it was only half full. Melody knew the exact day she'd stopped writing in it — the twenty-fourth of June, last summer. The day before her parents told her about the divorce.

I'm going to take this diary to Claymore with me, she thought. That's where I live now, so that's where my diary should be. She stuffed the diary into the bottom of her overnight bag, locked the drawer, put the key back on top of the molding, and left her bedroom.

As Melody walked back down the stairs to the pool house, she thought about what she'd put in her diary. She supposed she'd write about the divorce, but mostly she wanted to write about her new life in Claymore and what it was like to be a cheerleader on the number one squad in South Florida.

Maybe by the time we go to Nationals, she thought, I'll have started a new book.

ABOUT THE AUTHOR

Jeanne Betancourt has written many novels for young adults, several of which have won Children's Choice awards. She also writes the popular Pony Pal series for younger readers.

Jeanne lives in New York City and Sharon, Connecticut, with her husband, two cats, and a dog. Her hobbies include drawing, painting, hiking, swimming, and tap dancing. Like the girls in CHEER USA, she was a cheerleader in middle school.